The Course of Fortune

A Novel of the Great Siege of Malta

Volume 1

Tony Rothman

iBooks

Habent Sua Fata Libelli

iBooks
Manhanset House
Shelter Island Hts., New York 11965-0342
Tel: 212-427-7139
bricktower@aol.com • www.ibooksinc.com

Library of Congress Cataloging-in-Publication Data

Rothman, Tony.
The Course of Fortune, A Novel of the Great Siege of Malta / Tony Rothman. —
1st. American ed.
p. cm.
1. Siege of Malta, 1565—Fiction. 2. Malta—History. 3. Religion—
Christianity—History. 4. Fiction—Christian—Historical Fiction.
I. Title.
PS3569.A6887R8 2011
813' .54—dc20

Volume 1: 978-1-59687-427-5, Hardcover; 978-1-899694-24-2, Trade Paper
Volume 2: 978-1-59687-428-2, Hardcover; 978-1-899694-25-9, Trade Paper
Volume 3: 978-1-59687-429-9, Hardcover; 978-1-899694-26-6, Trade Paper

July 2024

The Course of Fortune

A Novel of the Great Siege of Malta

Volume 1

Tony Rothman

Also by Tony Rothman

Fiction

Firebird
Censored Tales
The World is Round

Nonfiction

Sacred Mathematics: Japanese Temple Geometry
(with Fukagawa Hidetoshi)
Everything's Relative and Other Fables from Science and Technology
Doubt and Certainty (with George Sudarshan)
Instant Physics
A Physicist on Madison Avenue
Science à la Mode
Frontiers of Modern Physics

CONTENTS

Map illustrations by Renee Zhan

To my Mother

Without whom it certainly never would have happened

Rien n'est plus connu que ce siège *où la fortune de Soliman échoua*

—Voltaire

Author's Note:

The Course of Fortune was originally written in 2002–2004. At the time I was unaware that several other authors had just finished or were just finishing their own novels about the Great Siege of Malta, which evidently forestalled the publication of this one. Those works remain unread by me. My own aim was, in part, to write as historically accurate an account as possible, and to that end I relied on the earliest sources and best scholarship I could find. At the end of Book V, the reader can find principal references, along with my acknowledgments of the many people who aided me by giving generously of their time and expertise. But let me thank at once the eminent Maltese historian and former Justice of the European Court of Human Rights, Giovanni Bonello, for acting as advisor from start to finish, providing me with his new and unpublished research and correcting errors. Without his help, I am sure the result would have been much different and much lessened. Thanks again, Vanni!

Sardegna
Gozo
N
MARE ME
Comi
Pantelarea
Linos.
Lampedusa
Africa
Djerbé/Los Gelves
Zuara
BARBARIA

Sicilia

Malta

Pozzallo

Cape
Passero

Mgarr

Birgu

Mdina/
Città Notabile

Zurrieq

ITERANEO

Tripoli

GREAT PORT-MALTA
1551-1553

Gellows' Point

St. Elmo's Chapel

Castle St. Angelo

Marsamxett Harbor

Mt. Sciberras

L'Isola

Marsa

Fountain

Book I

Turgut

Prologue

"Sultan of the Ottomans, Allah's Deputy on Earth, Sun of the Heaven of Prophecy, Star of the Most Happy Constellation, Lord of the Lords of this World, Possessor of Men's Necks, King of Believers and Unbelievers, King of Kings, Emperor of East and West, Majestic Caesar, Seal of Victory, Refuge of All the People of the World, Shadow of the Almighty Dispensing Quiet on the Earth ... "

His Majesty, having been roused in the depths of night by the explosions of gunpowder that had set the Royal Arsenal ablaze, and having seen with his own eyes the flames that destroyed the greater part of the Imperial Armada, ordered in his fury that the agents responsible for this perfidy be brought before him for interrogation; and now after his title, inspiring of awe no less than the scimitar he wielded against the Infidel, had rolled like thunder across the sea of silks gathered before him to melt away among the lofty minarets of Constantinople, the last of the prisoners rounded up the previous day was dragged, shackled and terrified like the others, into the pavilion of the *Divan-i humayun* of the Sarai itself, where the *bostancis* threw him unceremoniously to the floor and forced his submission with the heel of a boot until, at length, His Majesty ordered the vermin to rise.

I lifted my eyes to behold Soliman, by his own subjects given the title Lawgiver, in Christendom called grudgingly and simply the Magnificent. I faced the most powerful man on earth.

He did not see me. The Sultan's gaze was fixed on a place beyond, as if he were unaware of the bloodied and insignificant figure cowering so far below him. The Pasha at his side addressed me then, barking to the *dragoman* that lest the prisoner deceive himself, he could be certain that only death awaited; were I, tho', to reveal my accomplices who had attempted to ruin the Turkish fleet, I would be granted a swift beheading and be spared the *bastinado*.

At that instant my hands began to tremble of their own accord and my bowels threatened to desert me. Yet, it were as the Pasha's very threats served to steel my soul, and I regained a portion of myself. How often in those terrible four months not a year ago had my comrades and I faced certain death at the hands of the barbarians, to be spared by the Will of God alone? Truly, what could such weak threats mean to a man who had survived that living Hell, when each morning we awoke to face the end of the world? Death, I welcome you.

The *dragoman* began to render the Pasha's words, but in my exhaustion I uttered without thought, "An interpreter is unnecessary, *Hazretleriniz*, I speak Turkish." The chief *bostanci*, infuriated that the prisoner had dared speak without leave, struck me across the face, opening the wound on my mouth, and I again fell into the grip of those surrounding me. At this moment the Sultan for the first time revealed an awareness of the prisoner who had been brought to him, and motioned with a nearly imperceptible elevation of his ringed finger that the *bostancis* should desist.

"How is it," asked the Pasha at a nod from His Majesty, "that the infidel comes to speak Turkish?"

Only then, in the brief respite from punishment the question granted me, did I begin to perceive my surroundings. I stood in the Imperial Council Chamber itself, its dome and walls covered with ornate tiles, the color of sky. On the divans about me sat crosslegged the aghas, while men of lesser rank stood. Pages scurried this way and that, signaling to each other in their rapid sign language, for they are forbidden to speak. Behind me, in the courtyard, hundreds of janissaries stood at the ready in their red and yellow silks and unmistakable headdresses folding high over like the loose sleeve of a robe. How often, in the thick of it, had we cringed at the sight of those headdresses, so comical at firing distance and so terrifying at swordpoint? Everywhere plumes of ostrich, bright flowing robes and great turbans surrounded me, and yet for such a mass of people all was miraculously quiet, such was the discipline of my captors. I had been here once before.

Taking a deep breath, I answered the Pasha. "I was a slave of His Majesty for four years, on a galley and here, in Constantinople. It is a common fate, *Hazretleriniz*."

My answer only served to convince the Pasha, who I now understood to be the Grand Vizier himself, that I was a spy and should be executed forthwith. Once more His Majesty interceded. Speaking for the first time, he pointed out that an execution without interrogation availed them nothing, and were they to learn the origin of the agents who had set the Arsenal afire, patience was required. The Grand Vizier repeated that torture would be the simplest expedient, but the Sultan, with a flick of his wrist, ended the discussion.

His Majesty's reproach to the Grand Vizier was made without rancor or humor. His people say he has never smiled, that not once in his long reign has his demeanor ever failed to reflect the loftiness of his station. Not when he massacred the Serbs and Hungarians at Belgrade, or when he wrested Rhodes from the Knights of Saint John after a siege of six months' duration. Not when he erased the Hungarian Empire from the face of the earth or marched unopposed through the gates of Baghdad. Not when the shattered remains of the Christian fleet, defeated by his galleys at the island of Djerbé, were dragged without masts and rudders to Constantinople and the captives, among them myself, were paraded before him on the banks of the Golden Horn as they trudged into slavery.

Yet, when His Majesty finally rested his gaze upon me, and in the brief instant before I lowered my eyes in awe, I did not behold the Sultan of the greatest empire on earth. I beheld an old man. Weary and exhausted. His splendid white turban surmounted a drawn face covered with a rouge incapable of hiding the pockmarks that disfigured his complexion. His white beard blended almost seamlessly into the silk robe draped over a brittle frame. I saw a man who had not long to live.

His Majesty remarked on the patch over my left eye, the scars running along my arms and cheek, and guessed I had seen war.

The Grand Vizier granted me leave to answer. "His Majesty is correct," I whispered. "A year ago, when His Majesty dispatched the largest armada since times of legend against the Isle of Malta, God saw fit that I serve there under the Knights of Saint John, and to survive."

My words had the effect of lightning. E'en the guards and the Pashas seated nearly out of earshot snapped their heads toward me. The Grand Vizier grew instantly furious, shouting, "Liar!" And if I wasn't a liar, I was certainly a spy, for rumors had recently raced through the capital that the Grand Master of the Knights, in order to forestall a second invasion, had sent his agents to Constantinople to effect exactly what had transpired two nights ago. Again His Majesty raised his hand, intrigued by my answer rather than angered. What proof could the prisoner offer that he fought on that accursed isle? Few enough had lived to tell the tale.

I pointed to a Pasha standing nearby, having about five and thirty years to him, and resplendently dressed in a red robe with a bejeweled dagger thrust through the sash. "That is *Kapudan* Piyale Pasha," I said, "the Lord High Admiral of your fleet, who laid siege to the island."

"It proves nothing," the Grand Vizier shouted angrily. Everyone knew the Grand Admiral. I could easily have seen him while a slave, or while he was parading through the streets of Constantinople.

"If it pleases Your Excellency, ask the *Kapudan* if it is not true that the other leader, Vizier Mustafa Pasha, would not sleep in the house they had taken for headquarters because the bed was too hard."

Immediately the Grand Vizier summoned the Admiral, and with a laugh Piyale Pasha confirmed what I had just said. "Yes, beloved Mustafa indeed complained that his back ached. Did the *kafir* walk into the Turkish camp?"

"Not I, but I know one who did—often."

"A daring exploit, if true."

"Aye, more daring exploits in so short a span of time can hardly have been witnessed in the history of the world," I nodded, agreeing with the *Kapudan's* sentiments.

Despite all evidence, the Grand Vizier remained reluctant to accept the truth of my words and, surely, the more truthful they were the more they pointed to my part in the conflagration. Why were they wasting time with the dog? Seeing the impossible nature of my predicament I despaired of answering, but now His Majesty in his wisdom pointed out that, had the prisoner truly lived thro' the siege, he could provide useful intelligence, e'en as they decided whether to torture him or take his head, and his further narration would throw a light on the right course of action.

"What information may I provide His Majesty?" I bowed, seeing no choice in the matter.

Then the Sultan of the Ottoman Empire, King of Kings and the Shadow of Allah on Earth, said that he was most desirous of learning how his armada, the greatest ever assembled, consisting as it did of two hundred ships and tens of thousands of fighting men, with siege cannon the likes of which mortals had rarely set eyes on, was defeated on that insignificant piece of rock by a few hundred Knights, a few thousand mercenaries and a few thousand more irregulars unschooled in arms. Not merely defeated. When the Turkish fleet departed, it left twenty thousand dead on that rock whose name shall never be uttered.

"It was God's Will," I answered, "the Will of Allah."

This reply hardly satisfied His Majesty, who warned me that my life hung by the thread of the responses I gave. He was particularly curious about the role of the Grand Master and the heroic deeds attributed to him.

I, it need not be said, required no further warnings to understand my peril, but I had neither the knowledge nor the wisdom of kings and, as in most affairs of men, no single account could provide the answer he sought. Yet, if it pleased His Majesty I could tell him of the defense of Malta that saved Christendom from an invasion by the Turks. I could tell him of the extraordinary events I witnessed as a man of arms, events that would be seared in my memory until the moment of my death. I could tell him of Grand Master Jean Parisot de Valette, who I sometimes knew and under who I sometimes served, whose steadfastness in the face of overwhelming odds might well be said to have seen us through that terrible, great siege. And I could tell him of others, equally valorous, tho' they'd be unsung in the pages of history. But it was a long story, and hardly mine alone.

The Sultan bade me continue and to tell the story as I saw fit. He would decide just how long it would be.

One

The worst is the stench. His Majesty in his experience has no need to imagine one hundred fifty or more men, naked as the day they were born, chained three to a bench eight months of the year, pulling at their oars ten, fifteen, twenty hours at a stretch with nowhere to sleep save buttressed upon one another and nowhere to exercise their functions except at their places. The soldiers plug their nostrils with herbs or hashish to prevent themselves from gagging on the thick air, but it is to no avail, so evil are the odors rising from the galley deck.

Vermin have the run of the ship and gnaw unceasingly at the prisoners' heels unless they are caught and eaten, for slaves can expect no food but for the soaked biskets or olives the officers thrust down their gullets to prevent them from fainting. The groans of the timbers and creaking of the blocks and cables only add to the endless maledictions of the captives to create a chorus of the damned. At season's end fierce storms, thunder, lightning, driving wind and howling rain drown out the cries, but there is no respite. Through all is the drumbeat. Fettered leg to the foot brace behind you as you rise. Beat. Free leg forward to the stern brace. Beat. Push the oar-loom with all your might over the scarred backs of the prisoners before you. Beat. Plunge the oar into the water as you fall backwards to the bench and pull for all you're worth. Beat. God help a slave if he misses time. The *gumi* will flog him mercilessly with the lash or stick until the wretch has fainted on the oar and will flog him again until he appears dead and then throw him overboard.

No one pities the man whose sufferings end this way. Many, seeing the hopelessness of their situation, pray to God for a swift release. Some beg to be flogged to death or drowned. Why most perish but some survive I have never discerned. Some do survive, for a year, for five, for ten. An iron constitution is not enough. A man must also have an iron will or a foolish belief in salvation.

I had once believed in salvation, but after four years of slavery, I had at last ceased to pray for its arrival in this mortal life. A gun-caster by trade, I'd taken pride in my work and in my skill at arms, which was considerable. *Vanidad!* All dreams had ended this past season. If I believed ought now, it was only that Fortune had turned on the Mediterranean since ancient times. It had turned against me as it had turned against every other wretch aboard this galley. Each of us, from the noblest born to humble Pietru at my side knew that in the eyes of our captors we were worth nothing more than a ransom, and if a ransom weren't to be had, we were worth nothing. We bent our backs to the oar. We avoided the lash when we could, grabbed for *peksimet* or beans as they were thrown at us and, during the winters when we'd been locked up or hauling stones for Turkish forts, we traded stories with our jailers and begged for meat.

I cannot tell you the date of that morning, tho' it was early summer *Anno Domini* 1564. The day was like most others at that time of year—clear, bright. The sun was well up and we knew that by midday the heat would add to our misery. The only sounds were the usual grunts and curses, the splash of oars in the blue sea, the flap of the sails in the breeze and the caw of the seabirds that followed Cocia-Cocia's galley as it cruised between Zante and Cephallonia, guarding the great galleon of His Majesty's Chief Eunuch as it made toward Venice.

From my bench I could see Cocia standing on the poop dressed in his bright pantaloons, with his swarthy face and bald head, threatening the watch officer at the *tavola del fischietto*, as the Christians call it, the whistler's table. Cocia-Cocia was a Calabrian turned Turk. As I regarded him, he waved the flat of a scimitar at the *badbani*'s head, shouting at the dog to increase the tempo. Pietru, a stocky Gozitan farmer who had seen more than his share of misery, glanced at me and spat on the deck. Together we heaved the oar as the beat picked up, and Pietru, in a language I barely understood, muttered, "*Mur hudu f'sormok*—take it up your ass." I found no mirth in it. Cocia-Cocia boasted that as he must go to Hell for eternity, he wanted to give the Christians a taste of the tortures awaiting him there. Truly, Christians damned him as the Executioner, not because he was feared up and down the Italian coast, which he ravaged every year, but because once aboard his ship you were not likely to leave.

This season Cocia wasn't plundering. No, he had been engaged to escort the Chief Eunuch's galleon from Constantinople to Venice. This vessel, laden with the richest goods of the East, boasted twenty large guns, innumerable smaller ones, carried aboard two hundred of His Majesty's feared janissaries for protection and loomed over the small fleet surrounding it. The Chief of the Seraglio wasn't about to put into peril his merchandise or that of His Majesty's wives and concubines, and so we slaves heaved the oars, cursed and felt the sun bake our festering sores as it climbed into the sky.

Suddenly, all was commotion. The shouting and outstretched arms of the crew brought the prisoners' eyes starboard. Not half a league toward the horizon seven galleys under full oar and canvas were heading straight for us. Nothing is so graceful, or so dreaded, as a galley dashing into battle at top speed. At first we could make out only the great triangles of the lateen sails, but within moments the colors—the red and white emblazoned with the eight-pointed cross—told every man aboard the same thing.

"It's the Knights," said Pietru.

Pietru Galea ne'er spoke much, but he needed utter not a word more. By the True Cross of Caravaca, those ships were galleys of the Knights of St. John, for three decades past famed throughout Christendom as the Knights of Malta. The Knights Hospitallers, the last Crusaders, the sworn enemies of the Infidel. We sucked in our breaths. These seven vessels were the entire fleet of the Knights and that could mean only one thing: Cocia must at last face Commander Romegas. The very name Romegas was enough to put dread into the heart of the stoutest corsair. No Knight had taken more prizes, no man knew the Mediterranean better—its coasts, its ports, the smallest inlets. His disdain for danger was legendary. Nay, I say it was truth; once he joined battle, Romegas would sooner die than retreat, damn the odds.

Brilliant vermillion with pennants flying, drums and trumpets sounding ever louder, the enemy ship bore down on us. I have killed men in duels and have run for my life under a hail of arquebus fire, but I can say truly that, with each pounding heartbeat, I had never been so divided between joy and terror as on that morning. Joy at the thought that Fortune's wheel might at last turn for good, terror at the knowledge that if the Turk went down, every slave, chained, went with it.

Seeing that Romegas intended to ram us, Cocia ordered the crew to wheel to starboard, to bring the forward guns into position. As the drumbeat quickened, the *gumi's* blows rained more violently on our backs. "*Hijo de puta!*" I cried out in Spanish, knowing that the slave driver wouldn't understand me. A miracle took place then. Seeing that we were turning about, the enemy gunner let off a shot with his port *sacra*. The ball hit the Turkish gunner square in the face and blew his head to pieces, splattering his brain all over me and everyone else around him. A fragment from the Turk's skull hit Pietru, whose nose had been crooked from birth, and straightened it so perfectly that not even a crease could be seen from then on. Pietru told the story often.

We the slaves, tho', were not about to aid Cocia in the slightest and, as if on a signal from On High, the lot of us dropped our oars. The galley stalled. Romegas got off one shot with his thirty-six *libbre* piece, and an instant later his ramming spur ploughed straight into our broadside. With a great roar, our oars snapped and splintered as the ship lurched to port and heaved men overboard. We had two hundred arquebusiers and bowmen aboard, and those who still had their footing let loose. In all the smoke and noise there was little for the slaves to do but keep their heads down. Romegas, tho', leapt aboard the Turk, leading a dozen of his men, brandishing a rapier in his hand, but otherwise protected only by a small buckler and the white cross that striped his red tunic. Crying, "I've got your eggs in my palm now, Cocia!" he took down two corsairs at once and the mêlée began.

Cocia refused to decline the contest and received his enemy with the same ferocity. He immediately dispatched two Knights with cuts from his scimitar. All the while, making his way astern, Romegas was shouting, "Cocia, you old bastard, come to me," while his foeman answered, "The Devil's own son is waiting for you, Romegas!" The two met in a single combat. Today Fate went against the renegado; he received a blow on the back and fell across one of the slaves' benches, not three paces from me. In an instant the prisoners were upon him, pummeling him senseless with their fists. Romegas, now master of the vessel, watched from the poop as the slaves passed Cocia from one bench to the next, each man giving him a blow. Some slaves so thirsted for revenge that they tore at him with their teeth. Pietru took flesh from him and spat it out in triumph and I cannot deny that I did the same. By the time Cocia had been passed to the last bench, there was little left of him, and they threw him overboard.

As a small, long-tailed monkey leapt nimbly to his shoulder, Romegas ordered the Christians unshackled and the Turks chained. We watched in wonderment and disbelief as our bonds were removed; we embraced each other with tears in our eyes and cheered the Commander. I myself knelt at his feet in thanks. Only then did I perceive how as of old the Knight's hands shook with a tremor so pronounced that he needed to clasp one with the other to steady them. That harsh face saw I had my eyes upon it, frowned and turned away. He didn't recognize me.

Suchlike scenes were at that moment being enacted amongst the other galleys. Truly, seeing that Romegas was upon them, several of the Turkish escort fled altogether. The galleon, tho', was not about to yield the fight. Mayhap I will describe in its proper place that sanguine engagement, which lasted five full hours and which resulted in great losses on both sides. But the end of it His Majesty knows all too well: the Knights seized the *sultana*, whose cargo alone was valued at eighty thousand Venetian ducats, attached ropes to it and prepared to tow it home.

Seven mornings hence, when the sun was still low and the limestone glistened white like bones, the small fleet passed into the mouth of a great harbor, unequaled anywhere in Christendom. To starboard, a long hill sloped downward ending at a star fort that stood sentinel above water's edge. To port, three bodies swung from gallows erected on a rocky prominence that jutted into the harbor's entrance. Ahead, the imposing castle of the Knights of the Order of St. John of Jerusalem. I had come again to Malta.

Two

I was born in that most noble city of Granada without taint of Moorish or Jewish blood. Nine days after my birth I was baptized Francisco in the Church of Pedro and Pablo, where the ceremony was witnessed by the best citizens of the town, but my mother failed to see in the name she had chosen for me the omen it was. Like St. Francis himself, I would not be destined for the life of a merchant, the trade of my father.

My father Fernando had been cursed like all Spaniards with a great hunger: to rise above his station at any cost. He had inherited his business from his own father, a successful merchant of cloth and silver, and had slowly widened the firm until it included shops in Sevilla, Valencia and Avignon. He traded with the Florentines, the Venetians and sometimes even the Turks, and every three or four years received goods from China. Fernando's success allowed him to marry well; my mother's father had been one of the most respected goldsmiths in our city, working only on commission and once accepting an order from Emperor Carlos himself.

Luck smiled on Fernando when he helped finance a shipment of quicksilver to Nueva España, a shipment that landed safely and returned his investment three times over. His Majesty well knows the fruits of success, and I am told they changed my father's behavior markedly. From that day on he wore nothing but silks and furs and never failed to carry a sword, tho' if he'd fought a single duel in his life, no one knew of it. He bragged everywhere that he was to be knighted and hurried along the day by buying himself a coat of arms. Sometimes Fernando de Barai mistakenly signed himself "Don," a slip he confessed he was not legally entitled to. He spoke incessantly of honor, became quick to take offense and no one could distinguish his bearing from that of a prince. I remember vividly the house he built while I was yet a child, a house that to the envious eyes of Granadans across the river seemed hardly short of a palace. Visitors would marvel at the gardens, where they would bask in the scent of violets and oranges and gasp in delight at the peacocks and marmosets roaming freely. In those gardens guests would often have their first cup of chocolate, for the drink had only recently appeared and was considered a great rarity.

My parents naturally expected me to get enough of an education to carry on the family business, and they sent me to school for my elementary and *gramatica*, where I learned to read and to write from printed books. There, at the foothills of the snowcapped Sierras, not a stone's throw from the Alhambra and the Emperor's new palace, I learned another lesson: school was not for me. His Majesty appreciates that a child knows nothing beyond the rising and setting of the sun, but it did not take me long to discover that I loathed the daily recitations of arithmetic and Latin. "Why don't they just crucify me?" I said along with my Paternosters, and the thought of a merchant's life began to fill me with a real if unnamed dread.

I did not know what I was good for. The stars had blessed me with a certain nimbleness of feet and deftness in my fingers. With the clarity of years I see that one of my father's worst traits was beginning to show— that incessant striving for place—but it was tempered by my mother Anna's piety. I never parted from the crucifix she gave me; I grew tall and muscular. I began to display a certain Devil-may-care courage born out of that indescribable disaffection with my position. My classmates called me "*Esforzado*," which meant "reckless" no less than it did "fearless." I brawled with my friends on the town squares, winning more than I lost, and with everyone traded stories about the exploits of Cortés and Pizarro. News of Pizarro's death in Lima at the hands of treacherous assassins was the talk of the town and sparked in all the young men the heated desire to become conquistadors. By the time I was twelve I still knew nothing of what Fortune intended for me. I prayed twice daily, certain only that I would never pass thro' the gates of the university the Emperor had built in Granada not long before my birth.

When I look back on the path that brought me to His Majesty's palace, an abrupt turn took place when I was eleven. That year I met Blaij Vergã. A group of us had skipped school to watch an old-style jousting contest down by the bridge. A scuffle broke out in the crowd and soon it was an out-and-out fight among my classmates. One of them, Blaij, knifed Luis, who fell to the dirt, dead like a stone. I was close enough to see it happen.

"You killed him," I said to Blaij later, after everyone had scattered and we were alone.

"He was stealing coins from me," Blaij answered, spitting on the ground.

"But you killed him."

"If you say anything, I'll break your neck."

He might have too. Blaij was the strongest among us at school. Nobody knew who his father was and he lived with his mother, who worked as a weaver. She wanted him to be a silversmith, but anybody could see that getting a loan from a Jew without interest would have been more likely. Blaij was too proud, too headstrong and always spoiling for a fight. The next day the police showed up at school and questioned the entire class. Blaij denied everything. I kept my trap shut, but one of the other boys squealed and Blaij was sent away from Granada for a year.

He came back even more of what he had been. Gruff and growing powerful, with wild, unkempt black hair, he talked incessantly about his exploits, how he had followed the army as a kitchen boy, how he had learned to shoot and drink and about all the women he'd met. The thought never crossed my mind that he might be making some of it up, especially the women, and his stories produced an undeniable fascination in me. I admired and imitated him. Blaij was absolutely fearless. Facing three boys or six, he would never back down. We sometimes fought ourselves, testing each other. He was the stronger, yes, if only by a little, but I was the more agile and it was always a close contest. Of course my parents didn't want me sullying my good name with such a bad influence. Of course their advice misfired. Blaij and I became friends. I think we hated each other.

I lost sight of Blaij for several years when I turned thirteen and my father sent me to Sevilla to learn the business. The old proverb says, "*Quien no ha visto Sevilla no ha visto una maravilla,*" "He who has not seen Sevilla has not seen a wonder." Truthfully, Sevilla was wondrous and I ran all over the city gaping: at the great cathedral, at the churches, the convents, the squares and monasteries. I forced my way up the crowded steps to the Orangery, the ancient mosque that flanked the north side of the cathedral, and walked through the Moorish door above which a relief showed Christ driving the traders out of the Temple. Beyond that door courtiers, merchants and ship owners from all over Europe gathered to dispute the price of merchandise in the Americas. People were then flocking to Sevilla and it seemed the number of souls there increased visibly every day. They were coming to make their fortunes, for through Sevilla and Sevilla alone flowed the gold and silver from the Newfound World.

From the top of the Golden Tower you could cast your gaze over the barges on the banks of the Guadalquivir and the masts of ships and the goods destined for the Indies piled high on the quay. When a fleet came in, the whole town ran to greet it with as much dread as joy, for entire fortunes were made or lost with the fate of a single ship. Once amid the crowd I watched some Indians being led off the boat. As the savages walked down the gangplank in their strange dress they were met by cries of astonishment. Some of the women e'en fainted at the sight of them and had to be carried away. What astounded me was the finery of the dress I saw there. Not a few Sevillans sported gold-braided doublets and almost everyone else wore silk or velvet. Each lady seemed intent to outdo the next and every dress was embroidered or full of lace or swanskin, and every gentleman swaggered with a sword fastened to his waist by a silver chain.

I thanked the stars for my good fortune and might well have thanked my father for his wisdom in deciding well for me, but when I arrived at his shop, in the center of the old town, the first thing the accountant said to me was, "Go and fetch some water from the square." His tone offended me.

"I am here as an apprentice, not a servant," I answered, puffing up my chest, at which he threatened to strike me. I was nearly a man then, a tall and strong one, and I might have made him think better of his insult, but out of respect for my father I did his bidding. With such a start I became an even more reluctant merchant than before, natheless it was lucky for me that I went after the water, for on the square I saw a paper that Don Jerónimo Sánchez de Carranza had opened a fencing school for common people.

The science of arms had recently become the rage and Don Jerónimo was to become the greatest master in all Spain. At the time I had no idea of how eminent he was—or e'en if he was eminent. I knew only that he was a rather strange man. Dark, bearded and wiry, dressed usually in an ragged doublet and a tattered cloak, he spoke of Plato, of geometry, of the circle of defense.

"Maestro, all I want is to learn how to fight!" I pleaded after hearing out his introductory.

"Get out of my school, you ill-bred urchin!" he cried and no less than kicked me through the door, shouting at my back, "Does an adept study the geometry to become a great mathematician? No! He studies the geometry to improve the powers of reason in other spheres, to think with logic, with method and without emotion!"

Only a week later did I dare return, begging Don Jerónimo's forgiveness. He glared at me with the utmost disdain but did not turn me away. Instead he lectured with flailing arms that the base, the vulgar, dishonor the Skill, just as the Ass of Cumas dons the skin of the Lion to deceive its opponents, and that the way to the Sun is blocked by many thickets. Sitting on a bench before him, I thought, here, truly, is a madman, and I almost departed of my own accord. A full year went by before his assistant Gaspar told me that Don Jerónimo studied the alchemists, among them the late Paracelsus, who was famous throughout Europe, and my Master saw little difference between perfection of the Skill and the attainment of the legendary philosopher's stone.

None of this meant anything to a beardless youth, but I kept my mouth shut and learned what I could. For two years I trained daily in Carranza's school, learning the postures—to defend myself with dagger, to parry a threat with mailed glove or cloak, the wrestling holds required to disarm an opponent, the cut and the thrust. Don Jerónimo advocated the thrust as more suited to the new Spanish *espadas*, rapiers, which were designed to penetrate armor and were becoming the favored weapon across Europe. He railed at the Italians, who saw the best defense as a counterattack, and who launched their assaults from static poses.

"No!" Don Jerónimo would cry, "The Skill is a dance. Each step must flow into the others. That is the origin of *técnica*!" And so we danced around that imagined circle, learning to step aside from an attack, deflecting it, or to circle our opponent as we searched for an opening, or to force one by varying the rhythm of the dance. Sometimes Don Jerónimo would seize me by the arm to demonstrate the *mandoble*, which with the two-handed broadswords carried by knights of old had been unheard of. Sometimes he would stop a bout, grab my shoulders and spin me around, shouting, "Simpleton!" and he would explain that when facing an opponent, the *diestro* should present the smallest target, which with those heavy weapons of the past had also been impossible. Mostly, Don Jerónimo insisted that in the heat of combat the *diestro* must keep a level head and his blood cold and gaze upon his adversary as he would a problem from Euclid. The advice was sound, tho' I wasn't old enough to take it. Fortune would ensure that I would take it soon enough.

Inescapably, Father learned that I was spending the money he had given me on the science of arms, but to my great surprise he approved, for it accorded with his noble aspirations, and the episode ended happily and without rancor.

Another chapter ended less happily. During my second year in Sevilla, Don Jerónimo suddenly disappeared for more than a month and the lessons were taken over by Gaspar. When Don Jerónimo returned, he appeared years older, saying no more than he had been ill and that it would pass. Only under my persistent questioning did Gaspar divulge what had happened: Don Jerónimo had been summoned before the Inquisition. The Inquisition! The word itself filled me with an incomprehensible dread, tho' I knew no more than Luther was the Devil incarnate and *El Santo Oficio*, the Holy Office, was defending Spain from his vile heresy. Gaspar explained that Sevilla, being the center of commerce between nations, was full of forbidden books and secret Lutherans, and that Don Jerónimo's brief incarceration had been entirely common. The Inquisitors may have found his ideas strange, but not Lutheran.

Life in Sevilla went on unchanged. The Church authorities confiscated books daily at the docks, which I loudly applauded, and if anything the city seemed to become e'er more festive. Jubilation greeted news of Luther's death and there was dancing in the streets, but the Inquisition knew it had a long battle ahead. On many feasts you could see the Bishop leading a solemn procession into the squares, where a priest would mount a platform and read an edict of faith, wherewith he invited the crowd to denounce all who held opinions heretical, suspect, erroneous, scandalous or blasphemous against our Lord and the Holy Catholic Faith. He admonished us especially to guard against those who spoke favorably of the Law of Moses, the sects of Mahomet and Luther, and all those who possessed books written by heretical authors. After speaking for half an hour the priest would lead the crowd into the church, where each and every person renewed his vows. The spectacle terrified and exhilarated me.

I resolved to denounce every heretic I met and from that day on I listened to conversations with a sharpened ear.

But in my small sphere, everyone shared the true faith and I encountered no heretics in Sevilla. By the time I left I had learned far more about swordsmanship than finance and my father's partners were glad to be rid of me. Before I returned to Granada, Father ordered me to accompany a shipment of silver and Chinese wallpaper to Burgos. Burgos lay over one hundred leagues to the north and the journey on muleback took nearly a month. We outnumbered the only brigands who troubled us, and when we entered the city, some agents of the Holy Office inspected our saddlebags for offensive books, found nothing and politely demanded a bribe. At Burgos we followed the Friday procession from the town to a convent that stands a crossbow shot across the river. There we witnessed a great miracle. In the convent is a crucifix, the height of a real man, which is made of neither wood nor stone. Its hair grows and when one touches the limbs, they move. When I set my eyes on this wonder I fell on my knees and wept with joy. The townspeople told us that four hundred and twelve years after the birth of Christ, robbers captured a ship, which was carrying the crucifix in a chest. But when the thieves tried to open the chest, they fell down as if dead and a great storm blew up, forcing them to Santander. They recognized their fate as a sign from God and sought out a hermit, who advised them to take the chest to the Bishop of Burgos. Finding the Bishop asleep, they awoke him. He had been dreaming of a crucifix lying on a ship that sailed the water. Astounded by this, the robbers invited the Bishop and priests to the ship. As the holy men knelt before the chest, it opened of its own accord and the Bishop brought the crucifix with great solemnity to the convent where it rests to this day.

Upon my return to Granada, life changed quickly and unexpectedly. My parents kept three slaves, one of whom was a fetching Tatar girl with slanting eyes. I was at the age when the blood had begun to boil. It was not long before those eyes caught mine and I willingly surrendered my innocence. I had her only twice, and am certain I was not alone, for about a year later she was found to be with child. I denied responsibility and she was turned out. I do not know what became of her.

Blaij and I again took up our comradeship. By now we were men, young, strong, daring. Vergã had started a beard and girls blushed as we passed them in the streets. Blaij boasted that in the past two years he had had dozens of women and remarked straightforwardly that he had killed another man in a fight over one of them. He would have joined the army a year ago, except that his mother had begged him to remain in Granada. Vergã was already a man you crossed at your peril. I admired this in him. It made him exciting and simple. He was absolutely fearless, and he was absolutely dangerous.

He was also in matters of the flesh indisputably more advanced than I, and soon after my return to the city he introduced me to the Granadan whorehouses where we spent all our free time among the *mancebas*. For on two years I abandoned myself to this dissolute life, whoring, drinking and gambling, coming home at all hours of the night, when at all. My parents despaired that I had become incorrigible. They took the only course available to them and arranged a marriage.

I'd ne'er set eyes on the girl, but she was sixteen and from a family as well off as our own. The match was a good one and I could hardly object, for it would join the fortunes of our two houses. When I finally met Isabella, I was pleasantly surprised. She was black-haired, pretty and well spoken, in her secluded life had read more books than I and she did not overly paint her face. We went for strolls together on the town and once by accident I caught a glimpse of her ankle, which excited me greatly. Sometimes she donned the veil to meet me at night, which was a great risk, and once I caught her alone in her garden dancing the *chacona*.

"How dare you!" I cried, shocked at her lasciviousness. Isabella apologized profusely, swearing by the Mother of God she would never do it again, all the while secretly smiling. Our affection for each other grew and, following the current fashion, I paid some troubadours to serenade her at her window. My parents were pleased that their son would uphold the honor of the family and Isabella's parents were pleased that her future looked assured. Plans for the wedding went ahead, which would take place after Holy Week. Guests would come from far and wide and the banquet would be grand.

It was not to be.

One night during the *fiestas*, I returned home late, Carnavale mask in hand and walked into the big room. My father, surrounded by his paintings, was standing behind the table, face ashen, and my mother sat on a stool across the room, weeping.

"Mother! Father! What has happened?"

Father merely lowered his eyes to the table, on which lay a flat, green book that had been tied by a ribbon. With a frozen heart, I approached the table and slowly lifted the cover, letting it fall back onto the table. My fears were confirmed.

"This is a forgery!" I cried, "the work of a *linajudo!*"

Father nodded, trembling from head to foot in anger. His pride already screamed for vengeance. But there was also resignation written on his face, for he knew the damage had been done. I, tho', was far from resigned. In fury I dashed from the house and sought out Vergã.

I found him masked in the clutches of his *manceba* and got him out of bed. Once he sobered up, he agreed the papers must be false.

"Everyone knows your family is one of the purest in Granada," he said with a strange sneer in his voice. "There is no taint of Moorish blood."

It was inconceivable. The Moors had been expelled from Granada or converted more than a half-century ago. They lived in their own *aljama*, dressed like Arabs, fasted on Saturdays, spoke *algarabía*, not Spanish, wrote in a secret language. There had been many edicts forbidding them to do these things, but the infidels had bought the Emperor with great sums of money and he repealed his own laws. But for business dealings, my family never had anything to do with the Moors, and never would.

"It is the wedding," I said. "Some swine intends to prevent my marriage to Isabella."

"He has," Blaij replied, offering me his flagon. "You'll never live this down."

"By the Holy Scriptures I shall."

I stayed in the brothel that night but spurned my whore's advances. The *mancebas* had their own ideas about who was responsible. Some Agacio de Antonio who I barely knew was in love with Isabella and had been slandering me all over town. The whores' gossip only served to inflame me, but I wanted proof and in the morning I stormed over to the Town Hall with Vergã. I slammed my fist on the desk and demanded of the clerk to know if someone had been snooping around our family records. When the bastard refused to say, I stretched my arm across the desk and practically strangled him. Blaij merely unsheathed his dagger and pointed it at the dog's throat. The whores had been right, as usual. Agacio de Antonio had murdered my happiness.

We arranged the duel for that very night. Carnavale was then in full flight. As we walked to the far end of town, toward the caves across the river, we pushed our way through throngs of revelers, harlequins, swine, donkeys, monsters that terrified children. We dodged rotten eggs and knocked aside tricksters who intended to do us harm. Soldiers stormed a wooden castle and defeated the Moorish defenders, then after their victory led the prisoners through the town in chains and ceaselessly shot off their arquebuses. But nothing could distract me from my intent.

"You had better cool your blood," Blaij said cheerfully, seeing my determination.

"Do not be concerned on my account," I answered frigidly. "Just make certain Agacio has said his prayers."

To reach our destination we needed to pass by the Morisco *aljama*. The quarter was silent as a grave and most of the houses boarded up for the night. All the Moriscos must be across the river getting drunk at the festival so they would not be exposed as the false *conversos* they were. There had been trouble here of late. Moors were forbidden to carry weapons, even a sharp blade, but searches had been turning up some knives, and the criminals thrown in prison.

Blaij spat on the ground. "The dogs should all be thrown out or put to the sword."

From the depths of my soul I agreed.

When we arrived at the caves that honeycomb the Sacromonte hill, where brigands and gypsies secreted themselves, my adversary was waiting. He had come without a second. That was an insult, but I didn't care. His death was assured. Blaij, sitting casually on a rock and swigging wine from his flagon, demanded an apology as was the custom, but to no avail.

"Those papers were no forgeries," Agacio replied. "Your great grandmother was a Moor."

Blaij was about to say something, but I silenced him with a wave of my hand. By the Incarnation of the Holy Word, I'd had enough of this man's arrogance and his insults to my blood purity. I kissed my crucifix and drew my sword.

My adversary and I saluted, and we began to circle. Not so tall as I, he was a good swordsman, but untrained. He carried himself with a haughtiness that was unbearable, his moonlit smile nearly laughing. He thought himself assured of victory—and that mocking, snickering smile was meant to enrage me. But ice ran through my veins. Three times Agacio on a pass thought he had found an opening and thrust. Three times I stepped aside from his blade, deflecting it from the path of danger. Now it was my enemy's turn to anger; I saw him grow heated and careless. Our swords clashed there at the mouth of the caves, and the caves returned the sound, made louder and stranger, as if bellowed forth from the depths of Hell. In his vain assaults Agacio grew ever wilder and more desperate. Then he withdrew his dagger and advanced on me. I caught him in a *prise*, twisted the knife from his hand as I tripped him backwards over my knee and plunged the knife into his heart.

I caught my breath, spat on the body and was about to walk off when Blaij, having lazily applauded my success, rose from the rock on which he had been sitting and drew his sword. "Now, my turn."

"What is this?" I asked, startled.

"He was," Blaij said with a glance at the body, "after all, my cousin. You have defended your honor. Now I defend mine."

I could only stare at him in amazement. "You're a lying bastard."

Blaij shrugged. "Come, Señor, what are you afraid of?"

He suddenly hurled himself at me with such force that he knocked me to the ground, but his speed was so great that he himself tumbled beyond. We both got to our feet and the fight began. I could not overcome his natural power, and each time his blade struck mine, I feared it would fall from my hand. But neither could he, with my speed, find the opening he wanted. At first I thought I was a dead man, so impossible was it for me to believe that Blaij Vergã was attempting to kill me. Only after I convinced myself that my life was in dire peril did I regain my wits and my feet. We fought and fought, that unearthly, hollow groan filling the glade. We fought until our exhaustion was so great that neither of us could stand and it seemed that the victor would be he whose heart gave out last.

Suddenly, Blaij held up his hand. "Enough," he said with a deep laugh that unnerved me. "I just wanted to see if you could really fight."

Panting, I merely stared at him anew.

"You're such a cunt. Where we're going, I'll need a companion with balls."

I told him right then I'd fuck his mother. "What are you talking about anyway?"

Blaij sneered and began to piss on the ground. "You think you can stay in Granada now? Hah. Those papers may be real, mayhap they aren't, but everyone thinks you're a Moor. You know, Señor, what happened to that Morisco woman last month?"

"No," I answered, wringing the sweat from my hair.

"You should spend more time with the *mancebas*. They threw her in some secret prison and tortured her for slaughtering a kid ten years ago, and because she rests on Thursday nights."

"The Holy Office?"

"Holy Office, police, in God's name what difference does it make? They suspect you of being a fucking Morisco, you'll end up in the shit-hole. Forget Isabella. She won't see you now. You'd be better off dead than alive."

I raised my sword and held it to Blaij's throat. "You're a madman," I said. "I should kill you now."

"You won't," he said, not even bothering to shove the blade aside. "But be careful. Someday, my friend, I may lose my temper." He shrugged and walked away.

Blaij may have been more dangerous, more unpredictable than I had suspected, but on that day he wasn't a madman. As he had foretold, Isabella refused ever to see me. My father, knowing too well that a life without honor was a life not worth living, very nearly poisoned himself but, rescued by my mother Anna, he at last agreed to move the family to Sevilla. I refused to go and could think of nothing but killing myself or redemption. The priest-confessor listened, but in the darkness of the church I could see that if *El Santo Oficio* did not already know of the baseless accusations, it soon would. In such a despair as I had never known, one night I slipped out of the house carrying only my purse and my sword, and with Blaij Vergã, who mayhap would think only twice before putting a dagger in my back, headed to the coast. I never set eyes on Granada, the garden of Spain, or my native land again.

Three

We took horses to Malaga. I remained despondent over the events whose outcome I had not entirely felt, but His Majesty knows the resilience of youth, and from the abyss yawning within me arose a grim determination to put the past at my heels and face what destiny Fortune had chosen. "The Devil take them all!" I snarled as I spurred my horse through the city gates.

Blaij's humor altogether bested mine. "Cheer up, my friend," he said when the sun had barely risen, casting a harsh light on the road ahead. "Four days from now we're in Malaga. They need soldiers to fight Dragut. We sail on the first ship. Three weeks we're in Tripoli. You'll be skewering the Turks and fucking Moorish whores. A month from now you'll have forgotten Granada. It's all very simple, Señor."

I could not help but laugh aloud, for Vergã espoused the plan for the one hundredth time with the same gruff abandonment as he had proclaimed it for the first. Why I laughed, I can hardly say, for in truth I wholeheartedly approved of the brash plan. My desire to face the infidels had become as ardent as Vergã's own. The Turkish corsairs had raided the coasts of Spain on and off for decades with the connivance of the treacherous Moriscos, who shared their barbarous religion.

And Dragut.

The very mention of his name conjured in my mind an indistinct and enormous figure who cast his shadow across, lo, the entire Mediterranean. Even the most ignorant schoolboy knew that Dragut was Soliman's appointed successor to the legendary Barbarossa. The most feared of the Barbary corsairs, Dragut roamed the sea at will. To the infidels he was the Drawn Sword of Islam—and it was true: He had all but taken over North Africa and he raided Sicily, the Kingdom of Naples and even Tuscany almost every year. Half of Christendom lived in terror of Dragut's depredations, but half hardly satisfied his appetite and Carlos knew the Sword of Islam would soon strike Spain itself.

"So, Señor, would you like to face Dragut one on one?" Blaij asked me without warning as we put more leagues of the road behind us.

"Nothing would give me greater pleasure," I replied to the challenge without a thought.

"And tell me, what would the brave soldier of fortune Francisco de Barai do if he met him?"

"I would kill him, naturally," I answered. By the Sacred Nativity of Christ, I did not doubt for a moment that the outcome could be otherwise. Was I not a Spaniard?

But Vergã merely snorted, "Of course," and fell silent.

That evening we put up at a filthy *venta* toward Loja and handed over the raw meat and eggs we had bought to the innkeeper. In my brief life I had stayed in worse, yet the place was hardly above a kennel, or perhaps a fox's lair from which the large *ventero* was trying to smoke out the fox, for smoke belched so thickly from the pipe serving as a chimney that Blaij and I quickly fell to coughing out our lungs and retreated to a bench outside.

"Are you bound for Malaga, Señors?" the innkeeper asked in a heavy voice as he brought our food and poured two glasses of wine from an old goatskin. His clothes were no better than a vagabond's, torn and threadbare, and as I regarded his wife lingering nearby in a dirty peasant's dress, I attempted to find in her wrinkled face the pretty girl she might once have been. I failed.

Blaij nodded in answer to the question as he downed the wine, which stank of goatskin.

"Then you'll be joining up with Doria," the wretched *ventero* said simply, as had he foreseen the answer.

Again Vergã nodded, this time with a grunt, no doubt wishing the fellow and his foul breath would go away, but I found myself smiling. Somehow, tho' our host walked with difficulty and numbers of his teeth were missing, I perceived in him the remnants of a certain dignity. Do not ask me to explain.

Doria.

The *ventero* had put his finger on it. The idea was fantastic, enormous. Inescapable.

Andrea Doria, the great Genoese Admiral, had, as His Majesty well knows, been in the employ of the Spanish Crown for near a quarter century, since long before my birth. Carlos had offered an emperor's reward for Dragut's destruction, yet Doria's own hatred for the corsair was greater than an emperor's. Now into his ninth decade, the oath he'd sworn by the Mother of God to apprehend the fox remained in force with vigor undimmed. Iron! With his own fleet of galleys, the Captain General of the Sea—His Majesty will appreciate Doria's true and proper title—had hunted Dragut across the north coast of Africa. *Anno* 1549, two summers before Blaij Vergã and I quitted Granada, the chase had set every city square in Spain alive with surmise and advice, but had turned up empty-handed. Only a year ago, *anno* 1550, news had reached Doria that Dragut was at Monastir, but by the time the Admiral got there, his foeman had slipped away. The Christians then moved to besiege Dragut's own stronghold, Mahdia—"Africa" the town was called—and stormed it after two months. But Dragut was nowhere to be found. The Devil had walked across the sea and the sea had swallowed his footprints.

"Then you have heard the news?" the innkeeper asked us then.

"Nay," I replied, "what's that?"

Our host's eyes lit up at the chance to tell his tale and he pulled up a stool and sat himself beside us. "Dragut, Dragut—" he could hardly refrain from laughing, so good he thought the story—"Dragut prevailed upon the Sultan himself to write to the Emperor, demanding—demanding, do you hear—the return of Monastir and Africa. Can one credit such effrontery? Who does the Sultan think he is? Of course the good Carlos was enraged. Tunis is under royal protection, he told the Grand Turk. He had rightfully reft those places from Dragut—'a corsair odious to both God and man'—that is what the Emperor said. So once again he's sent Admiral Doria after the Sword of Islam with orders to take him alive or dead. They must have set sail from Genoa a month ago, at the beginning of March."

Blaij slapped the table with the flat of his hand. "So much the better. We'll be just in time."

His Majesty will himself be able to judge the accuracy of the innkeeper's story, which I recount with no greater detail than I recollect. But that was the essence of our plans. The innkeeper advised us to go to

Sicily. "If you can get there," he told us, "you can certainly meet up with Doria and, God willing, share the glory."

"How do you know all this, my friend?" I asked, surprised that the humble innkeeper could reveal himself to be such a lively fount of knowledge. "Did you hear it with your own ears?"

"You are not the first to pass this way, Señors—but tell me, young man, your clothes are too fine and too new for you to be a soldier. You are a gentleman."

Blaij answered instantly and without a trace of humor. "What would a gentleman be doing in this dung heap?"

"I make no claim to be a gentleman," I retorted no less quickly, "tho' I am hardly so lowborn as yourself."

"Señors," the innkeeper said at once, interposing his bulk between us, "*Por la Cinta de San Francisco*, I will have no blood spilled in this establishment on account of insults of such poor quality."

I had to laugh. "He is correct, Sir, I am no gentleman. I am just a merchant's son who has little taste for sums or bargaining." Once the moment of heat had passed, I was overcome by the sharp need to seek out a priest to ask why God had seen fit to deprive me, Francisco Perez de Barai, of my rightful heritage. My face must have turned crimson with shame, until I reminded myself that Francisco's lot was not so bitter as Job's. I crossed myself and renewed my determination to face whatever the Lord had put in my path.

Before sending the *ventero* off to buy some food for the morning, we brought our saddles and gear to the room given us. "Have you been to Madrid?" the innkeeper asked suddenly.

"No, never," I replied.

"I was once, years ago. They reckon the streets there are perfumed daily with ten thousand turds, and they say, 'that which one shits in the winter, one drinks in the summer.' Heh, heh, heh."

Madrid was far away, God high above and luckily our bed was enough removed from the latrine pit to make the smell bearable. In the morning, tho', I had good reason to exclaim, "Eh! Look at this!" when we awoke to find ourselves fleabitten from head to toe. "By the Blessed Virgin, my own mother wouldn't recognize me!"

"Lucky for her," Blaij replied. "Let's be gone."

We relieved ourselves outside and paid according to the board, but the innkeeper claimed that the breakfast eggs and chicken had cost him a *real* more than we had given him.

"You're a lying shit," said Blaij, "no better than your turds of Madrid."

"Leave it," I said, pressing my companion's arm, and put a few coins on the table.

As we two saddled up, Blaij turned to me. "You really are a fool," he laughed with some wonderment.

"Leave it," I repeated, not intending to admit that my judgment of the *ventero* had been faulty.

As that moment the innkeeper lumbered hesitantly into the yard after us and said, "Be careful at the port. They're looking at documents these days." His wife nodded. "Are your papers in order?"

"In order," Blaij replied. I merely nodded.

"God be with you," the innkeeper said, and without looking back, we continued on our journey.

At Malaga the harbor teemed with ships and we had no trouble finding a galiot bound for Tripoli. The Captain outfitting the expedition with letters of marque from the Crown, Dimas de Gustaldo, asked for no papers. The recruits before him were over fourteen and thus of military age. They intended to fight the Turks and that was proof enow that they were not Mahometans. Gustaldo did tell us to go find some arquebuses. Blaij and I sold our horses, bought morions at an armorer's and at a gunsmith's found matchlocks made locally.

Whether Blaij's stories of his exploits as a camp follower during our years apart were true I had never determined, but he had learnt somewhere how to shoot.

"You move the fuse here, my friend," he said, pushing the lit match through a small tube atop the barrel. "Fix it in these jaws." I did as he told me. "Push aside this powder cover. Pull the trigger."

As I pulled, the jaws moved the burning end of the fuse into the little pan of gunpowder fixed aside the barrel, and the whole flashed, a tiny hole in the barrel passing the spark to the charge inside. "How do you hold it?" I exclaimed, wondering at the ungainly operation even as I received a palpable kick.

"Against your shoulder, Señor," Gustaldo interrupted the lesson. "They haven't used the chest since your grandfather's day."

Either way the weapon struck me as unbearably clumsy and I held the repugnant thing at arm's length. "I'll stick to my rapier," I said, slinging the gun over my shoulder.

"A lot of good your rapier will do at thirty paces."

Vergã was right, of course. Over time I came to value the arquebus as utterly trustworthy as it was simple. If nothing else, a better club at close quarters has yet to be devised.

The expedition might prove to be a long one and Captain Gustaldo advised us to procure extra clothing and provisions. Blaij thanked me for the money I lent him, and by the end of the morning we had dressed ourselves in bright red blouses, purple leggings, new knee boots and yellow pantaloons striped with red. A peacock strutting in all its splendor hardly appeared as glorious and formidable as we two.

"Dragut will tremble before you," said Vergã, sizing me up with approval.

I paused before my reflection in the shopkeeper's mirror. "Of that there can be little doubt," I replied with the utmost solemnity.

As the innkeeper had foretold, the harbormaster on the dock, accompanied by armed men, was checking papers to prevent Moriscos from escaping to Barbary. Well he might. The Emperor had issued edicts to prevent Moriscos, under pain of death and confiscation of property, from changing their residence, yet the secret plots of the conversos to flee Spanish shores continued unabated. I offered my papers to the harbormaster, but seeing that we were Christians, he waved us aboard the galiot. Within an hour, under sail and oar, we were bound for North Africa.

Four

Our galiot set forth with seventy-two oarsmen, mostly *buenas boyas* who rowed to keep their asses out of prison. The wretches heaved two by two in eighteen banks. This small galley, what Your Majesty calls a *kalyata*, could hardly expect to best a full galley—of twenty-four banks and oarsmen that rowed three by three—in a head-on clash, but if naught else we could outrun one.

At first no danger presented itself. With little to amuse them, the forty arquebusiers aboard and the smaller number of crossbowmen crowded amongst them reflected my own discomfort at the newer profession by trading heated volleys over the merits of their chosen weapons.

"I spit on the arquebus!" one of the crossbowmen would cry, averring that any donkey could fire a gun, and that a gun held not a single advantage over the crossbow. It couldn't shoot as far, it couldn't shoot as true and it couldn't shoot with the same force.

"Go tangle yourself in your damned winding tackle and break it!" came the answer from the arquebusiers.

"*Por las Novenas de Señora Santa Elizabet!*" one of the rowers shouted.

A bow required more skill than either, and a real archer could launch six shafts in the same time it took an imbecile to fire an arquebus.

Listening to these feisty, never-ending debates, I perceived that e'en in that spring of 1551 crossbowmen were a dying breed, yet one had to admire the grip wherewith they clung to a weapon soon to be extincted by brutish simplicity.

The clash with the infidel we half expected came too near on the day we passed within fifty *brazas*—one hundred sticks—of a full Turkish galley. A Christian slave somehow managed to cast himself into the sea and made for us. But one of the Turkish crewmen likewise cast himself into the sea and, gaining swiftly on the other, mounted his back, just as he reached us. We pulled both of them from the water, like crabs stuck together, the first one half-dead from drowning, and gave him succour. The other we chained up. At this, the Turkish galley sent a caique our way, threatening to engage us unless we handed back the prisoners. Captain de Gustaldo freed the Turk and paid ten ducats for this slave who had placed all of us in such dire jeopardy. The exchange thus effected, we continued our voyage.

On this, my first sea journey beyond the waters of Spain, I plugged my nostrils with anything at hand to be rid of the ever-present smell of shit, but my measures proved worthless and on more than one occasion I lost a meal. God Almighty, what I would have given for a storm to wash the whole foul mess overboard! As oars splashed, I slowly grew inured to the evil, as I did to the steady diet of biskets, wine, sardines and salted meat. I sang racy songs with my comrades and joined the friar for evening prayers. Day by day my impatience to reach our destination increased until the Captain, seeing my distemper, at last asked me why I had undertaken this voyage.

"To fight the infidels of course," I replied, surprised. "For His Majesty the Emperor and for Spain." At that the Captain smiled, and so I added, "To test myself."

Now he laughed. "Ah, that is a better answer from a young matelot. Tell me, do you fear Dragut?"

"By the Life of my Father, how could you suggest it?" I raised my head proudly.

"You should."

Of one thing was I certain: Blaij didn't fear the Turk. He'd said so often enough and I'd wager my immortal soul that he'd wade into battle without a thought to his own life, leading his men to victory. Even now, aboard this galiot with his beard ripening, he seemed a natural leader, slipping without effort into the easy companionship of the soldiers, joking and boasting of future exploits, commanding the esteem of all. As much as I admired him, his recent actions could not but leave me unbalanced. More than once I e'en thought to off him just to avoid trouble, but then laughed. Why? We'd been like sparks and tinder since childhood, and that was all there was to it.

Several weeks out of Malaga, as we headed down the coast of Tunisia, a strong headwind beset us and Captain Gustaldo decided to put in at

Mahdia—"Africa"—the very town the Christians had wrested from Dragut only a year past. Excitement consumed every man aboard. Even at a distance the legendary fortress, whose five-*brazas*-thick walls made it the most impregnable city on the entire continent, commanded our attention. With eye riveted upon it, we put in to the smaller of the two harbors, one surrounded by a curving, iron-topped fence to protect the galleys. The sun was going down then, spreading a soft, rosy light over the rocks and sand. Birds whose songs I had never before heard sang from the palm trees, and it was far easier to imagine that we had landed in a paradise than at the site of recent and ferocious events.

We tied the ship fast and made our way across the beach and thro' the palms, gaze always held captive by the massive towers and bulwarks rising before us. Our Franciscan held that the Romans themselves had built the town where we found it, on a narrow slip of land that jutted a third of a league into the sea. Far above us loomed the castle, which sulked atop a rocky eminence on this peninsula's center, commanding the entire city. How was the thing possible, to have taken this place? I asked myself over and over again on the approach. As were he reading my thoughts, our friar Lepercio could no longer forbear instructing his flock and told how the inhabitants of Africa had thrown off the yoke of the King of Tunis, admitting neither Turk nor Christian within the city walls.

" 'I would render you the richest people in all the Mediterranean,' Dragut told the people from without the gates," Lepercio recounted, " 'if you only allow me to become a citizen of your great and beautiful city.' "

"Dragut is fair-spoken sure for a corsair," Captain Gustaldo interrupted, and the rest of us laughed.

"Verily silver-tongued," the friar gravely replied. "Yea, the most eloquent of all the infidel corsairs. But a corsair all the same, and the Africans had no intention of falling for a corsair's sweet words."

"They fell," observed Blaij succinctly.

"Truly," Lepercio answered, "but only because Dragut cunningly bought a Moor, one Ibrahim-Barat by name, with promises of most valuable and curious gifts, and that he should become a partner in all of the corsair's undertakings. This treacherous Moor, who commanded that very tower before you, opened its gate at the assigned hour. Dragut led in five hundred men during the dead of night, and only as the sun rose did the citizens confront their misery. They ran for their arms, but," ... Friar

Lepercio paused for breath, crossed himself. " ... *Por la Incarnation del Verbo Divino,* the corsairs cut them to pieces."

"What happened to Ibrahim?" I asked, stooping to gather up a handful of sand from the beach.

"Would you trust a viper in a bargain?" the friar replied with a question.

"No," I said, "I would not."

"Then you have your answer."

"I take it you don't know," I said, letting the sand run thro' my fingers. Everyone laughed again as we approached the city gates. There, signs of the recent struggle became more pronounced: the trenches dug by Doria's men, the walls pockmarked by cannon fire, one or two half-buried cannon balls themselves. On the far side of the faussebraye, ditches studded with iron pikes that had impaled any enemy who breached the outer works.

Seeing Spaniards before them, the guards opened the gates with a hearty welcome and we walked, footsteps echoing, thro' those immense walls. Our company spread out in search of food and lodging, such as was to be had. Blaij and I bought some bread and melons from a local shopkeeper and decided to see the citadel for ourselves. We began walking up the hill.

"It's unearthly quiet here," I remarked, gazing over the nearly deserted streets around us as the gloom of the place became manifest. A chill ran down my spine.

"The Captain's set us ashore in a damned cemetery," Blaij said, and for one of the few times in my life, I saw Vergã cross himself.

It was true. We had entered a graveyard. A large mosque, no different from those in my native Granada, dominated the town, and doves cooed on its windowsills, but we found no infidels worshipping there. As we approached the summit of the hill and the citadel, the few soldiers standing guard paid no attention to us and so, shrugging, we walked unhindered through the castle gate.

Of a sudden, loud voices and the most cheerful laughter accosted our ears from the quarters on the opposite side of the bailey. "Thank God!" I exclaimed. "I had begun to fear this place was bereft of the living."

"And some decent food," Blaij added. After three weeks at sea the vision of a well-cooked meal proved irresistible and without further thought we strode across the square straight to the hall whence all the noise was coming. With the door wide open and the smell of game beckoning us ever more seductively, the only question was which of us would get in first. We entered. Before us sat three men at a rude candlelit table, eating and drinking merrily. Each wore over his clothes a black vest fronted with a white eight-pointed cross. Tho' neither of us had ever seen one in the flesh before, no one needed to tell us that these men were Knights of Malta.

"I hold," the first of them was speaking with his elbow on the table and a raised cup in his hand, "that to no one is learning more suited than to a warrior."

"*¿Cómo?*" replied the second. "What a warrior needs above all, it goes without saying, is skill at arms."

"Without *scientia* of the ancients," answered the first, "how is *un homme armée* to know the stratagem wherewith to best his foe?"

"What is more," asked the third, "does Homer praise other poets? Bah. *Juro à Dios*, the bard chooses to sing of warriors. *Pourquoy? Parce que le métier des armes est la plus haute uocation.*"

"Of course the calling of arms is the highest!" exclaimed the second, who was stouter than the others, as he poured all three of them a new round of wine. "And I ask, was Achilles learned? As I detest that whore my stepmother, what did the *bestia* know except how to use a sword?"

"I put it to you," interrupted the first, downing his cup, "that the proper *exemplum* for our study is not Achilles but Odysseus, whom anyone will acknowledge was the most learned—"

"—the most crafty—"

Blaij and I, I need acknowledge, followed this lively exchange with difficulty, for it was a garble of French and Spanish with a sprinkle of Latin, depending not entirely on who was holding forth. It was only then that the voluble first speaker, a Frenchman, became aware of our presence and broke off the argument. "*¿Vellaco, y qué tenemos aquí?*" the Knight asked in a lightly accented Spanish, peering at us dubiously.

"Francisco Perez de Barai, your most gracious ... " I answered clumsily, bowing, "at your service." Blaij, no less clumsily, followed suit.

"Fra," said the second Knight, distinctly amused. "You may address him as Fra. What brings you to our forlorn castle?"

I told them that we had sailed with Captain Dimas de Gustaldo to meet Admiral Doria.

"*Pardieu*, the whole Mediterranean, I'd wager, is rushing to Doria's aid," the first Knight said with a noticeable weariness in his voice. Tho' he was seated, anyone could see he stood taller than the others by a head; in age I guessed he had lived onto ten years longer than ourselves; he regarded us with a face that might have been chiseled from marble and he stroked a finely trimmed beard, black as a raven's. "But tell me, my young friends, as you have so incommodiously barged in on us, what is your opinion of the matter under discussion? Should the man of arms have read Tacitus, Cicero, Herodotus ... Homer? *Siste viator*, speak, give us your mind on't."

If anything could have startled me more than having encountered the conversation we did, in the manner we did, in the place we did, it was being asked to expound on these questions, as were I a schoolboy. I had not taken to Latin then, and had long ago buried those ancient names. "I—I—I—"

"Yes, I see," said the Knight and pointed his cup at Blaij. "What about you, Señor?"

Vergã righted himself proudly. "Sir, I am a Spanish soldier and the only thing an enemy needs to know from me is the tip of my blade."

"Yes, *cavallero valoroso*, but what do you need to know of your foeman?" the Knight asked to the laughter of his companions.

"Only how well he fights."

"Surely Spanish rhodomontades is the most splendid in the world," the Knight said with a significant glance toward his fellows. "The Spanish are unsurpassed in their valor. This is why in a cavalry attack they first go for the enemy's horse. 'When the horse is down, *el humbre de armas* is done for,' is the expression, isn't it?"

The insult enraged both of us.

"Sir," said Blaij and we moved outside onto the square. The other Knights brought torches from the barracks, for it had grown dark, and Vergã and the unknown Knight unsheathed their blades. Blaij rushed him, as I had expected, assuming that his sheer strength would overwhelm his opponent. But the Knight, in the prime of his manhood, met the blow without undue concern and returned the attack. I saw in his skill a hint of the Italians, but rarely had I seen anyone fence with such controlled ferocity. He followed no rules, no school, but each movement was made with strength, foresight and precision. He outmaneuvered Blaij at every turn, ducking, leaping, attacking. Suddenly, he grabbed a torch from one of the bystanding Knights and with it knocked Blaij to the ground.

"You call that valor?" Blaij groaned, putting his hand to the side of his bloodied head.

"I call it battle." Now he beckoned to me. "Your turn, my friend."

We fought. He had a harder time of it with me. I had had the advantage of reconnaissance and my style was closer to his own, to the extent he displayed one, and thus more difficult to defeat. For half a watch our shadows, flickering on the stones around us, transformed us into terrible, supernatural dancers. But at the end of it, with a powerful circle *botte* he disarmed me and I found myself staring into the tip of his rapier. I had no choice but to yield.

"Someday you will best me," the Knight said graciously, offering me his hand. "That one, never."

"Do not underjudge him," I answered. "He is a fearsome fighter and grants an enemy no quarter."

"Where does valor begin?" the Knight asked, to the wind as much as to the young Spaniard at his side. He expected and received no reply.

"But, My Lord," I said, standing away from him. "I do not know who I have the honor ... "

"Fra Balthazar de Marans des Homes-Saint-Martin," he said, bowing lightly, "Brother of the Langue of France, of the Order of the Knights Hospitallers of St. John of Jerusalem, who afterwards called themselves the Knights of Rhodes, and now of Malta." Then he laughed, almost at himself. "At your service."

E'en years later, I do not think I perceived all the shades of Fra Balthazar de Marans des Homes-Saint-Martin's laughter. There, that night in the town of Africa, I understood only that I had been honorably bested by a fine duellist and a finer nobleman. We repaired once more into the barracks, where the Knights now invited us to join them for supper.

"If you are here from Spain in response to Doria's summons," Lord Balthazar said, filling our cups, "then you have a galley faster than any other on earth, or have flown with the Devil himself." A servant appeared then, a Moor dressed only in a linen smock girded by bryony; he bowed and piled high our plates with a king's feast of raisins, dates, figs and partridge. Fortune had at last smiled on our aim to procure a meal. We dug in and ate ravenously.

Blaij, tho', smarting yet from his defeat at the hands of Fra Balthazar, remained sullenly silent and thus I answered the Knight. "Neither, Your Lordship. We had no direct call, but our Captain undertook this expedition once the Emperor ordered Admiral Doria to set after Dragut."

"Then your arrival is opportune indeed," said Fra Balthazar. "Doria has trapped Turgut at the isle of Los Gelves, not two days from here, and he has sent galleys to all corners of the Mediterranean for succours and reinforcements."

"Then we must hasten thither immediately!" I exclaimed, even rising from my chair. Blaij, too, motioned me toward the door, so anxious was he, so anxious were we both, that we might have missed the engagement.

The Knight waved us down. "We shall wait for the sun; if the reports are true, Turgut will not be sailing soon."

"Why do you call the whore-monger Turgut?" Blaij asked, his first words since his defeat.

"For Turgut Reis is his true name," Balthazar answered. "As much as we justly despise his religion, he has proven a formidable adversary and deserves to be called as his people do."

Such had been the excitement of the past hour that I scarcely gave credence to the fact that I was dining in the company of three Knights of Malta. When the truth of it at last possessed me, I fell silent, struck dumb as by a bolt. What did I know of the Knights? Only what His Majesty no less than everyone knew, that they were soldiers of Jesus Christ who had fought the Mahometans with unflagging vigor for countless centuries. That they swore allegiance to no one but the Pope and to Christ himself. That they were esteemed above all others for their valor and humility, and that across the Mediterranean enemies of Christendom feared no standard such as they feared the eight-pointed cross of the Knights of St. John.

"Why so silent?" asked Fra Alferez d'Angulo, the stout Knight from Castille.

Not wanting to appear overly awed by these valiant gentlemen, I passed to another subject and asked if any of them had ever set eyes on Captain General Doria himself. For a moment my silence spread to everyone.

"That is not a theme for gracious conversation," replied Fra Balthazar, turning to his cup.

Fra Alferez chuckled in reply. "You protest only because Doria changed his allegiance to Spain when France betrayed him."

"When France failed to pay him," rejoined the third Knight, who called himself Ramon Caravajal.

Fra Balthazar, smiling, demurred. "Rather I hold that Carlos has not studied Niccolò Machiavelli, or he would know that the greater the mercenary, the less you can trust him, for he is guided solely by his own ambitions."

Alferez, unimpressed by the proposition, belched loudly. "Niccolò for once appears to have been mistaken. Spain, I say, has contracted no poor bargain by employing Doria on twenty-five years."

"Certainly Doria has not," Balthazar answered, "and he has become ever more ruthless toward his fellow nobles." Then the Knight paused, reflectively. "Natheless, if one forgives his cowardice at Prevesa, one must admire Doria's extraordinary deeds, which leave all in amazement ... and he is held in great esteem by his people."

"Prevesa?" Blaij and I asked together.

At that the Knights burst into raucous laughter and slapped their thighs, so astounded were they by our ignorance.

"Thirteen summers ago," said Balthazar, upon regaining his composure, "Doria had Khair-ad-Din, Barbarossa himself, dead to rights in the Gulf of Prevesa. Outnumbered him five to one, I say—and yet he let the corsair get away by his ungodly inaction."

"I think, Balthazar," protested Caravajal, who had gotten up to void himself in the fireplace, "that you ill discern the cause of Doria's defeat."

All this elevated talk made Blaij impatient and confused me. Tho' we'd heard of Machiavelli—who had not?—I'd ne'er met anyone who had actually read him. And if this disputation over a dead Florentine seemed an odd occupation for Knights, more surprising still was their attitude toward Doria, the hero of Christendom, who they seemed to regard as a mere equal, if not an inferior.

"One is not granted sight of Doria often," said Balthazar, "for he is an old man. Yet, of course we have laid eyes on him. During last summer's siege he sometimes showed himself as we pounded the walls of this place for the better part of three months."

We asked Lord Balthazar to tell us about the siege.

For a moment the Knight lost himself to memory. "It was not an easy contest," he replied finally, the others nodding assent. "Under Doria's command we landed twenty-four galleys of Spaniards, Neapolitans,

Sicilians and us, the Knights of Malta. Our Bailiff, de Sengle, was to manage the enterprise, but Don Garcia de Toledo, son of the Vice Roy of Napoli, had his own thoughts on the matter. No little discord, I assure you, arose on that account, but we finally managed to set sail. When we had put ashore troops, artillery and ammunition, and had opened trenches, our commanders approached the walls, demanding that the garrison surrender.

"We did not know then that Turgut had strengthened the town with fresh troops and put his nephew Aisa in charge. Aisa threatened to put every mother's son among them to the sword should they but utter the word 'surrender.' To prove his resolve, he sent forth three hundred arquebusiers and was met by Don Garcia. The skirmish was warm and when Aisa sent out six hundred Moors on foot and horse to give succour to his arquebusiers, it seemed things would go badly for Toledo. de la Sengle, I'm certain, would rather have seen him beaten and whipped, but for the sake of the enterprise he sent us the Knights in. We charged with swords in hand and put an end to the rout. The Moors turned tail and disappeared into the olive forest nearby."

The other Knights, Caravajal and Alferez, nodded at the veracity of the account, but I was surprised at how dispassionately Fra Balthazar narrated their role in such heroic events. In the same tone he continued:

"We battered the place for weeks, but with ramparts such as these you may imagine we did not produce much of an effect. Finally a breach was made in the faussebraye and the Vice Roy of Sicilia sent in his troops, but they were massacred by arquebusiers on the walls or fell into the trenches the enemy had lined with pikes. Things went worse for us when Turgut secretly landed three thousand men on the other side of the peninsula and surprised the Knights in the olive forest where we'd been sent to cut fascines. But we had faced Moors before, and Turks, and were not about to retreat. The engagement went on 'til sundown. Eventually we got the better of them, tho' many of our brethren had been killed.

"de la Sengle occupied himself with the hospital as more and more wounded were sent thither. Assuredly the whole enterprise seemed doomed, until Don Garcia, full of fire and having read the ancients, thought to lash together two galleys and raise a siege engine fit with cannon on it, to build a *sambuca* as the Romans called it. Our troops built it out of sight and one night towed the engine with some *frigate* and galleys to a spot near the end of the peninsula, where they anchored it. With the rising of the sun, they started bombarding the wall with as much fury as they could muster and finally made a breach. The signal was given for the attack and sorties were made all around the fortress. The Knights were sent in on skiffs and waded thro' the water with swords drawn and at last got to the walls. To get through that breach we faced arquebus and crossbow, stone and boiling oil. Natheless Commander de Giou planted the standard on the ramparts, only to be killed by a ball the next moment. Copier seized the standard and held it aloft through the entire battle. The number of our dead was fearsome, but not a man having got that far was about to retreat. We finally found a path into the city and went on to sack it. Aisa tried to escape disguised as a woman but was recognized and we held him for ransom, taking seven thousand other slaves besides. The city was rich in booty and everyone was rewarded with much silver, gold and precious stones. We buried our brethren in the mosque you have seen."

Balthazar ended his story in that abrupt manner, pausing for a moment before draining his goblet. Blaij and I glanced at each other, hardly able to credit such acts of heroism, made all the more valorous by the simplicity of his narration. Only toward the end, when he described the storming of the walls, did any pride creep into his voice. I finally summoned the courage to ask, indeed, why he did not sing of his exploits as his ancient bard Homer would.

"We are Knights of St. John," he answered, "sworn to die for Christ. Not a man on those ramparts would do ought but uphold his vows." Did I trick myself into thinking I perceived a flicker of a smile cross his lips? or into imagining I heard in his voice something less than doubt but other than sincerity? I set forth no further question, yet Fra Balthazar's voice did darken then.

"And to what end?" he asked. "Turgut escaped. He has now vowed eternal war on the Knights, which we cheerfully accept. But we cannot hold this city surrounded by a foreign land. If Carlos had read the Florentine he would understand. We are undergarrisoned here, as we are in Tripoli. What a bargain Malta turned out to be! To the Knights— Malta, in return for a solitary falcon to be sent each year to the Vice Roy of Sicilia on All Saints Day. A good price, wouldn't you say, my young friends, a falcon for an island? Except, the Emperor demanded the Knights must also accept Tripoli and defend it."

I began to think that Fra Balthazar had drunk a little much, but Caravajal and d'Angulo were assenting to everything he said. Finally, the nobleman concluded his speech.

"We cannot hold this place, I say. We should abandon it as soon as possible and mine the walls."

"Here, here!" said the two other Knights and all three rose from the table.

Fra Balthazar addressed us. "My *cavalleros*, it is getting late. Unless you have found better lodging, I suggest you stay here for the night. In the morning we shall set out to Isle of the Lotus Eaters, and this time, God willing, we shall capture Turgut."

Five

Fortune had granted us an opportunity that would surely ne'er appear again in our lifetimes, and our excitement that we would capture Turgut kept both Blaij and I awake much of the night. Yet by the time we rose in the morning, the Knights had already returned from their Paternosters and were readying to depart. We greedily stuffed our mouths with fruit and nuts and followed them and their servants down the hill. I now perceived the reason for Africa's forlorn appearance. The siege and the taking of slaves had left the city almost empty, a town of ghosts and spirits. Only at the main square did we encounter any number of people, Moorish slaves washing their linen in the public fountains. The women, wholly naked but for a piece of cotton to hide their private parts, wore large bracelets that circled their necks, wrists and ankles. I turned, disgusted at the sight of them.

"They are cheap here, if you are interested," said Fra Balthazar, laughing at my revulsion. "Give them a *piccolo* and they will show you everything."

All of us keened to be after Turgut and we walked—fairly skipped—laughing and joking in the highest spirits down the path to the harbor. There, we were met by a Knight directing a team of slaves who, putting their backs to a huge capstan, hoisted an entire galiot from the anchorage. What an extraordinary vision! To my eyes it appeared nothing less than a sea monster rising from the depths of the ocean, with great streams and rivulets of water coursing from its back.

"There is no simpler way to clean it," observed Balthazar, anticipating my question. "It is not even one of the Order's boats, but the Religion values cleanliness."

Anxious to rejoin my own crew and give them the excellent news, I was about to run off when the Knight robbed me of speech by asking whether I was infected by *la maladie de Vénus* or other contagion.

"N—n—no," I stuttered, dumbfounded.

"Then why not sail with the Knights?"

Thus, as the previous evening, I was reduced to jabbering, then mute silence. I managed to nod my assent and sprinted around the barrier to tell Captain Gustaldo both that Doria had trapped Turgut at Los Gelves, just down the coast, and that we would meet him there in two days' time.

"Turgut?"

"Yes," I smiled, "Dragut's true and proper name."

Everyone pitched in with vigor to load the boats. Such was our enthusiasm for the enterprise before us that by noon the wine, vinegar, water, grain, bread, chickens and livestock had been carried aboard, and all was ready. The day was glorious in every respect. The Knights strutted in their battle finery, tunics of red emblazoned by white crosses.

"The white cross of peace on the blood-red field of war," Balthazar remarked. "Such is the tradition." Each man's servant carried a half-suit of armor aboard, tasses, cuirass, vambraces, brassards, plumed helmet. After Fra Balthazar's Moor stowed his master's gear below deck, he handed the Knight, wrapped in cloth, one of the mightiest swords I had ever set eyes on—no rapier, but a two-handed battle sword in commoner use a century ago.

Balthazar saw my gaze fixed on it and asked the reason of my surprise.

"It is a sword such as only Knights of olden times would carry."

"Yes," he said, turning away, and he laid the weapon amid his other gear.

Naturally I was curious to learn something about the formidable Knight in whose presence I so unexpectedly found myself, but on the short voyage to Los Gelves it proved well nigh impossible, so circumspect was Fra Balthazar de Marans des Homes-Saint-Martin about his past.

"I hail from Navarre," he replied simply when I asked, "and was sent to Paris to study." Hardly another word slipped from his mouth, and not one as to how he became a Knight, tho' he did admit to being seriously wounded in Italy and of being restored to health by a mysterious and beautiful woman who fed him milk from her breast.

Seeing his reluctance to speak of himself, I requested that Lord Balthazar tell me something of the history of his order, the Religion he often referred to it. I should say I beleaguered him until he had no choice in the matter. With a good-natured chuckle, Balthazar yielded to my onslaught and began to speak of the Knights of St. John. Yet it was an uncertain discourse, for so ancient was the illustrious order, stretching across five centuries to the time of the First Crusade, that e'en a professed Knight confessed some ignorance about its shrouded past. When the Crusaders arrived in Jerusalem *anno* 1099, Balthazar related, they found there a hospice already administered by Benedictines from Amalfi, and at its head was a Brother Gerard. Some said Gerard was a Frenchman. Others claimed he hailed from Amalfi like the merchants who had originally established the hospice as a resting place for pilgrims to the Holy Land.

Neither could Balthazar say to exactly which St. John the hospice had been dedicated and, indeed, laughed when I put the question to him. Like most Knights he had always believed it to be the Baptist, but some maintained it was John the Almoner or John Hyrcanus. There were, after all, a surfeit of Johns to choose from. It was true that Gerard admitted any pilgrim to the hospice, Greek or Latin, without regard to religion. Infidels themselves were not refused alms and the poor of Jerusalem came to regard Gerard as their father. When the Crusaders laid siege to the city in 1099, the Governor ordered all citizens to join the defense against the Christians, but Gerard desired to give them succour and threw down loaves of bread from the parapets instead of stones. The Arab guards caught sight of this and brought the monk before the Governor, accusing him of treason. But when the guards attempted to produce the loaves as evidence of his crime, they had turned into stones, and the Governor released him.

So great was the charity that the Blessed Gerard bestowed upon the sick and wounded of the Crusade, that many of the soldiers, having recovered under the care of the Hospitallers, renounced all thoughts of returning to their native lands and joined the order. Upon their deaths, not a few of them willed the Hospital their unimaginable riches. And so the order flourished. Gerard, tho', wishing to perfect his design, proposed that his brothers and sisters take up the habit, which was naught but a black robe with an eight-pointed cross fastened to it on the left side, near the heart.

Fra Balthazar recollected that not many years later—when he begged me not to ask—the second Pope Paschal recognized the Order of St. John and exempted any payments or bequests made to the Hospital from the general tithes. Of e'en greater significance, thought the Chevalier, the

Pope granted the Hospitallers permission to choose a successor to Gerard without interference from any power on earth, be it secular or ecclesiastical. Thereat the Religion became a fraternity owing allegiance to no king, no nation. By the Angel of Peace, Balthazar reflected, could a more extraordinary circumstance be imagined? After the Blessed Gerard's death, the order chose Raimond Dupuy to lead them, the first Master. Fra Raimond understood that the pilgrims journeying to Palestine must be protected from the fanatical hatred of the infidels. He divided therefore the brothers of the Hospital into those who would serve the sick and those who would bear arms. In this manner the Hospitallers became the Knights of St. John, monks of war.

"Is it not a singular distinction," I asked at hearing that strange phrase, "to be at the same time a friar and a soldier?"

"Of course it is," replied Balthazar, "but what greater honor is there than to wage war in the name of Christ?"

There were others of the same ilk, of course. The Knights Templar, near as old as the Hospitallers, had from the start seen themselves as warriors above all and warriors alone. But once the Saracens had forced the Crusaders from the Holy Land, the Templars lost sight of their reason for being. They decayed into sybaritism and sin, practiced pagan rituals and the unspeakable crime in mass orgies. The last Grand Master of the Knights Templar had been burnt at the stake two hundred years ago and the Pope bequeathed all the Templar's vast holdings under his control to the Order of St. John.

Balthazar then spoke of the Teutonic Knights who, like the Hospitallers, had at first been nurses, but he seemed to know less about them except that, like the Templars, they slowly fell into irresolve and decay. Their despicable end came only twenty-six years ago, when their Grand Master committed the ultimate sin of accepting the Lutheran heresy. That event, for which no words were adequate, left the Knights of St. John alone as monks of war, the last of the Crusaders.

I regarded Fra Balthazar. As I came to know him, I admired ever more his prowess at arms, but not only. His good cheer and quick wit delighted his fellows and his nobility of spirit served as a beacon for everyone around him. Yet, there were moments when he seemed to feel the entire weight of the Knights' history resting on his shoulders.

Naturally I begged him to tell me how the Knights came to Malta. He recounted that after the fall of Acre and the exile of the Knights from the Holy Land, the Pope granted them leave to take Rhodes, and after some trouble they did. At once they built a hospital and remained for above two centuries. On Rhodes, they perfected the form of their order. So great were their numbers from all over Europe, and the Babel of voices that ensued, that the Religion had already long ago been divided into tongues, or langues, each representing a different nation. Indeed, Balthazar observed, many believed that the eight-pointed cross represented the original eight langues of the order. These he recited: Provence, Auvergne, France, Italy, Aragon, Germany and England. But as they were seven, he was inclined to believe the eight-pointed cross represented the eight beatitudes, tho' even here there were arguments. Later, the order added to Aragon the Langue of Portugal and Castille, of which I had already met two members, Caravajal and d'Angulo.

His Majesty well knows the circumstance which forced the Knights to abandon Rhodes, for it was one of the young Soliman's first acts as Sultan of the Ottomans to lay siege to that splendid isle. Balthazar did not then narrate the events, which His Majesty certainly remembers, saying only that he did not believe a more ferocious contest would take place in the future history of the world. Yet he spoke of the honorable terms that His Majesty, impressed by the valor of the Knights, granted them after six months of desperate struggle, when the outcome became inescapable.

For seven years after they quitted Rhodes, the Knights wandered the Mediterranean, like Odysseus himself, while they carried out tortuous and never-ending negotiations with the Pope and the Emperor for a new home. Finally, Carlos granted the destitute nomads in perpetual fiefdom the isles of Malta and Gozo in return for a solemn Mass to be said every year on the day the deed was signed. And the falcon. That solitary falcon to be sent to the Vice Roy of Sicilia on All Saints Day, without any deputation and by any messenger the Knights thought proper. On the twenty-sixth of October, *anno* 1530, Grand Master Philippe Villiers de l'Isle Adam sailed into the Great Port.

"From that day to this," concluded Fra Balthazar, "we have been known as the Knights of Malta."

His Majesty will appreciate the force wherewith this history struck a young man's imagination. Almost without pause I asked Balthazar, "What

must one do to become a Knight of St. John?" setting forth the question
in as passionless a tone as I could muster.

"You must remember, above all, that we are monks," he replied.

I broke out laughing.

Balthazar raised his hand as if to knock me, then he too fell into
laughter. *"Vertu de Dieu!* Yes, I know my friend, you have ne'er seen monks
so skilled at sword or drink, tho' in the second we do not differ so
markedly from our more timid brethren. Natheless we are monks. To join
the Religion a novice must take vows of poverty, chastity and obedience.
Novices must remain a year at the Convent—Malta—and perform three
caravans aboard a galley, each of six months' duration. Afterwards, most
Knights return to their homelands, but when called to the defense of the
Convent, they must report at a heartbeat, under pain and disgrace of losing
their habit." Balthazar briefly paused, stroking his fine beard. "Do you
know what chivalry means, Francisco?"

For the first time he addressed me by name, which gave me such pride
that I could scarce concentrate on his question. Vainly did I attempt to
put into words visions of gallant knights on their jousting lists and fair
damsels draping their colors over the lances of their champions. E'en as at
length I stuttered, "Nobility of spirit ... bravery, deference to the fair sex,"
Balthazar interrupted.

"'Chivalry,'" he said," comes of course from an ancient word of my own
tongue, *'chevalier'*—'horseman.' In those past ages, only nobles, 'twas
presumed, served on horseback; only they might become knights and
practice chivalry. So it continues in the Order of St. John. According to
the ancient custom, only those of high birth are permitted to become full
Knights, Knights of Justice. The langues are quite strict about such
matters, and becoming e'er more so. Anyone wishing to become a Knight
of Justice must present proof of four quarters of nobility, in some langues
eight or sixteen. Nor does any langue tolerate the slightest taint of Hebrew
or Moorish blood. You, a Spaniard, know that to name a man a Jew is the
greatest insult. Call a Knight a Jew and you put your life at peril."

I cannot convey the effect these words had on me. I burned with shame,
even as I told myself I had no cause to feel shame. I did everything within
my power to contain myself, to display no outward change of countenance.
I did not turn from Fra Balthazar. I received his gaze straight on and
returned it, eye to eye, man to man. If my face reddened during that

moment of disgrace he did not perceive it, or if he did, his chivalry was such that he revealed nothing.

And if, on that brief voyage, I had dared fancy myself a Knight of St. John, those hopes had been abruptly shattered forever. It was well, I consoled myself, for a man to learn his place sooner in life rather than later. If naught else, I was no nobleman. The same grim determination I had felt in Granada to put the past at my heels returned.

The watchman's cry brought me out of this most unpleasant reverie.

"Ah!" exclaimed Balthazar. "Look ahead. We have arrived at our destination, Los Gelves, Djerbé, the land of the *Lotophagi*."

Six

The sight that greeted our arrival at Djerbé was by far the most fantastic and incomprehensible I had ever beheld.

Dozens of galleys lay just outside the mouth of an inlet or harbor, forming a giant necklace about it. Great earthworks had been cast up on either side of that place, and on its left side Turks and Moors hauled stones and cannon up to the unfinished parapets of a massive bulwark. In plain view of the enemy and the Lord above, the infidels were raising a tremendous fort.

An ungodly quiet encompassed everything. You could hardly imagine a more placid evening on the Mediterranean, as if we had happened onto a colorful fishing village just when all the villagers were out in the late day's sun to haul in their supper. Our eyes descried no canvas anywhere, and battle pennants draped themselves limply around the bare masts as those galleys rocked gently in the water.

Becalmed.

Suddenly a small boat, a *fusta*, strayed too near the earthworks on the right side of the harbor. The corsairs let off a furious bombardment from their batteries. Smoke and flame enveloped the platforms, and eventually the distant roar of the cannonading reached our ears. In the midst of this, the *fusta* crew was hauling for all it was worth back to the line of galleys and somehow managed to reach safety.

"Francisco," said Balthazar, reading my thoughts, "the reports were truthful, it seems. The *capitana* there—" he pointed to the largest galley of them all, outfitted with a black canopy and Genoese standards hanging from the masts "—is *La Tempérance*, Doria's own. He has blockaded the channel. It can mean only one thing—he has trapped Turgut within and the corsair has no way out."

We glided toward the nearest of the Religion's two galleys, set apart from all the others by the brilliant vermillion wales and pennants of the

Order staked on the poop and forecastle. When we had met it, Balthazar and several other Knights jumped aboard. He and the Captain of the other vessel embraced like long lost brothers.

"Yes," the Captain told Balthazar, "Dragut is trapped in the road like a scared rabbit, but no one dares go in after him because of the gun batteries he has emplaced." He threw his chin toward the earthworks that had just moments ago made their presence so plainly felt. "They've been going up for weeks now and guard the mouth of the channel to good effect. No one can get in."

"What then is the plan?" asked Balthazar, seating himself on the wale of the Order's galley.

The Captain of that vessel, de la Roche, spread his arms wide and laughed heartily. "To wait. The Admiral has charged us to wait. Dragut must either break through the blockade or at length starve. We've got the dog-whore this time. He must be shitting in his trousers."

To my eyes, the tactic appeared clad with iron. The island—Los Gelves to the Spaniards, Djerbé in these parts—was of a fair size, five leagues from end to end, judging from the time it took us to sail by it. Turgut had put into a deep haven that no one could reach except through a narrow channel at a place called La Bocca de Cantara, where Doria's entire fleet was now anchored. By the same coin, the corsair had no means of escape, none, unless he forced passage past this Bocca de Cantara. But succours and reinforcements had begun to arrive from every quarter of the Mediterranean, and there was no chance of that. It was a matter of time. Turgut, at long last, had been routed.

It was a matter of time. The Admiral, of infinite patience, decided we would wait, and wait we did. For days, for weeks. The walls of the fort rose before our eyes. Whenever one of Doria's galleys tested the waters close to the harbor mouth, the infidels would commence their salvos and the ship would pull out of range. We spent most nights aboard, should the corsairs attempt to force the issue by running the blockade. Other nights, a few of the galleys would row to a deserted promontory of the island, which was but a league westward of the harbor, so that the crews could sleep on solid ground.

On one of these evenings, the better part of a month after our arrival, the entire expedition from Africa found itself reunited around a campfire

on the beach. Much of our early excitement for the undertaking had by
now faded and Blaij, who I'd only seen in recent days from hailing
distance, had grown impatient.

"How long do you think this will go on?" he chaffed, motioning me to
bout with him on the sands.

I shrugged, e'en as I indulged him. "How might I know? The Admiral
believes time belongs to him. We'll sit here until Turgut surrenders, or
until he starves."

"Bah," spat Vergã, at length stepping away, "this is a campaign for
women."

The Knights, tho', reveled in their inactivity. Fra Balthazar proved to
be in exceptional spirits and, sitting on a log, one hand on his knee, a cup
of wine in the other, he spoke expansively of Odysseus. "This island, Los
Gelves, is none else but the ancient Isle of Lotus Eaters. Fed by the natives
the honeyed fruit of the plant, Odysseus's crew succumbed to a great
torpor, forgetting e'en they had a homeland to return to."

"The air of these parts must infect people so," interrupted Blaij. "Doria
has already forgotten, and soon we will too."

The younger soldiers awarded Blaij a few chuckles, but Balthazar only
raised his hand for silence and carried on with a tale about a married
French noblewoman who, so smitten by the sight of a particular
nobleman, had him conducted blindfolded to her bed, where she awaited
him nightly with *tres bonne uolonté* and many sighs, but never a word. Even
as the rest of us urged Balthazar on, intent on discovering whether the
gentleman in question e'er found out who she was, Blaij impeded all
progress. Angrily, he paced about the fire, swiping at pieces of driftwood
and seaweed that had washed ashore.

At last, Balthazar broke off and deigned to address him. "We can see,
Brother Vergã, that you are eager to get on with it, as befits a Spaniard.
But do you propose a plan?"

"I do. We go in after Dragut and put an end to him."

Fra Balthazar nodded thoughtfully. "It is plain to every fool here how
the fox prevents our entrance to that harbor, just as we prevent his exit.
And you would have us bluster our way through on a galley and get
everyone blown to heaven?" Thereat the Knight stood and bowed to the
entire company. "This *cavallero valoroso* reminds me of another Spaniard I
once knew, who walked about without a sword. When I asked him why,

he replied, 'I am so fiery in my temper that but a whiff of wind invades my ears, I turn and whip out my sword, and the first who comes my way is a dead man, as sure as he were born.' This whiff of wind having caused him to lay low five men, my fiery Spaniard offered to the Mayor a signed document, wherewith he forswore the carrying of a weapon."

Balthazar crossed himself just as Ramon Caravajal, the Castillian Knight, let out a tremendous fart. "*Exactamente,*" Balthazar said and everyone else doubled over until we pissed in our pants. The Knight hardly paused. "Show your bravery at all costs, tho' it mean the lives of your fellows, is that your intent? By God, the Spartans would have you stripped of your citizenship and run out of the city for proposing a plan that so recklessly endangered your comrades." He paused and looked Blaij straight in the eye. "Do you call this valor, Blaij Vergã?"

The challenge was direct and we were all certain that another duel would erupt within a moment. To everyone's astonishment, Blaij contained his temper. "No, that was not my plan," he said without retreat.

Lord Balthazar bowed slightly. "Go on."

With the tip of his sword, Blaij made a few scratches in the sand. "I say we take a small company of men, at night, and ferry them another league west of where we sit now ... "

"And then?" asked Balthazar as Blaij paused.

"We circle around the road, creep into the Turkish camp and capture Dragut if it is possible, kill him if not. That will be the end of the corsair and the campaign will be over."

"Simply walk in?" asked Balthazar with some irony and some incredulity.

"The haven he has put into is a league long, longer. The enemy's camp is far removed from danger, and after these weeks of farting on their fires, his guard will be down. He won't expect us." Thereat Vergã shrugged. "If we die in killing Dragut, what better death could one wish for?"

I must say, the audacity of Blaij's scheme greatly appealed to me and I was hardly alone; a murmur of approval ran around the campfire. I would not have dared call Lord Balthazar a coward. In the weeks since we'd stumbled onto that dinner in Africa, I had come to admire his nobility and modesty of spirit, and on this night of sparring, hints of a deeper past. He seemed constantly to strive, after what tho' I could form no conception. I, Francisco Perez de Barai, on the other hand, had come to fight and, as

I knew I could never join the number of those Knights, I would fight without them. I seconded Blaij.

So did Romegas. At least that's what the Knights usually called him, after his ancestral home. He was born Mathurin d'Aux de Lescaut de Provence. I see you recognize the name, Your Majesty. Aye, no one knew then that this Knight, only three or four years older than Blaij and I, would become to the scourge of the Infidel and the spark that touched off the great conflagration. Then we perceived only that his dark, savage face displayed an unsurpassed fearlessness and that by repute he was already one of the Order's best sailors. On his buckler he'd inscribed *aut cum hoc, aut in hoc*, either with this or on it. This man, who had professed but four years before, stood up immediately and volunteered to pilot the boat to our destination, wherever that might be.

The moon was on the wane and we decided to move at once. Fra Balthazar put aside any misgivings he might have harbored and assumed command. As we boarded the Knights' galley, he turned to the newcomers and said, "Did you know that Turgut was once a slave?"

This was news to us.

"Yes," Fra Ramon confirmed. "*Anno* 1540, Dragut had been captured by Doria's nephew Giannettino, an extraordinary stroke of luck. When his captors paraded the corsair before the young leader, still beardless and wet behind the ears, Dragut bellowed, 'What! Am I now a slave to that fuck-face boy?' So incensed was Giannettino, that he flew at Dragut and tore out his mustaches and beard and would have sheathed his sword in the bowels of his impudent prisoner had he not been restrained by his own guards. Aye, Dragut served four years as a galley slave, his will unbending. He might have died behind the oar, defiant till the end, had not Barbarossa on his last voyage purchased his successor's freedom for three thousand *scudi*, a king's ransom, yea."

Seeing that we had been rooted to the spot by this history, Balthazar leveled his gaze at us and answered the unuttered question: "You should know the quality of the man you face and perceive what Fate may have in store for you," he said, and the oars dipped into the quiet waters of the bay.

Seven

To reach our destination was scarce an hour's haul across the water. With each passing moment our anticipation mounted—the palms of my hands grew wetter and my pulse raced ever faster. The rowers had been ordered to silence and with the same command I stilled my beating heart. Natheless, by some means sensing my apprehension, Fra Balthazar crossed the gangway between the oar banks and stepped to my side amid the forward armaments, where I had stationed myself.

"This is what you have traveled so far for," he said, "yet you are disquieted."

"Excited," I replied.

"Of course," Balthazar nodded in the darkness. Then, granting no preface, he said with a challenge, "Tell me, what is your valor?"

Tho' I perceived that the Knight was engaging me to turn my thoughts from the coming perils, in no manner could I comprehend what he was at.

"I understand your friend's valor—what he conceives to be valor—but I do not understand yours."

Now the strange question recalled to me Blaij's taunts and my guard went up. "Lord Balthazar," I answered, offense finding its way of its own accord into my voice, "I might take that as a slander, but do not mistake me: I desire to fight the Infidel no less ardently than my friend."

The Knight only slapped me on the back, laughing. "No doubt that is true. He is merely a brighter peacock than you are. But consider: Niccolò holds that a good man cannot take up the profession of arms, for no man can be judged good whose work requires him to be rapacious, fraudulent and violent. What say you?"

I shrugged, recalling the Knights' conversation in Africa we had barged in on only weeks ago. "I have always believed that the profession of arms is the noblest of all."

"And this I too have believed," answered Balthazar. "But Niccolò reminds us that the ancients established militias because there was no glory in it, and after a war a soldier's greatest desire was to give up his arms and return to his ploughing. After a conflict, tho', mercenaries return home and, having no other skills, band together to become highway robbers and wreak havoc in their native lands."

By the Entrails of God, I had never given the matter the slightest thought and knew not how to reply, but luckily at that moment Fra Ramon stepped up to us in that cramped place amid the guns and spared me further interrogation. "It is the mark of our age to quote the ancients, and no one is better at this sport than Balthazar."

"I accept the compliment," replied Balthazar, bowing perceptibly. "I do hold with Niccolò that what is truly golden in Tacitus is that one must honor past things and obey present ones, wish for good princes and endure bad ones, and anyone who does not brings ruin on himself." He then faced me directly. "Francisco Perez de Barai, I am no far seer. My campaigns these ten years past have been legion and I have thrilled in my duty. Of the Knights, few, I say, are held in higher esteem. Yet Niccolò does disquiet me."

I have said Balthazar was always striving, tho' to what end eluded me, and at that moment I began to fear him too. This time, fortunately, he himself turned the conversation from a too serious color by relating an incident he had witnessed in Gayette, not far from Napoli: Two chevaliers, an Aragonese named Lunel and a Castillian named Tamayo, were approached on the street by a peasant carrying a basket of fish. Tamayo wanted to buy them, but Lunel took the best of the lot. The wrangling grew fiercer by the instant until Tamayo declared that *his servants were finer gentlemen than Lunel*.

"*¡Juro à Dios!*" exclaimed Fra Ramon with alarm, and Fra Alferez too; he had at that moment joined us on the gun platform.

"*Ouy.* Lunel's hand had shot to his sword. But Tamayo fled forthwith and ceased not his flight until he reached Spain, where he became a priest in order to avoid his adversary. For an entire year, Lunel sought out Tamayo, but that one refused to fight, claiming his new habit forced him to decline all such challenges. So the despairing Lunel was reduced to posting *affiches* on city walls up and down Italy, proclaiming that he was not at fault that a gallant combat would not be seen. Hah! What a story!

"So you see," shrugged Balthazar, "not all habits are alike."

The amusing tale left us in raised spirits as we sailed along the coast of Djerbé in the still night. When we had passed well beyond the last campfires of the enemy, nine of us took the galley's boat to the beach and jumped ashore—three Knights, Blaij, myself and four other soldiers. Lescaut remained aboard, much against his nature, but accepting the necessity of it.

By then the moon was setting and we could soon scarce see past the tips of our noses. The Knights forbade us from lighting torches or even the matches of our arquebuses, lest we be sighted by the barbarians. Thus we walked in near total darkness, guided only by the *Via Láctea* above, through the palm woods of the Lotus Eaters. Balthazar had left his beloved broadsword aboard, taking only a rapier with him, and we all carried our weapons in our hands to silence them. After an hour, so I judged, Caravajal collided head on with a large stone and let forth an oath: *"Por las Reliquias Santas de San Juan de Latran!"* When our eyes adjusted to it, we perceived we had stumbled onto an ancient temple left by the Romans. For a few moments we rested there among the ruins, fortifying ourselves with wine, and continued.

After another span, well before we ought to have reached the enemy camp, we heard the first voices. Balthazar hushed the company and every man froze in his tracks. Then other sounds, not human, began to be felt. Faint creaking and groanings and scrapings now reached our ears from beyond the trees that surrounded us. None of us could fathom what such sounds signified or portended. On all fours we crept in the direction of those strange noises for what must have been a hundred paces, until we passed out of the trees, and Balthazar motioned for three of us to follow him up the slope of a shadowy rise.

In my life only one sight caused more shock and bafflement than the one that confronted us when we first arrived at Los Gelves, and that was this one, the sight that greeted us from the crest of that lonely eminence: On the far side, innumerable torches waving to and fro. A log road faced with two rows of planks shining darkly under the torchlight. Turbaned officers standing on rocks, shouting orders. And below them hundreds, nay, thousands, of men—Turks, Moors, natives of the isle—every one of them grunting and groaning, as with hand, rope and glistening sweat they

hauled entire galiots, galleys and galleases on wooden rollers across this
road, which vanished in both directions into the darkness. We watched
for what seemed an eternity as the procession of sea-going vessels, moved
over land by human sinew and the will of Turgut alone, passed before our
unbelieving eyes.

At length we scrambled down the incline to meet our fellows,
motioning for them to confirm what we had just witnessed. When they
had satisfied themselves that the spectacle before them was not a dream,
we all retreated together back to the palm trees, each of us whispering his
astonishment.

"As I came naked out of my mother's womb!" exclaimed Caravajal
under his breath, "I would ne'er credit such a scene—had I not seen it
with my own eyes."

"It is beyond anything I have ever heard told," agreed Alferez.

Balthazar planted the tip of his rapier in the earth and nodded slowly.
"Again Doria's inaction! Everything from the start has been a ruse. That
fort at the head of the channel, the earthworks. While we have been biding
our time at La Cantara, Turgut has marshaled every soul on the island to
build this road. You see where it must go—there to the eastern shore and
the sea."

"How could the dog have mustered so great a force of men?" Caravajal
wanted to know.

"We might have foreseen it," answered Balthazar after some reflection.
"The inhabitants of Djerbé are Mahometans, no friends to Christians."

A silence descended upon us for a moment then, with the realization
that the entire fleet had been tricked.

"We must warn the Admiral," I offered finally.

Balthazar nodded solemnly and sighed. "I fear we are late. We cannot
get to Doria by daybreak, and by daybreak Turgut will have set sail ...
There is only one chance if we are to prevent Christendom's greatest
debacle in o'er a decade—"

"To take Dragut or kill him," Blaij said. "The reason we came."

Again Balthazar nodded. "Will the two of you come with me? You
must understand we have almost no chance of success and less of getting
out alive."

Both Vergã and I assented.

Neither would Caravajal, who I began to perceive was a true Spaniard, be left behind. "You'll want a Knight by you, Balthazar," he declared, "not just two beardless youths. And believe me, when I lay my hands on Dragut, I'll cane him to death, and when he's dead, I'll have him flea'd and his skin curry'd, and I'll make a drum out of it, which I'll beat twenty years after, that the son-of-a-whore may remember me in the other world."

"Very well, Ramon," answered Balthazar, "let us pray 'tis not the other way 'round. Alferez, lead the others back to Romegas as quickly as possible. If we fail, you must get to Doria." They agreed and the Knights embraced. d'Angulo with the four soldiers then disappeared into the trees, leaving two Knights of Malta and a pair of untried youths to prevent the escape of Turgut from the Isle of the Lotus Eaters.

Eight

The plan was desperate and failed desperately. We followed the road at a distance, southward toward the harbor where we guessed Turgut would have established his camp. We guessed rightly but were too late. The tents had long been struck, the campfires doused. Under cover of the palms and shrubs, we managed to get within fifty paces of the water's edge, where the log road ended. There, under the starlit sky, a giant wooden frame fitted with block and tackle strung to two great capstans bestrode the road's terminus. This, then, the engine that had raised the now distant boats from the sea. Not far from that mechanism a small circle of men with torches about them engaged in animated deliberation. Tho' from our vantage point we could scarce distinguish one from the other, one turban stood out as by far the largest and finest.

Blaij and I glanced at the Knights, who nodded.

What struck me about this figure was not the opulent turban, nor the resplendent surcoat that reached his knees, nor the commanding presence, sensible e'en at a distance. It was the beard, the snow-white beard.

"He must have over sixty years," I whispered.

"Which puts him twenty winters this side of Doria," Balthazar replied with a noticeable condescension. "And I say pray for your life if you believe that number has diminished him." Then the Knight's voice brightened. "There are only eight of them, fair enow odds. What say you? If we are to proceed, we have no choice but to rush them."

"As I abjure the law of that whore Mahomet," Caravajal hissed his assent, "I've got you in my hands now, Dragut."

Infected with the Knights' enthusiasm, Vergã and I had already loaded our arquebuses and lit the matches on our final approach to the deserted camp. "I told you what I would do if I came face to face with that devil," I said with a glance at Blaij and he nodded. Before Lord Balthazar could bridle the two fools at his side, we raised the guns to our shoulders and fired.

We missed, and we did not get a second chance. The circle of men scattered with a start and we four, casting down our guns, emerged from our hideaway with rapiers unsheathed. Blood-curdling screams on our lips, we hurled ourselves toward that dispersing circle, but had scarce crossed twenty paces before a guard of another half-dozen men emerged from the shadows beyond the hoist and met us head on, instantly surrounding us. At Balthazar's command we dropped our arms.

So ended my first engagement.

Turgut, or he who I perceived was Turgut, approached Balthazar and Caravajal, eying them from head to toe. He commanded something to one of his officers in a language I had never heard and, without a glance at Vergã or myself, turned away with his retainers, striding quickly in the direction of the boats. The rest, six of them, marched us at swordpoint back along the log road, their haste to reach the galleys evident. Each time we faltered, they cursed us and cudgeled us on the shoulders. Blaij sometimes glanced at me with smoldering eyes, not letting me forget my brash vow.

I can't say precisely how long the march was. Half a league, less, over shoals, marsh, sand. Events had unfolded with such speed that I scarce had time to comprehend the dire peril into which Fortune—or Folly— had careened us. But at the sight of the boats at the far end of that road, in the water and ready to sail, the gravity of our predicament dawned rapidly enough. Lord Balthazar had no need to tell us that once aboard those vessels we would enter a living hell from which there was likely no escape.

He slipped then, on the curve of the logs, falling flat on his face, but when the guard took the cudgel to him, Balthazar spun over, tripping the corsair with his feet. At the same instant, Caravajal yanked the baton from the infidel nearest him and bashed him in the face. Blaij and I needed no further encouragement. We shoved our startled captors aside and dashed off the road.

"That way!" cried Balthazar, pointing toward the sea. "It is far too low a price to sell our souls to God!"

We ran as if all the demons of Hell were after us. And they were. With shouts and drawn scimitars, the corsairs pursued us across the rocks and

brush. The firing began. A ball caught Balthazar in the flesh of his right
shoulder; still he stumbled forward. When we reached the shelves
overlooking the sea, despite his wound, he did not hesitate to jump, and
with no thought at all we three followed, grabbing the Knight who now
had only one useful arm, and together hauling with all our might out to
the open sea. The infidels stood on the rocks above, cursing and shooting
at us with ball and arrow, but God's Will spared us.

"*Juro à Dios*, were I a fish, God would have given me fins!" sputtered
Caravajal. Truly, none of us swam worth a tin *maravedi*, but that morning
we managed to make it around the curve of those shelves, remaining
underwater as we could, praying the corsairs would abandon the chase or
believe they had killed us. At length, with the lightening of the sky, it
seemed that our foes' desire to escape Doria overcame their will to
recapture us their prisoners, and the voices became fainter. Yet we would
not risk coming onto land and swam further along the reefs. Only after
an hour in the water, not less, did we dare drag ourselves ashore.

With Caravajal grumbling every step of the way that the Drawn Sword
of Islam had been in his grasp, we marched several hours more along the
shoals of the same channel that had sheltered Turgut. At last, when the
sun was well into the sky, we reached the fort, now abandoned, built by
the wily corsair with such successful art for the sole purpose of deceiving
his enemy. We had feared the Christian fleet would already have set sail
in pursuit of its quarry, leaving us castaways on a hostile island, but our
galleys remained where we had last seen them, placidly guarding the
harbor entrance.

"Then Lescaut has not alerted Doria," Blaij said.

We could not then fathom what had taken place, whether d'Angulo
and the others had reached Romegas, or whether the young sailor had
been delayed. At the tip of the channel we stood long, waving our arms
and hailing the nearest vessels without effect. Luckily, upon collecting
our wits, we found an abandoned skiff not far from the fort and were able
to row out to the nearest galley without being fired upon.

The first business was to tend to Balthazar's injury. Fortunately, the
ball had been largely spent by the time it struck him and shattered no
bones. The ship's surgeon asked Balthazar if he wanted to be made
senseless with a sponge soaked in mandrake, belladona and God-only-
knows-what-else, but the Knight scoffed and told the man to get on with

it. To his credit, the physician was swift; he removed the ball without difficulty, even as he remarked that he disbelieved the prevailing notion that arquebus balls were poisonous. Rather he was certain that the very heat generated by the ball's passage thro' the air purged it of all toxins. He cleansed the wound with the newest mixture of spirits, myrrh and egg yellow and dressed it with linen, averring that a wound should not be exposed to air. In Lord Balthazar's place, I should have slit the throat of the young Granadan at his side, but he bore his ordeal stoically, saying only that if I insisted on fighting with so ignoble a weapon as an arquebus, I should improve my aim, and once the surgeon had finished, Balthazar desired to know one thing and one thing only:

"Where is Romegas, and why is Doria still here? Take me to the Admiral at once."

We set off in a felucca and within the turn of a glass, the four of us, looking hardly better than galley slaves ourselves, stood on the poop of Doria's *capitana*, *La Tempérance*. Balthazar now perceived the answer to his first question. Lescaut had beaten us. The dark sailor faced the Admiral as Fra Alferez described the unbelievable scene we had witnessed last night.

Doria refused to believe it. If the fort had fallen silent, he insisted, it was only because Dragut intended to lure the Christians into a trap.

The past hours had overbrimmed with so many wonders that the sight of Doria, old, withered, invincible, sitting in a carved, lion-armed chair under the canopy of this his magnificent galley of twenty-six banks, now seemed hardly more than natural.

Balthazar stepped forward, bowing. "*Eccellenza*," he addressed the Admiral in Italian, "Brother Alferez tells you the truth. *Per la mia fè*, Caravajal and I saw that log-hewn road with our own eyes, and with these two matelots were dragged along it, nearly chained to a galley bench. This wound bears witness to our narrow escape. I say that Turgut has set sail five—nay, six—hours ago. Even now we may have lost him, and if you do not hoist the red pennon this moment, we will certainly have seen the last of him ... until he deigns to be seen again."

What Balthazar failed to say was that if the Captain General did not after the corsair this moment, he would become the laughing-stock of all Europe. Natheless, stubborn Doria refused to credit the news until he had proof of it by his own eyes. Thereat he commanded his Captain to head for the channel, but the young Romegas could not disguise his fury. Half a day would pass before the Admiral would see with his eyes what we had seen with ours, and if the chase had not been lost by now, it would be by then.

All of us bid the Admiral farewell and boarded the Knights' galley. Romegas personally lofted the red pennon atop the foremast. The other galley of the Religion which had joined this useless enterprise unfurled its sails as well and we left Doria with the dog to hold.

And so the Knights sped northward into the Mediterranean after he who they called Dragut, knowing naught other than Dragut had vanished in the great expanse of the sea. On the second day of the chase we received an unwelcome hint of our foe's whereabouts when we met a Sicilian galley heading south to join the blockade we had just abandoned. Coming aboard, the Captain of that vessel, a certain Corbinelo, reported the most extraordinary event. Such was his agitation that he began jabbering away in Sicilian until he realized from all the blank stares being cast at him that nobody could understand a word, and he thereat passed to the *lingua franca*, the jargon sailors used in all the ports of the Mediterranean.

"Don Juan de Vega, spedir due bastimento parlar Doria que rinforzo venir, ma musulmin Dragut gantar nave ... " He babbled on.

What I made of this mess of Italian garbled with Spanish and sprinkled with Arabic was that Don Juan de Vega, Vice Roy of Sicily, had sent two ships including the *patrona*—his vice-flagship—to inform Doria that reinforcements were coming. That very morning, tho', the Christians came within sight of Dragut and the corsair, with an impudence one could scarcely credit to one who was now fleeing for his own life, himself broke off the escape to attack the *patrona*. He attacked it, and he took it. Worse, aboard the *patrona* was Buccar, son of the King of Tunis, who had given succour to the Christians, and who was now being hauled God-knows-where as Dragut's prisoner. Corbinelo himself barely escaped with his ship and his freedom.

Years later I would hear that Turgut had indeed sent Buccar, his prize, to His Majesty Soliman in Constantinople. There the prince died, shackled in a dungeon—punishment that he, a Mahometan, had aided Christians.

Many aboard took Corbinelo's report as an ill omen and near lost heart. Why had de Vega waited so long? But Romegas now demonstrated the severity for which in the coming years he became so feared. The moment Corbinelo had departed, Lescaut turned to the slaves and bellowed "*Remate cani!*"; he growled to the watch officer on the *spalla* to begin the beat and ordered the *comito* and his men to take their sticks to the slaves' backs. The dogs rowed.

To no avail. The watch pounded the drum, the *comito* lashed the backs of the rowers with his *cerchio orario* and the galley flew northward under oar and sail, but the Devil had left no footprints. The Knights guessed their adversary might have put in at Lampedusa for provisioning, and with a good breeze we made for that island. From Djerbé it lay over halfway to Malta. The soldiers, tho', numbering no more than one hundred on each galley, hardly embraced this decision with enthusiasm, for they'd begun to ask what we would do should we truly overtake the corsair, whose fleet outnumbered ours ten to one. On the first evening I put the question to Lescaut, but it was plain that the dark, trumpet-voiced Knight was not a man who took well to commoners. I flattered myself that our boldness on Los Gelves would have won his esteem, but when I bowed before him, asking how he intended to take Turgut should we actually find him, he merely scoffed and turned away.

Vergã, tho', with his brazen if foolhardy plan to stride into Turgut's camp, had captured Romegas' attention, and watch by watch they traded jests on the poop. Anyone could see that Blaij would strive to imitate Lescaut's daring. For my part, His Majesty knows that youth is a time of wild swings from heat to ice. Verily, one day I burned with desire to best Lescaut in a single combat, for these Knights esteemed nothing so much as skill at arms. On another day I listened to Balthazar, who did not scorn learning, and believed with all my heart his was the higher ideal. At yet other times, when Balthazar waved for me to bring him food or polish his armor, I took pride of his notice, just as I smoldered with anger at the debasement of it—as were I no better than a common house servant.

Above all, Vergã and I were simply elated at being numbered among this rowdy company, the company of the Knights, and each of us was determined to make ourselves worthy of them.

Early morning on the third day we approached the harbor of a small, wooded island. The place could not have been more than three leagues from end to end, without even so much as a proper hill to break the terrain. A tall stone tower overguarded the harbor, but it had been entirely abandoned, and no town of any sort opened its arms to returning sailors or lent cheer to the landscape, which but for some trees and shrubs was entirely barren. The only sign of life on this atoll was the beach itself, which seethed with tortoises. From the murmur of voices around me I understood we had come to Lampedusa.

When we descried no sign of Turgut's red and white banners with the dreaded blue crescent, as many among us were relieved as disappointed. Heated arguments soon broke out over the best course of action. Turgut had slipped through our fingers, and the more sober Knights argued that there was nothing for it but to provision the ships and head on to Malta. Romegas thought otherwise. "Dragut must be fleeing toward the Levant," he told Captain de la Roche of the other vessel, "I'm going after him. If nothing else we'll know the whore-dog's movements and I'll take any stragglers."

Thus was our expedition divided, which soon enow revealed itself to be a fatal mistake. For a few hours the slaves occupied themselves by filling the water barrels from nearby pools and catching for food tortoises on the beach and the rabbits that everywhere overran the island. To no one's surprise Lescaut's crew finished first. When Blaij and I volunteered to accompany him, he laughed in our faces, and so with Fra Balthazar and the remaining Knights we watched as Romegas' galley vanished over the horizon.

Not long after, de la Roche's vessel set sail, but we had no sooner cleared the harbor than we sighted a ship heading toward the island from the east. The gay colors told us it was a Turkish galley, a large one. Quickly the Knights conferred. The rowing gang, the *ciurma,* was exhausted after two days of fruitless chase and could not outrun the enemy. We had only a hundred men under arms. Yet the vessel appeared to be alone, not belonging to Turgut's fleet, and such a fat calf would surely prove an excellent prize. The Knights did not require more than a few grains of sand to make their decision: They would take it.

Moment by moment, as the two ships approached, it became ever clearer that we held the short end of the stick. The enemy's galley was larger than our own, fully manned and—not shrinking from battle. Seeing our predicament, de la Roche ordered everyone on deck and declared, "Gentlemen, ready yourselves to dine with Christ tonight or to wear chains in Constantinople." Turning to the chaplain he said, "Bless us quickly, Father, for this is likely our last day on earth." The friar made the sign of the cross over everyone, then walked among us, laying his fingers on my forehead as I knelt before him. Blaij too asked for his blessing. For an instant our gazes met and we nodded solemnly to one another. I wondered whether either of us had imagined this fate when we had galloped thro' the gates of Granada.

The ships now came within firing distance and de la Roche maneuvered to ram, but the Turks had the same idea and neither was able to gain the advantage.

"*Remate cani!*" shouted de la Roche suddenly and the galley lurched forward under our feet. The artillery from each ship went off at the same instant, both center guns, both pairs of culverins, both pairs of *sacres*. As clouds of smoke enveloped us all and wood from the foe's ship flew into the air, our own galley reeled under the impact of direct hits. Still we dashed forward to ram, but did not have a good position. The great wooden figurehead of an infidel Moor, bolted to our ramming spur, only grazed the other ship, snapping oars, but otherwise doing little harm. Likewise, their spur only caught amongst our oars and the two ships locked themselves together as the foes crowded the opposing wales.

The battle was long and bloody. We fought, rapier against scimitar, arquebus smoke blinding us, Turkish arrows flying past our heads. Balthazar, already wounded in his right arm, natheless managed to swing a broadsword, calling the Knights forward. I did not fence. I hacked. When a man went down next to me, his throat pierced by an arrow, I picked up his buckler and when that buckler was smashed, I found another. For on three hours we struggled, neither side gaining over the other. None of us rested for an instant. The Turks threw an anchor over our starboard wale so that we would be unable to pull away. They outnumbered us, by fifty men if not one hundred, but the Knights, steeled by their faith, had taken a vow not to retreat. My throat was on fire, from thirst and smoke. After two hours, I did not know by what force I remained standing. With other soldiers Blaij attempted to cut the rope that bound us to the Turkish ship. A Turk leapt across the space onto him and took a cut into his arm before Vergã dispatched his attacker with a thrust to that foeman's bowels. At the same moment an arrow passed clean thro' the flesh of my thigh. I collapsed onto my side, not seeing what happened next, but I felt the galley pull free. A few minutes later the cannon went off. Cries went into the air all around. We had blown a large hole in the Turk, but one of our forward guns had exploded, killing at least ten men and putting a huge hole in the forecastle of our own galley.

I tore the shirt off a dead man next to me and staunched the flow of blood from my leg, while a fellow soldier confronted a foeman who saw me as easy prey. They killed each other in front of my eyes, my nameless comrade's entrails spilling all over me and covering me with his shit. Finally I limped to my feet. Turks were now jumping into the water, swimming to shore, which lay some three hundred *brazas* behind us. The battle had turned. We pressed our advantage and soon the boarding began. By then it was apparent that the Turkish ship was sinking and our own so badly damaged that it would never get halfway to Malta. We could take no prisoners and slaughtered every Turk we found. Without thought I entered into that murderous frenzy, my heart pumping and arm swinging. By the time we finished, we counted over two hundred dead on deck and below. We threw them overboard.

"Do you see," remarked Ramon Caravajal, who remained standing among us, "how the Turks and the Moors float on their bellies and the Christians float on their backs? It is always thus."

He was right, and since then I have never seen it otherwise. Nay, during the rampage we spied one Turk floating on his back and asked a group of cowering infidels who he was. They told us it was a Christian who had pretended to convert to the Mahometan faith. Then we slew them. We freed what few Christian slaves were still alive and found plenty of loot to be divided, but there was little time to get it aboard our ship. We took the better part of it before the Turkish galley went down.

Our galley limped back to the harbor, but half the *ciurma* was dead, and more than that number of soldiers. There remained the question of what to do with the escaped Turks. No one could say how many had got away, but they posed a danger to our own survival on this deserted island.

Those who could walk went off to scour Lampedusa and kill or capture whoever they found.

As we sat exhausted on the beach, surrounded by the other survivors and tortoises, Balthazar asked me how I felt now, after this my first battle. My chest yet heaved, my heart yet raced, but his question did much to bring me out of the frenzy I'd been in for the past hours. I could hardly credit how easy it had been to enter the spirit of the thing, and how exhilarating. How much greater now was my appreciation of Vergã, who had fought with valor against the Infidel, and my admiration for the zeal of Lescaut.

"You acquitted yourself well," he said, "but methinks courage is more than a willingness to die."

I was too tired to be angered—too tired, for certain, to comprehend and made no reply. Balthazar, tho', seemed not to need one and went on somberly. "As on Gelves, the price was too low to sell our souls. There is a time to die, even for Christ. This was not it."

I still had no idea what the Knight was at. "Do you accuse me?"

"Not in the least," he said. "I just wanted to know how you felt."

"Yours is a good life," I replied, "but I smell like shit." And I limped into the sea to wash myself off.

That night the ship's surgeon, his assistant and barbers were kept busy. Until daybreak they walked among the survivors, sewing up wounds and amputating limbs. They nursed slaves as well as Christians, but when they found a slave they ajudged to have inflicted wounds on himself to become useless as a rower, the *agozzino* flailed the dog 'til his bones showed and cut his nose off. Lord Balthazar had the new gash on his right forearm sewn up, and I the puncture in my thigh, which turned out to be not so serious as I had at first feared. Later, the scouts returned with the news that they had captured a few Turks and we the survivors camped out where we sat on the beach. As he spread his cloak on the sand and readied for sleep, Balthazar remarked that the Grand Master should be pleased with his tenth part of the spoils—if we could ever get it back to Malta. The morning would be soon enough to tell.

Nine

Sunrise revealed the damage. On two hundred had survived the engagement, Knights, soldiers, freed Christians, Turkish slaves. The force was sufficient to row the galley to Malta but the ship's carpenter had been killed, his tools lost and every appearance announced that the galley was irreparable.

"This way," Balthazar said suddenly, glancing at Blaij and me. "Can you walk, Francisco?"

"Well enough," I dissembled.

"Take your weapons."

Vergã and I followed Balthazar two coves westward of the harbor. He refused to say whither we were bound, and we made our way through a light wood that showed signs of being harvested by marooned sailors who had preceded us. When we reached the inland extremity of the second cove, the Knight ordered us to climb down a steep path. We did so, I with difficulty, and faced a hole in the cliffside, the entrance to a cave.

"Let us see if we can find some carpenter's tools," he said, climbing up to the entrance.

But at that instant a figure bolted from the darkness, shoved Balthazar forcibly aside and jumped onto the path, aiming to escape. It was a Moor, a Moor dressed in finer clothes than any common soldier's. Blaij, who yet had legs to run with, was after him immediately with sword drawn. I hobbled behind. This fugitive, tho', was no athlete and in his fright slipped on the loose rock underfoot, falling against the wall of the cove. He had trapped himself. Blaij raised his weapon and was about to off him when I lumbered up.

"*Calla!*" I shouted, unsheathing my own sword. "He is unarmed."

The fever of battle still embraced Vergã and he paid no heed to my words.

I could not countenance it. "He is of no danger, I say. The Knights will hold him for ransom. Can you not see he wears the robes of a gentleman?"

Still Vergã ignored me. I have no knowledge of why I acted as I did, but at that moment, as Blaij readied to slay the helpless fugitive, I threw myself at him with such violence that he dropped his weapon and tumbled to the ground. I fell atop him and hit him squarely on the chin with the hilt of my rapier. In that rage I felt each chain on my sensibilities slipping fast and, despite his struggles, I would certainly have run Vergã through, had not Balthazar's voice reached down to us from on high, commanding me to desist. I obeyed. In the meantime, the Moor had made a second attempt to escape. Glaring at me, Vergã grabbed him as he tried to scramble up the path and we hauled the infidel back to the cave.

For some long time our prisoner refused to utter a sound. Rather than wait for him to speak, Lord Balthazar told me to see if I could find anything within that might be of use in repairing the ship. Naturally I took his words for a jest, but as my eyes became accustomed to the darkness I perceived in the back a soft glow, a light. I approached it, thinking the Moor had lit a fire, only to find a small lamp sitting atop an altar before an old wooden board, a faded image of the Madonna with the Child. From her eyes dripped real tears. I glanced about. To my poor eyes I might have been standing in a treasure room. Surrounding the altar were heaped piles of offerings, bread, biskets, jugs of wine, knives ... I smelled cheese and oil, I lifted to my lips salted meat, I pressed wool and linens to my chest, I let coins fall through my fingers ... Here was everything a mariner could need to stay alive. Overwhelmed, I dropped to my knees, suddenly perceiving the reason for yesterday's victory in battle: the Blessed Mother had saved our lives.

That was scarce all. I found no carpenter's tools, but grabbed a jug of wine and started back, only to descry at the other end of the cave the dim outlines of a tomb. I stepped over. Mats spread across the ground, and the still-glowing remains of a fire told me the Moor had slept here. I picked up a smoldering torch, blew upon it until it flared and passed it over my surroundings. Aye, against this wall of the cave rested a stone coffin about which were also piled heaps of gifts, no fewer than at the Madonna's altar. The entire cave, I now saw, overflowed with provisions. On this side, tho', against the tomb, the clothes left behind were Turkish. I limped back to the entrance of the cave.

"Where are we?" I asked Balthazar with wonder filling my voice.

"The cave of the Blessed Virgin," he answered. "I had seen it once, years past. Have you found anything wherewith we might repair a ship?"

I shook my head.

"That is unfortunate," he said, besitting himself at the cave's very entrance, "but we have wine, and Francisco, you have hands. Open this jug. At least between the three of us we are a whole person. Ah, this is the life, my friends." The source of Balthazar's good humor remained a mystery but there, with three of us wounded and a Moor sitting sullenly before him, the Knight told us what he knew of the cave in which we found ourselves.

"This sanctuary is sacred to both Christians and Turks alike. Tho' the island is deserted of men, the light you see on the altar has never gone out. Any galley slave lucky enough to escape will find succours here, left by Turkish corsairs and Christian sailors who touch shore. The tomb there is a Turkish marabout, a saint by their beliefs. The Madonna, I say, works many miracles and only Knights of the Religion, who sometimes take provisions to Trapani, may remove anything from this cave without fear of their lives. Lest any ship of any nation try to remove these supplies for profit—lo! the Blessed Virgin will not allow her to get out of the port. Many are the ships that have perished in a storm, attempting to steal from the Madonna!"

He then asked the Moor in the lingua franca, *"Quy estar toy?"*

To our surprise, the Moor answered in respectable Spanish, "I am called Abdallah al-Waryagli and am a *chavush* from the Sultan's court to Algiers."

"An emissary? Ahah! It is right you saved him, Francisco," Balthazar turned to me, "for he will fetch a good ransom." Then he addressed the Moor. "You were on the ship we fought?"

The infidel nodded. "Will you repair your galley?"

"Nay," replied Balthazar, "the task appears impossible. We are stranded on Lampedusa until the next ship."

"Will she be Christian or Turkish?" asked the Moor.

"Only the Almighty knows."

"If only Allah knows, then perhaps it is I who shall be ransoming you."

"Usanza de guerra," Balthazar laughed, "the usage of war."

The motto of the Mediterranean. If I had not already learned it, I would soon enough.

Lampedusa afforded us little to do but survive and talk. With two hundred men ashore, the cave would prove more a temptation than a salvation and the Captain stood a guard by it. So our men spent their days fishing or catching tortoises and rabbits, and their evenings about the fire, where they were forced to drink water instead of wine. Many fell ill.

To our astonishment, Lampedusa proved not wholly uninhabited. A few days after we arrived, the men stumbled across two fishing villages at the far end of the island. Their existence on this forlorn place caused us to wonder not a little, but the simple people were terrified of us, believing that any stranger would carry them off into slavery. Several Knights commandeered a boat and set off for Malta, intending to send a rescue, but we ne'er heard from them again.

Balthazar remained cheerful, dipping into his inexhaustible treasury of stories collected over his years of campaigning. Yet, the lock on his own past remained remarkably fast and I could not pry it. En route to Lampedusa, he did let drop in a moment of confidence, "Do you know, Francisco, I am an abbé. *Moy foy*, can you imagine?"

"Assuredly I can," I answered with confidence. "Indeed what could be more proper for a Knight of the Religion?"

"Ah, but you do not understand," Balthazar said.

I did not. The late King François, Balthazar recounted, had bestowed upon him an abbey, but why or for what purpose, the Chevalier gave me not the slightest comprehension. "I was ill pleased, sitting in those ruins."

At that I smiled, thinking that his discomfort at the inactive life was a bond we all shared.

"One day I sold some wood from my forest, equipped myself and set off to war. There have been many to choose from in our age." Then he fell silent and I gleaned nothing more, except that the Abbé had e'en fought on the side of the Turks a few years ago when the outcast King François was allied with the Padishah against Spain. Leaning over the *ballestriere*, Balthazar remarked, "The scimitar is almost useless for defense. It must be used to strike, and then it is fearful. Perhaps therein lies the secret of the Turks."

Not another word.

His Majesty knows that the weather in the middle sea is largely constant over the summer months, but not always, and that season the winds were blowing strong. On our second night we suffered a gale, which further damaged the ship, and a number of us took refuge in the crumbling tower that overlooked the harbor. Maugre the storm that raged about us, the fire was warm and the conversation lively. Caravajal started things off with a song he'd collected on his own travels:

> *Quy uoudroit garder qu'une femme*
> *N'aille du tout à l'abandon,*
> *Il faudroit le fermer dans un pipe,*
> *Et en iouir par le bondon.*

"He who would be sure that his wife does not lead a life of abandon," the Knight translated freely, "should shut her up in a cask and enjoy her thro' the bung-hole."

"In vain, in vain!" Balthazar shouted merrily and countered the attack with his own story about a Frenchwoman whose husband was so jealous of her virtue that he jailed her in an impregnable chastity belt, pierced by only a few little holes to *pisser* through. But the wife revenged herself by applying her charms to a plain locksmith, who without difficulty forged a key to the belt.

"Thereafter, my friends, the two indulged in their pleasure at their will, the husband being none the wiser." With a wink Balthazar raised his cup: "To Venus, the goddess of love, and Vulcan, the ironworker and locksmith of the gods, with whom she took her pleasure despite his ugliness."

"Balthazar," Fra Alferez interrupted, biting into the rabbit he held between his hands and turning the conversation to an altogether different color, "with your reverence for the ancients, you will be amused to learn that the Emperor Carlos has appointed as his personal physician a certain Andreas Vesalius. I have met the man. Can you imagine, he refutes Galen's claim that the thighbone is curved."

"How so?" asked Balthazar with marked curiosity.

"By cutting apart the bodies of thieves! Extraordinary! His opponents shower him with ridicule; if the thighbone is found to be straight in modern times, it is only because our tight trousers straighten them! They ran Vesalius out of Padua for his nonsense. Why Carlos appointed such an imposter, I know not. "*¡Voto a bríos!*"

A strange smile played upon Balthazar's lips, as if he both welcomed the intelligence and yet could not absorb it. But he had only an instant to consider d'Angulo's news, for one of the German Knights leaning over the fire offered an even more fantastic tale.

"When I was fighting at Mühlburg against the Lutherans," he related in a mixture of Spanish and French overladen by a German accent, "*I ecoute* much talk about a Polish monk, a Kopernik, who dies four years before. By the sins I confess, this monk *imprimer un livre* in which he to affirm that the sun does not *viajar* about the earth. He to insist that the *mundo* circles about the *sol*."

For a moment a baffled silence descended over the circle. The same strange smile that had played across Balthazar's lips a moment ago returned and suddenly—everyone broke out laughing.

"*¡Por Dios!* That is the most absurd thing I've ever heard!" Caravajal erupted. "Why, if the earth were moving, we'd have a constant wind in our faces! Never a calm day at sea!"

Balthazar, after stroking his beard for a moment on't, nodded his assent. "Methinks if you dropped a stone from a height, it could hardly fall straight, with the earth moving beneath."

"By the Mother Without Blemish!" I belatedly sputtered with true alarm, "no more heretical idea has ever been put forth. Surely it goes against the Holy Writ!"

"Of course it does," replied the German. "Even the dog Luther railed against it. Then all was forgotten."

So it was, for days, for weeks. No one paid any attention to the Moorish prisoner, who was chained up in the tower at night but left unshackled during the day, when he was put to work with everyone else. One evening it fell to me to bind him. I found him at his prayers, his robes no longer fine, but soiled and tattered like our own. He preserved only his turban with care. As I ran the chain through his shackles he turned his head up to me and asked in a deep voice, "Why did you save my life?"

Having no ready answer, I shrugged. "I say now as I said then, you were unarmed and anyone could see you would fetch a ransom."

The Moor shook his beard. "I think not. How many helpless sailors did you slaughter on our galley during your intoxicated bloodletting? You, a limping, wounded man, had no reason to spare me."

"And I have no reason to discuss it with you, a slave."

The prisoner bowed his head. "I offer apologies," he went on. "But I also ask, with Allah as my witness, for you to accept my gratitude."

"Do not ask. *Usanza de guerra.* That is all."

"My life is yours."

I found myself staring fixedly at the man. With the Moors their dark skin always makes them look younger than they are, but I judged the prisoner to have five and thirty years or forty; with his beard still black I couldn't be certain. "I do not want your life," I said and turned away.

But the barbarian insolently declined to remain silent in the dark tower. "Only the Almighty God may refuse it," he said, with a resonance in his voice that caused the stones to sing.

I struck him.

"You, infidel, if you ever use the Lord's name in my presence again, I shall snap your neck, harbor not the slightest doubt."

The Moor, rubbing his jaw where my blow had landed, natheless righted himself and found the strength to answer, "It is always thus with unbelievers from the House of War."

I beat him until he was senseless and walked out of the chamber. Blaij had been right to intend to kill him.

A few days went by when it again fell to me to bind the Moor for the night. At the sight of me he pressed himself against the corner of the tower with the greatest suspicion in his eyes and thoughts. We spoke not at all as I fettered him and I departed, not seeing him for yet another span of days, when for a third time my turn came to perform the ritual. That evening Balthazar accompanied me to the tower. As on the previous occasion, the prisoner cowered at the wall, shooting at us the same gaze of fear and hatred. Balthazar paid no heed.

"You are a *chavush*, an emissary from the Sultan to Algiers?" he asked simply.

The prisoner nodded with equal economy. "I am."

"What was the purpose of your undertaking?"

"I was carrying dispatches to Turgut."

"Where are the dispatches?"

"At the bottom of the sea."

"What was their contents?"

"The dispatches were sealed."

Balthazar gazed at the prisoner serenely, attempting to judge the truth of his words. He knew that a *chavush* was generally informed of his mission and often given extraordinary powers. "We can put you to the question."

"Yes," the Moor replied with the same serenity. "But on this lonely island, when our fate is in the hands of Allah, and only Fortune knows whether the next ship will be that of the True Faith or of the unbeliever, of what benefit would it be to you?"

Without a further word Balthazar turned on his heel and left. My blood boiled at the prisoner's insolence before a Knight of Justice and cried for me to strike him e'en again. Yet, because Balthazar had regarded him with dispassion, I would do the same. I handed him the bowl of tortoise stew we had brought.

"They will torture you," I said.

For a moment the Moor regarded me his warder with a gaze such that I had ne'er before beheld, as if the entire history of his race and the hatred and fear it bore towards Christians was encompassed in the infinite recesses of his black eyes. "Yes," he said at length, "they will."

"And so you deserve it, an enemy of Spain and Christendom and messenger for the Beast of the Apocalypse."

I spat on the floor and exited. But as I walked through the arch, the Moor called forth, "Christians are quick to blaspheme our Sultan—may the Blessings of God be upon him!—until they require an ally. Then the French King François crawls on his belly to Soliman, begging his mighty sword to defeat Carlos."

I turned, aching to run the infidel thro' once and for all, when I recollected that Balthazar had briefly fought against Carlos in that most strange alliance between Frenchman and Turk; it was beyond me to deny the truth of it. "Soliman is the Antichrist incarnate. François himself proclaimed as much."

"Truly he did," the Moor replied, as he greedily spooned the stew into his mouth, "to the ears of Europe, just as he secretly sent emissaries to the Sublime Porte with hasty assurances that those public words were empty of all consequence."

I could find no answer to this, many of those events taking place beyond the cast of my memory. François had died when I was yet a youngster in Sevilla. Instead I said to my adversary, "You hail from Barbary, yes?"

"Algiers was my birthplace, that is true," he replied, looking up from his bowl.

"What would you call an Argierian Morisco who gives succours to the enemies of Spain?"

The prisoner held his spoon still.

"A dead man, I would call him." This time I did leave him, chained to the wall.

Another span of days passed and a ship appeared on the horizon. Cheers went up as the red and white sails became visible, imprinted with the unmistakable eight-pointed cross, and we knew that Romegas had arrived. Verily, Turgut had fled whither God alone knew, and Lescaut returned to Malta, learning there that his comrades had never arrived. Forthwith he returned to Lampedusa and we were saved.

The evening before we set sail, I bound the Moor again to his wall. "In two or three days you will be wearing chains in Malta," I told him. "Pray that your Sultan ransoms you quickly."

"All who are captured by the knight-pirates pray for a quick release. Have no fear, I will so pray."

He made his reply with the same impassive countenance he so often turned toward me and I saw my warning had had little effect. But that word, *pirates*, fell unexpectedly on my ears. It was a word I had not heard much and the sound of it far from pleased me. Had the infidel uttered "corsairs" I might have accepted the esteem implied therein. But *pirates* ... Hidden in the strange name was something of the outlaw, the thief.

"Y—you dare call the Knights of St. John *pirates*?" I stuttered in disbelief.

"What other word should a man use for those who live by sucking the life blood of the Sultan's rightful trade?"

Each time I confronted this Moor my own anger was the outcome and now it mounted by the heartbeat. "You have made me regret more than once I spared you!" I erupted, "and be certain that had the Knights not their own intentions, I would put an end to you now!"

But again my bolts fell uselessly against his armor and the prisoner merely shrugged. "My life, as before, remains yours, and if death will spare me the torture of the knights, I welcome it."

At this answer frustration overwhelmed me, robbing me of all reason, and I could find naught within but a growl: "You will always be an enemy to me."

The Moor, tho', had passed well thro' his fear. "And I," he answered with peace, "whose grandfather and grandmother were dragged through the streets of Granada in shame, and forced to profess the false religion and speak an alien tongue, shall forever be an enemy to haughty Spaniards. Yet I bear you, Francisco, no malice."

I saw no more of the troublesome emissary before we set sail, except to briefly behold him chained to a galley oar.

Ten

Lampedusa cannot lay o'er thirty-five leagues to the west and south of Malta, and even with an overcrowded galley with upon five hundred souls aboard, we reached our destination on the third day after setting out. His Majesty has, I believe, never beheld the Great Port of Malta with his own eyes, but I may assure him, once seen, the sight is ne'er forgotten. As we sailed into the harbor that would play such a crucial role in the mighty events yet beyond comprehension, I quickly understood why the Knights, who at first viewed the Emperor's offer of the island with such disdain, had at last relented.

The Port is far from wide—across its narrower stretches a man may swim in a small part of a watch—but it is close on a full league from end to end. The vista formed by its stark prominences and basins and some of the fairest waters of the Mediterranean delights a mariner's eye, and its confines can easily shelter the largest fleet. As a sailor enters, he sees rising along the northern bank Mt. Sciberras, as the locals know it, but it deserves to be called a mountain only to the same degree England deserves to be called a country. This "mount" is no more than a pleasant incline, not above five hundred paces wide, that divides the harbor from Marsamxett to the north, an inlet all agree to be scarcely less splendid than the Great Port itself. Towering all of thirty or forty *brazas* above the two harbors, Sciberras gradually slopes down between them to end as a narrow spit of land where both waters merge with the sea.

We sailed into the Great Port with this rocky peninsula to starboard. But tho' His Majesty's troops will always remember the earth-trembling battle at Fort St. Elmo guarding there the harbor entrance, on the day I first beheld it only an ancient chapel and watchtower occupied the place, and the water lapped quietly against the limestone that everywhere underlies this island.

Were His Majesty to sail into the Great Port, as I did, his eye would surely be drawn to the southern flank. Thence protrude into the harbor a number of large rocky fingers, promontories, which betwixt them form smaller inlets ideal for sheltering vessels. As the first of these outcroppings passed by larboard, all of us espied there three or four corpses swinging from the gallows erected on that forlorn rock. It could be naught but a warning that we were entering the realm and justice of the Knights.

After this Gallows' Point a small first inlet, then a second finger—entirely barren—jutting into the harbor, and that one followed by a second and deeper channel. The natives call it Kalkara Creek, tho' it is far wider than anything I have ever heard termed a creek, it being perhaps a hundred *brazas* across, nearly the breadth of the harbor proper. They say the word *kalkara* in the Maltese language means "lime-kiln," which is hardly surprising, for the island is nothing but an enormous limestone quarry.

Then you are face to face with it. Even as our galley glided past Kalkara Creek, it was eclipsed by the shadow of the fortress, whose walls drop down like a hand-wrought cliff to the water's edge. Standing at the very tip of the third finger that juts into the harbor, it was not so magnificent as a few citadels I had seen in Spain, yet somehow the fort embraced the entire character of the island. Shorn of ornament, even then with patches of green thrusting thro' the cracks in yellowed walls, it presented a sullen stone face to the world, proclaiming that here on desolate Malta the Knights had made their stand and here they would remain, immovable as their faith. The proud banners waving high above from the cavalier and ramparts only added their defiance: our standard has here been planted, on Castle St. Angelo, stronghold of the Knights.

A few moments later we had rounded the stone apron that skirts the fortress at water level and put into the third inlet, Galley Creek, which was hardly smaller than Kalkara. From the seaward side, I would have said St. Angelo was impregnable; from this side I began to have doubts. The cavalier surmounting it was recent and the stronghold also boasted a mighty new bastion. And yet the new joined ancient and crumbling walls, which stood atop a wide open slope running up to them from the water. My heart skipped a beat; I would not place my faith in those walls against an enemy host.

"You see, my friend," remarked Balthazar cheerfully, joining me on the *ballestriere*, "e'en the Knights of St. John run out of money."

As the *ciurma* raised its oars for landing, the galley slid past the new bastion and past a ditch separating the castle from a small town which occupied the full landward end of the peninsula. There, beside the walls of this town and dozens of other vessels, the crew moored the galley and everyone prepared to disembark.

Before I could ask what the place was called, Balthazar passed his arm across it and said, "Welcome to Il Borgo. Should you remain in Malta, she shall be your home."

The first sight of this town, which one could seemingly walk across in less time than it took to polish your boots, hardly called out any great welcome to my soul. The walls surrounding it, made of the same infernal limestone as everything else within sight, blocked from view most of the buildings within, excepting a square clock tower and the tops of a few churches. On the embankment directly before us stood a row of small stone houses—quarters for galley captains, I learned—pressed against the wall so snugly they fair became part of it; and here and there plainly dressed townsfolk walked along the quay beside the galleys and round ships of all flags. I searched in vain for the great crowds that should have appeared to celebrate our arrival, and only the church bells ringing evening prayers lent the air about this place any cheer. Truly, if Sevilla was a marvel, Il Borgo was a hovel.

Appraising my expression, Balthazar asked, "Would you rather live yonder?" and pointed across Galley Creek to yet a fourth tongue of land jutting into the harbor. Thereon rose a few modest houses and two large windmills with spinning vanes, but otherwise the place appeared mostly deserted. In truth, I saw little to choose from and with a marked lack of enthusiasm I shrugged.

Only at that moment did it dawn on me that Vergã and I had ne'er made any plans for coming to Malta. Poor Captain de Gustaldo must surely be wondering what had become of us.

"By the Devil!" I exclaimed loudly. "What are we to do now?"

Balthazar turned to me and Blaij, who had stepped within earshot. "I say to you matelots, mind your tongues while in the Convent. Penalties for blasphemy can be severe."

Vergã and I began to learn exactly then in what respects Malta was a convent. No sooner had we set foot on the dock than we were accosted by a pair of cloaked women who begged alms in such a forward manner that their true business was made plain. Hoisting the Knight's cuirass onto my shoulder I said, "If my memory hasn't failed me, Fra Balthazar, you had placed great weight on a vow of chastity."

He offered no reply.

E'en as we stood there disengaging ourselves from these insistent women, Romegas's men were herding together the captives from Lampedusa and chaining them. With cudgel blows to the shoulders, the crew marched the infidels past officials who examined them for sickness, through the nearest gate and out of sight. I paid little attention to this business and saw nothing of the Moorish emissary, who was surely amongst them.

The moment had come for Balthazar to decide what to do with us his charges. Custom forbade us from staying at the auberge—the hostel—of the Langue of France, where Balthazar himself might remain while on Malta should a room be empty. And tho' with few brethren residing on the island at any moment, the Order always had need for mercenaries, common soldiers were expected to fend for themselves.

"But come," Balthazar said, "let us see what we can do." At that, he led us into the Borgo, upwards across a square and along a narrow street to the Auberge de France, a modest building of two stories near the center of town. To be sure, a free suite was available and, leaving there his armor, Balthazar took us back across the ditch into the castle, where he spoke to the Captain of the Guards about hiring us. The Captain agreed and for the night we would be quartered at the castle; in the morning he would send us over to the barracks.

By then the bell had struck complines and Balthazar bid us good evening, saying that the Grand Master would want to receive him in the morn for a report of all that had transpired since Africa. Balthazar confessed he was not looking forward to the audience. He also suggested that we visit the Hospital to learn whether our wounds, which had shown signs of putrefaction, might be further treated.

That warm night, as we ate eggs on the cavalier of Fort St. Angelo overlooking the dark harbor, Vergã and I attempted to understand what in the name of God we had gotten ourselves into.

"Chalk!" I cried, standing and spreading my arms over the whole of Malta. "The entire island meseems is made of chalk! The harbor, this castle, the walls, the auberges ... Yellow! Everything is yellow!"

"I haven't seen a single tree," growled Blaij. "Even Lampedusa had trees ... What do you think of the women?"

Again I threw up my arms. "How might I know! They are completely shrouded. Perhaps they shield themselves from the plague!"

"This Borgo is a town I'd piss on," Vergã said gloomily, "compared to Granada—"

"—Sevilla! If here live three thousand souls, I'll sell mine."

"Two thousand. And hold your tongue, Señor."

I bit my tongue and sat down again, as my leg was yet not fully healed; indeed it showed some lingering signs of putrefaction. "All the same, we have yet seen little ... Would you remain in this place?"

My companion shrugged. "Lescaut said I might profess."

"Hah!" I laughed, tossing over the wall an eggshell, which blew back into my face. "You are no nobleman. You know not who your father is, Señor, yet alone your grandfather."

With a sullen eye Blaij glared at me, e'en as he knew the truth of it. "Lescaut said that to their custom exceptions can be made, tho' ... "

"Tho' ... ?"

"They never are."

Both of us laughed. But as I stood once more, becoming fully aware of the strength of the sea wind, Blaij went on. "I'll show them what Blaij Vergã's sword can do. Then they must let me become a Knight, and I will win honor and reputation."

"You have a long road to plough, Blaij Vergã," I chuckled. "Methinks a good sword arm is not enough to bring one into the graces of these Knights." Above our heads, the big flag of the Order snapped loudly in this breeze, forcing one to raise one's voice against it. "But let us speak of quality. Lord Balthazar is a man of rare quality, one can sense it. Some of the others ... " I shrugged. "Tell me, is it possible for a commoner to best a Knight in quality?"

"Eh, you must be bred to these things over generations," replied Vergã, abruptly losing interest. "They can't be learned."

"What of their arrogance and condescension?" I blurted out. "Can that be learned?"

My companion only got to his feet and, with a dismissive wave of his hand, walked to the edge of the tower. "Stop blathering, Señor," he said, gazing out onto the dark water far below. "We cannot be Knights and that is the end of it."

"For my part," I replied with such assurance as I could muster, "I have no desire to be one."

"*Mentiroso!*" Blaij exclaimed instantly, turning on me with equal hardness and amusement.

As right as he may have been, I'd ne'er admit such a judgment. "Very well," I persisted, "you desire to be a Knight. We shall make you one, this moment." Did he remember the vow, as Fra Balthazar had taught us?

Blaij nodded, perplexed, as I looked around, making certain no prying eyes witnessed this sacrilege.

"Kneel," I said, "take the vow."

To my surprise, Vergã did so, there on the cold stone of the fortress cavalier below the flag of the Order. Having no Bible with us, he merely raised his hand.

"I do promise," he said as the ancient ceremony required, "and vow to God, to the ever Virgin Mary, the Mother of God, and to St. John Baptist, to pay henceforward, by the assistance of God's grace, true obedience to the superior which it shall please him to set over me, and which shall be chosen by our order, to live without any property and to preserve chastity."

I answered with the equally ancient formula: "We own you for a servant of the gentlemen that are poor and sick, and for a person devoted to the defense of the Catholic faith."

"I own myself to be it so," Vergã responded, gravely.

As he rose I made as if to drape him in the black mantle of the Knights, and reminded him that if he ever turned his back and deserted the standard of the Cross, he would be stripped of the holy sign and cut from our body as a rotten and corrupt member.

I say, Your Majesty, we performed this ritual with the utmost solemnity. Yea, we were young and overbrimming with Folly, and there is always in youth something of the jester, ridiculing the sacred. Yet in that mock ceremony we were fully sincere, and when Vergã told me to kneel and accept the vow, I refused, saying again I had no desire to become a Knight. Aye, at that moment I felt a bitterness in it.

Luckily, this rite or ours went unnoticed; otherwise I can hardly imagine that our stay on Malta would have lasted but a single night. We sat down again on the cavalier and peeled two more eggs.

"So," I mused, "why should you not be a Knight? Who would fight the Infidel with greater zeal?"

"Romegas," came Blaij's immediate and earnest reply. "If I fear death less than him, may the Sins of the Dead never be pardoned—but there's a man who'd cause the Devil himself to take to his heels. *Juro à Dios*, twenty-two and he's captured at least five Turkish ships and freed hundreds of Christians. Two of those ships he took in a single engagement."

From what we'd seen of Lescaut in action, I had no reason to doubt Vergã, but then he continued: "Go on aping Lord Balthazar and his ancients, for all I care. I shit on it."

The insult sent my blood pounding until, strangely, I imagined Balthazar asking of Lescaut, "Is this true courage, this fearlessness?"

"I have many times in my life," the Abbé had remarked on Lampedusa, "witnessed men in action who held no fear of death. But methinks this cannot be called courage, because they have no idea of what danger is. They wade into battle with a foolish, dull-witted grossness, without the deliberation and resolve to put honor above every danger in the world. It is this deliberation, I say, that marks true courage."

Did it? My judgment of the Knights would change time and again. One thing I could say, as the stars came out above the wind-buffeted cavalier: In the élan wherewith these men went into battle, I had never seen the like—whether it was Balthazar taking on eight corsairs without a care, the crew of our undermanned galley attacking a Turk with twice its numbers, or Lescaut abruptly abandoning Doria for Turgut. Little wonder the dreaded corsair held the Knights responsible for all his misfortunes. These warriors were truly the modern incarnation of the Maccabees, those holy martyrs who took on vast hosts and defeated them with nothing but their own prowess and the aid of God. If this was not courage, I did not know what was.

Eleven

The morning after our arrival in Malta, Fra Balthazar rose late with the church bells ringing First Paternoster. It was neither Sunday nor Wednesday, and so he was not obliged to attend Mass. Custom, natheless, required that he recite one hundred and fifty Paternosters throughout the day. As he confessed to me only hours later, Balthazar often failed in this obligation, but he knelt beside his bed in the Auberge de France and said the Lord's Prayer with unusual conviction, feeling a sharp sense of unease at what the day would bring. Rising, he dressed and exchanged his woolen sleeping gown for the black habit of the Religion. The auberge bell would ring for the first meal of the day at precisely the Angelus, noon, and so he set out to Grand Master's residence in the fortress to secure an audience with His Eminence, Juan d'Homedes.

The Monsignore, I learned, was among some little esteemed, not only because of his stubbornness but because he was a Spaniard and, tongues wagged, more devoted to the Emperor Carlos than to the Order. As it happened, he received Lord Balthazar only when the sun was well up, and then in the magnificent garden he had built by his summer home on that deserted prominence across Galley Creek. In that garden full of ponds, paved with mosaics and smelling of herbs from distant lands, Balthazar knelt before the Monsignore and kissed his ring. d'Homedes, white, bearded and dressed also in the robes of the Religion, waved the younger man to his feet and embraced him like a father. But there in the garden, where he was surrounded by trees bearing dates and figs and apples of paradise, and where water streamed from marble fountains, Balthazar understood he had much explaining to do.

He was, in almost every respect, too late. During the weeks we had been stranded on Lampedusa, Lescaut had already informed the Grand Master about the debacle on Los Gelves and Turgut's astonishing escape.

"So Doria let the dog get away!" d'Homedes said in his dry voice, as he paced along the garden paths with the younger Knight beside him. The Grand Master frequently boasted that he'd lost an eye in combat. As a result, Knights on the wrong side were unsure whether the old man could see them, as indeed Balthazar was at this moment.

"Yes, Monsignore," Balthazar answered, grasping his rosary. "A few of us attempted to capture Turgut but—"

"What possessed you to take two untried soldiers?" d'Homedes turned straight on Fra Balthazar, glaring at him with the eye.

"I have in truth been asking myself that question, Eminenza—"

The Grand Master paused at the garden gate to regard the great horse and rider he'd commissioned to be carved there from alabaster and painted. "The Captain General of the Sea returned safely to Genoa weeks ago. He has announced he will not after Dragut, no, for he must ferry the Emperor's son, Philip, from Italy to Spain. How convenient ... " The Grand Master again cast that eye at Balthazar. "And you quit Africa ... "

"With but a single company ... We received Doria's summons—"

"Already Europe is laughing." d'Homedes scoffed and snapped a fig from a branch; considering it briefly, he popped it into his mouth. "Where is Dragut?"

"I fear he must have gained the Levant, Monsignore, Constantinople."

Balthazar fell silent then, perceiving that the Grand Master's distemper was directed far more broadly than at his misadventure with two young Spaniards.

Verily, d'Homedes began to pace anew, with hands locked behind him. "We receive daily reports from Naples and Sicily that the Grand Turk is readying a fleet ... "

The Monsignore did not finish his thought, for at that moment a tall Knight in hose and doublet strode into the garden, bowed and kissed his ring. Balthazar recognized the sunburnt face and blond curls as belonging to Nicolas Durand *dict* Villegaignon, Grand Prior of France and nephew of the great l'Isle Adam, admired by all as one of the handsomest men of the age and no less esteemed for his valor at Algiers and his learning. Villegaignon had moments ago arrived from France through Sicily, where he had spoken to the Vice Roy, Don Juan de Vega.

"The common opinion in the court at Paris," declared Villegaignon, "leaves me in no doubt that Soliman intends to attack the Religion. Yet

Don Juan imagines that the coasts of Naples and Sicily lie in greater danger than the territories of the Order; he will spare no men or ships to protect Malta, Tripoli or Africa."

Balthazar hesitated to contend with Villegaignon, whose mind by reputation was adorned with every sort of knowledge and whose reasoning was as cold as it was acute, yet he understood the older Knight to be in the wrong. "Where an invasion will fall we do not yet know, Brother Nicolas," he answered, again squeezing the tasseled string of beads in his hand, "but I say the Religion has not the forces to garrison Africa or Tripoli. They must be abandoned."

Villegaignon's celebrated blue eyes regarded the younger Knight with amazement. "How say you, Brother? We should immediately send succours thither and undertake their defense. Moreover, I tell you the defense of the neighboring isle here, Gozo, is untenable. We must destroy the castle and send the inhabitants to Sicily, where they can be employed by the Vice Roy for rude labor. In exchange, we may press him for troops for Tripoli."

At this Balthazar shook his head decisively. The reasons behind Villegaignon's argument he could hardly perceive; he did see with every clarity that the Knight was repeating past errors. "Nay, Brother Nicolas, tho' it is apparent that you have given the matter much thought, you are mistaken. Far better to demolish the walls of Africa, which stand in a foreign land surrounded by a hostile people. With God as my witness, we have not the men to defend that place, which has never proven to be of any value to us, and each time it changes hands between Christian and barbarian, we lose ever more Knights in the bargain. As for Tripoli, the Religion has never wanted it and the whole garrison there is composed of nothing but old and infirm Knights who have repaired thither for the benefits of the air. With the small resources we possess, we would do better to fortify the walls of Malta and Gozo."

"Gozo must be sacrificed," said Villegaignon. "Thereon live nothing but farmers and peasants and we cannot protect them."

"Five thousand souls inhabit that island," rejoined Balthazar, "if not six. You would ship them all off to Sicily like so many cattle?"

Villegaignon answered dismissively: "The expense, my young man, would be far less than attempting to defend the place."

"Messeri," interceded d'Homedes at that juncture, "I find it difficult to credit that Soliman the Grand Turk would be readying a fleet such as our agents inform us for the sole purpose of attacking this inconsiderable rock. He must intend to fall on Naples and Sicily."

"Eminenza," Balthazar responded, "if Turgut has the Sultan's ear, I say beware. The corsair holds no one so responsible for the setbacks of the Turkish fleet as he holds us. And rightly so, for no one has caused him such woe as we the Knights."

The Grand Master had wearied of the discussion. "Truly," he said at length, pulling a new German timepiece from the folds of his robe, "this is a matter for the Council. I shall at convene it at once. Brother Nicolas, I expect you at the Castellan's house at nones."

With those words, Balthazar knew he had been dismissed, for he was not a member of the Council, which consisted of only the most senior Knights and officers of the langues. Natheless, d'Homedes might have seen fit to call for his testimony. Fra Balthazar de Marans des Homes-Saint-Martin bowed and strode out of the garden shaking his head, recalling the words of the poet:

De mon bien, on mon mal,
Mon esprit m'est oracle.

Balthazar's soured spirit was plain when he found me clasping a shining halberd in the Borgo. Vergã and I had been roused an hour before dawn with the morning Angelus to guard the Order's slaves, then employed at strengthening the city's walls. Without prologue Balthazar asked where the Moorish emissary was to be found. I had not seen him, and as we searched among the gangs of Mahometans along the ramparts, Balthazar recounted his meeting with the Grand Master and Villegaignon, which had left him so troubled. At length we discovered the Moor hauling stones with the other infidels on the landward extremity of the Borgo. Lord Balthazar commanded me to take the prisoner aside.

"What do you know of Soliman's invasion plans?" Balthazar barked abruptly.

The word "invasion" took me by surprise and the Moor only shook his head, glancing at his bleeding hands. "My Lord, I told you on the isle of

Lampedusa, with Allah as my witness, that the dispatches I carried were sealed."

"That is not what I asked," snapped Balthazar. "You are an emissary of the Grand Infidel to his dog-*puta* Turgut and I am not a child. You have knowledge of what transpires in Constantinople. I want to know what that is."

"Sir Knight, my position is not so exalted as you believe. I know no more than Soliman desired that Turgut return to Constantinople and, by happy accident, that almost certainly has transpired. I ask permission to write to the Sultan to secure my ransom."

"Certainly," said Balthazar, "once we rack you."

Balthazar called for guards to lead the prisoner away, and seeing that I yet walked with a perceptible limp, ordered me again to the Hospital. The distance was not great—nothing in the Borgo was great—and I set off whither the Knight pointed. Tho' I had spent only a few hours in this town and most of that on guard duty, I dimly perceived that Il Borgo was not entirely as I had yesterday believed it to be. As I made my way through the narrow, unpaved streets, puzzled by the strange, flat-roofed houses rising to either side, a babble of Spanish, French, Italian, Greek, Portuguese and almost every other tongue you could imagine accosted my confused ears. What a mélange! Criers accompanied by trumpets and drums barked out edicts on the squares in what I supposed to be Maltese, the language of the locals. I could make out not a word of it, and days would pass before I learnt it was more akin to Arabic than any civilized tongue. The Knights disdained those harsh sounds, and the natives spoke naught else but sometimes a few words of Italian. In the Knights' estimation, this was no great loss, for the Maltese were nothing but rude and unlettered peasants who in their daily prayers could not distinguish the Lord Almighty from Satan.

On this hot summer day near the feast of Saints Peter and Paul, the sun burnt your skin in instants and mosquitoes the size of sparrows carried off the pieces. Mahometan slaves hurried along the streets in burnooses or tattered cloaks. Many lacked ears or noses and they all wore iron rings about their ankles, but otherwise they went about their business freely. I shoved aside a kneeling beggar and tripped over pigs. At the square, near the clock tower whose clangorous bells rang out the hours from morning till night, a woman stripped near naked and chained to a great pillar was being flogged to the taunts of the crowd. Women aplenty passed me in the Borgo, but as I'd grumbled to Vergã, white mantillas shrouded nearly every one of them from head to toe and I could discern nothing of their charms. To be sure, it is common knowledge that Maltese women often squint, on account of having to peer with one eye through the veils they constantly wear. In the inns and taverns it is another story.

Maugre these signs of life, Fortune had truly dropped us into a convent, an austere and yellow one ruled by the Religion's own Church of San Lorenzo and the Bishop's Palace. With four or five other churches crammed into the tiny Borgo, and a saint's image on near every corner, I was swiftly convinced that the inhabitants of this convent must be more Catholic than the Pope himself. Where was a sprig of green to give joy to the heart? Oh, Granada!

The Holy Infirmary was the pride of the Order. I found the magnificent structure where Balthazar said I would, pressed close to the eastern ramparts of the Borgo, overlooking Kalkara Creek. As I entered its cloister, I at once sensed the dedication of the Knights to this their sworn duty, the care of the poor and the sick. A shaft of light fell into that great, quiet courtyard, as if sent from the hand of the Almighty himself to illuminate this sacred space. In vain do I attempt to describe the feelings which flooded over me at that moment. Unbidden, tears streamed to my eyes and I cried like a child, knowing then that here was a place truly good, truly blessed and sanctified by God.

Almost immediately a Serving Brother approached me with the utmost humility and when I composed myself I told him of my injury. They would gladly see to it, he replied, but by custom I should first bathe and make my confession. Bathe I did, and in the chapel there, yet under the spell of the holy place in which I found myself, all the turmoil of the past months cascaded forth. For a full watch I emptied myself to the chaplain of battles and duels, Knights and whores, all in such a stew that I am certain he made nothing of it. I shook, sobbed, I cried in exaltation, truly beside myself; the Lord Christ stood above me surrounded by a nimbus of light, with his hands opening my chest, commanding the words I knew not whence they came to my mouth. And when his spirit left my side, I veritably collapsed into the chaplain's arms. He blessed me, telling me to attend Mass from hereon and say fifty Paternosters a day and that number of Ave Maria's. Then he asked if I had any last testament to make and, as I did not, he led me upstairs to the ward reserved for wounded soldiers. In my unruly, unbridled torrent I had omitted only the one, why I had left Granada.

The infirmary was immaculate. I do not think I had ever seen a cleaner building. Gradually, I became attuned to a peculiar sensation, rather the lack of it; for one of the few times of my city life, I was unaware of the smell of shit. The physician received me with the same courtesy as the Serving Brother, bidding me in perfect Spanish to sit down on one of the dozens of canopied beds that occupied this spacious and sunlit room. I held no doubt, having on the stair glimpsed three full stories and numerous wards, that this the Sacra Infermeria of the Order was the largest hospital in Christendom.

When I told the young man, who introduced himself as Doctor Jean de Vigo, of the arrow wound I'd received weeks before, that the ship's surgeon had cauterized it, but that it yet remained pus-filled, he at once ordered me to remove my breeches. Nodding at the fetid red and white mess, he remarked that suppuration was a natural and good part of healing; he'd drain it and apply a digestive of egg yolk, liquid spirits and rose oil to speed along recovery. The galley surgeon, I recalled, had applied the same preparation to Balthazar's shoulder wound.

"Tell me, did the ... *surgeon* on Lampedusa use a boiling mixture of ... oil of elders to cauterize your wound?" Doctor Jean asked with affable curiosity and a slight hesitation that gave his voice a pleasing gravity. Hardly pausing, he sent an assistant to the nearest apothecary for the mixture with orders that it be prepared fresh.

I shook my head in answer to his question. "I recall only a hot iron."

"Mayhap that is ... *good*," the physician replied, admonishing me with a finger to his mouth to speak in a low voice. "Or mayhap not. The French master, Ambroise Paré, has ... observed that boiling oil of elders is of *no* help when treating a wound, and the mixture I have just called for serves equally ... *well*."

"It does?" I asked, having no notion of it.

"Yes," he said, continuing to speak in a whisper, "I do not know of another time before him when such an ... *experiment* was made ... "

The strange word "experiment" was new to me, and the hesitation wherewith Doctor Jean pronounced it showed that he was uneasy with the term as well. "Have you read the works of Paré's student Paracelsus?" he asked, holding out to me a small book he'd been carrying.

Paracelsus's name was familiar to me, for he was renowned as a healer and alchemist, but no, why should I have read him?

Doctor Jean chuckled conspiratorially. "Some say before he died he made a pact with the Devil to become young again. Then there are those who say the guzzler fell down a flight of stairs in a drunken stupor. I have heard his tomb has become a place of pilgrimage for the sick, like a ... *saint's*."

The conversation halted then and Jean de Vigo bowed, for hereon the Grand Hospitaller himself entered the ward making his daily rounds. Dressed in the same black habit as everyone else, he carried a glimmering silver service in his hands and bade me with all good cheer to take some fruit and cheese. The thought of accepting food from one of the highest ranking Knights of the Order set my hands atrembling, but the Grand Hospitaller insisted in all humility that he was here only to serve "Our Lords the Sick." As I bit into an apple, Doctor Jean showed to the Hospitaller the book of Paracelsus and for a few moments the elder Knight joined us in conversation.

"Was Paracelsus not a Lutheran heretic?" I asked.

"I have no knowledge of this," Doctor Jean replied, admonishing me again to keep my voice low, "but he insists on this page—" he poked his finger at it—"that the ... *theory* and *practice* of medicine should remain undivided, and he asks, 'What would you do if your speculations did not accord with findings based on practice? Both must be *true*, or both must be *untrue*.'" Doctor Jean glanced up. "I believe the Order practices such a view."

"Does he follow the ancient traditions?" the Grand Hospitaller asked with genuine interest.

The physician shook his head. "No! And he dares even to write in German! He maintains—let me again quote his words—'He who would become a good physician must find his faith in the rational light of ... *nature*, and not undertake anything without it, for Christ would have you draw faith from knowledge and not live without it.'"

Doctor Jean read the passage with evident satisfaction, e'en as the Grand Hospitaller wrinkled his brow as he attempted to discern the meaning, which escaped me altogether. After having Doctor Jean recite the passage again he shook his head. "This last seems to me dubious. Perhaps it should be discussed with Bishop Cubelles."

"Perhaps," echoed Doctor Jean, stroking his striking red beard and putting his nose again to the book. "But consider: Paracelsus further avers that a good physician must ... desire to learn and gather experience. 'He must consult with magicians and astrologers, for they have a greater regard for honor than money; he must not be married to a bigot, should not practice self-abuse—'"

"Here we can agree," interrupted the Grand Hospitaller severely.

"'He should not have a red beard.'" The physician looked up abruptly.

"Ah, of course this presents difficulties for you, Doctor Jean," laughed the Hospitaller, laying his hand on the other's shoulder. Then with more gravity he added, "Paracelsus's reliance on astrologers and magicians troubles me. Please, discuss the matter with Bishop Cubelles."

With his secretary at his heels, the Grand Hospitaller set off again on his rounds, stopping to converse with the other patients, offering them fruit from the silver service and at times assisting the attending physician with treatment. By then the assistant had brought the digestive Doctor Jean had requested. He lanced the pus-filled blister on my thigh, washed the wound with salt water and vinegar, applied his mixture and dressed it with clean linen. As he worked he mused, "A few years ago the Florentine Girolamo Frascastoro—the same illustrious physician who wrote that most renowned poem '*Syphilidis, sive morbi gallici*'—published a work in which he claimed that disease is spread by ... um, spores ... *contagium vivum*, he named them, which he says travel between organisms and infect them by direct contact, or perhaps through an intermediary ... or perhaps borne by the air ... Have you ever encountered such a thought?" Doctor Jean looked quizzically at me as he finished dressing the wound. I made no answer. "*Vive valeque*," he said and bade me farewell.

As I walked out of the Infirmary, the last thing I noticed were lists of Hospital regulations written on parchments and hanging by chains on the doors, rules that forbade the sick any food but that ordered by the physician, the playing of cards, dice or chess, the making of noise and the reading aloud of books.

Twelve

That evening at sunset, Blaij and I crossed Galley Creek to the empty spit of land the Knights called Monte del Mulino and the natives simply l'Isola. Whatever its name, for us it was the place where soldiers slept in dirty and crowded quarters. E'en as we walked into the barracks to the sound of dice rolling on the filthy floor, the talk was of one thing and one thing only: a Turkish invasion. But no one could say what each man would give his blood to hear—where and when the descent would fall. The Knights, tho', heeded the apostles and went about their business untroubled, and the rest of us had no course but to follow their example.

So, the next morning Blaij and I arose at the Angelus. By primes, knowing nothing of the Order's many edicts governing slaves or of a soldier's duties guarding them—or that little attention was paid to either—we were marching back to the Borgo, up toward Kalkara Creek and to the prison where the galley slaves were locked up at night. Everybody laughingly called it the bagno—the baths—but except for a small stone house near the Hospital, this bagno was wholly underground, cut from the living rock. We descended into the lightless place and herded all the dogs out. Once we got them into the sun and counted, I saw the Moorish emissary was missing. Puzzled, I grabbed a torch and went down again into the dank labyrinth, where I roamed amid chests and makeshift Mahometan altars and finally found the infidel lying in his own dirt against the wall of a large vaulted cell. I passed the torch over him and told him to follow the others or by God I would flog him.

"You must flog me," he replied calmly, "for my limbs are so swollen I cannot walk."

"Lord Balthazar had you racked yesterday?"

"With the Council's permission, but two turns only. He is wise enough to understand my worth decreases with each turn of the wheel."

In the inconstant light I saw little but rope burns. The Moor's humor under the circumstances evoked some reluctant admiration from me, but the outcome of the questioning held a far greater interest this morning. "What did you tell him of the Sultan's plans?"

"I am like the raven whose skin and bones make a meal too poor for a king. I told him nothing, for nothing is what I know."

"The Sacra Infermeria treats even infidels," I told him, unable to decide whether he continued to lie or whether he truly had nothing to tell. It was, I decided, none of my concern. "Lord Balthazar may perhaps have you admitted."

Now the emissary laughed outright. "How like the barbarians! First you torture me, then you would nurse me. It has always been thus with the House of War, has it not? When the Franj invaders sacked the Holy City, they put every man, woman and child to the sword, seventy thousands they butchered. For a full week the streets ran crimson with the blood of Muslims. The Franj burned ten thousand Jews alive in their temple and destroyed the tomb of Abraham, may peace be upon him. Yet you ask why the House of Islam declared jihad on the unbelievers. 'Fight in the way of Allah against those who fight against you, but begin not hostilities.'"

There as water dripped behind us, I slowly perceived that by the derisive "Franj" the Moor meant the Holy Crusaders. The *chavush's* voice, rich and deep as befitted an emissary, impressed me, and the conviction of his words, but I found no strength in his disputation. "The Crusaders retook the Holy City in the name of the Lord Jesus Christ," I rejoined, "and three days of pillage is the usage of war, concede it."

"The spoils of war belong to Allah and the Messenger."

For a long time neither of us spoke. At last I took Abdallah al-Waryagli to the Hospital.

Returning to my duties, I passed the Conventual Church in the Borgo. Seized again by the presence of Christ, I stepped inside and knelt before Our Lady of Filermos and the hand of the Baptist himself and gave thanks for the sign that had been granted me yesterday at the Infermeria. Never since childhood, when I'd once stared into the jaws of Satan and Hell itself, had I felt so powerful a presence as in the Hospital. Hands clasped before these holiest relics of the Order, I felt today a like presence and knew that my journey to Malta had been ordained.

Why I could not guess, and despite my fervent prayers, the relics granted no further sign to make my purpose manifest. Natheless, after only a single night I forsook those filthy barracks and found more permanent lodging atop a small house in the Borgo. The room was scarce larger than the bed occupying it, but Frugality had declared herself my patron saint. My purse from Granada had been lost God knows when, and our part of the spoils from the Turkish ship would not see me far. As I patted the bed, I consoled myself that it was softer than the pallets of the past nights and that I looked through a window onto Galley Creek rather than into a dark cellar.

Vergã had also fled the overcrowded barracks for the Borgo and at sunset, as the bells struck the Ave Maria, he came to fetch me for supper. We hied to the most popular tavern in town. No shingle marked it from above, but the noise alone told us what we'd find below. Under lanterns swinging from wide stone arches, it was all sailors, merchants and even Knights throwing cards and dice, crying, "To the Turk with you, robber!" and swilling whatever came into their hands. There we quickly discovered what everyone else in Christendom already knew: that Maltese whores were the most numerous and industrious in the whole of the Mediterranean.

We'd scarce sat down and ordered wine and partridge when five or six *quiracas* fell into a cat-fight over us, three of them spilling over a table and uprighting it altogether to the cheers of everyone around. While those on the floor kicked and screamed—and a few men willingly entered the fray to untangle the damp knot of legs and under-clothes—Blaij and I invited the two pleasing wenches who remained standing to join us at our table.

Their names were Innocenza—aye, such she called herself—and Flaminia. Like all Maltese women, so I judged, Innocenza and Flaminia were short, narrow of waist and ample of bust, with eyes like coals and hair to match and—most astonishingly—of fair skin. How unlike their menfolk, who stood a few fingers taller than the women, whose skin might have belonged to an Arab's, whose chests resembled barrels and heads nothing so much as cannon balls. From the moment I stepped off the galley, I would have sworn the Maltese men and women came from different races altogether!

Following what I perceived to be the prevailing fashion, Innocenza and Flaminia wore their hair in curls and their dresses girded high under their bosoms, which showed them off handsomely and which they employed at once to great advantage. To a man who had just spent three months on a galley in the company of filthy soldiers, the scent of their perfume—had it been but oil and vinegar—was well-nigh irresistible and I fairly drowned in it.

All this I took in before even a word had been exchanged. Tho' bartering names was easily enough thro' the pointing of fingers, carrying the conversation forward with these *quiracas* proved difficult. At once they began chattering at us in Maltese:

"Spanjoli! Imkabbrin, mahmugin jintnu, bhas-soltu."
"Qatt ma tiehu xejn min fuqhom. Oime ghal xi Franciz."
"Ahjar induru ghal xi kavallier."
"Jien nghidlek: qaxxar lill min jrid ikun imqaxxar."

You can be sure this strange dialogue left both Vergã and I baffled. Flaminia, positioning herself on my lap in the most skillful manner, turned to the lingua franca:

"Aia! Commé ti star?" she asked, which I naturally took as, "How are you?"

"Muy bien," I replied in Spanish, *"por los Ojos de mi Dama."*

At that she poked my nose, expressing her happiness in the language of the Frank: *"Mi star bonu,"* and went on to say, *"Mi star contento mirar per ti."*

"Gracias."

"Gratzia."

My little one wasted no further time in getting to the meat of it.

"Dara mi vino, ebriacar mi, mio cuore," she ordered and I called out, *"¡Bebamos otra, rápido!"*

Thusly, as more wine filled our cups and our lips swelled with the words we shared from all the languages of the Middle Sea, Vergã and I stepped into the Maltese way of life.

Beneath all the noise, a Florentine merchant who was sucking on chicken's feet leaned over to us with a conspiratorial wink and advised,

"Messeri, in this tiny city you'll find *puttane maltesi, italiane, greche, spagnole, arabe ... di ogni razza che ti stuzzica il nerbo.* Beware, tho': the Maltese pox is more virulent than any, being a combination of all the others." He raised a cup to us, wiping his brow. "*Oimè!* It must be this excessively hot climate that increases their wantonness beyond mortal limits."

"*E di chi è la lascivita'?*" retorted Innocenza sharply, releasing her arm from Vergã's neck. Speaking with a slight cough that only increased her charm, she told us, "Anyone with eyes can see friars and priests leaving the convents at night, straight to their mistresses. The Prior in Rabat— Oh, I know him—"

"—and the Mother Superior of Mdina," Flaminia interrupted in a voice as gentle as a turtledove's, while she cooled herself with a small fan she held on a stick. "After Holy Week, she disappeared from her convent and, it's true, they found her in the hermit of Mosta's hut with his pestle in her mortar. *Nirrahom jiggidmu it-tnejn li huma!* O Madonna, do you think a whore can betray any sacraments? A few drops of holy water and all the sins from her soul are washed away."

A French Knight next to us cried out, "Does not St. Augustine tell us, *'Anima certe, quia spiritus est, in sicco habitare, non potest.* Surely the soul, because it is spirit, cannot dwell in dryness.'"

Paying no heed, Flaminia gave another reason why it was better to be a whore than a nun. "It is good to be called 'Signora,' eating and drinking like a signora, having a feast and marriage day every day."

Vergã and I nodded to each other. No less than in Spain, every Maltese *quiraca* would murder her sisters to find a man to support her. Walking the streets of Birgu—as the natives seemed to call Il Borgo—it was nigh impossible to distinguish the whores from the married women.

"Well it might be," suggested Flaminia, "for we give all the good things of a wife and none of the bad things."

"Except the *morbo gallico*," interjected the Italian merchant.

"The Neapolitan malady," objected the French Knight.

At which a German interjected, "The Spanish scabies."

And a Spaniard concluded, "The American pox."

Of no consequence. The number of Knights at the nearby tables, each surrounded by their own *quiracas*, gave a fair enough view of how seriously members of the Religion took their vow of chastity. Flaminia watched me as I regarded the picture and without prompting offered, "By the Blessed

Mother, each Knight has a mistress and every Grand Master two."

"You two are not Knights," Innocenza observed thro' that delicate cough. "What is your business in Malta?"

"To become Knights, of course," Flaminia answered for us, "and make us their mistresses."

The nimble wit of these beguiling wenches had already captured us and their presence now inspired Blaij to a rare height. "You must each swear not to publish my exploits," he set forth, kissing Innocenza soundly between her breasts, "otherwise all the women on this rock will fall in love with me and I shall have to contend with too many of them."

The declaration elicited only a laugh from the whores, but all three of us solemnly swore. Unhindered, he went on to recount our exploits at Gelves, during which, tho' outnumbered five to one, he had all but captured Dragut with one hand, only to see him get away when I jostled him and his shot went awry—

"*Calla, picaro!*" I exclaimed, instinctively feeling for my dagger.

Dismissing me with a sneer, Blaij went on to narrate the sea battle at Lampedusa, which required little by way of exaggeration. To be sure, I washed away his insult with a gulp of wine, and neither of us erupted on this occasion for which braggadocio was invented. He finished by showing off the wound he had received in the arm, for which he had yet to seek treatment.

The women were no more impressed with this souvenir than the boasting, nor were they insensible to the unease between us. "Messeri, you two are not entirely friends," Flaminia observed.

"'Tis true," I answered, "this wretch would not disown killing me should it suit him."

Blaij lifted his mug. "Eh? When did I ever say I'd kill you?" he responded with something between a laugh and a growl. "It was you who near off'd me on Lampedusa."

"And well you deserved it," I replied severely, "attempting to kill an unarmed man, infidel tho' he was."

"What is the cause of this?" Innocenza asked, taking Vergã's cup from him and finishing it.

"He once stole a woman from me," Blaij said, this time without jest. "I can't trust him. Who can trust a rich poltroon who acts only for himself?"

Now my dagger was out, instantly, its point jammed into the tabletop.

"Hah! Finally it comes, the cause of this enmity! And what do I hear? Barefaced lies!" To the whores I said, "I ne'er stole a woman from this one."

"You did," Blaij answered without retreat.

"Who?" I exclaimed, incredulous at his falsehoods.

"Carmesina."

For a moment I gaped. Carmesina? Then: "That whore! What was she to you?"

"Everything," Blaij answered sullenly. "And you knew it." The gaze he leveled at me at that moment was full of hatred, pure hatred.

"Did you know what she meant to him?" Innocenza asked.

"No woman ever meant anything to him."

"*Picaro*—"

Blaij and I were on our feet, truly ready to throttle each other. Flaminia used the opportunity to snatch my glass and drain it. "Madonna! Why not get this over with now, rather than letting such a wound fester?" she taunted. "Kill each other off, you two, or put it in the well."

The proposal suited both of us.

"A wager then," said Blaij, staring me in the eye. "We race the lice. Mine wins—we fight to the death. Yours wins—we put it aside ... "— He shrugged—" ... for a year."

"Done," I answered and we sat.

We had taken up this method of gambling aboard the galleys. With my dagger I scratched a circle on the rough tabletop. We each placed a personal louse at the center of the circle and waited to see which one would cross the line first. After several moments of turnings and wrigglings, my louse won.

Vergã and I shook, agreeing to forget such matters for a year.

At that moment none other than Lord Balthazar entered the cellar and did us the honor of joining us, towing several women in his wake. The hour was already somewhat late, the bell just striking complines and this, naturally...

"A gentleman," he narrated to the much widened circle, "one evening approached a woman, who tho' somewhat advanced in years was yet quite handsome and desirable. 'How can you make love to me?' she asked, 'when

I am at my complines?' To which the other made answer, 'Your complines, Madame, are preferable to any other woman's primes.' Hah!"

Balthazar shouted, slapping the table, "I say, what a wit!"

Maugre his exclamation, the Knight appeared to be in less than an exuberant humor. "Have you news of the invasion, Fra Balthazar?" those around him asked.

He responded with an ambiguous motion of his head. "Today we again received word that a large Turkish fleet was being readied in Constantinople. By now it will be underway. But we still have no knowledge of where an invasion will fall. The Vice Roy of Sicilia has decided to send succours to Africa with Antonio Doria, one of the Admiral's too many relatives. The Council, not three hours past, decided to ship the entire population of Gozo off to Sicilia. Do you know how I name this? Folly, I say it again, folly! Fortune and Folly, the two muses of man. It shall ever be thus." He lifted his cup in a salute and drank.

"What would you have them do?" one of the merchants asked, pulling up his stool.

"Defend this place, of course!" replied Balthazar. "We the Knights are not so numerous, and any idiot can see that the fortifications of Malta are insufficient. The castle our stronghold is a fair piece of work, but what else? Birgu itself is surrounded on the landward side by hills, a stew pot for Turkish siege guns." He paused then, surveying the tavern. "Look at these Knights," he said as he passed his arm across the tableau, "they have sold their slaves to support their mistresses and have fucked and gambled away everything they own. They have brought themselves to such rack and ruin that they cannot even afford their own roofs and must needs beg alms at the auberges. In heroic ages the Knights of St. John wielded swords, not pricks. Who be these weak wretches, half of whom are riddled with the pox and of no use to anyone? They could forego half their caravans were they not obliged to pay for all this whoring. If we are to fight the Turk—and we will fight the Turk—we must remake ourselves, of that I am certain. Of course men must always remake themselves, mustn't they, especially in these times when they are buffeted about so completely by the winds of Fortune. The world is changing, into what I am at a loss to perceive, but how shall the Knights remake themselves?" He paused, glanced about bemusedly, added, "With that let me come to the amen of my Paternoster," and he crossed himself.

As Balthazar completed his sermon, half melancholic and half befuddled, a wandering musician, a troubadour I suppose, entered the tavern with a lute in his hands and began singing: *"Syphilus, ut fama est, ipsa haec ad flumina pastor ... "*

Balthazar slapped his thighs and guffawed. The words, from the same poem of which Doctor Jean in the Hospital had spoken only yesterday, told the story of the shepherd, Syphilus, who blasphemed the Sun for a draught that had scorched the land.

"The Sun, my friends, lost no time in retaliating with an unknown pollution, which struck Syphilus straightaway. Farmers began calling the contagion Syphilis, and the evil plague spread to all the towns and would not spare e'en the King himself ... "

"Ah, what a fine note on which to finish the evening," concluded Balthazar, rising as the music continued. "Two days hence is the feast of Saints Peter and Paul. Allow me, my friends, to invite you to the Auberge of France for lunch, as my guests. The noon Angelus, precisely."

With that, Fra Balthazar drained his cup, plunked it on the table and left the unhappy *donne meretrici* behind him, saying he was expected elsewhere.

L'hora della ruffiana had sounded long ago, and Blaij followed Innocenza out the door. Only then as he steadied her gait did I espy her shoes, which lifted her so far above the ground that it was a wonder she found it possible to walk at all. I contemplated with relief and a strange sadness that I might see less of Vergã from this night on. To be sure, one did not have to be a seer to perceive that these fair wenches were ministers of all that belonged to both gentry and soldiers on Malta. I gave Flaminia my arm to steady her and she led me to her tenement.

Thirteen

If rumors of war are a contagion, the Grand Master did not so much fear them as he would the plague. E'en Birgu's whores knew that to strengthen the town's fortifications would take years, and d'Homedes seemed to reckon that if a Turkish attack were only weeks away, then to bask in the scent of the flowers in his magisterial garden was the more profitable occupation.

That's what you might have heard from French tongues. In truth the Monsignore didn't remain wholly idle. Under the glare of his eye, Knights, slaves and we the soldiers bent our backs to repairing the castle's old walls and to fortifying the landward side of Birgu and l'Isola. We hauled barques ashore and fashioned gabions wherewith we barricaded the stretch of land between the Borgo and l'Isola. And so if the Turks foolishly attempted to put into Galley Creek, they would be exposed to fire on three sides. Able men were issued arquebuses from the armory and a few rounds of ammunition in order to increase their skill.

But e'en Turkish slaves laughed that these were half measures, and under them the whispers of a descent infected the Borgo not so much with terror as a strange St. Vitus's Dance, a morbid festivity made ever gayer and frenzied as the calamity approached.

On the feast of Saints Peter and Paul, this most holy Saints' day, the streets of the Borgo came fully alive. Garlands had been strung everywhere between rooftops, green garlands from the countryside, and beneath them—endless processions of priests and Knights, monks and nuns, all dressed in fine gold and silver robes or mantles pressed, carrying through the streets the standards of the langues and the holy relics, everything accompanied by a festive clangor of bells and the swoop of finches.

As noon approached, I left off guarding the slaves, wiped my brow and scampered down from the earthen terrace the workers had just raised near the end of Galley Creek. The hour had come to lunch at the Auberge de

France. I collected Vergã and we pressed through the throngs of townspeople, pigs and chickens that greeted the priest as he splashed everyone with holy water. Would that it had been a rainfall! Fifty paces away, work on the walls continued. What an extraordinary sense of the ordinary this clash of military discipline and religious festivity lent to the Borgo, and without a thought I joined the priests in the singing of hymns.

A moment later the air changed. As we crossed the main square en route to the auberge, our way was blocked by a crowd of peasants moving in the direction of the fortress. Rarely had I seen people more destitute. Wearing as they did the meanest goat's wool, and some even carrying yokes across their shoulders slung with capons and egg baskets, I thought they had come to market or were availing themselves of the paupers' meal the Grand Master served by his own hand each evening before vespers. But the tower bells told us it was noon.

The auberges stood barely around the corner and, sensing something amiss, Lord Balthazar had also stepped outside. Speaking a few words to these people, he told Vergã and me that lunch would wait. We followed, crossing the bridge into Castle St. Angelo. The crowd surged past the guards and up to the old Castellan's house atop the fortress, where the Grand Master made his residence and where the Council met. The Council members were just dispersing for lunch, and as they descended from the chamber the black robes also found themselves confronted by this angry delegation, with shouts rising on all sides. Guards came running from the barracks just below and, with a glance at each other, Vergã and I retrieved two pig-stickers from the nearby armory.

Now the Grand Master himself appeared, demanding the reason for all the commotion. The leader of these peasants stepped forward, explaining they were from Gozo. They had heard of the Council's decision to ship them off to Sicilia and at once got into their boats and sailed the few leagues from that island to Birgu. Many had brought their entire families. Aye, from the top of St. Angelo the Grand Master—all of us—could see the several barques that had arrived in Galley Creek, overladen with women and children.

At the sight of this invasion, the old man instantly flew into a rage. "The Religion cannot feed so many unwanted mouths in the Borgo!" he shouted. "It is impossible!" Without waiting for a response from anyone, he walked over to the parapets and ordered the cannoneers there to blow the vessels out of the water should the passengers make any move to disembark. "Do you hear me!"

The cannoneers, glancing at the Seigneurs of the Council for guidance, nodded in fright and aimed the artillery directly at the vessels in the creek below.

I could hardly believe what was unfolding before my eyes, but others did. Seeing that the horrible threat was about to be carried out, terrified Gozitans turned and sped headlong from the fortress and down to the quay to warn their loved ones of the danger. At the same instant cooler heads on the Council surrounded the Monsignore, prevailing on him not to carry out this action. At length he relented, but there and then repeated the Council's decree: The Gozitans would be removed to Sicily.

The leader of the peasants at once knelt before him on the stone. "Eminenza," he said with great humility, speaking in the simplest Italian, "we beg you to change this cruel decision. If the Turks fall on us, we will run to the castle, as we have before. We would rather die than leave our homes and island to be sent to a foreign place where no one knows us, and we do not know how to live. Please, we beg you ... "

E'en the face of Villegaignon, who had been so relentless in advocating their expulsion, softened at this pitiful speech and the Grand Master, visibly moved, replied that the Council would reconsider. In a better humor now, His Eminence invited the Gozitans to return for supper, but this relieved Balthazar little as we again crossed the bridge over the ditch.

"This will end badly," was all he said as we reached the Auberge de France. There he begged our forgiveness, for lunch had already begun and to attend after the bell was forbidden. He would invite us again soon. That evening fireworks lit the sky in honor of the saints.

It could not have been two days later when several hundred Calabrian shepherds arrived in Malta, sent by the Vice Roy of Sicilia as his contribution to the island's defense. Nay, they would be ferried on to Tripoli as irregulars. Balthazar was incensed.

"These goat herders have ne'er fired an arquebus in their lives," he said as we watched those hundreds sitting idly on the dockside, "and are terrified of the prospect of fighting in a foreign land." So it was. On the point of being shipped off, the greater number of them vanished completely, no doubt hopping on any boat that would take them back to

Calabria. To ease the fears of those who remained, the Grand Master put twenty-five Knights at their head, but these rascals had been in prison for God only knows what reason and the Monsignore was as glad to get rid of them as he was of the Devil himself. All this time not a single preparation was being made for the defense of Gozo.

As I had foretold, I saw little of Vergã. Now that he had a mistress to support, he lost no time in signing on with Romegas for an expedition to reconnoitre the Turks and pick up what booty they could. My own mistress, Flaminia—if one could call a whore I had known so briefly my mistress—had lost much of the wit she mastered on the evening of our first acquaintance. The skeletal fingers of dread were beckoning her to their embrace.

"Blessed Mother, *salvar mi*, what are we to do?" she cried, spinning around in her little room before the image of the Virgin she had surrounded with candles.

I regarded my dark-haired beauty with some pity, for she knew that if the Turks overran the island, the men might die gloriously but the women could look forward only to rape, slavery and perhaps, she had heard, the Sultan's harem.

"I do not know," I answered truthfully. "No one e'en knows whether an descent is to come and the Grand Master does not appear to be overly alarmed."

"*Por Supuesto* he would be unconcerned!" she exclaimed angrily. "Those Knights! *Imorru ghand ix-xjaten!* They carry themselves as if they rule this island!"

"They do. Malta is the fiefdom of the Order."

Flaminia shook her head, not understanding what the word meant.

I knew not the Maltese word for it, e'en if the language held such a word. "The islands and everyone on it belong to the Religion," I told her in Spanish.

"Yes," she sighed. "As we own pigs."

"As you own pigs."

Flaminia suddenly threw her arms around me and smothered me with kisses, promising me eternal devotion should I save her from the Turks. For the love of me she'd give her eyes to the fleas, she swore, but the *mancebas* of Granada had taught me to treat a whore's protestations of fidelity with some disdain. Natheless, tho' lacking any schooling whatsoever, Flaminia was not insensible to the dangers of her profession and the advantages of remaining faithful to a single master.

"O Madonna, is there a more wretched life?" she wailed despondently, becoming e'er more frantic. "We wait for the Turks to fall and each day we are in danger of being robbed or beaten ... We are always at the whim of the Knights and their dreaded diseases ... That *spendut* Pascale is on the loose; he has murdered a poor girl and no one knows what has become of him. O Madonna, make a miracle happen and catch him! If you don't, I will not consider you the Madonna anymore!"

This speech gave my ears little pleasure, for one pays a wench for her grace in conversation, not for her complaints. Flaminia's affront to the Madonna especially startled me and I slapped her soundly for it.

"Oh forgive me, burn me up if ever I uttered such words," she begged, tho' whom she begged I knew not.

But the prospect of an attack had possessed my *quiraca* and her tongue could not be bound. She carped incessantly about the Knights until, at last tiring of it, I said, "Why do you moan so? You will take up with the first Knight who comes along, for he will be able to offer you more gifts than I."

Hard pressed to deny it, Flaminia lowered her eyes. That modest gesture did her more credit and elicited from me more esteem than all her false kisses. She then admitted her dream was to build a house for herself and be buried in consecrated ground.

"I am not the one to build it for you," I answered, continuing in this vein of openness, "for I traded wealth for Fortune and have nothing to my name save a small share of the spoils from a Turkish ship and the *denari* they pay me here each day as a hired soldier."

After this declaration I was certain Flaminia would have no more to do with me, but to my surprise she seemed to accept the state of affairs. Desiring to return the evening to a more pleasant color, she lost little time in arousing me with the required caresses and then mounted me on the bed, allowing me to satisfy my lust. While we lay there sweated in the summer heat, she stroking my hair, our respite from argument was interrupted by a voice from the street calling the *quiraca* to her window. A Mahometan slave in her burnoose stood below. Flaminia bade me wait while she descended. I had already dressed and was about to depart when she returned with a few small bottles. She placed them on the table, making no comment.

"And what might those be?" I asked sharply, fastening on my sword.

At first Flaminia refused to answer, but when I threatened to hurl the lot out the window she confessed they were love philtres. This one was especially potent, composed as it was of the heart of a dove, the liver of a sparrow, the womb of a swallow, the kidney of a hare, all reduced to powder. To set the spell in motion only a drop of her blood was needed— and to make the person desired swallow it.

"You are a witch!" I exclaimed, as much confused as alarmed, tho' in Spain I had never put much stock in philtres.

"No," she laughed, caressing me. "All the women sell them, *mio cuore*. May God strike me dead if I am a witch."

Hardly reassured, I pushed her to arm's length, saying, "And what commerce do you have with infidel slaves?"

"Why," Flaminia answered with surprise written across her face, "all the best recipes come from the slaves, and the best talismans for warding off the Evil Eye."

Indeed, as I glanced about the room, I now perceived that several trinkets hanging from the window and above the Madonna herself were talismans. I took one of these in my hands but could make nothing out of the mysterious letters covering its faces.

"*Te faccio na fica*," Flaminia said with a wave of her hand.

"Ah!" I exclaimed, casting the amulet away from me in fear and disgust, "this is infidel magic!" At that moment I saw the fires of Hell opening to swallow me for merely having laid a hand on such an unclean thing.

"*Mio cuore*," said Flaminia with some incomprehension, "there are many who cast the Evil Eye on you. I knew a woman who had the Eye put on her and from that moment her milk flowed from her armpit instead of her nipples and she never had any more children. The Moors and the Jews know how to stop these things."

"There are Jews on Malta?" I asked severely, with disbelief.

Flaminia shrugged, confused. "A few slaves, no more."

"And what business might you have with them?"

"Only the trading—" My wench broke off, frightened again. "Blessed Mother! Francisco, surely you cannot think—"

"At this moment I do not know what to think!" I cried, putting my hands to my head and spitting out the words with such disdain that tears welled up in Flaminia's eyes.

"My Francisco," she pleaded, "I would never ... Nothing is worse than being caught with a Jew. To be taken by the Turks is better—"

"In truth?" I fairly shouted, entirely overcome by dark suspicions.

"O Madonna, yes!" Flaminia sat hard on the bed, not having the least understanding of my anger. "All the *meretrici* know it ... "

For the first crime, she confessed, the wench would be flogged and sent away from the island for ten years. The second time she would be hanged. As for the Jew, she could not say: Flaminia had never seen a Jew again after he had been caught.

Reassured finally that I had not been sharing my whore with an infidel, I ended the conversation and made to depart, picking up an egg from the shelf, but Flaminia begged me to leave it, saying it distracted the Evil Eye. I left her, deeply disquieted about whether I had fallen into the clutches of a Maltese wench or a witch.

It could only have been a day later, as we labored on the walls to prepare for the invasion that might not come, when I caught sight of Abdallah al-Waryagli moving among the slaves, handing out bread loaves from a basket.

"I see you walk now," I said, hailing him.

"Yes," he replied, "with a limp. Yours is gone."

"Nearly. The pain lingers some."

"Indeed."

Thus we fell into an easier conversation than on past occasions. To my remark that he was no longer hauling stones, he nodded. "Yes, because of my station your Lord Balthazar has secured for me some leniency. As you see, I now labor at the food wagons." The Moor chuckled softly. "There is also the prospect of renting a room next to the prison—if I can pay for it. The Knights do not object to slaves finding their own work."

"Perhaps you should sell potions to the *quiracas*," I remarked, sitting down against the rough stone wall and leaning my halberd against it. "All the infidel slaves seem to."

"That is not my skill," Abdallah al-Waryagli answered, lowering himself with pain to my side. "But perhaps I can sell my pen to slaves who need one." The *chavush* had begun dispatching letters with any round ship bound for Venice and the Levant in order to secure his ransom. "Unfortunately," he mused, "I cannot hope that one of my letters will reach the Sultan in less than a few years. So you see, for me the prospect of an invasion is welcome. If I do not die in the sack of Malta, I shall be free."

The emissary then asked for news of the Turkish movements.

"I know little more than you," I said. "I fear the Grand Master also knows little more than you and is concerned less."

"Were the Grand Master a truly wise man, he would have no need of information," Abdallah al-Waryagli answered, offering me a loaf of bread. He continued: "In the affairs of mortals, surely the deity who blinds them is the most powerful. Had not the King Ferdinand and his Queen Isabella profaned their oaths so promiscuously and forced on my grandparents the unholy choice of abandoning their native land for Cezayir-i Garb or abjuring the One Faith, Spain would not now tremble before the corsairs, as the unrighteous justly tremble before the sword of vengeance."

The emissary's slanders of the good king and queen and the favorable terms they granted the Moriscos naturally inflamed me, but recalling our previous arguments I saw no profit in attempting to convert the barbarian. Instead, taking the bread proffered, I remarked, "They say that when the poor give to the rich, the Devil laughs."

"I have heard his laughter. It is loud and unpleasant."

I then asked the *chavush* to tell me of Turgut, who he surely knew.

The emissary shrugged, tossing a pebble onto the walkway. "I have had the honor of speaking with him on occasion, but of the small things in his life I am ignorant. Turgut Reis was born in a little village of Natolia, across from Rhodes. This was some sixty-five years ago. When he was but twelve he left his parents, who tilled the soil, and enlisted in the service of the Great Sultan. Since that time Allah has smiled on his undertakings. There is no sailor who better knows the waters of the Levant. There is no wiser soldier, unless it has been Khair-ad-Din himself."

That there was no craftier soldier mine own eyes had forced me to agree.

"And with the passing of Khair-ad-Din, Outstanding of the Faith, the Sultan made Turgut the *Beylerbeyi* of Santa Maura. Since the Knights evicted him from Mekdia, Turgut has abided his time in the environs of Cezayir-i Garb. This you know. Perhaps you do not know that seven years ago he and his brother attacked Gozo with eighteen galleys, but Allah caused his brother to be killed and Turgut fled, vowing revenge. He believes he will die on Malta, as a teller of fortunes prophesied."

"He comes then to fulfill the prophecy."

"Perhaps. By the Truth of the Messiah, a great conflagration is advancing, for after the loss of Africa and the events at Djerbé, neither he nor the Knights will rest until one of them is driven from the face of the earth, as ash is scattered by the wind."

For a moment both of us remained silent. "You are also of Argier," I said.

Abdallah al-Waryagli both shook his head and nodded. "I was born in Cezayir-i Garb, yes, but my father, a merchant, found it more profitable— and safer—to live in Constantinople, where I was raised. There is a city! Not another in the world compares to it."

Had he seen Sevilla? I asked.

Abdallah laughed. "Such glorious mosques as rise in Constantinople are not to be found anywhere else. But that is not the important thing. I tell you, in the Sultan's empire, birth counts for nothing. Christians and Jews live in peace. You see none of these haughty Knights, who believe they can make fire without sticks, yet who have nothing on which to base their lofty esteem except the divine accident of their birth. In my country only ability counts and a man who possesses it may rise to the greatest heights. I, a merchant's son, became an *chavush* of the Sultan's court. And Turgut ... Had the rulers of Spain lived by the laws of the Prophet, the Moors and Jews would never have fled, and Turgut would be Carlos's ally rather than a dreaded enemy."

Abdallah al-Waryagli's speech hit me with a great force—it convinced me he was lying and I rose to my feet, thirsting for a *terzo* of wine.

"But do you know what I miss most of all?" he asked, as I picked up my pig-sticker.

"No, what is that?"

"My wife and children," he said.

I nodded. Fortunes of war.

"There is one other thing." Then Abdallah al-Waryagli said as near as I could make out "*yoghoort.*" Shaking my head, I bade him good-day.

I began to fear that among all the Knights of Malta, only Lord Balthazar showed any concern for the prospect of an invasion. Late in the day, after I had been relieved, he approached me with a Maltese servant who carried two broadswords across his shoulders.

"This way," said Balthazar and I followed him thro' the town gates, past all stables and houses pressed against the walls and up a dusty path to a nearby hill. From the crest I was able to survey much of the island and, but for a small monastery and chapel by us, I discerned no end to the barrenness in which prickly Indian figs seemed the most abundant life. Balthazar had been correct about Birgu. It was surrounded by hills, a stewpot for Turkish guns.

"Do you have news?" I asked him; there was none. If, tho', an invasion was in the offing, it was time to begin exercising his arm. His new servant handed me one of the two-handed swords. The weight of it astonished me. What was one to do with such a weapon?

Balthazar's first blow knocked it from my hand.

"Hold it tighter," he said.

I did as he instructed but my previous training was of no value. One could not dance with such a sword. One could not thrust with it, except by grasping the blade itself. This was not a weapon of skill. It was a weapon for giants of old to stand before one another like trees and hack off each other's limbs. For two turns of the glass Balthazar instructed me on how to parry his blows with an angled blade, but it was of little use.

"This is not a rapier," I said.

"No."

"Then why?"

"Had I wished, I could have sliced you in half, from head to toe. Further," he smiled, "a soldier's skill with the *montante* is highly valued and is paid more."

I laughed. That he could have sliced me in half there was not the slightest doubt, but as I sat down exhausted on the nearest rock I understood, now that I had come to know Balthazar somewhat, that his preference for an ancient if mighty weapon went far beyond its weight—or its pay.

"How did you become a Knight?" I asked him.

"As every other Knight here," he replied, as the servant handed him wine. "I spent a year on Malta at the Convent, I performed my caravans and I professed."

"Lord Balthazar," I ventured, also taking wine from the servant, "no one is as loquacious as you when a tale is to be told, and no one so circumspect with the subject turns to himself. *Why* did you become a Knight?"

"Ah, that my friend, is a different question," he replied and fell silent.

A lone rabbit darted among the Indian figs by us and a solitary falcon soared far overhead, with the wind in our ears adding to the silence and forlornness of this place. Yet I could do naught but chuckle. "Your sealed lips demonstrate my argument, Lord Balthazar. Please. What have you been hiding these past months?"

With no other Knight would I dare such presumption, but as I expected, Balthazar's good nature manifested no offense. "I told you," he said, "I am an abbé, if in name only. At your age, I shared your desire to see the world, to demonstrate my prowess. The siege of Rhodes yet loomed large in the world's imagination. What prodigies of heroism those Knights performed! For six months Grand Master l'Isle Adam and his handfuls held out against Soliman's ten thousands. At last they surrendered, but as Carlos himself said, 'Nothing in the world was ever so well lost.'"

Despite the Emperor's high words I remained not entirely satisfied. "What more?" I asked.

"One day," Balthazar went on, "when I was on campaign in Italy, I had a vision." He passed his hand through the air. "In the sky, above the enemy troops, framed by the sun's rays as if by a golden crown, I saw the Lion of Judea rear upon its hind legs and with all its strength loose from its jaws a deafening roar. At that moment I recalled the words of the psalm, 'my soul is among lions.'"

"You were called."

"Yes," he nodded, "I was called."

Tho' yet unconvinced he had fully revealed his soul, this admission explained much to me about Fra Balthazar. I did not press him. Instead, as the insects buzzed around us in the evening air, I asked, "Why have you befriended me?"

The Knight shrugged and for a rare instance a look of perplexity crossed his face. He took a long drink. "You are eager; I perceive in you quality. As a merchant's son, you may never become a Knight, but you are more than merely impressionable; you retain perception enough to profit from what is best in us. As Socrates asks, 'What is the good?' so shall you. That, I have come to see in these months past, is your valor. Now, to your weapon."

He placed too high a faith in my aspirations, but again we stood. This time while he flailed at me, Balthazar exulted with childlike glee. "One must keep one's eyes wide in this age. And what an age! The ancients have been rediscovered, yet scum like you abandon weapons of honor for guns that require no skill and cover you with smoke. Have you read my friend Rabelais? I can't get over that scene where Gargantua whips out his tool and bepisses the Parisians so soundly that he drowns two hundred sixty thousand four hundred and eighteen people, not counting women and children, then steals the bells of Notre Dame. And this Kopernik fellow, saying the earth moves! Can you credit it? Who can make sense of this age? Does it go forward or backward? Do you know, Francisco, I met Rabelais once …

Our swords clanked into the evening.

Fourteen

Over the next fleeting days little changed. After the pitiful scene atop Fort St. Angelo, the Council thought better of its decision to ship the Gozitans off to Sicily. But neither did the Grand Master provide ought for the defense of those people, as had he expected battalions of warriors would spring from the earth to protect them. In Birgu, the strange dance of death whirled with ever greater anticipation and festivity. Taverns overbrimmed with song and drink, ships sailed to and from the Port; I spent hours with Flaminia, even as I worried that she dabbled in the black arts. The Council members wondered aloud what happened to a grain ship that had sailed to Sicily.

The Knights did nothing to alter their customs and so the day after I served as Lord Balthazar's jousting partner, just before noon, I stepped up to the Auberge de France for the postponed meal. Of that selfsame limestone, it stood plainly with the other French hostels on a narrow street not a stone's throw from the Hospital, and only large, ornamented windows above and below lent it any elegance. At exactly the Angelus, a small bell atop the building sounded and Lord Balthazar appeared on the street. He collected my weapons and led his guest to the refectory.

We stepped into a dining hall for monks. Cloaked by silence absolute, Knights stood arrayed behind long rows of tables, waiting for what I did not know, and I was sensible enough not to ask. Shortly, the senior Knights of the Langue—the Grand Crosses—filed in without a word and took their places behind the head table. After a pause, the Pilier, the Langue's chief officer, followed, stepping onto a raised dais upon which sat an armchair covered in blue velvet and surrounded by plush cushions. At once I recognized this Pilier as none other than the Grand Hospitaller himself, who had cheerfully accommodated me not many days earlier. By custom, the Hospitaller and the Pilier of the Langue of France were always one and the same.

The contrast between Knights carousing at the taverns and the Knights standing noiselessly here in the refectory was almost too much to bear. But e'en in this conventual eatery the martial face of these monks intruded. The banner of the Langue of France framed the Pilier's solemn visage as by a halo; tapestries and trophies of glorious campaigns decorated the hall. Sumptuous silver services set every place in the room, velvet draped the benches of the senior Knights—and yet the tables at the rear for the Serving Brothers lacked even linen.

A motley crew if there ever was one, I perceived it by force now. Balthazar had put it well in the tavern—a man who owned naught but a sword and a horse could become a Knight if he passed the tests of nobility. A bastard born into the greatest family of Europe could not. Aye, some of these men might sit without much distinguishing themselves at the paupers' table standing at the back of the hall.

Amidst all this, my eye rested on only one, and my heart skipped. She was young, with perhaps fifteen years, and beautiful. His Majesty knows a young man's heart is lightly turned, but I thought I beheld an angel. She stood among the senior Knights with grace and bearing, in a splendid white dress and veil modestly parted. A thrilling, frightening shudder passed through me, which I could not comprehend. By the Tears of the Madonna, it terrified me. So transfixed was I by the heavenly vision that I entirely failed to see the signal made by the Pilier and Lord Balthazar was forced to nudge me onto the bench.

After the chaplain recited grace, the Pilier blessed a silver credence at his place to ward off poison and motioned for lunch to begin. A dozen servants and novices appeared to serve the first course. My eyes grew as a silver bowl of soup containing an entire pigeon was set before me. During this course silence continued its reign and shrouded the soup with gloomy effect, but the moment the Pilier had finished, he sounded a small bell and suddenly the hall burst into conversation. The servants set down dishes overfilled with figs and melons, and I sighed with relief.

Course followed upon course. A entire capon, a leg of mutton, a side of beef. For every portion the younger Knights received, the senior Knights received two. Between courses cheese, fruit, fennel, celery. Wine. Wine from Sicily, wine from France, wine from Spain, wine from Portugal, wine from Greece.

"It is all out of the Pilier's own purse," Balthazar confided to me, "for every Pilier would become a Grand Master, and what better way to win the votes of his Knights?"

The Pilier undoubtedly received many votes, or at least many toasts, for one was made with each sip of wine. Natheless, throughout the restrained cheer my eyes were riveted on the maiden sitting amongst the senior Knights.

Balthazar was not insensible to my distraction. "She is Isabella Guasconi, daughter of a Florentine nobleman from Rhodes."

Isabella ... The name of my lost fiancée pierced my heart as a rapier and I shuddered, convinced that God had loosed from his hand an unfathomable omen. "Is that her father?" I asked, indicating the Knight sitting at her side who was so solicitous of her.

"No, her father is long dead. That is her guardian, Jean de Valette, *dict* Parisot, of the Langue of Provence, next door. He also appears to be a guest today."

Astonishment is written clearly on your face, Your Majesty. Aye. During an ordinary meal in those weeks of uncertainty, I first beheld Jean Parisot de Valette, who was to become the greatest hero of Malta, nay, of Christendom. It is strange to think that as I sit before you, he walks the slopes of Sciberras, for in the months since the end of the terrible siege, so many stories have sprung up around him that I have begun to doubt he was—is—a breathing man. His Majesty will easily comprehend how those of us bereft of destiny expect an aura to surround those such as he, declaring to all who pass that this person has been touched by God, has been chosen by Providence for a greater purpose.

But no signs or portents surrounded de Valette when I first caught sight of him. At the head table sat a man already well past fifty. Despite the robes he wore, a leonine physique revealed itself. The locks of his hair yet touched his shoulders and his beard, grey-streaked, framed a narrow, austere face. He jested well enough with his fellow Knights and his ward, but no one gazing upon him would be drawn to a man of good cheer. His thin lips seemed only to frown and if any aura surrounded him it was of severity, and a profound melancholy.

The conversation was all of invasion, moreso, the fate of Malta, each voice colored by the same intense indifference that touched every part of our lives during those weeks. The French Knights, including de Valette and by him Villegaignon, demanded that the entire Convent be moved forthwith to Tripoli. Truly, at the last Chapter General the French declared Malta to be a miserable piece of stone and voted to transfer fifty Knights a year to Tripoli until Malta was abandoned. This after they first spurned Carlos's offer of the island because Tripoli—which the Emperor insisted be thrown into the bargain—could ne'er be defended. What a *volte face*! The Spaniard d'Homedes refused to have anything to do with the plan. He did appoint a Frenchman Gaspar de Vallier as Governor of Tripoli, "undoubtedly," said Balthazar, "to rub the noses of we the French in our own folly."

"If the French King François had not allied himself with the Infidel," a voice countered with disdain, "no Spaniard would ever have been elected Grand Master."

I clenched my teeth e'en as Balthazar laid his hand on mine. Who would have guessed at such squabbles within this monkish brotherhood that owed allegiance to no king? Aye, the dissension was more extreme. de Valette and Villegaignon raised their goblets: "To the return of our true and proper home, Rhodes."

"*Pardieu*," whispered Balthazar, shaking his head sadly, "will they never learn? Two decades ago the Knights undertook an expedition for that dream and it ended in complete disaster."

The lunch went on for a good three hours and with each bottle of wine the arguments became more spirited. Yet hardly any Knight sided with Balthazar to remain on Malta. And this maugre his simple reasoning: no more crucial location existed. Malta lay at the exact center of the Mediterranean and was nothing less than the portal between East and West.

Finally, the bell rang, signaling that everyone might depart. At that moment Parisot, disputing with one of his neighbors, grabbed his goblet and splashed wine onto the auberge floor.

"*Oimè*," sighed Balthazar as we left the refectory. "He'll receive a *settena* for that affront, no less—"

"A *settena*?" I repeated, even as I guessed.

"Confinement to his house for a week, on his knees in prayer. The man's temper is uncontrollable." Balthazar retrieved our weapons and together we walked out into the Borgo. "Eh, for Parisot a *settena* is a mere trifle. Some years ago he near beat a layman to death, God alone knows why.

The Council threw him into the *cavea* on Gozo for six entire months."
This time Balthazar didn't wait for my question. "*Cavea, guva.* Call it what
you will; pray you never see the inside of one. In France it is an *oubliette*,
the place where you are forgotten. And who would not be forgotten in a
dark hole in the ground? Six months—not bad!"

Against my will I swallowed.

"Of course that wasn't the end of it. Once Parisot was released, the
Council had him exiled to his beloved Tripoli for two years. Did the sun
there drum any sense into him? Nay, it drove him mad. He brought back
as a slave a *nigro* who was not liable for servitude and the Council had to
punish him again."

"Truly?"

"Aye, tho' I never learned the outcome. Of course, since he now knew
Tripoli so well, the Council appointed him Governor of the place until
two years ago." Balthazar glanced at me. "You believe that Vergã is a man
to cross at your own peril. Hah! Vergã is a peasant with a sword. Parisot
de Valette is nobleman with a brain."

I must have imagined that some warning to his companion colored
Balthazar's voice, for he continued without pause. "I also say his spirit is
indomitable. You have just gazed on a man who lived through the siege
of Rhodes. If you are lucky, someday he will tell you about it."

A week passed. The Council debated whether to seal off the entire Great
Port with a chain of the largest galleys available, equipped as they were
with heavy artillery. But like a group of squabbling hens, or made mad
by the July sun, they became numb with dissension and failed to carry
out the plan.

Once again Balthazar and I stood on the hills, he strengthening his
arms, I my distaste for ancient weapons, and I put it to him that disputes
among the brethren of the Order struck me as more than passing strange.

"How so?" the Knight laughed boisterously as he took a swing at me.
"Truly, my friend, you cannot be such a simpleton to believe that an order
composed of knights who swear allegiance to no king finds it congenial
to swear allegiance to one another? Indeed, you remind me of the absurd
and preposterous events that took place here *anno* 1533, merely three years
after the Knights put to shore. A French Knight, the nephew of
Commendatore Servier of Provence, fought a single combat against a

Florentine—mayhap on the very ground where we now stand. Nobody remembers the cause, undoubtedly some pox-ridden harlot. No one e'en remembers the Florentine's name, but unfortunately, he killed the Frenchman.

"*Allora*," Balthazar continued, motioning me to a better stance. "Now this Florentine was one of sixty gentlemen who resided in Birgu at the manse of Fra Bernardo Salviati, the General of the Order's galleys, and—as it happened—a Cardinal and nephew of the Pope. The family and friends of the Frenchman now invaded Salviati's home, where the Florentine was holed up, mauled and wounded. The Italians of Birgu counterattacked and inflicted even more damage to the French than had been visited upon them. Thereat the French appealed to Grand Master l'Isle Adam, and Salviati, in a gesture—I presume—of atonement, ordered ten of the fiercest Italians to be chained to his *capitana*. Hold that sword tighter! Did this appease the French? To no degree. I tell you they boarded the galley and murdered several of the Italians, wounding all the others. They would have killed every man aboard had not Salviati himself, hearing that his *capitana* had been profaned, personally led the *contre-coup* against the French.

"Lo! Thus the affair began. The French incontinently withdrew to the three auberges, armed themselves with arquebus and halberd, grabbed the banners from the refectories and raced through the streets in full armor shouting, 'France! To arms! To arms!' Salvati had fortified his home with cannon dragged from his galleys and had barricaded himself within. Thereat the French removed a cannon from the Post of Provence and began firing at Salviati's house."

"A civil war!" I exclaimed at hearing this extraordinary tale, while Balthazar continued to swing away. "A veritable civil war!"

"*Vertu de Dieu*, it was! True to their nature, the Spaniards jumped in on the side of the Italians, and eventually forced the French to retreat. By some miracle, only one French Knight was killed in all this mayhem. No, a solid parry, blade angled—*Voylà!* The Grand Master, fearing for his life, declined to intervene, but once passions cooled, he defrocked a dozen Knights, sewed the ringleaders alive into sacks and drowned them in the harbor."

"Hold!" I said, exhausted by the instruction and the tale, which was surely among Balthazar's best. Indeed, I could no longer hold my sword aright, so disarmed was I by the telling and so wondering was I of the character of these Knights.

But neither instruction nor storytelling proceeded, for at that moment a well-garbed Knight rode by us thro' the scruff, with a falcon on his glove and followed by two servants and his ward.

"*Holà*, Navarre!" he shouted.

"*Holà*, Parisot!" cried Balthazar in return.

de Valette himself. As I stood petrified, the party trotted over. de Valette removed the hood from the bird's eyes, untied the jesses, and loosed the magnificent creature into the air after its ascending prey. "You are not duelling, I trust," he said in a tone too dark for a jest and too light for a threat, "under pain of imprisonment."

"Nay," laughed Balthazar, natheless with some alarm measurable in his voice, "mere exercise."

Then de Valette asked in an altogether sunnier spirit, "So, what news? I have been cooped up at my home for the past days."

"None, I fear. Romegas has yet to return with booty or reconnaissance. Work on the fortifications continues, but these are childish measures. Sciberras remains vexing, for as you well know those heights look down upon St. Angelo and the town."

Neither Balthazar nor de Valette remarked further on the latter's punishment; truly it seemed not to make the slightest difference to either of them. Only now did Balthazar present me to the Knight, mentioning that together we had encountered Turgut.

"Ah, yes," de Valette answered, with no discernible humor now, "I have heard of you." He then, speaking more to the wind than to me, told of how he, also, had twice crossed paths with the infamous corsair. "Ten years ago in battle, God saw fit that the galley I commanded should be captured and myself, grievously wounded, thrown into irons. One day Dragut caught sight of me behind an oar and secured for me better conditions until after a year I was released in an exchange of prisoners. On a later occasion it was I who boarded a galley and spied my old enemy. '*Holà*, Señor Dragut!' I called out. '*Uscança dy guerra!*'"

For a moment de Valette fell silent, lost in memory.

"Did he reply, My Lord?" I ventured slowly, intimidated by every aspect of this imposing Knight.

de Valette only chuckled. "''Y mundança de Fortuna!' Dragut replied. And he laughed. He laughed! A change of fortune indeed! We are lucky to have such foes, do you not agree, Navarre?"

Balthazar nodded. "We are, Parisot."

"My Lord," I spoke up again, resolving to put aside my fear. "Fra Balthazar has told me you lived thro' the siege of Rhodes. I would be grateful to hear the story from your own lips."

Thereat de Valette regarded me strangely, severely. He nodded, tho' I could not discern whether this marked assent. Without another word he turned his horse and would have ridden off after his falcon had not his ward then raised her own voice.

"*Voulez-uous me présenter uotre amy, Frère Balthazar?*" she said.

Caught in this breach of etiquette, both of us bowed clumsily to the slender maid above us. "*Mademoyselle Guascony, permettez moy de uous présenter Francisco Perez de Baray de Grenade,*" Balthazar said.

I bowed again. "*A vuestro servicio, Señorita,*" I said and kissed the proffered hand.

"*¡Por favor, contad conmigo!*" she said, and galloped off after her guardian.

It would be my pleasure to seek her out at the earliest opportunity, I thought, watching the senorita's long dark hair stream behind her as she rode away. When the party had well vanished, I asked Balthazar how Turgut might have possibly recognized de Valette on a galley.

Balthazar shrugged, smiling. "None among us has shown such zeal for the Religion. So far as I know, having professed, he has not once returned to Provence his home. *Pardieu*, Parisot seems never to have left the Convent, save for his chastisements and war against the infidel. If any face among us is known to the enemy, it must be his. And now, my friend, let me give you good advice: that girl is spoken for and you would do well to stay clear."

Fifteen

I was hardly of an age to take sound advice. The next morning I sought out the Guasconi residence in the Borgo. To find the house, which fair overlooked Kalkara Creek on the landward side of the town, proved simple enough, but so taken aback was I by the size and quality of the manse facing me that I swallowed long before putting my fist to the elegant door. The servants received me in travel garb, as if they were about to depart for a journey. Natheless, one of them led me into the big room where Isabella and her mother, dressed also for the road, soon appeared and cordially greeted me. At once I was struck that today Isabella's hair was of a lighter shade, near saffron, and I perceived that following the current fashion she had dyed it to suit her pleasure. Startled, but collecting my senses, I bowed and apologized for arriving at what appeared to be an inopportune moment.

"Allow Messer to accompany us to Città Notabile," urged Isabella. "He will amuse us with tales of his adventures."

Her mother Lady Emilia assented. As if to remove themselves from the unpleasant talk filling the Borgo, they were off to spend several days at their second house at Città Notabile, the island's old capital, which lay two or three leagues inland. Balthazar and a few of the other Knights had spoken of it, tho' from the tenor of their remarks I perceived that members of the Religion avoided the Città like the plague. This of course made me all the more eager to see the place, and I was overjoyed at the opportunity to get out of suffocating Birgu. To my good fortune, this rude and uncivilized island had left the ladies bored enough that they would readily accept the company of a common soldier. We collected horses from the stables outside the town walls and six of us set off—the two women, two servants, a slave and myself.

There was no road. As our party trotted along the well-worn paths, the relentless austerity of the island never ceded to a welcome. One could easily have surmised that some pagan sun god had purged Malta of all but the heartiest life, for under the clear vault of heaven, beside those green prickly figs, we discerned nothing but a few olive groves planted near and far, an infrequent vineyard or windmill, some lonely cotton fields and a few head of cattle trying lucklessly to find a tree to shade while they grazed.

Lady Emilia intended not to speak of current events. Fanning away the mosquitoes she remarked, "Ah, this *mal aria* is dangerous to the health. It is the peasants, you know—soaking their hemp always in the marshes! Such a pity the Knights were forced to abandon the fertile valleys and snowcapped mountains of Rhodes! What could they have been thinking when they accepted this horrid place, where there is hardly a spring of fresh water? No wonder they are constantly drunk! And wood! Heavens, we must bring it all from Sicily. At least the Emperor threw that into the bargain!"

"Mother, you are harsh," Isabella replied, seeing the effect this bitter landscape produced on both Lady Emilia and me. "Smell the thyme—isn't it delicious? And we are blessed with a surfeit of melons and fruits of all kinds and figs—and the honey is wonderful."

"Well it should be," answered her mother with small enthusiasm. "Or the island is wrongly named."

Isabella laughed gaily. "Did you know, Francisco, that the Romans called this place *Melita*—'honey'?"

No, I hadn't, but surely I mused, the word "Malta" could mean only "limestone."

"I do not believe so, Milord!" teased Isabella, her grey eyes sparkling. "I have heard it speaks of 'safe haven' in an ancient tongue. Oh, I have forgotten."

Isabella pouted then. For an instant her thin lips seemed to droop to her narrow chin in true frustration, but this flicker of gravity on her bronzed, oval face made her only more beautiful to me. She was hardly a finger taller than Flaminia, and to a greater degree than the Maltesa her figure was still as much a girl's as a woman's, but there any commonness with the *quiraca* ended. Isabella's speech, so refined, spoke of a high education. Yesterday I had wondered at the ease wherewith she flitted between French and Spanish, and now I learned she spoke Italian and Latin with equal freedom.

"Who should be surprised by this?" she answered with a distinct rise in her voice. Only rude people spoke fewer than five or six tongues. "Monsieur Parisot is as well able to converse in Greek, Arabic and Turkish." The last he had learned while a galley slave.

"He is your guardian, I am told," I said, stung well enough.

"Yes, he held me in baptism. He is my Godfather. Let us race, Messer Francisco."

The spell of haughtiness had vanished as abruptly as it had come and Isabella spurred her horse forward. Letting loose a yell, I whipped my horse after her. We galloped along the crests and ridges, laughing heartily, for a moment abandoning all our cares to the wind that whistled about us. At length we slowed our mounts and waited for the others to catch up. All the while I could hardly take my gaze from this girl, and the exhilarating, terrifying constriction of the heart that convinced me God had put her in my path refused to loosen its grip. Surely, my purpose on Malta and she were intertwined.

My sense of Fortune immanent increased when a snake slithered across our path and one of the servant's horses balked. Isabella herself took it as a favorable omen, reminding me how the Apostle Paul, having been shipwrecked by a tempest on Malta, was bitten by viper and cast it into the flames, threat purging the entire island of venomous serpents. To this day anyone born on St. Paul's Feast is protected from snake bites and their spit is a rare curative for many illnesses.

We continued on our way. I recounted to Isabella and Lady Emilia how Vergã and I had well nigh captured Turgut on Djerbé, how I had saved Balthazar and Caravajal from the galleys and how we had defeated the Turks at Lampedusa. Isabella and her mother listened to my exploits with rapt attention, and thus pleasurably passing the time, we arrived well before the Angelus at Città Notabile.

The city was an impressive sight. Ringed by high walls, it sat on a steep rise at the exact center of the island, commanding the plain around it—indeed all Malta, every rock of which seemed visible from this place. As we trotted through the outer fortifications and the main gate, I thought that Notabile could be no larger than Birgu, yet it was in every way more

pleasing, for its rich cathedral overlooking the walls and the streets lined
with splendid and elegant mansions. Yes, Isabella remarked, the ancient
and noble barons of Malta all lived here. And she warned me to watch my
tongue, for they were not much fond of the Knights, regarding them as
little better than feudal lords and usurpers.

"How is it then, Lady Emilia," I inquired, "that you, so close to the
Knights, have a home in this city?"

She laughed. "After Rhodes, Grand Master l'Isle Adam granted my late
husband a tract of land nearby. I still see to it. Nor do I mind coming to
the Città. Madonna! With so little for a widow to do on this island and
such a lack of lively conversation, one is grateful for any neighbor who
has opened a book." She frowned. "Especially now, when the talk is so
unsuitable."

Beyond the gates, Bailiff Giorgo Adorno of Genoa himself greeted us.
Adorno had been dispatched by the Council to Notabile a few days earlier
with a handful of Knights to calm the fears of its inhabitants. But lacking
even a cannon he also had little to do at this outpost other than twiddle
his thumbs, and he was more than pleased to escort us to our destination—
not Lady Emilia's home as it turned out, but that of a neighbor who had
invited her to lunch. We dismounted, turned the horses over to some
stable hands and, walking hardly more than a few steps, arrived at the
ornate door of a large mansion, the home of one Matteo Falzon, Malta's
richest landowner.

Several other nobles and their wives had already gathered at the house
for the repast, but Falzon himself was nowhere to be found. Ushering us
into a garden courtyard that reminded me of my father's house in Granada,
his wife apologized profusely for his tardiness; she had no idea of why the
master should be late. But shortly Falzon did appear, a tall man of about
Balthazar's age, who wore a pointed beard, a short mantle, knee breeches
and hose. With like apologies, he explained that he was head of Città
Notabile's ancient council, the *Università*, and he needed to levy a fine on
a city resident for allowing his pigs to roam the streets. Falzon ordered
the servants to bring wine and soon, amid the fig trees and twittering
birds, the feasting began.

I could follow the conversation in Italian well enough to realize that
Isabella had spoken truthfully. As we drank, these Maltese landowners
complained that the local wine was not as fine as Sicilian, and they

complained that Sicilian wine was too costly. They lamented the destruction of Malta's forests, which had once covered the island with a dense green, only to vanish with the need for firewood and ships. They grumbled about lazy peasants and the cost of slaves, tho' Malta's slave market was the largest in the Mediterranean and prices ought to be low.

Most of all they complained about the Knights. The Knights treated them with contempt. The Knights ignored the old laws and overturned the decisions of the parish *università*.

"This Adorno has been appointed by the Council without consultation of the *Università*," protested one Giuseppe Callus, a doctor. Indeed, said he, so completely had the Knights trampled on the liberties of the Maltese that from time to time there had been talk of open rebellion. The others nodded. Such was the loathing for the Order among this company that they refused e'en to utter the name Città Notabile, because the Knights used it, and instead spoke of the town by the ancient "Mdina," walled city. And as more and more peasants left for the harbor to work, Mdina was becoming the Quiet City. The prostitutes of Malta were not alone in their detestation of these recent overlords.

Through this lunch Mademoiselle Guasconi's face reddened with shame and embarrassment, for of course she was the ward of a high-ranking Knight of the Langue of Provence. I wondered again why Lady Emilia associated with people so opposed to her own customs, but she parried each barb with grace and riposted with wit. Arrogant, true, but the Knights brought to the island wealth, work, commerce and—let us not forget—fine wine. Without the Religion, Malta would be forever doomed to be a tiny backwater, of no interest to anybody, and Matteo Falzon would hardly be able to import his expensive Italian furniture.

"The Knights have also brought to Malta the pox, let us not forget that," retorted Falzon to the lady's remark.

"I think you may only lay at their feet—or other part—quantity, not quality," Lady Emilia rejoined.

"And now they have likely brought us an invasion," Falzon added humorlessly.

At that pleasant moment, which returned the fear that worked itself into every crevice of the day, I excused myself to the pot and used the opportunity to visit the house. It was indeed a mansion belonging to a rich man, covered with imported rugs and tapestries, and whose doors were of the rarest wood. One room—a study I presumed—even boasted a shelf holding a few dozen books. I glanced at them. And I froze. Erasmus.

When I returned to the lunch, the guests were all standing and strolling about the courtyard, twittering like the birds about the statuary and the nymphaeum. I took Isabella aside. "Señorita," I whispered gravely, "the master is a heretic. He reads Erasmus. We must leave this place at once."

"Shh," she hissed. "There is no Inquisition on Malta, Señor. He is leader of the *Università*, a lettered man. I am certain it means nothing."

"Means nothing!" I blurted out, quickly lowering my voice again. "This is the Conv—!"

But the conversation proceeded no further, for at that moment the cathedral bell began to clang.

And it clanged ceaselessly. I froze in mid-utterance and every other guest did the same, gaping at one another with incredulity. Then as if the bell's resolve finally shattered our disbelief, we bolted as one out the front door and around the corner to the cathedral square. From every street and doorway people appeared, running toward the stiletto shrieks of the tocsin. As a crowd gathered before the old Norman church, a mounted rider pronounced the words each person feared most in the world.

"Captain Romegas has returned. He has sighted a Turkish fleet off Sicily. They have burned Augusta there and are sailing towards Malta."

Sicily lay only twenty or twenty-five leagues to the north. If they had followed Romegas, they could be here at any time. Tomorrow. Today.

"Is it Dragut?" a voice from the crowd shouted.

"It is," the rider answered. "Dragut and Sinan Pasha."

Immediately a great wail arose from the square. Each person standing there crossed himself and another voice cried out, "How many ships?"

The messenger paused, running his tongue over his lips, considering. "More than one hundred."

At this, sobbing broke out all around and more than a few of the women collapsed straightaway into their husbands' arms

"We must get back to the Borgo at once," Lady Emilia said.

"No, Signora," replied Matteo Falzon. "The corsairs will attack the harbor. It will be safer for you in Mdina."

"But apart from Signore Adorno and his few men," Lady Emilia said with alarm rising in her voice, "there are no troops in Città Notabile."

Adorno was himself standing nearby and added his voice. "The Signora is unfortunately correct," he said to Falzon. "You above all, Signore Falzon, know the Knights have put all their efforts into fortifying Birgu. Mdina sits high above the plain, it is true, but its walls are thin, rotting—they cannot stand against modern artillery."

Lady Emilia, having understood she could no longer ignore the events in which we were all immersed, was growing visibly frantic. With clasped hands and a sob catching in her throat she turned to her daughter, anyone. "What are we to do?"

"Signora," Falzon repeated, attempting to calm her, "Remain in Mdina. You have a large house and I assure you it will be far safer. Any attack must fall directly on Birgu."

For myself, no decision was to be made. "I must return to the garrison," I said. "Every man will be needed. *Addio.*"

Adorno grabbed my arm: I must see the Grand Master himself and implore him to send more troops to Mdina—at once. With that charge and only the swiftest glance at Isabella, I retrieved a horse from the stables and galloped full tilt to the Borgo.

The news had arrived at Birgu only scant hours earlier. Balthazar learned it when Romegas himself had marched into the Auberge de France. Lescaut had captured a stray Turkish galiot and learned from the slaves he freed that Soliman had sent Dragut and Sinan to Sicily with orders to take Malta en route to Tripoli. Arriving at Sicily, Romegas discovered that the infidels, failing to take Catania, had laid to waste Augusta and were moving south. Immediately all gathered at the auberge hurtled across the ditch to Fort St. Angelo, where the Council was in session, but the news off the galley traveled yet more swiftly and half the town, Balthazar observed, attempted to stampede with them over the bridge.

Romegas and the other Knights with him broke into the Castellan's quarters to find the Grand Crosses and other Seigneurs of the Council gathered in the big hall above. The news that even as they spoke a large fleet was sailing towards Malta threw the entire assembly into alarm.

Several objected. Romegas could have no definite knowledge that the Turks planned to sail south; if they were already under oar, they would have arrived on the Knight's heels and at this very moment be sailing into the Great Port. All was yet rumor.

"Brothers, they are coming," replied Lescaut. "Doubt it at your peril. Every Sicilian will tell you."

As if the Almighty had deemed it necessary to put an end to the Knights' inconstancy, at that instant another brother, Antoine Gotto, burst into the chamber. He'd himself been on Sicily and escaped on a barque with a renegade slave from the Turkish army. He led the poor Christian by the arm before the Council and that one, weeping for joy at his salvation, confirmed everything.

"How many men do we have?" asked the Grand Master, seeing there could no longer be any debate.

Turcopilier Sir Nicholas Upton—Commander of the light cavalry— replied that he could at this moment muster fifty Knights. The old Spaniard Bernardo de Guimeran declared that some one hundred Knights stood awaiting his orders. Altogether fewer than three hundred brethren seemed to be on the island. Another five or six hundred arquebusiers, hired soldiers and Maltese awaited in the barracks or in the Borgo. Someone present asked whether a swift galley could be sent to Antonio Doria, who was then ferrying succours to Africa and Tripoli. But the reply came that just this day news had arrived: Doria's fleet had been wrecked in a storm on the shoals at Lampedusa. Over one thousand men perished, including Doria himself. No reinforcements could be expected.

"And thus we are to face a fleet of one hundred galleys," said finally His Eminence, "ten thousand men, at least."

"We are in want of everything," muttered one of the French Knights. "If we had taken the threat of an invasion to heart, we might now be prepared."

"We have our courage and our duty to the Order," answered Lord Balthazar himself, "and that is enough."

To a man the Knights cheered him.

But now the noise from without the Castellan's quarters was such that the Monsignore was once again forced to confront a crowd atop the castle. Followed by the Seigneurs, he stepped outside onto the balcony and told the townspeople that he was convinced the Turks planned to invade Provence and were only taking the southern route by Malta because it was the quicker road to their destination.

Balthazar listened to this speech with disbelief, unable to decide whether His Eminence was mad or merely lying in order to calm the simple people before him. Indeed, soon the Council sent criers throughout the Borgo to let it be known that the enemy would fall on Provence.

"*Mort de Dieu*—if they believe their own words," Balthazar said to himself as he returned to the auberge and to his armor, "then theirs is a fatal blindness."

Sixteen

An hour later, watchmen atop St. Angelo sighted the enemy fleet. As the ships appeared on the horizon, specks floating toward Malta in a crescent that stretched across the sea, those eagle-eyed sentinels counted: one hundred, one hundred one, one hundred two ... one hundred five galleys. And more: galiots, transport vessels, *fuste* ... one hundred forty ships.

The watchmen did not wait to complete their count. The instant they perceived the formidable danger approaching all on the island they sounded the alarm. The clanging began and continued even as I galloped through Birgu's gates and sped to the Auberge de France to hand to Balthazar Adorno's plea for more troops. I could not find him anywhere. I ran back to the langue's stables outside the walls where the Knight, now in full armor with a broadsword girded to his waist and his two-hander strapped to the saddle, was preparing to mount. He put his arm on my shoulder, nodding calmly, without apprehension, as if everything was somehow unfolding as it must.

"I shall ride with the Turcopilier," he said. "Fetch your arquebus and join de Guimeran, who is assembling his men on the docks as we speak. Remember, Francisco, on Lampedusa we fought for our lives and for booty. Today we fight for honor, the survival of the Order and for God." He then embraced me and I ran for my helmet, my powder and my gun.

E'en as I reached the docks, moments later, hundreds of men were gathering, the greater part arquebusiers like myself, perhaps a hundred Knights in armor among them. Time did not permit us to form ranks. Commander de Guimeran and his ensigns were waving everyone into all available skiffs, *fuste* and feluccas with orders to row across the harbor to Mt. Sciberras. Three or four hundred men piled into the boats with no thought of tomorrow, nearly sinking them under the weight. Yet somehow, by the Grace of God, within two turns of the glass we had ferried everyone across.

The men climbed up the steep paths to the heights of Sciberras and then down to the tip of the peninsula where the old watchtower stood near the equally ancient chapel consecrated to St. Elmo. de Guimeran ordered every man to silence and we hid ourselves there behind the tower and the chapel and in the brush. The Turkish fleet was now almost upon the island. One hundred ships under fair winds and colorful sails had closed in on the Port so that it seemed you could reach out your hand and touch the fatal picture. Nearest of all was the *capitana* of Sinan Pasha, the Turkish Admiral. A huge galley of twenty-eight banks, it headed almost directly towards us, as if Sinan knew we lay in wait and was determined to blow us to heaven. But he stopped not far offshore and waited as a small galiot entered the Great Port to test the waters, where it found no danger and returned to the fleet. Through all this old de Guimeran ordered us to keep our matches lit, but no more. Only when Sinan himself steered his Reale into the Port, so close to our right that you could spit on it, did the Commander order us to fire. Three hundred arquebuses opened a broadside. Our fusillade, ferocious, unending, sent half the galley sails into tatters. Turkish archers got off a few arrows but our bombardment had taken them completely by surprise, and before they could react, we had sent a dozen of them into the water and killed a great number of the *ciurma*. Astonished by this unexpected resistance and not knowing our true numbers, Sinan ordered his galley to retire to Marsamxett, the large harbor north of Sciberras. Our men waved their morions and let up a great cheer.

But Sinan was only one of two commanders. While we engaged Sinan, Turgut's ships steered toward the southern flank of the harbor, on which stood St. Angelo and Birgu. Seeing that the Turks had begun to land, de Guimeran ordered us back into the boats and once again across the Port to Galley Creek. We accomplished our embarkation as Sinan's gunners amused themselves by bombarding us from Marsamxett, tho' he did not follow us, so seriously had we damaged his ship. We made our redeployment in good order, not having lost a single man, but e'en while we scampered into the boats at the base of Mt. Sciberras, the cannonading from Fort St. Angelo began, and it was only while crossing the harbor under that thunder did I finally spy Vergã, sitting behind the oar of a small skiff not far from the *fusta* in which I found myself. We embraced on the opposite shore, genuinely overjoyed to see each other alive.

"As I abjure that dog-*puta* Mahomet and spit on his Sepulchre," he shouted, "we showed them what Spaniards can do."

"That we did," I answered, catching my breath, "but I fear we shall have to show them more. Turgut is surely putting his men ashore, and he will not be so easy to capture this time as last."

As we reformed our escuadrón there on the docks of Birgu, with the roar of St. Angelo's cannons unceasing, vespers had already come and gone, but the midsummer sun stood yet high in the sky, the air was yet warm, and sweat dripped from every one of us. The Knights in their armor must be roasting alive, I thought, surveying the scene around me. Our company had landed near the landward extremity of Birgu town and the quay was deserted except for we the soldiers. Hardly had we set foot on the docks, every one of us instinctively flinching under each cannon shot, when we suddenly descried, as if in answer to the bombardment, a stream of people pouring over the hilltops—not men of arms, but the Maltese, peasants, farmers leading their animals and carrying their few possessions toward the city gates.

E'en at a distance the terror that gripped these people was sensible. Under the din of artillery they ran, they stumbled, they screamed, they stampeded to get into the Borgo, for from the landward heights they could well discern Turgut's corsairs putting ashore south of Gallows' Point. I think it good that the disembarkation of his troops was hidden from our view, for tho' I felt none of the frenzy which had gripped me at Lampedusa, nor fear, this was the bravery of the ignorant of which Balthazar had spoken. There on the docks I did not comprehend that by morning twelve thousand Turks and corsairs would stand on Malta.

The cannoneers atop St. Angelo had better discerned the danger and opened fire with the heavy artillery as the enemy skirmishers waded ashore. This put such a fright into the attackers that they abandoned their plans for a direct assault on the castle and instead began a march to the south and west, inland, skirting the fortifications. But now the Turcopilier and his men, who had gathered their horse and foot on the plains there, formed their ranks.

"We have not the men to defeat such a multitude," said Turcopilier Upton, unsheathing his sword, "but we can sell our lives at a high price and make the Infidel wish he had never set foot on this island."

The chaplain blessed them and those fifty horsemen charged.

The cavalry caught the enemy from the rear at the far end of the Great Port as it wheeled north toward the village of Birkirkara. The Turkish arquebusiers turned, surrounding the Knights with fire. A ball glanced off Balthazar's helmet, but he galloped forward undeterred, unsheathing his sword. He discerned no janissaries among this rag-tag lot. He had never directly confronted that elite corps but knew that by custom the Turks held the janissaries in reserve, and he doubted they had yet put ashore. Before him were merely undisciplined corsairs, who knew not how to obey the commands of Turkish generals. He did envy the foemen their loose, cool robes. But those robes would also do naught to protect them against a ball or a sword. Balthazar swung and took a head from an infantryman. The mêlée went on for a watch before the enemy found its wits and regrouped. Upton ordered a retreat and the cavalry fell back to the infantry.

It was a feint. The enemy charged and found itself confronted by Sir Nicholas' arquebusiers, who had hidden themselves behind a line of large rocks and let loose a fusillade that felled dozens of infidels on the spot. Natheless, so many were the enemy that their numbers showed no decrease. The Knights could hack away for hours and ultimately they would succumb to these legions. Perhaps, indeed, the hour had come to sell their lives. Balthazar jumped off his horse and took his *montante* in both hands. With his first blow he cut a man's shield in half and with his next he cut the man in half, from his scapula to his hip. He grasped the sword by the bridge and impaled another foeman through the chest, freeing the weapon with a kick of his boot. As blood spurted all over him, Balthazar thought he heard the heart pop. He spun, grasping the blade, and clobbered a further attacker over the head with the back end of the sword. Once more clasping the hilt by his hands, he severed another head, which sailed off on a fountain of blood, landing among the arquebusiers. Yet, as the circle of bodies piled up around him, he remained alive and at length the corsairs retreated.

Sir Nicholas, a large man, now urged his troops forward again, inspiring them to attack the enemy. This they did, with horse and foot falling on

the rear of the infidel column, making considered retreats, taking cover
among the rocks, attacking once more. In that way skirmishes went on
'til darkness, Turgut's men continuing their march inland, the Knights
picking off stragglers and taking prisoners from among them. The
Knights had lost only four or five of their number, the infantry twenty or
thirty. The soldiers gathered up the Turkish heads and carried them back
to St. Angelo, where they were mounted on pikes for the enemy to see.

Covered with blood and tissue, Balthazar returned to the town brushing
away flies and wondering wherefore he remained alive. He had fully
expected to die that day, by so many men did the infidel outnumber the
Turcopilier's company. Why had not the enemy put up a stiffer fight? He
could find no answer except that these were hired corsairs, not janissaries,
and he had nowhere seen Turgut.

Now in the Borgo, Balthazar was finding it, like the rest of us, nearly
impossible to make his way through the streets. In the space of a single
day the population of the town had doubled or trebled. The Sacra
Infermeria overflowed, not with casualties, for they had been light, but
with common people searching for food. We slept seven men in my small
room, weapons and all. In the dwelling Flaminia called home, soon she
was joined by eight or nine sisters. Everywhere it was the same: eight to
a room, nine, ten ...

At length Balthazar pushed through to the auberge, where his servant
washed him clean with seawater. After being dressed in a leather under-
jerkin and battle tunic, the Chevalier trudged with a sense of unease to
the ramparts of St. Angelo and there stood among the sentinels who
watched the Turks continue their disembarkation. From the other side of
cavalier he saw a glow far to the north, behind Sciberras. He thought the
village of Birkirkara must be burning. Then he went to find something
to eat.

I do not know where Balthazar ate, but I saw with my own eyes what
a brisk business the taverns did that night, skinning everyone in sight.
This caused no end of brawls and even a few deaths over legs of mutton.
The dance of death that had gripped the town was no longer a dance. Fear
and the madness of demons possessed the Borgo. A leg of mutton, a flagon
of wine, a place on a floor to sleep. Tempers flared over trifles and deaths
followed. Vergã claimed he killed a peasant who tried to rob him of his
meal. Flaminia became frantic that she would be unable to sell her potions.

When one of the other women in her cramped room by chance knocked over the image of the Blessed Mother, the *quiraca* broke down in tears, weeping uncontrollably, and no one consoled her.

The situation three leagues inland was worse. Matteo Falzon had prevailed upon Lady Emilia and her daughter to remain in the Città Notabile. Within only hours of the news that enemy was sailing toward Malta, it seemed to Isabella that farmers and peasants had begun to stream into the town from all over the countryside, this one carrying a stool, that one a spinning wheel across his back, another a scythe, a woman lugging a milk churn, still others driving cows or pigs. In her short life she had never seen a picture that compared to it.

Isabella watched with horror and pity this human river fill Mdina. There was no end. She and her mother opened their home to the priests and nobles from nearby Rabat, until no fewer than four families occupied the house, twenty people at least, who would sleep on the floors and carpets, upstairs and down, but this was nothing compared to the plight of the common people who had no shelter at all and must night among their animals on the squares and streets.

The sun was burning this July. As Isabella pushed her way through the throngs of people to find food for those gathered at her house, the air had already become infused with a sensible thickness. She managed to find a side of horse at the market, which she bought for four *scudi*, highway robbery, and had her servants take it back to the house. Passing the city gate she spied the Bailiff Adorno atop it, mounted the stairs and asked him in Italian how things stood.

Surveying the scene, he shook his head. "In the past hours six, nay seven thousand people have passed through this gate, and still they come. There are no public cisterns in Città Notabile. We do not have water for one thousand, yet alone for ten, as there soon will be here. With so many people in such a small town we can expect only one thing—the peste."

"Have you had any news from the Borgo in the last hours, Signore?" Isabella asked.

"*Si*," Adorno nodded. "Some farmers from that direction and a rider from the town." He paused when he noticed the slender girl's expectant eyes. "The enemy fleet was upon Malta by the time we received the alarm this afternoon. As we speak they are landing a large force, and fighting has been taking place all day at the harbor."

"How many are they?" Isabella asked.

He shrugged, putting his foot on a step. "No one knows, Signorina. Ten thousand, perhaps more."

"And how many men do you have in Mdina, Signore?

"Not twenty soldiers. Perhaps among the farmers we might smoke out a few hundred who can bear arms. I have heard nothing from the Grand Master. I do not know whether your young friend reached him with my request for more troops."

Isabella glanced in the direction of Birgu. "I hardly know to call him a friend, Signore, but I think he will have tried."

The evening star was already shining brightly, Isabella realized, and she scurried home.

Seventeen

His Majesty perhaps remembers the unexpected and terrible sequence of events that unfolded over the next week, events that have been recounted by Christians and Mahometans alike since that year, *anno* 1551, and that will be recounted so long as people tell of the past. Events that neither your troops nor ours understood at the time. Events that were perhaps understood only by God.

By sunrise next all the enemy troops had put ashore, Turgut's on the southern flank of the harbor—Rinella it is called—Sinan's on Mt. Sciberras. Our sentinels reckoned twelve thousand in all, several thousand janissaries among them. That the Sultan had sent such a number of his elite, who alone the Knights considered worthy adversaries, proved this invasion was no casual undertaking, but an enterprise meant to rid the Mediterranean of the Knights once and for all. Yet, if I may be so bold, Your Majesty, the crucial blunder lay in dispatching one armada under two commanders.

We the soldiers stood atop St. Angelo, gazing across the harbor at the enemy gathered on Sciberras and on the shore below Gallows' Point, awaiting an attack, but not perceiving that one was underway. We waited and we waited and were answered by nothing but the call of gulls.

Finally, Turcopilier Upton shouted in disgust, "If the infidel-pricks cannot summon the courage to attack us, we must summon the courage to attack them!" With that, the corpulent commander mustered his Knights and rode forth from the castle. Again we waited and again our expectations were disappointed. Only weeks, e'en years later did we begin to piece together what was then transpiring on the opposite shore.

His Majesty had put Sinan Pasha in command of the armada, with strict instructions to undertake no action without the consent of Turgut, who had agreed to act as counsellor or lieutenant. They say Sinan was originally an Italian of the Visconti family who'd turned Turk. The truth of it I never learned, but his name caused Christians to tremble hardly less than that of Turgut himself. Corsairs regarded him as a leader whose fearlessness in action was matched only by the length of his deliberations.

Many tell that when he stood on the heights of Sciberras with Turgut and looked upon St. Angelo across the harbor, Sinan spat out in alarm, "Is that the castle you told His Majesty could be so easily taken? Do you not see that we would need wings to scale those walls?"

"No eagle ever built a nest so easy to snatch!" was Turgut's derisive reply.

"Hah!" The venom in Sinan's contempt startled all those about him. "Half the artillery in the world would barely suffice to take that fortress, and we have brought few enough heavy pieces with us."

Thereat, an old corsair, brother of one of Khair-ad Din's lieutenants, entered the dispute. "I myself was a slave on this island, and with stones I carried on my own shoulders I built that rock on which flies the haughty standard of the infidels. I tell you, before you can demolish that work, winter will come." The old man paused as if there were more. There was: "To capture St. Angelo you will not only have to take it down stone by stone but kill every man inside."

Such a speech far from pleased Turgut. "It is but July!" he shouted.

"The bad weather will be upon us in eight weeks," Sinan answered, "and if we delay here we will be unable to capture Tripoli, that which we came for."

At this Turgut flew into a rage, so incensed was he at the irresolve of the others. He named them all cowards and rogues, that he was the sworn enemy of the Knights of St. John and he would see them expunged from the face of the earth or die in the attempt.

Natheless, Sinan and his lieutenants saw that four months or six would be necessary to take the fortress and they wouldn't countenance the attempt this late in the season. Turgut, tho', would not easily surrender the prize he so eagerly sought and the dispute went on.

"Everyone aims at the same meaning, but many are the versions of the story," His Majesty has written, and a few who were there swear it was Turgut who perceived the season to be far gone and he who advised they give up St. Angelo. Whatever the exact truth, after long debate the corsairs came to an agreement: to march on Mdina.

By this time, the Turcopilier and his men had circled around the Great Port to the northern slopes of Sciberras, and on the banks of Marsamxett harbor engaged the enemy in the same sort of skirmishing they had undertaken the previous day. During the same hour, Romegas and the Knight Scipion Strozzi took their galleys into the Port. Seeing they were barred by the Turks from exiting, Romegas immediately barked to his crew, "All provisions astern!" Strozzi followed suit and the galley prows were raised nearly clear of the water. Having elevated the forward armaments, the two Commanders immediately began bombarding the enemy atop Mt. Sciberras. Often their balls overshot the mountain to land in Marsamxett harbor. One, guided by the hand of God, fell straight through the prow of a Turkish galiot, sinking it.

Heartened by the inaction and disarray among the Turks, Upton's troops attacked the enemy with abandon. But now, leading his cavalry forward under the midday sun, Sir Nicholas, his sword raised high, of a sudden keeled over and toppled from his horse. Balthazar, not far from the Turcopilier, galloped over and jumped from his mount, as did several others. Removing his helmet, they found no blood or holes in Upton's armor; he hadn't been felled by the enemy. The heavy Knight was yet alive, but incapable of speech. He appeared in severe pain, with great rivulets of sweat streaming down his brow.

"I fear it is the heat," said Balthazar. "Let us move him to safety."

Balthazar and his fellows did so, but within hours the Turcopilier had sent his soul to God.

Earlier, when Upton and his men set forth, I had caught sight of the Grand Master himself walking down the steps of the Castellan's house and, as I was certain Balthazar had found no time to pass on Adorno's request for more troops, I would do it myself. I knelt before the Monsignore, who close up I now judged to be about eighty, and kissed the ring he extended to me.

"Eminenza," I said, somewhat foolishly, "I was at Città Notabile yesterday when the enemy arrived. Bailiff Adorno urgently requests more troops. And artillery."

By now, of course, d'Homedes had received the request several times over. Natheless, he replied that as we spoke a squadron of Knights and arquebusiers was preparing to march overland to the old capital and, if I wished, I could join that number. The Grand Master had, it transpired, also sent urgent dispatches to Sicily for succour and reinforcements. Most of the sailors hadn't the heart to run the Turkish blockade and they fled, yet once the Turks began to remove their troops from Sciberras, Romegas and a few other stout-hearted Knights volunteered to make the attempt.

Vergã was among the first to join this most desperate mission, by which he intended to prove his worth. They sailed north, navigating in full view of the Turks practically the entire day, but somehow managed to elude them. Once at Sicily, the Knight d'Appelvoisin found a guide and made his way to the village of Sta. Caterina, where the Vice Roy was in hiding. He shouted to the sentinels that he was a Knight of St. John, but hearing only "St. John" they thought this stranger was giving the wrong password for the day and shot him. God, however, willed that d'Appelvoisin survive and the Vice Roy told him that Andrea Doria was presently in Spain; only when he returned could he send a fleet in relief. Tho' only Romegas's men knew it, Malta was on its own.

Within a glass of my conversation with His Eminence, perhaps twenty Knights and eighty arquebusiers set out to Mdina, dragging a cannon. Among the Knights in our escuadrón was Ramon Caravajal, whom I had not set eyes on since our arrival from Gelves. He asked how I was growing into the life of arms.

"It is to my taste," I replied. "And assuredly the outcome of this contest lays in the lit fuses of the Spanish arquebusiers. If only we had another hundred—nay, another fifty—the fate of the Turks would be sealed!"

Fra Ramon slapped me on the back, laughing at this. "A right answer from a fellow Spaniard! I say, moreover, that we be given chariots and armor of gold so that we may charge the enemy like the legionnaires of ancient Rome. That would show 'em!"

To which I replied, "Methinks we ought not to keep guard in towns and defend stone walls. Nay, we should be invested as the corps of an Invincible Order and reserved for only the most dangerous missions!"

"A true Knight of St. John!" Caravajal laughed once again, but soon the boasting fell aside. He told me that Fra Alferez had been killed in yesterday's action and, in truth, with every step we ourselves anticipated an engagement. Having a better idea this day of the numbers of the enemy, I felt far from confident of the ability of even a century of Spaniards to defeat them. Yet were I to die, I resolved, I would prefer it to be with honor and glory, sword in hand, than cowering behind a stone parapet. Whether that was true valor, as Balthazar would call it, I could form no conception.

No engagement came. As we trudged toward the old capital, we didn't know that the enemy had decided to move its siege guns by boat to St. Paul's Bay on the northern side of the island, where the Apostle himself had been shipwrecked. The corsairs who'd landed the previous afternoon continued their march inland, sacking and burning small villages, but their path too was northward. We clashed with nothing en route to Mdina except a broken wheel on the cannon, which we repaired.

When Isabella awoke that morning and set out to the market to find food, she found a city transfigured. Every street, every corner, the cathedral, the square, the markets were filled with people, packed as close as pigs in a pen. The air was by now so thick with the smell of excrement that Isabella could hardly breathe, and she walked with her silk handkerchief to her mouth in order not to vomit. She could find no food for sale except a goat, for which the farmer wanted more money than he would ask for a slave, a price so exorbitant that Isabella thought she must speak with her mother before buying it. When the girl again encountered the weary Bailiff Adorno yet at his post, he told her that five or six thousand people had streamed into the town overnight and, as far as he could reckon, twelve thousand souls now occupied Mdina, whose usual number was perhaps a tenth of that.

"O Mother of God!" Isabella exclaimed, near tears. "How can we support such a multitude?"

"We cannot," Adorno answered simply. "We have neither the food nor the water. I said to you last evening we can expect only the peste, and of that there is now not a doubt under Heaven."

"Do you have at least men of arms?" she asked.

"We have men," he replied, with a glance at the crowds huddling below him. "Between the arquebuses in the armory and the farmers who bear their own weapons, we may be able to put a thousand guns on the walls." Even as he spoke, his soldiers were handing out arquebuses to those who knew how to use them, who then took their places on the curtain. The enemy was nowhere in sight.

Isabella returned home sobbing. When Lady Emilia asked the reason for her distress, Isabella dried her tears and told her forthwith that they must begin giving food to people on the street.

"How can you speak so?" asked her mother. "We have a score of people in this house and not enough in our cellar to feed them."

"We are yet rich compared to those who have slept in the open air," her daughter answered, "and we can follow no better example than that of the Knights, who feed the poor with their own hands each day."

Her mother still protested, saying that it was inconceivable that they should share their food with the rude peasants on the walls.

"Rude they are," Isabella acknowledged harshly, with reddened eyes, "but if the peasants on the walls die, we will surely die with them." Thereat she had her servants gather up the stores of bread and wine and made her way back to the city gates.

When our escuadrón arrived at Città Notabile, we found it much as Isabella had hours earlier, full of such a powerful smell that it fairly knocked one over, like a cannon ball. No galley was ever afflicted by such an evil. The Bailiff Adorno and his men embraced us as we dragged the field piece through the Greeks Gate, and all the men on the wall cheered. He now had a garrison of one hundred soldiers, a thousand farmers and a cannon. Not long after we arrived, Isabella, who'd been distributing food and wine to the men, herself approached the Bailiff. At first not noticing me, she told him that he must begin rationing food at once or that everyone in the city would surely starve.

When at last she caught sight of me, she started, as if I were a spirit back from the dead. "Señor Francisco," she said, extending her hand, "you persuaded His Eminence."

I let her believe that. There was little time to speak. With our increased numbers, Adorno immediately sent Knights out on foraging expeditions and to scout the enemy. Over the next hours some food entered the city, not enough to see Mdina through a siege. Adorno ordered that each person receive only two cups of water per day. In that way he reckoned the water in the city might last six days. More alarming were the reports that the Turks had put into St. Paul's Bay, not two leagues to the north, and that the corsairs marching across the island had sacked Mosta village, even closer. Reports, nay. From the ramparts we could survey the entire island.

E'en Birgu was just visible in the distance. Were those not ships in St. Paul's Bay? The Bailiff sent out the Spaniards on several sorties to verify what our eyes told us. Yes, Mosta had been gutted and the enemy was closing. Yet we encountered only a few renegados and corsairs, who seemed to be taking orders from no one, and that day none of the enemy appeared at Città Notabile.

As evening fell, I sought out the Guasconi residence in Mdina, but not knowing its location I pushed my way through the clogged streets to the Falzon mansion and knocked at the door. At first no one answered, so fearful were those inside to open. Only after I persisted, banging with the hilt of my sword, did a servant finally crack the peephole and, recognizing me from the previous day, allow me in. The place was full of people. I asked for directions to the Guasconi house, but Matteo Falzon now appeared to see what all the racket was about and invited me to tarry a moment.

Great was my unease at standing before this man who I took for a heretic, and it grew greater still when he invited me into the very room where on the shelf stood the forbidden work of Erasmus. I watched every motion of this man as if he were a necromancer readying to bewitch me. Standing taller than most of the Maltese, he was also fairer of skin; as I had learned yesterday, most of the barons on this island traced their lineage to Sicilia or Aragon. Yet, ushering out the two others who sat there, he now spoke neither of Erasmus nor of sorcery. He merely offered me a glass of *aqua vita,* which I refused, and then he asked for news from the harbor and whether Mdina could expect succours.

I told him I did not believe reinforcements were on the way; with so few Knights on the island, none were to be had.

"Do you think we shall be able to withstand a siege?"

I hesitated.

"Speak, Messer, as a soldier."

His words fed my vanity and, in truth, after Los Gelves and yesterday, I flattered myself a one. Still I hesitated. "No," I at last answered, shaking my head. "I have seen the numbers of the enemy. They are legion. The Knights themselves cannot defeat them. If we could move everyone in Mdina to St. Angelo, we might hold out until succours arrive. But there is no longer any room in Birgu. You must know that."

"Yes, I know that," said Falzon. "But I wanted to hear it." Then he muttered, as if to himself, "Those Knights have brought our land nothing but misfortune."

"Had they not come to Malta," I replied angrily, "Città Notabile would have fallen to Turgut years ago and you, Signore, would do well to remember that."

Falzon only smiled. "Have you ever been a slave to the Turks?"

I shook my head most slowly.

"I am trying to decide when the barbarians storm the city whether to allow myself to be taken or to kill my entire family. I do not think I possess the bravery to take their lives, nor do I possess the fortitude to live the life of a slave."

"You are a rich man and can be ransomed," I answered. "The enemy will not harm you."

Falzon knew better. "You find my books interesting," he said, having noticed my darting eyes.

"Erasmus is a Lutheran heretic, and in Spain you could be imprisoned for owning that book—perhaps worse."

"Here too, soon enough. As you must know, Erasmus remained Catholic, but that is of little consequence now, isn't it? I shall regret not having an opportunity to read this one." He handed me a fresh volume from the desk. *On Subtlety*, by one Cardano.

I glanced at the book impatiently and handed it back to Master Falzon. "I have never heard of him."

"Truly?" asked Falzon with surprise, leafing sadly through the work. "No man in Italy surpasses Cardano as an astrologer, a physician and as a mathematician. He says that if demons exist, they exist on a higher mental plane than man and will hardly comprehend our vain ambitions and insignificant achievements, any more than we understand the discourse governing the life of ants. Forgive me," he abruptly apologized, closing the book. "This is not a proper conversation under present circumstances."

I could find no response other than to nod and excuse myself, asking again which house belonged to Lady Emilia. Falzon called to a servant as he showed me to the front door.

"God be with you, Francisco," he said and I quickly departed.

The scene at the Guasconi residence was of similar aspect. Having been shown in, I found all the women on their knees in the sitting room before an image of the Virgin surrounded by candles. I crossed myself, silently watching them, but at length Lady Emilia sensed my presence, got to her feet and threw her arms about me, as were I the Savior himself. At once she burst into uncontrollable sobs, vainly attempting to stifle them.

"O Blessed Mother!" she cried, "O Blessed Mother ... " She repeated like that, as if under a spell. Finally, she released me and slumped onto a stool, but she was yet unable to contain her tears and sat, sobbing, into her hands. No words of consolation came to my mouth and I stood by silently, as dumb as an oak. When at last Lady Emilia found a voice to speak, it was a voice filled with despair.

"Have we remained here in Mdina only to give up our lives? Lord, why have you asked this of us?" She was not speaking to me and her eyes, swollen and red, encompassed infinite anguish.

"There is yet hope, Signora," I said.

She started, jerking her head back. "And where is hope? In that?" she pointed to my rapier.

I could find no answer. "In God," I said finally. I knelt before the Virgin and prayed.

My gesture provided Lady Emilia little solace. When I arose, she apologized for having yielded so readily to despair. Yet she despaired and angered. She cursed Falzon for placing her and her daughter in such mortal danger, and once she finished sending him to the Devil, her eyes flew wildly about the room and, voice catching, she summoned only the strength to ask where they would find food, water, and what would become of them when the infidels sacked Città Notabile. As with Falzon, I had few answers. At length Lady Emilia calmed down enough to request that I escort Isabella to the Benedictine abbey, St. Scolastica, where it might be safer for her, even if it required making her a nun that very night. I nodded my agreement.

On the street Isabella too asked whether we were all going to die.

The innocence and freshness of her voice sent a shudder down my spine, and I once again sensed the presence of Destiny intertwined. "Milady," I answered, struggling to find words, "no one can say what God has in store for us. But be assured, I shall give my last gasp defending you."

"Then I am not afraid," she said with a gravity I later learned was habitual.

At the small abbey near the city's main gate the nuns greeted us. Judging from the numbers of young girls sitting in the entranceway, Lady Emilia had not been alone in her thoughts. Natheless, the sisters agreed to take in Isabella if she desired. I clasped her hand and returned to the walls.

Eighteen

By dawn morning next the enemy had appeared on the plain below Città Notabile. There seemed no end to this host, the twelve thousand arrayed far below us like a sea painted by an artist who, blind to the natural color of things, had let his palette run riot. Nearly within hailing distance one could discern His Majesty's *spahis*, cavalrymen, mounted upon their beplumed stallions; the *silahdars*, the Porte's horsemen-sword bearers, attired in resplendent crimson surcoats girdled with broad belts and scimitars dangling from them; scouts hardly distinguishable from animals, crouching beneath leopard-skin capes tied across their backs and leopard-skin caps thrust upon their heads. Above all the janissaries. Perhaps I imagine what was visible to the eyes of we who defended the citadel, but in the years since, I have become too familiar with those bright costumes and now, as I cast my gaze back, they seem as clear to me as if I might embrace them.

The janissaries, *yenicheri*, new troops. Tales of their prowess were legion: They were the world's best marksmen, firing arquebuses a good two or three palms longer than our own. They scorned death no less than the Knights; they ate but one meal a day around a brass pot—they e'en fastened a spoon to their headdresses as a sign of their rank. Those headdresses. Aye, how to describe those useless adornments that rose from the janissary's head like a great white sock, flopping over like one as well? By their beliefs, a wise man blessed the first recruit with his sleeve, and from that day to this they have worn his sleeve atop their heads.

As soon as he had approached within battering distance, the enemy got down to digging trenches and positioning cannon. The sight of that purposeful activity put such a fear into the defenders that all along the walls the irregulars began cursing themselves for allowing themselves to be shut up in Mdina, which at this moment must be the most dangerous place in the entire world. Numbers of men began fastening ropes around the parapets on the side away from the enemy, lowering themselves into the ditches and fleeing the doomed city.

The cowardice enraged Adorno. "Shoot any man who tries to escape!" he bellowed there on the ramparts, and we did.

But the numbers climbing over the walls was so great that one of the soldiers walked up to the Bailiff and said, "Señor, we cannot afford to waste the ammunition." Thereat the Bailiff stormed up and down the lines of arquebusiers with a noose in his hand, grabbing the first man who flinched, threatening him—anyone—with execution should he display the slightest disobedience.

"Ramon!" Adorno shouted, "Take charge of these goats!" At once Caravajal herded up the goats assigned him, while the Bailiff divided the rest of us into other companies, putting Knights and friends at their heads as a further means against sedition.

The defenders' spirits were not lightened by the sight of dozens, nay hundreds, of carrion feeders circling above the city as were we already dead. I had never before seen such an apparition, and I tell you in the wheel of those birds the visage of Satan himself was taking shape above us. Under that portent, while irregulars deserted, those huddled within Mdina's walls awaited the onset of the first bombardment.

To say that the Lord Almighty showed His hand over the next hours would diminish the miracle that transpired. Of greater wonders people do not speak. That morning a nun, Agatha, who resided in the very abbey to which I had escorted Isabella, awoke, having been visited during the night by a vision of St. Agatha herself. The saint had taken pity on the plight of Mdina and told the sister that the townspeople should attend Mass in the cathedral and carry her image along the ramparts before the enemy. With these tidings the nun ran to the Vicar General; the news spread on stallion's wings. Fleeting moments after Agatha awoke, each person who had slept in the street or market knew of her vision. The Vicar General himself sought out Adorno, directly on the bastion, and even as the Turks readied to bombard us, the Bailiff and every citizen of the town who could squeeze into St. Paul's Cathedral attended Mass.

Afterwards, the Vicar, holding the image of St. Agatha proudly in his arms, with the Bailiff led a great procession from the cathedral. Falzon and his family, Lady Emilia and Isabella, all the nobles of the city, every

Knight, all the soldiers and many of the common people joined that demonstration. Together, as the enemy opened fire, we marched to the walls and mounted the ramparts.

For hours the enemy fired against the steep walls of Città Notabile, yet always their balls fell short. During the entire day, not a soul in the city was injured. St. Agatha had interceded on our behalf.

Night fell, and the bombardment let up some as the enemy seemed to go around to the weaker side of town, away from the sharp inclines that faced them and to the flatter plains westward. Naturally, this increased Adorno's disquiet and he and insisted we needed succours.

"Send me to St. Angelo," I volunteered, not knowing why. "I shall seek out the Grand Master and yet again request more troops."

"He will resist, as he has until now," Adorno answered. "Ask him, if he'll do no more, to send Villegaignon and anyone who will accompany him. Every Knight here knows that man's valor and his very presence will give them heart."

Only then did I realize that the full moon was unmoved by my bravado, and so I paced impatiently until the small hours of the night when she departed. Then, in utter darkness, on a side of town where few of the enemy seemed present, I crept out of a postern gate as silently as I had ever carried myself. After walking a good five hundred paces past a windmill, and hearing only a few shots in my direction, I mounted my horse and sped to the Borgo as if Beelzebub were breathing down my neck.

During those few leagues I could not but wonder by what means Fortune had guided me to the center of this conflagration in which I had so little stake. Of course, I was a foolish idiot. I'd set off with Vergã desiring to fight the infidels, but hadn't much considered that we would end up in straits so desperate that we, along with all the people of Malta, stood in mortal fear of our lives. Truly, I should have dwelt more on that eventuality, for with Birgu in sight a Turkish scout hurled his spear at me from his hiding place in the rocks. The javelin struck my horse, felling it and knocking me to earth. As I gained my feet the scout jumped to his and rushed me with a scimitar drawn. He was one of those animals cloaked in leopard skin with a hyena's brush rearing frightfully from his head. He carried a large shield as well, which put me at a disadvantage. But so desperate was I to achieve my mission, he would have had to chop me into little pieces before I would yield. The scout stumbled on the dying horse as it attempted to right itself, and this gave me time to yank the javelin. As my foeman turned to me I impaled him on his own spear, then, grasping my rapier with two hands, I took his head.

I carried it with me, stumbling the remaining distance to Birgu. Luckily, the sentries recognized me as a Christian and allowed me to pass. I gave them the scout's head, telling them to mount it on the walls with the others.

Fort St. Angelo was alive as had it been daylight and I found the Grand Master at the Castellan's house awake with several of his Seigneurs. Covered with blood, I asked him in the name of a city under siege for more troops.

For an instant, I could not tell whether the Monsignore saw me with his eye. But Adorno had foretold rightly: the old man wavered, vacillated. "The Borgo is overflowed, you see it, and the Religion cannot spare soldiers who must look after these people and defend the castle against another attack."

"E—Eminenza," I blurted out in heat, "it is Città Notabile that is now under attack. You, a Spaniard, would ne'er shirk from the graver danger, which lies there."

At once I regretted this outburst and began to apologize.

d'Homedes raised his hand. "For the moment you may be correct, young man, but it is too dangerous—even for Spaniards. Among so many thousands in the Città, can you truthfully tell me there are not sufficient numbers who are willing to die for their country and the Order?"

Agitated verily beyond control, I nearly responded that the Maltese, certainly the nobles of Mdina, would sooner see the Knights made galley slaves than defend those who had stolen their lands and liberties. Somehow I stayed my tongue and instead conveyed the Bailiff's request for Villegaignon. Thereat the Grand Master sent a messenger to find him and meanwhile asked me to more fully describe the situation in Città Notabile. When I had given him my intelligence, the Monsignore dismissed me, entering into deliberation with other Council members. Once Villegaignon appeared, the Grand Master admitted both of us to the Council's presence.

d'Homedes, with a flattery e'en a stranger would not mistake for sincerity, proposed to the Knight, "Brother, you are renowned for you valor and devotion to the Order. The Città is at this moment besieged and in need of succours. Those peasants are incapable of fighting and the Bailiff is surrounded by insufficient men. Are you prepared to lend them your skill in arms?"

The blond Knight, who appeared to be about forty, bowed. "Monsignore," he said with a certain coldness, "when I joined the Order I swore to obey my superiors in all matters. I have never failed to uphold my vows. I go whither you send me."

"Very well. Bailiff Adorno has requested your presence above all at Notabile. Due to the shortage of men the Council has agreed that you should take six other Knights and this messenger; go hence immediately."

"Eminenza," Villegaignon replied, startled beyond comprehension, "of what use are six or seven Knights against this host? Those miserable sheep the peasants will desert under the first thunder of artillery and, if I may speak plainly, you are sending us to be knocked on the head by the enemy. We'll be vanquished within moments to die a death which lacks the slightest opportunity for glory. I declare, we must send entire companies, every available Knight."

The old man refused to bend. "The Council," he said, "has agreed that all available Knights are to be used for the defense of St. Angelo and Il Borgo. Will you go or will you not?"

A second time Villegaignon bowed. "The Monsignore knows that fear has never made me decline danger. Whom may I take?"

"Take whomever you will, your friends." d'Homedes waved his hand and dismissed us.

Outside the Castellan's quarters, Villegaignon yielded to rage. "That cyclops has done this to dispatch me to Heaven and for one reason: he opposes moving the Religion to Tripoli. No matter, *magister dixit* and we have our duty ... Now, six Knights to their deaths."

"If I judge him aright, Fra Balthazar de Marans des Homes-Saint-Martin will not hesitate to accompany you," I said as we descended from the castle.

"Fra Balthazar and I also have our differences."

"Over Tripoli, yes, not over duty."

We roused six Knights from the auberges and their private rooms in town. As I had foretold, Balthazar readily agreed. Within an hour the party was armored, but horses were in such short numbers that we were forced to take eight unsaddled mares we found feeding in the castle ditch.

En route, Balthazar commented on my bloodied appearance, that for a second time I appeared to have been baptized by fire. "How do you feel now, my friend?" he asked.

"In need of sleep," I answered and, as we passed it, I pointed out what remained of the scout, whose body was already being picked at by ravens.

Balthazar, raising his eyebrows, remarked, "You are coming to love it, Francisco, I trust not so much as the rest of us."

To which I replied, "This campaign would do better with more Spaniards."

And Balthazar laughed.

At first light we approached Mdina. The crack of arquebuses reached our ears from both sides and as we neared the city the flashes from the gun muzzles became visible. It seemed impossible to reach the gates without passing directly beneath Turkish fire. Villegaignon quickly made a decision: He divided our company into two columns of three and four each with himself in the middle and ordered us to spread out. All at once he leaned forward over the eyes of his mount, brandished his sword and cried, "*Saint Jean! Saint Michel! à l'aide!*" The rest of our formidable party took up the cry and charged past all the prickly figs straight for the walls. So startled were the Turks by the illusion that we gained the ditch before the *spahis* had gotten their wits together for a chase. But as luck would have it we had landed in the ditch far from the nearest gate. Whistling, we managed to attract the attention of those above, who lowered down ropes for us. And so we left the horses behind and climbed into the city, in full view of the enemy with arquebus balls slamming into the walls nearby. Natheless, God protected us in the grey morning and all of us entered Mdina unscathed.

Villegaignon's presence lifted everyone's spirits immensely. When word spread that seven Knights had risked their lives to enter the city, the men redoubled their resolve to resist the enemy and, as Villegaignon walked through the Città, he was everywhere met with volleys of small-arms fire. He exhorted the inhabitants to be of stout heart, for soon a large company of Knights would arrive from St. Angelo, and he immediately ordered that the weaker side of Mdina's walls be buttressed with anything available. E'en as the Turkish bombardment intensified, balls now crashing into those walls, the Knights set their hands to it and, following their example, everyone in the city joined us—men, women and children. The entire day we hauled logs, dirt and carriages to reinforce the ramparts with terre-plein and make shelters for the arquebusiers and our single piece of artillery.

I had ne'er experienced the like. The narrow streets of Mdina, surrounded by stone houses, channeled and made greater the terrible thunder of the artillery so that one had to clasp one's hands over one's ears for fear of going deaf. And the same stones, the cathedral, the houses, reflected those sounds countless times so that one turned and turned, not knowing from which direction the volleys were coming. Amid that horrible din and pieces of the walls crashing down about us, I caught sight of Isabella working with the rest, and indeed Lady Emilia, and wondered at their bravery. We had not a moment to speak. Only the seven Knights and myself knew all the activity was a diversion.

"How long will they believe we are to be saved by these planks?" I asked Balthazar when I sat down next to him late in the day, exhausted, covering my ears as the walls shook and dust fell over us.

"Let us not speak of it," he said. "I would only have preferred a more useful death, for this one will avail us or Christendom nothing." It was one of the few times that Balthazar had found neither story nor joke to tell, but he went on: "Perhaps we will think of something better," he said, and I was reassured.

Adorno also realized that our measures were for naught when Villegaignon finally spoke to him in private and told him dispassionately how things really stood. "You must understand that what I have told the people is a lie. The Grand Master intends to be rid of me, and you cannot expect further succours but what my own valor and those with me might bring. I have come to die with you in Notabile and the only thing I can offer is that we make a brave resistance so that we weaken the enemy insofar as possible and make an end glorious enough that the Order shall remember our names."

At hearing these words, Adorno did not give way to despair. Nay, he climbed once more to the ramparts and ordered continual fusillades to be directed at the enemy. I found an arquebus and joined them.

With night the Turkish batteries fell silent. I slept at my post. Having had no sleep at all for two full days and near none for three, I hurtled quickly into a dreamless slumber that brooked no interruption until at dawn Balthazar shook me violently to my senses.

"Look there," he said, pointing toward the enemy position on the plain.

I rubbed my eyes and squinted, seeing nothing in the rising light.

"They've gone."

"They've gone?"

I peered out again and shook my head, glancing in every direction, north, south, to Birgu, to the sea. Lord Balthazar was correct. By the Angel of Peace, they had gone.

The same words, "they've gone," were soon on every pair of lips in Mdina, and no one believed them.

"It must be a ruse," was repeated as often as the other phrase, but plainly no enemy was in sight. Soon Villegaignon ordered scouting parties to search the area and learn whether the Turks had truly departed. We rode to Rabat, hardly two paces from Mdina, finding no trace of the foe, and rode farther to Mosta and some other villages and found them gutted but empty. Emboldened by this lack of resistance, the scouting parties spread out as far as St. Paul's Bay, and there we finally descried the Turks embarking on their ships.

The soldiers galloped back into Mdina, whooping and cheering with joy. We practically burst into the cathedral on horseback to offer thanks for this unfathomable deliverance. The bells of the Noble City began to ring in celebration, the people rejoiced and ran forthwith into the countryside to smell the flowers there. Balthazar and I fell into each other's arms, embracing each other. As the town slowly emptied of all those who had crowded into it, I searched for Isabella and her mother, but finding them on St. Paul's Square before the cathedral, words eluded us and we stood before one another, convulsing with laughter and tears and giving thanks to the Almighty.

At about this time, two Maltese youths returned through the main gate dragging a third young man before Villegaignon, who rested with Adorno nearby. They explained that this fellow had tried to hide behind a rock when he had caught sight of them scouring the countryside. Suspicions aroused, the two scouts gave chase—here he was.

"Who are you?" Villegaignon barked at the boy, who judging from his appearance, must have been a Christian.

He refused to open his mouth.

Villegaignon immediately commanded the scouts to go back to where they had found him and search the area diligently. No more than a glass had turned, when the boys walked up to Villegaignon and handed to him a packet of messages written in Turkish. Enough of the Knights had been slaves aboard infidel galleys so that finding a translator proved a simple matter. The messages contained details of the Order's numbers and disposition in Birgu and Mdina and were addressed to Sinan Pasha.

"Who are these from?" bellowed Villegaignon, but again the youth refused to speak. Without hesitation Villegaignon threw the boy to the ground and cut off his hand. "Who are these from?"

Screaming in agony the spy—and there could be no doubt he was a spy—named a Turkish slave in Birgu. Villegaignon ordered the slave brought to him. Long hours passed. When the slave, shackled, was finally dropped before Villegaignon and saw his confederate with a bloody stump for an arm and a hand on the ground nearby, he shat in his pants. And he talked. It seemed that the Christian, a Greek, had switched allegiance each time the tide of battle threatened to turn, thrice in as many days, or perhaps more often.

Villegaignon ordered both men made *tremenda ed esemplar giustizia*. As evening fell we who remained in the city watched the Knights string up the traitors and slowly flail the skin from the their bodies. Still alive, but looking more like calves hanging at the butcher's, the two were quartered and their pieces thrown over the walls to the birds.

The rejoicing in Birgu's taverns began at once, and the arguments over what caused the siege of Mdina to be lifted so mysteriously. They rage to this day, Your Majesty. As the years passed, the priests and many of the common folk who were there insisted that the vision of St. Agatha put such terror into the enemy troops that they lost heart and abandoned the enterprise. The soldiers averred that the sight of so many thousands on the city walls and the great fusillades Adorno commanded convinced Sinan Pasha that reinforcements had arrived, and that the eight mares we had abandoned in the ditch removed all doubts. Runaway slaves captured by the scouting parties at St. Paul's Bay later spoke of a note Romegas had left in a skiff on his return from Sicily, a note he intended the Turks to find. It persuaded the enemy that Andrea Doria had arrived from Spain and would soon be sailing to Malta in force. As the years passed, many garbed themselves with this story as the truth. Vergã, who had accompanied Romegas to Sicily, often claimed to have left the note himself.

For myself, I became convinced that each account of our salvation was true, but that the greater truth was the simplest: Turgut and Sinan decided they were wasting time at Mdina and that more important matters awaited to the south before the season turned. One thing is beyond any dispute: we in the taverns celebrated too soon.

Nineteen

His Majesty, who has conquered much of the known world, massacred the defenders of Belgrade and burnt Buda to the ground, may have slight recollection of Gozo, the small island lying but one-and-a-half leagues northwest of Malta. For those who walked forth from the gates of Mdina after that siege was so miraculously abandoned, the events of the next days tested our faith as no other in our lives had. The most devout, who better than others discern the hand of God in reversals of Fortune, found themselves utterly incapable of grasping in those acts the design of the Almighty. To the Gozitans themselves, those simple people whose humble prayers never lifted far enough to reach the ears of kings or popes, the events were not merely unfathomable. Their world ended that week, as on the fields of Armageddon. I stand before His Majesty fifteen years later and the tiny, rent world has yet to become whole, and will not for another age.

Half a day after the bells in Birgu and Mdina began to peal in celebration, the Grand Master was leading a procession to the Conventual Church in Birgu, where he had ordered a *Te Deum* to be sung. E'en as he set foot on the church steps, four or five Knights ran up to him from different directions with the news boatmen and riders had just brought: Sinan and Dragut were attacking Gozo. All the people on Gozo had fled to the decrepit castle there, on which the Turkish army was now advancing. They lacked any soldiers or defenses beyond the unsteady walls themselves. At once d'Homedes called the Council into session but, tho' they raised their arms to Heaven and argued 'til nightfall, the only conclusion they reached was that nothing could be done.

Four days later a barrel-chested peasant with a round face and a crooked nose stumbled into Birgu wearing little more than a filthy, torn shirt and laced sandals. Those of us who happened to be standing near the

embankment gate when he fair collapsed into our arms understood his
rude Italian with difficulty, but we well perceived that his presence before
us was a miracle.

Pietru Galea was among the Gozitans who had taken refuge in the
castle. Pietru, Your Majesty, was perhaps the simplest man I have known.
If you asked him for the story of his life, he would cock his big cannon-
ball head and gaze at you. He had no story. He existed. He planted in the
spring and harvested in the autumn. He caught birds in wooden traps and
cooked rabbit stew. He had a wife, tho' he would never understand the
need for marriage, and he had sired two children. They lived in a hovel
that was scarcely more than a cave of sod and rocks where pagan idols
hung from the roof next to crucifixes. Yet in the years I knew him, I ne'er
had a more worthy companion.

When word came that the Turks were ravaging the Maltese
countryside, Pietru gathered his wife and children to him and, much as
those who had crowded into Mdina, they made their way with their
favorite goat to the citadel. It stood at the island's center, a fortress from
an antique age, an old castle in disrepair surrounded by a town smaller
than Birgu. Houses trespassed on the walls both from without and within;
some of the houses formed part of the walls themselves. Defending the
place were two cannon, or three. By the time Pietru and his family pushed
their way through the gates, so had nearly everyone else on "Ghawdesh,"
as he named Gozo. No one knew exactly how many people that was, least
of all Pietru. Most say five thousand, others six; some, as if it were
necessary to tell tales, seven or eight.

When the enemy disembarked, Pietru said they captured a certain Paul
de Nas, who told them the castle was much stronger than it seemed and
might hold out for ten or twelve days. So Sinan and Dragut decided to
plant large batteries before it, as they had at Mdina. When the
bombardment commenced, the cathedral was overflowing and Pietru and
his wife—his woman as he spoke of her—could not find refuge there.
They made their way to one of the side streets and pressed themselves
against the walls of one of the old houses above. Each time the houses
shuddered under the siege guns, bits of stone and dust flaked off the roofs
and fell upon them. They endured this for more than a day. When the
children tried to run away Pietru's woman ran after them, screaming, and
gathered them back to her. They ate the goat's cheese and bread they had

brought. She and Pietru slept in each other's arms, both knowing this would be their last night together.

Pietru in his gruff voice spoke of the island's Governor, the Knight Galatian de Sesse. Watching the enemy from his quarters atop the keep, de Sesse could not doubt the mortal peril confronting him. On the second day of the bombardment his gun master, in desperation, fired off a few shots with the little powder left to them, but the cannon exploded and he was killed. At this de Sesse flew into a panic and called for the friar.

Pietru himself did not understand what was happening, only that with every passing moment he and everyone else trapped inside the castle was growing more restless. He left his wife, taking an old sword in his rough hand, and struggled down past the cathedral to the front gate of the citadel. People were saying that the Governor had moments ago sent a monk to the enemy leader.

"He is going to give us over to the Turks!" somebody cried.

At that, an extraordinary terror seized everyone within earshot. Pietru joined a crowd that climbed up to the Governor's quarters. He felt no anger, even betrayal. He felt a great a great confusion and a great emptiness, as if God had abandoned them.

"Allow us to fight the enemy!" a Gozitan soldier beseeched de Sesse in the name of all those present, but they saw as well as he did that among their weapons were fewer arquebuses than pitchforks and scythes. Pietru watched the Governor, shuddering from head to toe, slam the door in their faces and bar them from entering.

Sometime afterward the friar returned and as he passed into the citadel the people swarmed onto him to find out what had taken place. Shaking himself free, he refused to say anything, first walking, then fleeing to the Governor's quarters with the crowd at his heels.

Months and years later we pieced together the story. This monk went to Sinan Pasha, saying to him, "The Governor offers to surrender the castle should you preserve his life and effects and spare as well the lives of the inhabitants of Gozo."

"Get out of my sight, you impudent dog!" Sinan shouted, "and tell your governor that if he doesn't quit the castle at this very moment I'll hang him by his entrails at the gate."

But the Governor, terrified as he was, did not lack for the bravado of the Knights and he sent the friar back to the enemy camp. With a trail of

people behind him the monk once more descended, again shaking them
from his tail as he passed through the gate.

This time when he was escorted before Sinan the friar said, "The
Governor is agreed to turn over the island if you spare him and the two
hundred principal inhabitants."

Once more Sinan laughed, but perhaps he was in the mood for a bargain
and agreed to forty. "Now get from my sight, dog snout, and if I ever see
you again, I'll hang you from your balls alongside the governor."

Now it began, that terrible sack. de Sesse ordered the gates of the citadel
flung open and the Turks stormed in, without the least opposition. The
Gozitans stampeded in every direction, but there was no place to flee.
Turks began rounding them up, roping them like cattle, and tho' the
screams reached to Heaven, hardly a one of them resisted. One man,
Bernardo de Opuo, understood what was coming. A Sicilian who had lived
on Gozo for a long time, he had a wife and two fair daughters, of
marriageable age. When he saw the enemy rushing up the streets, torching
the houses, he took the decision Matteo Falzon in Mdina had been spared.
Rather than see his wife and children raped and sold into slavery, he lifted
his sword and slew all three. Pietru watched this with his own eyes. He
then saw de Opuo take up a crossbow and an arquebus and run headlong
to meet the enemy. He killed two Turks forthwith, one with a bolt and
one with a ball, threw down the weapons and met the enemy with his
sword, only in the next moment to be hacked to pieces.

The Turks broke into the Governor's apartments, carrying out trunks
and chairs on their shoulders. When de Sesse cried that this broke the
agreement, they spat on the ground and forced him to carry a chest on his
own shoulders, even as they marched him to a galley, stripped him naked
and chained him to a bench.

In the midst of the tumult, Pietru lost sight of his family. As the Turks
flooded in, the terrified wave of people bore him higher and higher up
the narrow streets. Flames now raced along the rooftops. A man carrying
a piglet refused to part with the animal and had his throat slit. A woman
stumbled and never got up. A dog with smoking fur chased its tail,
sending its yelp-shrieks into the unheeding air. Why Pietru acted as he
did, he never knew. At the moment the screams became so loud that he
ceased to hear them, he darted into one of the old houses that formed part

of the citadel wall. He did not see much, smashed chairs, emptied stores. There was a window. The grate had already been broken and a rope dangled down the outer walls. He did not think. He climbed. He was not alone. Near him others were climbing down or throwing themselves from the high windows, or hurling themselves off the parapets to their deaths. When Pietru reached the ground he did not look back. He ran, not knowing where. Away. Forever. Wholly across the island. He found a cave at the seaside and, as darkness fell, he crawled into it.

Only two days later did Pietru dare emerge and walk back to the citadel. He found a deserted ruin. His wife, his children, every person on the island had been carried off by Dragut and Sinan to God knows where. Pietru sat down in the midst of the echoes, and cried.

When this short man with bulging muscles staggered through the gates at Birgu, for a long time he uttered nothing more than "my woman, my children" over and over again. Only when we gave him food and drink was he able to recount his simple story and learn that a few others had also survived. Some hundreds had made that desperate flight down the castle walls, or had chosen not to take refuge in the citadel at all, and escaped with their lives. I told him to go to the Hospital; they might have a bed, or a bundle of straw.

The enormity of what had just transpired on Gozo made itself felt at once. That very evening, Balthazar shoved aside a whore who had already seen fit to get back in business and roared, as he got roaring drunk. "My God, where were the Knights? We stood by and allowed this to happen!"

"Hold, Lord Balthazar," said I. "You, I, everyone had just emerged from a city under siege. By the Saints of God, how would it have been possible during those scant hours to have accomplished anything?"

Overcome by genuine rage, Balthazar delivered the tabletop a violent blow with his fist. "What we lived through, Francisco Perez de Barai, was not a siege! Hardly a one of us was harmed. None of us was given to display the slightest valor, dost thou not understand?" You can be certain I took offense at those words but Balthazar went on, heedless. "We should have reconnoitred the Turks and dispatched every man capable of standing to Gozo once we realized the enemy had landed there. But, young man, at issue is not what transpired in those short hours when time had abandoned us. At issue is our inaction for the months past." Balthazar swallowed long and ordered another *mezzo*. "Villegaignon was correct," he said, wiping his lips. "We should have shipped them all off to Sicilia."

I could hardly countenance such speech. "Villegaignon showed no more concern for those people that he would have for offal."

Just as the observation was in my eyes, it served only to elicit from Lord Balthazar's the fiercest reply. "Do not presume to speak so, *cavallero valloroso*, of one so far above your station. I say he was correct. *Mort de Dieu*, I maintained that they stay and be slaughtered."

"You, My Lord, maintained they be defended."

That evening Balthazar was not to be consoled. Nor were my spirits any higher. Drunk myself, I left him and staggered to the bagno where the slaves were kept underground. I told the guard on duty to find Abdallah the Moor, convincing him the matter was urgent. The guard led him out into the corridor. I unsheathed my sword. Only the guard's quick-wittedness prevented me from running Abdallah through. As that one restrained me from the Moor, I pointed in my fever and said, "Ne'er again from your lips a word about the House of War." This time he remained silent as I staggered off.

At the same moment, Balthazar himself was stumbling to St. Angelo, where he sought out the Grand Master at the Castellan's quarters. Finding d'Homedes at sup, Balthazar bowed as he could, righted himself. "Eminenza," he declared, grape fully evident in his eyes, "you told the people the Turks were en route to Provence. We have seen plainly this week that Provence was not their object. Whither does the Monsignore suppose Turgut is sailing now, ships overfull with Christian slaves?"

For a moment Old One-Eye stared at him. Receiving no reply, Balthazar went on. "You can no longer doubt the report Romegas brought a week past: The Turks are sailing for Tripoli."

d'Homedes put down the fork in his hand. "Yes, that is true, Fra Balthazar, they are sailing for Tripoli."

"And when Turgut seizes that weak garrison, the ancient Order of the Knights Hospitallers of St. John of Jerusalem, Rhodes and Malta, having existed for five centuries, will be but one step away from complete destruction and the Grand Turk will control the entire eastern Mediterranean, from sunrise to Djerbé. I ask, what does Eminenza intend to do about it?"

At this the Grand Master got to his feet, casting his fiery eye at the drunken Knight who flailed his arms before him. "What do you think I intend to do about it, Fra Balthazar? The Council has been in session all day and shall resume within the hour. We have already sent word to the Vice Roy—"

"—which will arrive too late."

Only the regard the old man held for Fra Balthazar de Marans des Homes-Saint-Martin and the strict deference wherewith the younger Knight addressed him prevented the Grand Master from erupting completely. "Yes, it will arrive too late," he said, ancient voice dry as dust. "Leave me, Fra Balthazar."

Aye, the Council gathered that very night, as it had that very day and as it would each day hence, but naught was accomplished but the wringing of hands. The five or six galleys of the Order's fleet, as feared by the infidels as it was, could not challenge the Turkish armada. With the towns of Sicily burning after the invasion, no one believed the Vice Roy would send aid and, if he did—e'en d'Homedes did not flatter himself that Tripoli could hold out for so long. As Balthazar often observed, the garrison there was manned by only a few elderly Knights who repaired thither as much for the waters as for duty. And so, while the Grand Crosses of the Council met in their fruitless deliberations, Sinan and Turgut sailed boldly southward.

To my surprise, Flaminia met the events with a certain resignation, more a fatality. "What is the Knights' castle in Tripoli to me, *mio cuore*? I do not know where Tripoli is." E'en the sack of Gozo left her strangely unmoved. "Yes, God has sent the Turks against us in punishment for our sins. He has always done this and always will."

Natheless, with large stretches of her own island having been laid waste over the past week, the whore was fully desperate to discover the fate of her own family who lived in the little village of Zurrieq, a league or two to the south. She begged me to accompany her thither to find them, or bury them, and at last I agreed. We set off on a horse and a mule. That part of the island lay outside the main path of the corsairs and, by the Grace of God, the village had been spared. Finding her parents and sisters alive, Flaminia ran to them with tears in her eyes and embraced them.

They insisted we join them by the small stone house for barley bread, which had just come out of the oven, fresh goat's cheese and garlic.

A more sublime meal I could hardly recall, yet the conversation was beyond me, for these people spoke no Spanish or e'en Italian, and as we sat on rude benches under a trellis, they chattered away wholly in that strange, harsh tongue of Maltese. Sometimes Flaminia would break off to tell me what had been said. Of course, the family had heard about the fighting, but as it had not come directly to the village and as they'd set eyes on no corsairs this year, it all proved difficult for them to imagine. The invasion was nearly as distant to them as Tripoli was to Flaminia, and the most they could think to say was to curse Dragut with a life of bad Easters.

Flaminia's father was more concerned with finding enough dried dung to fuel the oven and that the Knights had been confiscating all the good wheat bread, leaving none to sell. The cows were not giving milk and her mother was convinced that a neighbor had cast a spell on them. She did not know what to do about this. Two Carmelite friars were also planning to exorcise an evil spirit from a nearby cave on the southern coast and had come to ask the local priest about the proper ritual. The priest himself was unsure, but they intended to go ahead with the rite as soon as they could.

"What do you think they should do?" Flaminia suddenly asked, turning to me for my advice.

Caught off guard, I fairly spit up the goat's milk in my mouth, wondering if everyone on this island was a damnèd pagan. "I can have no opinion on this," I said, glancing at the little carved effigies that hung from the trellis by the crucifixes, "for it certainly lies outside the province of God."

My answer meant little to Flaminia, for she lay her head gently on my shoulder and told me she would bring me to the exorcism. The invitation did little to entice me. As we finished our meal, a few curious neighbors thrust their heads under the trellis vines and, before I knew it, everyone was on their feet, singing and clapping to the sound of bagpipes. Of a sudden Flaminia grabbed my hand and we all joined in a round dance. Never had I participated in such a spontaneous celebration of joy, if joy it was. As little as these people comprehended the large events unfolding about them, I could not help but feel that this was some rustic prayer, a thanksgiving that all of us remained alive. The tears mixed with laughter and when we had exhausted ourselves, we fell into each other's arms.

"God be with you," the neighbors said as we departed.

Not having set eyes on them since Mdina, I finally called on Lady Emilia and her daughter in the evening, after Flaminia and I returned from Zurrieq. When Isabella received me, I kissed her hand, perhaps lingering longer than I ought. She withdrew it and I looked up, only then noticing the paleness of her face.

"I am sorry not to have called earlier," I said.

"As I am," she answered with a noticeable coldness in her voice.

How unjust, a woman's tongue. "Isabella, everything is in such tumult. The streets have yet to be cleared. I merely wanted to be assured of your spirits."

"Assured of my spirits!" she exclaimed, glaring at me. "Just how would you assure them in the wake of such horrors?"

Stung by her unforgiving demeanor, I decided I'd best depart. "Accept my apologies, Signorita. I have disturbed you and will return at some other time."

"No!" she cried suddenly, placing her hand on mine. "You shall take me to Gozo."

"*¿Cómo?*" I asked, startled.

"You heard correctly, Messer, I would see Gozo."

This was incomprehensible to me. "But Isabella, nothing remains ... no one remains."

"That is what I must see," she said, unrelenting. "That is what I must believe."

I also refused to retreat. "We can hardly reach Gozo and return in a single day," I replied.

Isabella insisted. A new Governor for the island had already been appointed and we could sail with his men on the morn, or hire a boat ourselves, or travel overland, resting at Mdina on the return. Her mother would never grant leave for the such a journey. What could dangers mean after the past week? And what leave? Lady Emilia had already returned to Mdina to take charge of the cleanup of the house there.

We hired a boat. By sunrise we were on our way, Isabella, myself and two servants in a Maltese fishing boat, a *luzzu*. As the boatmen took us along the north coast of the island, in an attempt to lighten the air all about us, I asked Isabella to speak of her guardian, Jean de Valette.

The attempt misfired and Isabella's displeasure at my question was sensible. "What would you have me say, Señor?" Her true father, Emilia's husband, had died near the time of her birth and she had no memory of him. Parisot had been the only father she'd known.

"He displays not the cheeriest countenance," I replied.

"No. Like all you soldiers, Parisot is a closed man. He has witnessed so much cruelty and bloodshed, and has suffered such grievous wounds in battle that have brought him near death ... I do not know. Perhaps because he has survived, he knows of what he is made, and that others are not made of it. And of course he is of the purest blood."

The last words were filled with a certain haughtiness and I took them to mean that de Valette—and perhaps she herself—held little truck with we commoners. "Fra Balthazar declares his temper to be uncontrollable."

At this Isabella laughed faintly. "He is known for his outbursts, yes."

"I saw nothing of him during the past days," I ventured.

Isabella sighed, truly not much interested in speaking of her Godfather. "He rode with the Turcopilier," she said without enthusiasm, "and went nearly without sleep."

"And Rhodes?" I persisted, my curiosity aroused by the stern and distant figure.

Isabella again shook her head, still displaying little eagerness for the conversation, then turned her gaze directly on me. "You have asked me no questions about myself, Francisco Perez de Barai."

"And neither you of me, Milady." Both her accusation and my reply surprised me, but having responded, I quickly thought better of it and softened my tone. "I know that you are the daughter of a rich landowner who came with the Knights from Rhodes. I know that you have been well tutored—"

"—in Florence as well as Malta," she added pointedly.

"—and that you are more clever by half than most on this backwards island, more clever than I. And I know that you are a noblewoman and I a poor soldier. And I know you are betrothed."

"Who told you that?" Isabella exclaimed, caught off guard.

"Balthazar said you were spoken for," I answered, lowering my eyes. Then, casting aside my fears, I gazed straight on her. "Is it true?"

Now it was Isabella who glanced away. "To a Florentine gentleman I have never met. I think the marriage will not come soon with all ... " She moved her hand over the island. "Or perhaps all this will hasten it ... But let us speak no more of marriages. Tell me of your life."

Hardly able to recollect a time before Gelves, I began to speak of the beauty of Granada and the grandeur of Sevilla, of fencing master Don Jerónimo de Carranza, who seemed truly to belong to a former life, and of my strained comradeship with Blaij Vergã. She shook her head at the foolishness of males and told of her years in Firenze, of the great works of artists named Donatello and Michelangelo that adorned the city, of the tumult that gripped Italy and that, all in all, her mother had deemed it safer for her to return to Malta.

By midday, immersed in this sort of conversation, we arrived at a fishing village called Mgarr on the Gozitan coast. No one greeted us. At length we found a peasant with a wagon who agreed to drive us inland. Along that road we saw not a living soul, only falcons and kites soaring high above. Strange, the first impression of Gozo was of an altogether greener and more fertile isle than Malta, a pleasanter place on which one might live. But every turn revealed the signs: bootprints, ruts where guns had been dragged, abandoned swords, even smashed furniture, bodies.

We saw it from a distance, of course, the citadel, what remained of it. But only when we were upon the place did the entire carnage become evident. The tendrils of smoke, the charred remains of houses, the smashed and deserted walls, the smell of ash mixed with earth and decaying flesh. Birds hopping, pecking. It must have been this sight that the Gozitan Pietru had witnessed a few days ago and told us about when he stumbled into Birgu. Bending to pick up a handful of dirt, I wondered for a moment what had become of him. A few Knights were already about beginning to clean up the place. I let the dirt fall from my fingers.

Why Isabella had insisted on casting her eyes over this field of sorrow, I knew not—perhaps to understand how perilous it had been for us at Mdina. As I had foreseen she could not bear it and began to sob. Without thinking she turned to my chest and I held her there.

Looking back, Your Majesty, I can say without exaggeration that the calamity visited on Gozo shrouded Malta in a gloom from which it never fully recovered. In people's minds, 1551 ceased to be the Year of Our Lord

1551 and instead became the feast day of another, less exalted calendar, the year of the *razzia*. Many named the sack the worst disgrace in the Order's history and, you can be sure, only that Governor de Sesse was nowhere to be found saved him from being strung up.

Aye, as Turgut and Sinan flew southward with five thousand souls in chains and the Knights argued impotently over how best to save Tripoli, news of Gozo shot with equal speed north to enrage every capital in Christendom. But Christendom did nothing, for by then it was too late.

On Malta we could do little but clean away debris and wring our hands along with the Grand Master and his Seigneurs. People gathered in the churches, in the taverns, on the docks, cupping their ears for every scrap of news from Barbary, knowing that any news was weeks away. Blaij Vergã had returned from the fruitless expedition to Sicily full of his comrades' praise for his bravery, many averring that he'd saved Appelvoisin's life. But confronted by the devastation of Gozo, e'en Vergã put aside his usual braggadocio. Truly, as we met on the embankment of Galley Creek, Blaij did naught but swear he would devote the rest of his life to battling the barbarians.

"By the Hatred I bear to all Unbelievers," he said as we turned southward, imagining in our mind's eye what must shortly take place there, "I will not rest until I see Dragut hanged and the empire of the Ottomans brought to its knees."

Standing at Vergã's side I also swore to volunteer for the first expedition against the enemy, but it seemed we had learned little from our lessons. As we bravely took oaths in the bright sun, we but dimly perceived that Fortune on the Mediterranean had turned her hand, and we wholly failed to see what had become plain: that the infidel trumpets called out the doom of Tripoli, that the Order would stand at the edge of the Abyss, that the Grand Turk's shadow would soon stretch, as Balthazar had declared, from sunrise to Djerbé, and that neither foe would now rest until the other had been expunged from the face of the earth.

Book II

d'Homedes

For several weeks, I had narrated to His Majesty the foregoing events. During that time, officers, pages and servants frequently interrupted my account with the urgent business of state. Now and again, with a raised hand, the Sultan would put to me a question, order me to hasten past one episode or to repeat another. Yet for the most part he merely sat above his prisoner on his resplendent jewel-encrusted throne, listening with the same impassive visage that wholly shrouded his thoughts from intruders.

The Grand Vizier Sokullu Mehmed never ceased to insist that Soliman's hours would be better spent writing the poetry for which he had been renowned as a youth and that I should be incontinently executed. With that inscrutable mask on one side and a towering foeman on the other, I expected each evening's sunset to be my last. Each morning the sun rose and I awoke with my head intact.

During my audiences many whispers flew about the throne room, giving me to learn that preparations were underway for a campaign against the Emperor Maximilian in Hungary. The Sultan had not himself rode before the army in a full decade, but his daughter Mihrimah pressed on him that a gazi's first and foremost duty was to make war on the Infidel. This harpy had an easy time of it, for in the wake of the siege, Soliman's most fervent desire was to deliver a swift and crushing blow against the Christians. Hushed tongues told how after Malta the Sultan wandered the streets at night dressed as a commoner to overhear the curses rained on him by his people.

So. One morning a bostanci threw open the door to the dungeon and growled that my usual audience would not take place due to the departure ceremonies. Surely, I thought, my day of execution had arrived, and I thanked the Lord for my deliverance. But no, the Sultan commanded that the prisoner accompany the army in order that his history be continued. The departure festivities filled several days and surpassed anything the people of Constantinople had ever beheld. Rank upon rank of *silhadars* paraded before Soliman on the banks of the Golden Horn, followed by legions of spahis, then janissaries and at last common foot soldiers. All in all two hundred thousand men, no fewer, set off to war and even before they marched through the city gates, poets sang of the coming triumphs of the great Padishah of the world.

The Sultan in his age lacked e'en the strength to mount a horse and so he was driven in a magnificent carriage, pulled by a team of celestial stallions. On the second day of this long, arduous journey to Belgrade, Soliman again commanded my presence to take up the narration where I had left off ...

Twenty

His Majesty has requested from me a more reflective account, overbrimming with good judgment and sense, rather than a mere description of events. Muhibbi has observed that the early part of the tale took place when I was not of an age to form a sound judgment about anything. I acted, sometimes observed. Did I reflect? Please, I am a Spaniard. There can be little doubt that I was a perfect specimen of the "dull-witted grossness" Balthazar so often despaired of. Fortune had yet to reveal what she intended for me and, having no notion of my purpose, I often behaved in a manner fit for goats. To my sadness, I cannot promise His Majesty in what follows the wisdom we are assured comes with age. Unlike Balthazar, God ne'er granted me the gift to stand apart from the world and view it entire. All I have found is life, and with life, struggle.

For days after Gozo, the air in Birgu rang with naught but curses against Dragut and prayers for the slightest means wherewith to save Tripoli. All in vain. Suddenly, the prayers were answered. At the beginning of August, no more than a week after the *razzia*, the winds blew into the Great Port a pair of splendid galleys. Some declared it luck sooner than Providence, but what was true is that Gabriel de Luetz, Baron et Seigneur d'Aramont et Valabregues, France's Ambassador to the court of Soliman, had chosen to stop at Malta en route to Constantinople. The moment Lord d'Aramont's colors announced his arrival, cannons boomed in salutation and a whole host of Knights and townsfolk dashed down to Galley Creek to greet his embassy. The Grand Master himself appeared with the warmest courtesies, presented d'Aramont with a mule and, followed by all the Knights, led him up into Castle St. Angelo. The evening next, d'Homedes hosted the Ambassador at a sumptuous banquet, where the Grand Master explained to him the grim situation.

Oh, it was a magnificent and somber occasion, Balthazar recounted. The Ambassador brought greetings from King Henri II and declared the zeal and affection this most Christian monarch bore for the ancient and valiant Order of the Knights of St. John. Cheers and goblets went up all 'round, whereupon d'Aramont spoke of the great displeasure Henri would reveal upon learning of the Turkish depredations against Malta and Gozo. The Ambassador's single regret was that he had not arrived earlier in order to have been of service to the Religion.

To this speech the Grand Master replied, with eloquent thanks, that Lord d'Aramont might yet render a great service if he would consent to sail for Tripoli and convince the Turks to leave off their siege.

To that the Ambassador readily agreed.

"I say, we might well be at a theatre," whispered Balthazar to his neighbor at table. "What can d'Aramont alone do against the corsair and Sinan Pasha? We have no means whatsoever to force their hands."

The plan was roundly applauded.

Late the same evening, with a loud bang on the door, Balthazar roused me from Flaminia's bed. "Be prepared, thou rascal," he said, "to set sail for Tripoli tomorrow eve."

"Eh?" I replied, putting on my nightshirt and rubbing my eyes. "What are you at?"

"The Grand Master has convinced d'Aramont to parlay with the Turks over Tripoli. *Moy foy*, d'Homedes has e'en offered a *fregata* to guide them. It will need a crew."

"You are going?"

Balthazar sighed heavily, expelling the world. "Of course. Would the Abbé Balthazar de Marans des Homes-Saint-Martin miss an opportunity to witness utter futility in the face and, meanwhile, enjoy the desert sun? Tomorrow."

Without another word Balthazar slammed shut the door.

Flaminia, whose spirits had been struggling to regain firm ground after the *razzia*, was no little displeased by this turn of events. "O Madonna," she cried, throwing her arms around me, "you may never come back."

I commanded my *quiraca* to withhold her tears. By the Angel of Peace, we were to accompany an ambassador, not to fight. Without fail I'd bring her something from the markets of Tripoli. A ray of sun crossed her fair face at the promise, tho' she remained fearful. I myself had no stomach for the discussion, or perhaps no head, for I felt curiously out of sorts.

Flaminia at once proposed an old woman she knew near Zurrieq who would cure me of any ailment.

"Flaminia," I replied severely, untangling myself from her embrace, "you trade in philtres and talismans. Now you would have me visit a witch because my head aches. Do you take me for a fool? Do you not see what sacrilege this is, that you put yourself in dire jeopardy, and me as well?"

"Why?" she asked with utter and disarming perplexity, as she threaded her fingers nervously through her tresses. "The Mother Superior visits her on all occasions, and well she should, for this woman knows every cure."

"Ah!" I exclaimed, mightily vexed and tearing at my own hair, "I say you are dancing with Satan himself!"

At that Flaminia started and crossed her naked breasts. "Satan! Why, *mio cuore?*"

I gnashed my teeth, pacing before this stupid wench, finally erupting.

"Because the Dark Lord surrounds us," I cried, "and his demons fight against the Almighty and the Church of Good for the possession of our souls. Do you fear for your immortal soul, Flaminia?" I demanded, casting my wrathful gaze on her.

Again she started, greatly confused. "Blessed St. Vitus, who was Our Lord's friend," she said, crossing herself a second time, "yes, I pray every day for my salvation. Mother always told us *Jekk ma toqghodx kwiet, jigi x-xitan u jiehdok bis-sodda b'kollox.* If we misbehaved the Devil would come and carry us away with our bed. Please, Francisco, don't let the Devil take me, I beg you." She began to convulse with tears.

I had frightened her terribly. "Forgive me," I said, abruptly sitting and enfolding her in my arms. As I stroked her hair, Flaminia sobbed her constant dream, that she wished for no more than a house and to be buried in consecrated ground. I perceived then that this simple soul did not understand, and that I could not express what she did not understand.

In the morning I kissed her, leaving her a little money that Vergã had repaid me after his profitable expedition with Romegas, and took my leave.

The French embassy was cleaning and provisioning its galleys and would indeed not sail 'til evening. With some hours to spare I hied to the

Guasconi residence to inform Isabella I was joining the expedition. A servant ushered me to the entrance of the sitting room but there hesitated with a fearful expression on his face, refusing to announce me. I perceived the reason. Before Lady Emilia and Isabella stood Jean de Valette, robed and towering, and raging in anger.

"The Spaniard d'Homedes is the Emperor's dog, a base coward and a traitor," he roared. "He has forsworn the duty of the Holy Religion—to wield the sword of Christ, to fight the Infidel's mortal hatred of godliness, to defeat his insatiable desire to consume all Christendom." Hereon Parisot began to pace, halting, beginning anew, clenching his fist. "But God is purposeful; he is a father to warn us, not to destroy us. If the Spaniard had fortified Tripoli, moved the Convent thither, we might have frustrated the force and fury of the arrogant Turk. But no, this scoundrel we call Monsignore has disobeyed Christ and consigned us to the tiny desert of Malta. We sit here defenseless, able only to pray to God for our salvation, just as the snake pockets the Order's riches to aggrandize his family—"

At that instant the Knight noticed my presence at the doorway and halted in his tracks. Malachi might have stood before me. The bolts loosed from his eyes pierced me through and through, robbing me of all strength. I attempted to turn, to flee, as if I, a corrupt thing, had beheld the Holy of Holies, but my legs refused to obey and I remained rooted ... petrified.

"What are you doing here?" de Valette's words exploded.

"I—I—I merely, I—I—"

Lady Emilia's intercession alone saved me. She rose from her chair, offering me her hand and bade me join them. Still quaking, I took the empty seat between her and her daughter, not daring the slightest glance in Isabella's direction. "Parisot," she said, "you will remember Señor de Barai, who displayed such gallantry in the recent events, who at risk to his own life led Fra Nicolas to Città Notabile in the midst of the siege."

de Valette's fury abated sensibly as he recollected our meeting and hearing of my reckless flight to the Council. He natheless demanded to know wherefore I now appeared at the Guasconi door, and I gave the truthful answer, that I was accompanying the French embassy to Tripoli and had come to pay my respects before departure. At the mention of Tripoli, de Valette's eyes again took on the aspect of brimstone and, with no prompting from any side, he loosened, if slightly, the seals on the past.

"d'Homedes is hardly better than the traitor d'Amaral at Rhodes," he said somberly, "d'Amaral who offered to sell his soul to the Devil to encompass the ruin of the Order and l'Isle Adam with it. Andrea d'Amaral, the Chancellor who coveted the Grand Mastership and reviled l'Isle Adam for attaining it. Yes, he ordered his servant, the secret Jew Diaz, to fire a crossbow bolt into the enemy camp with a message revealing the desperate state of the garrison, that powder was low, that the defenders believed God had forsaken them, and that one last assault by the enemy would be sufficient to compel l'Isle Adam into accepting terms.

"But the dog Diaz was caught with his hand on the trigger, and no sooner had the cords of the rack been tightened around his wrists than the true state of affairs revealed itself. That d'Amaral plotted with the Infidel to betray the garrison, that he had secreted away gunpowder and lied to the Order about the stocks. He was no better than the Jewish spies in the Hospital itself, Jews who would sell the Convent to the barbarians as they sold Our Savior to Pilate. Justly did the Grand Master behead and quarter d'Amaral and present his pieces to the langues. d'Homedes deserves no better, for he would sell Tripoli to the Infidel for his own name."

Lady Emilia and Isabella saw beyond this speech; its fervor left me stunned. Mine eyes beheld a Crusader, heir of the lineage that stretched back to the struggle for the Holy Land. Mayhap before me stood the last Crusader, an exalted Vergã or Romegas, who thundered not for profit but for the glory of God and the Religion. Despite this understanding, I was unsettled—nay, shaken—by what I had just heard, and excused myself forthwith.

"I shall accompany you to the docks, Francisco," Isabella offered.

"I forbid it!" bellowed de Valette and I departed alone.

Not long after, a mantled figure scampered up to me in the Borgo. Isabella had snuck out the back door of the house. "You have time, I think," said she. "Let us walk on the hills."

We left through the gate. A strong, fine breeze was blowing, portending a swift voyage to Tripoli, and the scent of herbs infused the air. Both young people perceived it was the first time we had been in each other's company away from prying eyes. Both of us felt the promise and danger.

"Monsieur Parisot despises me," I said as we mounted the nearby hills, "and the enmity of one so powerful must surely bring a bad end to the weaker."

"You mustn't think so, Francisco," Isabella answered, snapping up a twig of thyme and putting it to her nose. "It is no more than the way he is."

Wherever the truth lay, I confess I was then blind to any greatness in the man. "I have ne'er heard anyone speak so ... " I fumbled for the word.

" ... zealously," Isabella completed my thought. "Yes, he has no life but the Religion and cannot comprehend another."

"He is extremely jealous of you," I remarked, still having not collected my wits.

Isabella nodded and drew her black *faldetta* close against the wind. "As my Godfather should be," she said pointedly, "but let us speak no more of Parisot today."

"What should we speak of?" I asked.

"Oh, Francisco, you men! I would poetry in my life."

Her answer disheartened me and I said, "Then I fear you must find a poet, or become one, for I am not he." Whatever I was good for in the world, the pen was assuredly not my weapon.

"Do not be such a dolt, Francisco," she answered swiftly, "that is not what I mean, and you well know it ... If you could only see Firenze, you would understand what I feel, that what happens on Malta, this conflict, is not what will endure. Oh, I can hardly express it." She stopped then, parting her veil, and gazed on me. "We have not known each other long."

"No."

"Only a few weeks, and during the most horrible of circumstances. And yet ... " Isabella went on to say that somehow, for reasons she could not voice, she felt we had known each other our entire lives and that we had merely been separated until recent days, and that our destiny would be shared.

At hearing these words, I again felt the omen in the marrow of my bones, the omen telling me Isabella was right, that however often we might be torn from one another, our paths would be forever intertwined. Yet when I answered her, as is so often the case before women, my courage fled and my tongue betrayed me. I told her I felt as she did, but that tho' my heart yearned for her, it could never be.

She started, sadly, and pressed for my meaning.

"We have talked of this. You are to be wed—"

"Do not speak of it!" she said angrily, with downcast eyes. "It is only because Parisot demands it. If necessary I will flee. I have never set eyes on my betrothed."

"You will do your duty. That is not all. The events carrying us in their stream ... We can never ... " I faltered. "I am not high-born."

"No you are not, that is true ... " she said with a strange harshness before catching herself. "Oh, it means nothing."

She could not disguise the flush on her face. "Your hesitation says otherwise," I replied. "What's more, there is something I have not told you." Hereat, Isabella looked onto me, questioning. "We will speak of it when I return from Tripoli, not ... today."

"Very well," she said, glancing downward again, "but I think it cannot be of much importance."

"It is." I refused to say more and we walked along the hills in silence as the wind whistled through the saffron. Tho' we exchanged no words, with each step the wind and silence bound us e'er more closely, until neither the young man nor young woman understood where the one left off and the other began. The intensity of that tightening cord became so unbearable that both of us stopped abruptly on the hillcrest and gazed at one another with wonderment written openly across our faces, a terrible rapture that quickly overwhelmed our ability to withstand it, and with it a certainty that we must either fall headlong into each other's embrace or turn away.

"I fear I do not have the strength to stand here any longer," said Isabella and turned away.

We walked back to the Borgo, the spell not broken but cast once and for all time. At the main square's fountain, Isabella gathered her strength and faced me again. "*Mon chevalier*," she said, almost losing herself to tears. "Be so good as to carry this token of my esteem with you, wherever Fortune may take you." From the folds of her cloak she brought forth a silken kerchief. With a brave expression she handed it to me, and I brought it to my lips. Her courage at once deserted her and she fled headlong, losing herself in the crowd.

For some moments I stood motionless in the center of the square with the kerchief pressed to my lips, drained of every thought and understanding, until a rough, unfamiliar voice accosted me.

"Signore."

Coming to my senses, I lifted my eyes to see a stocky Maltese peasant with a crooked nose standing before me in laced sandals. Some instants passed before I recognized Pietru, the Gozitan who had staggered into Birgu a week ago with his sad story. Neither could I by myself quickly make him out, for his Italian was too pitiful for a Spaniard to understand and he often fell into that incomprehensible Maltese when he could not discover the words. At length, tho', I perceived he desired to join the expedition.

"I am far from the person in command," I replied.

"S—signore," he stumbled in a deep voice, loud as a singer's but full of gravel, "my woman ... children, the Turks have them. They are in Tripoli. I go find them."

I could not refute his supposition, tho' the undertaking seemed to me utterly hopeless. Natheless, moved by his intentions, I presented Pietru to the Captain of the *fregata* the Grand Master had lent the Ambassador and, as he still had a place for an oarsman, he took the Gozitan on.

That evening at sunset, three crews spread canvas and the enlarged embassy set sail for Tripoli.

Twenty-One

The *fregata* we sailed on was smaller yet than a galiot, designed to fly. Fly we did, for with the wind at our backs, Malta fell from us, league upon league. To what end our speed? The Ambassador d'Aramont had no fixed plan and the few dozens of arquebusiers amongst us would threaten Turgut only with death by laughter. Our single weapons were d'Aramont and the oaths we swore never to forget Gozo.

A grim humor possessed each one of us. Eying the gulls above, Balthazar began a solemn discourse. "Niccolò," he said, hand on the mast, "writes that countries living in freedom make the swiftest progress, for a man living in freedom does not hesitate to enter into marriage and procreate. He is assured that his children, born free and not slaves, may—through their own ability, their virtue—become great men."

Thereat Balthazar abruptly halted and walked to the forecastle, where he leaned on one of the swivel guns. I followed, only to have him turn on me, as had he just divined the full import of the Florentine's words.

"With this task upon us, my friend, I begin to fear we Knights of St. John are a relic of a past age. These ideas—freedom, liberty—would seem to share not much common ground with a body o'er which rules a Grand Master with the authority of a king, which owns in perpetual fiefdom an island and its unwilling subjects, and yet which does nothing to protect them." Again the Knight dropped into silence. "Natheless," he eventually went on, "relics, we know, can work miracles, and for that reason I believe we can be of aid to Christendom. One thing I see clearly—we must reforge ourselves just as the world is now reforging itself in the cauldron of this century. I have said as much before, so I quickly say Amen to this Paternoster."

Throughout this speech I stared at Balthazar in alarm. When he finally admitted to the Knights' value, I sighed a great relief, yet did not press him for a more exact meaning. Instead, I asked about a subject that at this moment also consumed me, one that he had skillfully avoided during every attempt I'd made to invade his past: women.

"Have you ever been in love?" I said abruptly.

Balthazar long fixed his eye on his inquisitor. At last he said, "A man who has ne'er loved has ne'er lived." He pushed the swivel gun away and, without a word more, made his way astern.

Watching the lonely figure, my gaze fell on Pietru, who was putting his back into the oar. The earnest expression on that round, burnt face showed no despondency but a fierce, e'en hopeless determination. Did this simple soul understand how futile his undertaking? With the wind, the *ciurma* was having an easy time of it and I was able to speak with the Gozitan two or three times during his rest periods. To understand one another hadn't gotten easier. Over and over again he grunted, "*Hakit Turok!*" as near as I could understand, which another oarsman said meant "Damn the Turks!" Pietru thrust into my hand a tiny doll, a wholly naked figure of a woman, but I could not discern whether it was a token from his wife or an image to cast a spell, or both. When I handed it back to him with a puzzled shrug, he laughed and slapped me on the back. Pointing at himself he said that I should call him "Xabaw"—that is "Shabaw." It meant nothing, as far as I could tell, but was how friends named him.

So swift was our passage that the embassy reached the Barbary coast two evenings after setting out. We struck the sails and lay by the wind until dawn, when we perceived to our distress that due to the pilots' ignorance of these waters, a strong current had driven us at least ten leagues off course. The blunder cost us the full morning. Finally the cape our destination came into view and suddenly we found ourselves at the rear of the entire Turkish armada. All one hundred and forty infidel ships, lying directly between us and Tripoli.

The Ambassador decided that the *fregata* should convey his intention to parlay to Sinan. All of us aboard, you can be sure, counted our heartbeats as Captain Cotignac slowly moved forward in the midst of the same fleet that only days before had brought the world's misery to Malta and Gozo. With great reluctance the Knights among us divested themselves of any sign of the Order.

"May God forgive us this cowardice," said Balthazar, kissing his crucifix.

The watchmen, tho', made certain the French colors were flying brightly, for France and the Ottomans remained on friendly terms, and they saluted the Turkish vessels with the *fregata's* light guns to assure them we had come in peace. An eternity passed while we held our breaths, expecting at each instant to be blown from the water. But the Turkish cannon returned the salute and the embassy passed, whole.

"Perhaps God has forgiven us," said Balthazar.

At length our vessel approached the Reale of Sinan Pasha. A few of the Knights climbed aboard and shortly after returned in the company of a Reis and his janissary, Reis for "Captain"; Turgut the Captain, I supposed. Two weeks ago I'd beheld a host of janissaries on the plain before Mdina. Now one walked close enough by me that we might engage in a single combat. Such was my blood instinct, but nay, we nodded to one another, e'en bowed as he stepped aboard. The fellow was a warrior bred. He swaggered in his yellow and red costume with a bold arrogance, twiddling his fiery moustaches with one hand and with the other shouldered the longest arquebus I'd set eyes on. With each step a mighty scimitar swung at his side, and to complete the spectacle, from that peculiar folding headdress he sported a plume that reached fair to his ass. Balthazar measured him from head to toe, nodding appreciatively.

Yet at this moment the janissary was, if no friend, neither a foe and had been sent with his Captain merely to escort the Ambassador to Sinan Pasha. This was accomplished in short order. The two met briefly, d'Aramont returned to his galley and, before a glass had emptied, twenty-five muttons and other refreshments arrived on board, a present from the Pasha to the Ambassador. Soon we were ferrying a veritable stream of Turks and Christians between the two galleys, as well as a small German clock and pieces of fine cloth from Paris and Holland. Sinan was delighted.

Everyone breathed deeply.

Thereat began an episode as strange and astonishing in its own way as Turgut's escape from Djerbé, and of greater consequence. His Majesty should recollect that a week before our arrival, Sinan and Turgut had put into Tagiora, but four leagues from Tripoli, and at Tagiora one Agha Morat welcomed them with a sumptuous feast. No one seemed certain whether His Majesty had appointed as Bey this eunuch—a born Christian with whom his father's favorite concubine acted out all manner of depravities—or whether he'd appointed himself. But the feasting went on for several days. When Sinan had finally rested, he sent a Moor to the enemy garrison. The Moor rode out to Tripoli with a white flag, stopping before the ditch of the castle where he planted a stick into the ground, attached to which was a letter addressed to no one in particular. He hailed those on the ramparts, crying out only that he would return on the morrow for an answer. Thereat he righted his turban and galloped off.

Gaspard de Vallier was the Religion's Governor of Tripoli, one of those Knights d'Homedes had sent hither out of annoyance. Learning of the message-bearing stick, de Vallier sent a Knight out for the letter and read with astonishment:

Surrender to the mercy of the Great Sultan, who has commanded me to reduce this place to his obedience. Do so and you are at liberty to go with your possessions. Otherwise I will put every one of you to the sword. By his own hand, Sinan Pasha.

de Vallier had but fifty Knights under him and some six hundred soldiers. Natheless, he immediately penned a reply and had it posted on the same stick:

This place has been entrusted to me to govern by my Religion. I cannot surrender it to anyone but to him commanded by the Grand Master and the Council. Against anyone else I will defend it to the death. Signed, Mareschal Gaspard de Vallier.

Well, upon receiving this answer, Sinan and Turgut betook their fleets to Tripoli and lost no time in opening trenches to the east of the city. It was at exactly this juncture that our embassy arrived.

Aboard Sinan's galley, d'Aramont pleaded in the name of King Henri to leave off the siege; Sinan refused. He showed the Ambassador the orders from Soliman, who was bitterly aggrieved that the Knights had reft Africa from Turgut and had so violated the oath they gave when quitting Rhodes, that they would never make war on the Great Sultan again. Of course, the Knights of St. John never took such a vow, but the Pasha went on with every complaint. Matters got worse when, maugre all the Ambassador's precautions, Sinan learned that our *fregata* had come from Malta.

"Why is it that you sail on a boat of the Knights of St. John?" the Pasha asked with great curiosity.

"Your Excellency," replied the Ambassador with grace, "we are negotiating on behalf of the Order. The Grand Master lent us this small vessel."

Sinan wouldn't accept d'Aramont's explanation. "For what purpose? Have the French allied themselves with our enemy the Knights?"

Not only was he unable to allay the Pasha's suspicions, Sinan refused to allow the Ambassador to communicate with the besieged until the castle had fallen. Hearing this, d'Aramont understood his journey was for naught and that he should continue forthwith to Constantinople in order to negotiate directly with His Majesty. But Sinan had taken a liking to d'Aramont and insisted that the embassy tarry a while. He would be pleased to show the Ambassador the trenchworks he was preparing for the taking of the garrison. He would be so pleased that he ordered the rigging of the embassy's vessels taken down.

Unable to refuse the Pasha's polite entreaties, the following morning Lord d'Aramont led a sizeable entourage to an opulent pavilion on the beach. We entered to discover a slave wrapping a magnificent turban about Sinan's head as he comfortably breakfasted. It was the first time I had actually set eyes on the Sultan's Admiral and clearly this renegado Italian had not led a pauper's life. Despite the little stomach he'd allowed himself in his fifty years, Sinan was strongly built and when he arose, his silks parted before him. He then personally escorted the entire retinue to a hilltop where we might comfortably observe the opening of trenches before the castle.

Thus Balthazar and I found ourselves guests at the siege of Tripoli. *Si, o reniego la que me parió, si no es Verdad.*

Twenty-Two

But it was true. To the east of Tripoli, with a magnificent view of the sea, the city and the castle, the embassy gathered upon this hilltop and watched the digging of the trenches and the emplacement of batteries, all the while listening to Sinan Pasha as he tenderly embraced the thirty-six pieces wherewith he intended to reduce the citadel. If my astonishment at this turn of events was unsurpassed, it grew. With a wave of his hand, Sinan dispatched his janissary and a few moments later, ascending from the trenches to be presented to the Ambassador, appeared our great foeman himself.

For a second time I had crossed paths with Turgut. At arm's length stood the man who had carried the entire population of a Christian island into slavery. My vow to kill him on sight burned in my mind. Did I act? No. To my e'erlasting shame, I did no more than bow with the others, and my thoughts lingered less on how to send his soul to Hell than on the fate of my entrails should the corsair recollect me from Gelves. He gave no hint of recognition. Balthazar was in sorer straits. The greater likelihood was that Turgut would remember *him*. A sensible shudder ran through the Knight's frame, but the white beard revealed not the slightest interest.

As Turgut exchanged greetings with the Ambassador Lord d'Aramont, for the first time I voiced to myself a sense that had been slowly building during the past months—that the events into whose stream I had fallen since departing Spain were of a measure larger than I had originally supposed; that the powerful figures amongst whom I found myself intended to change the face of the world and would perhaps succeed. At that moment my life faded into inconsequence.

The strangeness of our predicament rose yet again when the cannoneers and arquebusiers from the castle suddenly began firing at the slaves digging the trenches, causing no few injuries among them. At once a small force of Knights sallied forth from the castle gate. We watched in amazement as these horsemen, despite resistance from the enemy, galloped full tilt into the Turkish camp, almost to Sinan's very pavilion on the beach, where after a short skirmish, they managed to carry a Turkish prisoner back into the garrison. Seeing this, it was all for the Knights among us to stifle a cheer, but they held their tongues. Sinan decided, tho', that our embassy was needlessly exposing itself and led everyone back to his camp, warning us not to leave our galleys on the morrow, lest the Turks mistake us for the enemy. As for today, we were free to see the town, should we please.

"I bowed to Turgut," I spat, cursing myself as Balthazar and I walked along the beach in the direction of the galleys.

"As you may again," the Knight replied. "By such actions do we erode our vows to achieve a greater purpose. It is well to know one's weaknesses." Thereat Balthazar abruptly halted in his tracks, turning toward the garrison and the town next to it. "I must get into that citadel," he said without warning.

"¿Por que?" I exclaimed, startled at the proposal. "By the Penance of Mary Magdalene, what can you hope to achieve? The situation is hopeless. The Knights must capitulate or be slaughtered."

Balthazar continued to gaze on Tripoli, laying plans in his mind's eye. "If they are to capitulate," he answered, "mayhap I can help them receive better terms. If they are to be put to the sword, I, a Knight, am obliged to die with them."

There, with my feet sunk into the sand, I shook my head in incomprehension. "Is this valor, Fra Balthazar de Marans des Homes-Saint-Martin?" I said to the sometime Abbé, flinging his damnèd question back at him, "or stupidity?"

"I have taken my vow," he said mulishly.

In exasperation I threw up my hands. "Your vow will hardly alter the outcome, which is ordained!"

But his mind was fixed on his purpose and Balthazar at last ordered me to silence, saying that as the Ambassador was unable to communicate with the garrison, someone must. "I shall enter the citadel on the other side, from the town."

My sigh of capitulation was deep, but before we entered the town I must fetch the Gozitan Pietru, who intended to find his wife here.

"*That* I say is hopeless," scowled Balthazar.

Thus facing futility on every side, we returned to the *fregata* for Pietru, dressing him in some proper clothes so that he might at least pass as a servant. The Ambassador's chamberlain and geographer, Nicolas de Nicolay, accompanied us for our own safety, and together we took a caique back to shore, where hard by Sinan's camp the Turks had set up a slave market.

Into that place the Turks had unloaded the thousands of Christians they'd seized on Sicily and Gozo and were now selling them to the highest bidders. The slave masters had stripped every one of the captives stark naked and with blows of the stick forced them to run back and forth to show the customers they had no bodily impediments. The buyers, who came from near and far, visited the eyes and teeth of these people, as were they horses.

With this spectacle before him, tears sprang from Pietru's eyes. Suddenly, seized by an uncontrollable fever, he rushed headlong into the crowds of slaves, turning each one toward him, hoping to find his wife and children. At once I sped after him, lest the Turks discover that he was not a buyer but, in their eyes, another slave.

"Pietru," I said, grabbing him by the shoulder, "soft."

My words failed to reach him and he continued to struggle. With the strength of a bull he loosed himself from me, tearing off once more. By now, a Turkish slave master had noticed the commotion and was moving toward us both, bastinado raised. Luckily, Balthazar and Nicolay caught up with us and intervened.

From that moment on we stayed close. Balthazar, too, had his reasons for coming here. As we walked through this bazaar, as the Turks called it, the Knight had his eyes peeled for the traitorous Governor of Gozo, de Sesse. "I'll buy the scoundrel back if we see him," he said, "to stand trial. But he may prefer to be sold to an infidel so that he may ransom himself and regain his freedom."

Amid those thousands of slaves, so difficult to distinguish from one another in their nakedness, we did not find de Sesse. We walked, strolled in the bazaar for several hours, listening to the slavers try to drive up the prices of their wares by fair speeches: this one was strong, that one able to cook, another no doubt came from a rich family and was certain to fetch a great ransom. Time after time Pietru turned a woman's face toward him certain that she was his wife, only to meet with disappointment. Time after time, he lifted the chin of a child to find another's. Neither my hand nor the madness about him ever loosened its grip, and e'en as we left the market, stepping over scorpions that crawled about the earth, he continued to shudder.

"They must have been sold, Xabaw," I told Pietru.

"*Qatt!*" he replied angrily, "I find them."

Choosing not to argue, we headed off along the beach to the town itself. Soon we reached the western edge of the harbor, where a small tower stood above the docks and where fair palm trees stood guarding the main gate of Tripoli.

As we entered, the exotic, tropical paradise I had conjured in my imagination dispersed like a morning dream. To be sure, palms and fig trees provided shade everywhere. Strong walls surmounted by a great number of turrets surrounded the town, but most of the houses stood in ruins. Every street boasted wells and sculpted fountains, from which the Moors around us paused to drink. At the center of the town a triumphal arch of white marble loomed above us. Atop it, two great griffons pulled winged Victory in her chariot, but like everything else in Tripoli, it appeared decrepit with age. Balthazar, who had once been posted here, claimed the arch to be over a thousand years old, dating from Roman times.

But the Knight showed little interest in seeing the sights. With purposeful strides he suddenly set off across the town to where the walls broke off at the ditch before the castle. There, practically in full view of the enemy trenches, he turned to Pietru and me as the two of us caught up to him. "Getting in will be easy enow. Getting out I fear will be the difficult business. Go back with Nicolay. Tell him I will join you later."

I protested a last time. "Lord Balthazar, you averred you would come to hither to look Folly in the face, not to take part in it. Do not do this thing, which can have no good outcome. I beg you."

"Go." Balthazar embraced me, then without another word turned and, across the open space, hailed the sentry atop the castle walls. That one recognized his countryman and shortly thereafter let the bridge down. The Turks by now had caught sight of us but it was too late. As the arquebuses opened fire, Balthazar sped across the bridge and disappeared into the fortress.

Pietru and I found Nicolay at the fountains. Hard pressed to explain what had become of our comrade, we repeated only what we'd been told, that Balthazar would join us later. Despondently we made our way back to the *fregata*.

The Mareschal de Vallier embraced Balthazar warmly and, in the chapel where the younger Knight had found the senior, Balthazar told him forthwith what he had not told me: "The French Ambassador asked me to speak to you."

de Vallier shook his grey head in puzzlement.

"Ah," Balthazar nodded, at once understanding. "Gaspard, you may be unaware that the French Ambassador Lord d'Aramont has arrived and is, as we speak, negotiating with Sinan Pasha."

"Negotiating for what, Navarre?"

Again Balthazar nodded. "He has come at the Grand Master's behest to convince the Pasha to leave off the siege, but unfortunately God has not handed him a plum wherewith to negotiate, and Sinan is entertaining us as his ... *guests* until he has finished with this enterprise. What is your intention?"

"As I told that snout of a dog," replied de Vallier, putting his arm around Balthazar's shoulder and leading him out into the sun, "I cannot give up Tripoli without orders from d'Homedes or the Council."

"d'Homedes gave no such authorization. Gaspard, the situation is grave. If you can hold out, it may give us time to bring succours from Malta or Sicily. But the embassy is presently hostage to Sinan, and d'Aramont's golden tongue does not seem sufficiently pure to dissuade him from a siege or allow us to depart. Sinan has orders from the Grand Turk to take Tripoli and he has a month before the weather turns."

The two walked past the barracks toward the St. Jacque bastion and the Mareschal replied that he could hold out neither for succours nor the weather. Antonio Doria's fleet had been wrecked on Lampedusa and those reinforcements had ne'er arrived. Now but fifty Knights were under his command and six hundred soldiers, including those Calabrian sheep herders the Grand Master had uselessly sent hither. "I would sooner rely on the two hundred Moors who have served us so faithfully."

Now Balthazar put to him the other question: "Are you prepared to surrender?"

de Vallier halted in his tracks before the powder magazine, shooting at his old friend a gaze of disbelief. "How can you suggest it, Navarre?"

"I am not suggesting it, Gaspard. Remember Rhodes. After six months the slaves were dead, the powder and shot exhausted. The Council urged the Grand Master 'not to make the enemy's victory more splendid by our deaths,' and that 'when all human hope is gone, it is our duty to try to come to terms so that we may vindicate our loss at another time and place ... '"

"We have not reached that place," replied de Vallier.

"Of course not. But my opinion has always been that the Order would do well to abandon Tripoli. Look at these ruins. They may be of value to Carlos but they are of no value to us. We cannot defend the place, as has of this day become apparent to all."

The Mareschal's face reddened and he fair covered his ears. "If you speak further I may not hear you, Navarre. This borders on treason."

"Only to French Knights, Gaspard, who are married to tropical dreams," replied Balthazar calmly, "and who are more shamed by a humiliating retreat than heartened by the benefits of cutting off a useless and corrupt limb." They had now reached the Captain's quarters. "Perhaps you have something to bargain with. Gold, jewels, anything. Just tell me, Gaspard, what word to the Ambassador?"

"Be my guest for dinner, and tomorrow you shall have it."

Balthazar accepted the invitation, fearing that tomorrow would be too late.

Aye. Sinan began his bombardment hours before dawn, just as Balthazar was preparing to depart. The Knight, understanding that war throws all plans into disarray, resolved to remain in the castle and cast his lot with his fellows. Luckily, Sinan had directed his fire against the St. Jacque bastion, which had been reinforced with earth and was the strongest part of the fort. Tho' over the next day the outer facings gradually collapsed under the cannonade, the balls merely sank into the exposed terre-plein beneath, producing no effect. For several days the Turks kept up this useless endeavor.

Those of us stranded aboard the embassy's vessels knew only that the pounding didn't cease day or night. At every moment I wondered to the fate of Balthazar, praying that the Knight remained alive. Pietru and I played dice on deck, but e'en the Gozitan began to perceive that the straits of the Knights trapped within the castle were becoming more desperate by the hour.

Through all this, Sinan continued to serve the Ambassador at his opulent meals, cheerfully hosting his guest while the cannons thundered. On the second or third evening, Sinan's janissary ushered in a villainous Provençal from Cavaillon who had been seduced by a Moorish whore to betray his religion.

"You're wasting your time," the renegado-worm declared to Sinan. "You cannot level that bastion, which is the strongest in the castle. You must direct your guns to the wall of St. Barbe, next to it, which is crumbling with age."

Sinan immediately sent this advice to Turgut, who lost no time in getting to work. Within a day the effect was apparent.

Inside the castle, de Vallier and Balthazar watched the curtain collapse in a cloud of dust, leaving a tremendous breach. Quickly appraising the situation, the Mareschal ordered that trenches be dug behind the breach and artillery placed there. The *agozzini* took their lashes to the slaves, who at once began digging, but almost immediately balls began to crash into the thick of them. Half a dozen fell in the first moments as the enemy fire continued relentlessly, arquebuses joining the cannon. By evening most of the slaves had been killed. A officer ran up to de Vallier, who commanded from atop the St. Jacque bastion.

"Sir, the slaves—those that remain alive—are refusing to work. They would rather be beaten and whipped than exposed to this fire."

"That is hardly surprising," remarked Balthazar, observing the wholesale struggle now going on below between the slaves and the *agozzini*. "There is certain death at that breach. Soon enough the enemy will storm it."

Even as they debated the best course of action, a Serving Brother who had run over from the small harbor fort, that *chastellet*, approached the Mareschal.

"Sir, the Calabrian dogs at the tower have mutinied. They've blown up the powder magazine and some have escaped in a brigantine."

"Those base cowards!" cursed de Vallier, clenching his fist as tho' it would do some good.

"Gaspard," said Balthazar as another section of the wall below fell with a deafening, prolonged rumble, "at this moment we need Spartans. What we have are shepherds who have never faced a gun, yet alone a siege."

Without answering, de Vallier turned and climbed down to the bailey, where in the chapel he took the Holy Eucharist and prayed for deliverance. Peace eluded him. The Calabrian Captain himself rushed into the chapel to inform the Mareschal that his troops were deserting their posts. de Vallier rose quickly from his knees, ran from the church and—faced a garrison of mutineers.

"I've lived a day too long," he muttered, loud enough for his officers to overhear, "that I should be spared Turkish guns to be faced by this rebellion."

The crowd before him was not to be placated. A Calabrian, so frightened that he fairly danced in terror, cried out that their position was hopeless. "The Turks will storm the breach! The Turks will storm the breach!" he shouted over and over again, like a madman. As pitiful as the sight of him was, the other mutineers—who by now included most of the garrison's common soldiers—began yelling that he was right. "The while flag now! Now!" the cries went up.

At first de Vallier refused. "This perfidiousness causes me nothing but sorrow," he answered the men against him. "I say that the moment to demonstrate our valor has now come upon us."

"By my Sins, I am not the least surprised that you call for a useless defense," shouted one Majorcan Knight Fuster—even Knights had now joined the rebels. "You are a damned Frenchman and we know your damned Ambassador has arrived and he will save your damned fucking skin. The rest of us—. We can't expect any quarter from those damned barbarians. Why do you refuse to consider the safety of your men?"

Suffering these blasphemous insults with equanimity, de Vallier called for Commandeur Copier, the same who had fought so valiantly at Africa, to inspect the breach. Shortly Copier reported that it was not so terrible but that they could repair and defend it.

The rebels weren't about to take the word of a Frenchman and, under the continued roar of the guns, they sent their own man, a Spaniard, to look. Soon this Guevara returned. "How can you lie like such a whore?"

he demanded of Copier angrily, spitting at his feet. "By nightfall that entire curtain will be down and that will be the end of us."

Balthazar saw by the abrupt change in countenance of the mutineers that they had no intention of allowing the Knights to buy their own glory with the lives of their subordinates. With redoubled fury, shouts and curses exploded in the bailey until de Vallier understood that control of his forces had slipped from his grasp.

"I'll double your pay," he offered as a last resort, but they spat on the ground. Seeing no hope, the Mareschal begged the soldiers to grant him the space of a single glass, repairing immediately to his quarters and calling his senior Knights into council. Balthazar watched the deliberations unfold as had they been ordained from Above. Each man cursed the base cowardice of the rebels and each man ended by conceding no choice remained. When the council emerged to face that mob, de Vallier did the only thing left to him: he ordered a Serving Brother to hoist the white flag above the ramparts.

As the rebels cheered, de Vallier glanced at Balthazar with an expression of animosity, resignation and understanding. At least that is how Balthazar took it, for what else could be in the Mareschal's heart?

Twenty-Three

Thus the affair began. Sinan at once ordered the bombardment to cease. Balthazar offered to lead a delegation to the Turks to arrange terms, and with a solemn nod de Vallier accepted the proposal, but the mutineers refused to let Navarre pass. "It's because of you French that we've come to this fucking end!" the Majorcan Fuster shouted, "and we know you'll only barter for the tips of your own pricks."

The rebels conferred quickly among themselves and dispatched their own deputies, the selfsame Fuster and the Spaniard Guevara. Under a flag of truce they picked their way across the enemy trenches to Sinan's pavilion on the beach, where Fuster bowed and offered to give up Tripoli should the Pasha allow them their life and liberty, their possessions and if he would transport them back to Malta.

Sinan listened to the offer with attention. Then he broke out laughing. "Hah, hah, hah! The rashness of you infidels knows no bounds! Hah!" The Admiral could hardly contain himself, nearly pissing in his pants. "You cannot expect to hold out in such a weak place, any more than your ancestors did against Saladin at Hittin! A few more days and every one of you dogs will be dead. I'll make you this offer: If your order is prepared to pay the Great Sultan for the expenses incurred during this war, I will provide your passage to Malta."

Fuster sputtered that they had no authority to agree to such a plan, at which Sinan shouted that the jackals should get out of his sight at once. Then, popping a fig into his mouth, he added, "I will put every one of you to the sword."

His Majesty knows better than I whether Sinan's offer was genuine. Whatever the case, the delegation removed itself incontinently from the Pasha's tent and fairly collided with Turgut himself, who demanded to know how the negotiations stood. No sooner did the dread corsair hear from their trembling lips what had just taken place, than he raged into the Admiral's marquee.

"*Senin techruben yok kopek!*" Turgut lashed out at the Pasha. "To what purpose do you prolong this siege? Succours may arrive from Malta, the weather may turn. If you reduce the castle to ruins it will be of no more use to us than it was to the accursed knights." Pausing, Turgut helped himself to an apple. "You are the Sultan's *Kapudan* and meant to be more clever than a goat. Sign a treaty. When you control this place, you can read it as you like."

Despite his counsellor's haughty tone, Sinan recognized the music of good advice and forthwith called back Fuster and Guevara, swearing by the Padishah's head not to require payment of expenses. He then told them to summon the Mareschal.

A few hours later Gaspard de Vallier himself stepped into the Turkish camp accompanied by his lieutenant Commandeur Monfort. Fuster and the other rebels were pleased to let the Mareschal take charge again, reasoning that by the treatment he received they'd discover what to expect for themselves. But word of the mutiny had already reached Sinan and when de Vallier presented himself before the Admiral, the Turk said, "Have you brought the money which I demanded as recompense for the cost of the expedition?"

"You have pledged a solemn oath," replied de Vallier without exhibiting the least emotion, tho' knowing at once Sinan for a liar, "and our capitulation depends on its inviolability. Should you forswear it, we will fight to the last drop of blood."

de Vallier's icy calm sent Sinan into a rage. "It is not to dogs like you that a man should keep oaths!" he cried, declaring again that the Order survived only because Soliman the Lawgiver had generously allowed the infidels to depart from Rhodes with their lives, yet the moment they reached Malta they violated their own oath never to make war against him again.

The Mareschal replied that the Knights had never sworn such an oath, and he could prove it with the document signed by the Sultan's own hand, but Sinan had had his fill. With a snap of his fingers he ordered de Vallier to be taken. Then and there the guards stripped the Knight of his clothing, shackled him in irons and prodded him out of the pavilion toward the boats.

As he was led away, de Vallier turned to Monfort: "Tell Copier and the others they are to regard me as a dead man. They are to comport themselves as their duty and honor require in this dark circumstance."

Now Sinan cast his eye on the lieutenant. "Go back to Tripoli and tell your comrades that if I don't receive the money I demand immediately, I shall claim it from their own persons—by selling them all into slavery."

Soon Commandeur Copier knew of Sinan's decision. The Knights immediately comprehended that all negotiations were at an end.

"The only thing for it is to mine the walls and bury us and the enemy together," said Balthazar to Copier, who agreed.

"Men," he said, "if we are going to make an end, let us make the best one possible and deny the Infidel his prize." Thereat the Commandeur ordered some Knights to take pick and shovel in hand and begin undermining the bastions at critical places, and others to bring the powder caskets.

The rebels had no intention of being interred. Fuster stepped up to Copier and spat his refusal to be made part of this suicide. At once the enraged Copier unsheathed his sword and began beating Fuster with the flat of it. It availed nothing. Errera, another Spaniard, cried out, "I'd sooner give myself over to the Turks than bring this fortress down on my head!" A cheer went up from his fellows.

Copier now found himself in the same hard place de Vallier had before. Maugre entreaties and threats, nothing persuaded the mutineers. At Copier's order, the loyal Knights took lashes and cudgels to the rebel soldiers, only to be met by drawn weapons; Calabrians were fleeing hither and yon, displaying no more courage than the sheep they herded daily, and moment by moment swordfights broke out across the bailey. In the midst of this mayhem Balthazar himself strode up to Fuster, grabbed him by the throat and threatened to impale him unless he ordered his men to the task. Even as a wet circle spread over his pants, nothing could force Fuster to take part in mining the castle.

"It is for naught," said Balthazar, hurling the traitor to the ground and returning to Copier. "We would do better to release them to their liberty to fend for themselves. They are of no value to us."

That night the Council agreed that the mutineers should be let go.

What happened during the next morning of chaos, Your Majesty, only God can say with certainty. The Commandeur dispatched Monfort again to plead with Sinan to allow three hundred men to walk free of the castle. Once the lieutenant had departed, Copier advised his loyal Moors to escape inland while they could. He embraced their leader, who sallied forth across the bridge at the head of nearly two hundred Moors in full view of the enemy. As Balthazar watched from the bastion, the Turks gave chase. Some of the Moors escaped over the hills, others were captured. Because they had betrayed their religion, Sinan ordered them hacked to pieces, and they were, amid great shouts of joy.

Not long after, the Agha Morat himself appeared on a horse before the fortress walls and announced that Sinan had agreed to allow everyone inside to leave with his life, liberty and possessions. At hearing these words the Calabrians and other soldiers cast aside their few remaining arms and began streaming out through the breaches toward the Turkish camp, followed incontinently by the women and children who had been trapped inside the stronghold.

"Do not trust the Agha!" Copier shouted after them. "Wait until Monfort has returned!"

His words were as barley before wind. No sooner had the mutineers crossed the Turkish trenches than Morat's troops surrounded them, stripped them without regard to rank or station and threw everyone into irons.

Tho' the Knights didn't know it, when Monfort had presented Sinan with the request for liberty for three hundred, the Pasha once again sent for de Vallier. "Let us dispense with the demand for money," Sinan said to the Mareschal. "Go back to the fort and bring out your men. I will be happy to take them back to Malta." Of course de Vallier, now knowing Sinan's true color, refused to be a dog to this trick. Turgut himself took Sinan aside and suggested sending the perfidious Agha Morat to the fort.

At least this is what Ambassador d'Aramont told me. Regardless of the route of treachery, at last the loyal Knights found themselves abandoned within the castle.

"We must either blow this castle into dust at once or surrender," said Balthazar to Copier, glancing about the empty square. "We have fewer than thirty Knights left amongst us and cannot defend ourselves."

"Nor do we have the time to effect the mining of the walls," answered Copier. "The Turks can overrun us within moments. This is a sad hour for the Religion. I dare say the saddest in five hundred years."

Balthazar smiled. "Then I say we take the lesson of our brethren at Rhodes and do not make the enemy's victory more glorious by our deaths. We shall find another occasion when it is worth selling our lives."

The two men embraced each other. They and the remaining Knights cast down their arms and walked forth from the breach in the castle wall.

When the Ambassador and his party, including myself, arrived for dinner at Sinan's pavilion, which had been moved near to the castle, a horrible scene greeted us: Copier, Balthazar and the other Knights all lying on the sand, naked and in irons.

"A shameful injustice, I say!" exclaimed d'Aramont to Sinan, catching sight of the prisoners, "and a violation of your oath."

I felt hot tears streaming down my cheeks.

Sinan laughed, sneered. "One hundred thousand soldiers witnessed their oath at Rhodes," he averred again, "never to make piracy against the Sultan's ships." Just then, the ordnance of all one hundred forty vessels in the Turkish armada fired a victory salute, as if to seal the truth of the Pasha's words, and the heavens and earth seemed to split under the thunder of it.

d'Aramont refused to dispute Sinan, but e'en under the roar of the artillery he resolved that the Christians should go free. All evening, as Turkish musicians serenaded us and one hundred officers dressed in the finest golden robes served excellent meats and fine wines, the Ambassador bargained with the Pasha. At first Sinan agreed to let two hundred go, the oldest and most infirm, much as he had offered at Gozo. The rest he would keep in slavery.

But d'Aramont would make no exceptions and continued haggling. As the night wore on, the Ambassador ordered a sack of money and a silver cup brought from the ships, then a pavilion worth three hundred ducats. To all this Sinan refused. At last, d'Aramont promised liberty to thirty Turkish slaves from good families who were being held on Malta. I caught my breath, for I knew the Grand Master had authorized no such exchange. But the offer pleased Sinan and, as the sun rose, he agreed to release all the surviving soldiers.

The following evening, the French embassy, its galleys laden with Calabrian shepherds, treacherous Spanish Knights and a few disheartened brethren dressed in spare rags, set sail for Malta. After four decades the Christians had lost Tripoli, Agha Morat was proclaimed Bey and the Ottomans ruled the east of the Mediterranean, from sunrise to Djerbé.

Twenty-Four

The Knights made their way back to Malta sick at heart to have taken part in such a debacle, yet grateful to the heroic Ambassador for having saved their lives. The winds on that northward journey were against us and it took four days to reach Lampedusa, during which time the pilot of d'Aramont's galley died of ship fever, six galley slaves also, and the crew cast all the bodies overboard to feed the fishes. As we passed Lampedusa, Balthazar and I fell to reminiscing. But somehow, tho' our sojourn there and my initiation into battle had taken place only three months earlier, their importance had already faded under the patina of experience.

We put into Malta late the following night to find Galley Creek closed by a great chain stretching between Fort St. Angelo and the tip of l'Isola, a chain sometimes raised at night by a mighty capstan at the base of St. Angelo. Knights said each of its thousand links, manufactured in Venice, cost the Religion ten ducats, twice the price of a kiss from the most expensive Venetian whore, and the spectacle of it lifting from the water never failed to cause a gasp. A gargantuan chain barring our entrance was a far cry from the welcome we'd all expected to greet the Ambassador as the savior and deliverer of the Knights. Natheless, everyone understood it was well past *l'hora della ruffiana* and so d'Aramont sent a skiff ahead over the moonlit water to inform the Grand Master of the embassy's safe return and to have the creek opened. With his deputy he also dispatched a letter he had prepared, giving an account of the events at Tripoli.

We waited and waited outside the chain. Finally the messenger appeared in great perplexity. Upon reading d'Aramont's letter, the Grand Master had hurled it immediately to the ground, declaring that he would not receive the Ambassador until he had met with the Council in the morning.

"This does not bode well," remarked Balthazar needlessly.

"What could cause the Grand Master to behave so?" I asked.

"Be certain, my friend: he is not pleased to hear of the fall of Tripoli. But perhaps morning shall prove wiser."

Many of the Knights, exhausted after their long ordeal, refused to spend all night aboard the vessels and put ashore on the galleys' boats. Parisot, being informed by Mareschal de Vallier himself of our return, sent out all manner of food and refreshment to his friend the Ambassador. I, merely an extra hand on the *fregata*, received no opportunity to disembark.

Morning proved no wiser. As the sun climbed into the sky, the embassy received a message from the Grand Master that it might dock at Galley Creek. The harbor watch ordered the slaves to put their backs into the capstan, the chain fell beneath the water and our galleys slid to the quayside. But the silence around us was interrupted only by the caw of seabirds and no Knights or crowds came to greet the Ambassador as would have been proper.

"I do not like the smell of this," I observed.

"No one likes the smell of shit," nodded Balthazar.

As if to fulfill the truth of our presentiments, the Knights had hardly set foot on the embankment than a company of the Grand Master's men emerged from the town gate and surrounded them.

"Balthazar!" I cried, watching those guards slap bracelets on the Knights.

Balthazar managed only a glance in my direction before he was led away in irons.

I stood there stunned. The preposterous thought flashed through my mind that the Turks had captured Malta in our absence and, disguised, had lain in wait for our return. Those soldiers were as Christian as I was. When the disbelief fell from me I dashed toward the Guasconi home, no better idea—no other idea—entering my head. But nearing their residence I recalled that Jean de Valette lived but a street away and, realizing from the news we received during the night that de Vallier must have gone there, I impulsively pounded on his door. A slave admitted me into the sumptuous mansion, but I did not have time to take in my surroundings. I noticed only a coat of arms above the fireplace—a shield emblazoned with a falcon and a lion—as I was led into the dining room where de Valette and de Vallier were breakfasting together.

"They're arresting the Knights!" I blurted out, out of breath and forgetting to bow.

The two senior monks at once jumped to their feet. "Where is Lord d'Aramont?" Parisot demanded.

"I—I believe he is addressing the Council as we speak," I stuttered.

Without any hesitation whatsoever, Parisot ordered a servant to the castle to bring the Ambassador to him the instant he was freed. Again he faced me and this time commanded, "Find me Villegaignon!"

"W—where might he be, Signore?"

"At the Auberge de France, fool. Get him."

As I backed out of the room, this time bowing profusely, Parisot slammed his fist on the fireplace mantle. "d'Homedes is a disgrace to the Religion. God will punish him or I will. Gaspard, you are not to leave this house."

I found Villegaignon in his suite at the auberge. He well recollected our desperate ride to Mdina and mayhap for that reason deigned to hear me out. Truly, before I had finished he was on his feet. As we sped to Parisot's home I could not but be struck by this man's appearance. Tho' his blond hair and blue eyes and perfect physique indeed made him unmatched in beauty, a halo of haughtiness and condescension visibly encircled him. At this moment I hardly knew what to make of the rumors that swirled about him: the company he kept, the divers languages he spoke, his silver tongue for which he was renowned. As on that hill overlooking Tripoli, I felt once more surrounded by persons whose stature I could only dimly perceive and by events whose magnitude eluded me.

On this second entrance to de Valette's home, I was able to quickly take in the sitting room, which, tho' spacious, reflected the cast of its owner. A crucifix, trophies and standards of war; an image of the Virgin seemingly painted by Greeks; but no portraits or other artwork that, as at the Guasconi house, might lend the place some cheer. A pair of rusted shackles, hanging above one of the doors. Was a reminder so necessary to him? And a colorful parrot, sitting atop a cabinet, sometimes fluttering its wings and making human-like noises.

Leaving Villegaignon with Parisot and de Vallier, I overheard only Durand's first remark: "*Iuan d'Homedès est une crapule, Iean, et en accord auec les Italiens et les Espagnols, il est bien capable d'accuser les cheualiers français pour sauuer sa teste."* One did not have to understand French to comprehend the revilement.

Now I did stop at the Guasconi house. When Isabella proffered her hand, I could hardly restrain my tears. My gratitude at seeing her was boundless, tho' my incomprehension and anger at the morning's events had robbed me of speech and sense. "They've arrested Lord Balthazar!" I exclaimed, unable to get out a word more, and only under the persistent questioning of Isabella and her mother did I manage to recount everything that had taken place since my departure.

"What has happened to de Vallier?" asked Lady Emilia, alarmed at my story.

"He is presently with M. Parisot ... But I tell you, I shall not suffer Fra Balthazar to languish in prison. He has done all for me."

Isabella did not wish to believe the news. "Are you certain that is the fate d'Homedes has in store for him?" she asked.

I answered no. At this moment all certainty had fled.

Her mother then questioned me about the Ambassador. So far as I knew he was standing before the Council and de Valette expected him at his home afterwards.

"We shall see about this," Lady Emilia said and, after she threw on a cloak, the three of us returned to Parisot's house, where we found him engaged in the most agitated discussion with Villegaignon and de Vallier. The servant protested that they were under no circumstances to be disturbed, but Lady Emilia barged past and confronted Parisot directly. She entreated him with such melting eyes and voice that at last the Knight's expression, fixed on her, softened and he permitted his unwanted guests to enter.

Only near midday did the Ambassador appear, shaking his head in awe and anger. Parisot had ordered a royal meal prepared for his friend, but such was Lord d'Aramont's agitation that he could do little more than gulp down the wine set before him. Before the full Council d'Homedes had accused him of betraying the Religion.

"You have come to Malta as a spy in order to effect our subjugation to the Turks!" he ranted there in the Castellan's quarters. "You, Ambassador, are the representative of a foreign power, more a countryman of Mareschal de Vallier. You, Sir, insinuated your way into my confidence and exaggerated the weaknesses of Tripoli in order to effect its humiliating capitulation."

"This is absurd," replied d'Aramont coldly. "You have lost your mind."

Maugre his eighty years, the Grand Master paced and gesticulated before the Council members. "Had it not been for your secret commerce with the Pasha and the fatal weakness of de Vallier, having been seduced by your perfidious advice, Tripoli would ne'er have fallen."

"I was unable e'en to communicate with the besieged," responded d'Aramont without raising his voice. "Truly you are mad."

The Monsignore's accusations went on throughout the morning. Of the Ambassador's solemn promise to release thirty Turkish slaves in exchange for the Knights, d'Homedes declared that never would he honor a vow made to dogs and one so contrary to honor and religion. The Italians and Spaniards on the Council, incredibly, lent their voices to the His Eminence with shouts and cries of support.

Parisot heard out the Ambassador with the greatest of difficulty, for this outrage strained the shackles of decorum. "The villain has slandered your good name, Gaspard, you who have served the Religion honorably for decades and with valor. And he does this for one reason: because of his own cowardice, his refusal to have strengthened Tripoli against our great foe the Infidel. He has as well slandered you, Gabriel, the Ambassador of a sovereign power, and by rights you could have challenged him. He arrests Knights while the Calabrian dogs who caused this debacle run freely back to Sicily on any boat that will take them. With the Almighty strengthening my hand, I swear this perfidy shall not go unavenged."

"Jean," said Villegaignon, "are you suggesting a coup against the Grand Master?"

Before de Valette could make answer, d'Aramont himself interrupted. "Gentlemen," he said, "His Eminence has also threatened to detain me on Malta. I must quit the island at once and thus, with your indulgence, I will see to the provisioning of my ships. Would the occasion have allowed me to tarry longer."

No sooner had the Ambassador uttered these words than six or seven halberdiers burst through the front door, surrounded the table and declared that in the name of the Grand Master, de Vallier was under arrest.

"Ye shall not!" roared Parisot, jumping to his feet, overturning his plates and glasses and causing them to smash on the floor.

The rest of the company also jumped to its feet, but merely stood, rooted to the spot and gaping, having no sense of what to do. The bird, frightened out of its wits, began to fly about the room, making hideous sounds and attacking the guards with bared claws. A slave finally caught it and carried it away. The guard, with some deference, then presented de Vallier with the signed warrant for his arrest.

The Mareschal read it, turned to de Valette and said, "Jean, to his disgrace the Monsignore orders this and I must obey. He is our sovereign lord and we have sworn to him obedience. God willing, we will soon see the end of this affair." Thereupon, the Mareschal, with great dignity, laid his napkin upon the table, allowed himself to be shackled and was led away.

"Do not despair, Gaspard!" Parisot called after him. "We will indeed soon put an the end of this affair."

Slowly, after exchanging words of commiseration, the rest of us departed, sick at heart and speechless.

Twenty-Five

Isabella and I were left alone. Neither she nor I could comprehend the actions of the Grand Master, which bereft us of spirit and filled me with wrath. With the fall of Tripoli, the fortunes of the Religion had ne'er sunk lower, and yet the Knights themselves, as if to ensure their complete and utter destruction, had launched into war amongst themselves. Uppermost in my thoughts was Balthazar. Tearing at my hair, pacing, circling, truly beside myself in every way, I declared to Isabella I would free him with God at my hand. I owed everything to the righteous Abbé and would sacrifice my life before abandoning him to a foul dungeon and the mad designs of a tyrannical prince who would betray the Order to the wishes of a foreign emperor—

"Francisco, stop!" Isabella cried, facing the wild beast beside her. "I beg you. I cannot endure further misfortunes, should they be ordained by God." She insisted we ride to the country. "You will be of no help to your friend Balthazar at this moment, the way you are."

The young lady was surely right and I acquiesced. As we walked to the stables to fetch horses, a sharp change in the aspect of Birgu now struck my eyes.

The streets were all but empty of women.

Isabella nodded. "Only a day after the embassy departed, the Grand Master decreed that all women and children be sent to Sicily. He expects Dragut and Sinan to return." That thought was too terrible to contemplate, but would the Turks risk another attack so late in the season? "You'll not find your whore here," said Isabella sharply, as we reached the stables.

"Of all the women on Malta, the wenches are the most essential," I retorted, trading her barbs. "Does d'Homedes wish a revolt of the Knights on his hands as well?" Despite her prickly tone, Isabella's words fed my vanity, for I saw from her pouting lips that jealousy ran through her, and that pleased me greatly. "But why are *you* here?" I asked abruptly, eyeing the half-empty streets.

Turning to saddle her horse, my companion answered only that Parisot had been unconvinced that leaving was safer than remaining and Emilia had refused to go. "Have you the token I gave you?" she said, breaking off her reply and suddenly facing me.

Startled, I natheless collected my wits quickly enough to pull the kerchief from my blouse. "I have never parted with it and I ne'er shall part, as long as I have breath within me."

A hopeful but doubtful smile spread across the girl's visage and we trotted off. Head cooler now, I recounted more fully our strange experiences in Tripoli, which led me to believe that in these incomprehensible times anything was possible—indeed, ordained. Isabella listened with a horrified fascination and only beyond the hills, after the silence that descended, did I think to ask how she had spent her weeks.

With the barest hint of a grin, Isabella replied, "I have taken your advice, Señor, and have begun writing poetry." Startled again, this time a reply fully escaped me and, seeming my amazement, Señorita Guasconi frowned. "Tho' you would not know it on Malta, my Francisco, ours is an age of literature. Everyone must write, excepting perhaps stupid Spaniards."

"Were you a man," I answered, circling my horse around her, "I would challenge you for that insult."

"But I am not and you shall instead ask me to read my verses."

"Yes."

Now Isabella lowered her eyes. "Not yet. Someday perhaps when I am accomplished. Someday ... when Fortune has granted us a respite ... "

We hadn't ridden a league when suddenly on an open plain we came across a large circular pile of stones, what I at first took to be mere rocks half- buried in the earth. Upon coming closer we saw some of them had been hewn into great blocks and set atop others, likewise hewn. Strange spirals and scrollwork ornamented a few, but there was no order to the place and the ruin of it spoke of distant ages.

"They say a race of giants once ruled the island," Isabella offered, observing me climb about the place.

"It must be," I answered, looking all around at the stones too heavy for mortals to lift.

Abruptly, Isabella asked whether I danced.

"He is not a Spaniard," I replied with a careless laugh, "who does not dance as he emerges from his mother's womb."

And so we danced a courtly pavan there on this ancient altar. To that stately music, imagined by us, I bowed, she curtsied, we advanced and retreated, her palm touched my hand's spine. In the touch of those hands we felt warmth, fire; our faces flushed. We did not cease. The partners retreated and advanced, and the dance slowly changed to something less for a lord and lady than for goat-herders and shepherdesses. With their faces now red with heat, each feeling the other's close heat, they stopped, flustered but full of each other's warm glances, and not withholding those glances, they sank to their knees, palm against palm, on those difficult stones.

Isabella gazed at me without retreat. "Señor," she said, "before you departed for Tripoli, you were about to tell me something of import and promised you would speak of it on your return. I now hold you to that promise."

First I balked and found excuses, but Isabella insisted and I knew there was nothing for it. Slowly, reluctantly, I told all. I told her of my fiancée Isabella in Granada, and I told her how another man had ruined my family's good name and our *limpieza*, with accusations that Moorish blood flowed through my veins. No graver charge could be leveled against a Spaniard, and many a duel had been fought over such slanders. I had fought a duel and had killed a man. I told her that I viewed her name, Isabella, as an omen, an omen that only increased my certainty that she had entered my life for a purpose, tho' I knew not what.

Listening to the story, a cascade of emotions raced furtively across Isabella's face: confusion, disappointment, horror. This girl, raised by Knights, knew better than anyone the importance of blood purity, and now she saw her admirer for what he was: a marked man. At length she looked into my eyes with a kind of hopeless tenderness.

"Are you certain?" she asked, putting her hand to her throat, as if catching her breath.

"It is of course impossible. My family is one of oldest in Granada."

"Then you must return to Granada and clear your name of these vile slanders," she said forcefully as her thin lips bent into a frown.

"Someday ... when a respite is granted. Isabella ... " I did not know how to express it. The slurs, the knowledge that I could not become a Knight under any circumstances, had somehow given me a ... liberty to act as I pleased, to think as I saw fit. In that, mayhap, this injustice held some hidden benefit.

"Know one thing more," I said. "From the moment I first beheld you, I loved you. These events that sweep us along so powerfully ... No man has the strength—I rail at them, and they dash to earth every hope ... You will be married to a Florentine lord, yes, but whate'er happens, never doubt that I love you and shall always love you."

I concluded my awkward speech, which had welled unbidden from my heart, and Isabella glanced up with tear-filled eyes. Hesitantly she placed her palm against mine. For a moment it rested there, with warmth and uncertainty; then this ward of the Knights slowly turned and got to her feet. She had gazed upon a Moor. We started back, side by side, and Isabella told me that her betrothed hoped for a wedding in Florence next year. After that we rode on in silence.

That evening I found Blaij in his room and he at once complained that his wench Innocenza had been temporarily stolen from him. The man sitting before me was not the Blaij Vergã with whom I'd so aimlessly floated ashore at Malta. His first caravans with Romegas had proven profitable; in the taverns his crewmates all spoke of his fearlessness. This Blaij Vergã exuded a confidence and a power that went beyond bravado.

"You are doing well," I observed, seeing that he had taken the first strides to become a Knight.

"I am," he answered simply, flipping a Venetian ducat in his fingers. "This is the life. The wind, the seas ... women in every port. What more could a man want?"

Without further prologue I asked whether he had heard what happened this morning.

Blaij nodded, pouring me a cup of wine. "I have, my friend," he said with an amused sigh, "but so many tales are flying around this town one doesn't know what to think. One is true: the Grand Master has already sent fast brigantines north to Sicily and Naples with letters declaring that the loss of Tripoli was due to the Ambassador's treachery."

"Aye, d'Homedes knows better than to let Carlos believe otherwise."

"But you must know what's true and what isn't. You were there."

I accepted the cup he was holding out. Yes, I was there. "I know the situation was hopeless, that a mutiny deprived the Mareschal of his men, that he would have preferred to die defending the place and that now every Knight who survived sits in irons somewhere in the bowels of St. Angelo, among them the best man I have e'er known."

Blaij eyed me with a certain irony in his expression. "Why is he the best?"

I shook my head. "If you cannot see, I cannot explain."

"Spanish Knights say he contrived to turn over the fort, that he is a French traitor."

Now I leveled my gaze at Vergã. "I mean to set Lord Balthazar free and I want your help."

Blaij cocked his head and ran his tongue slowly over his lips, considering my request. "I say again, the Spaniards believe Balthazar to be a traitor, the Italians as well—and of course d'Homedes."

"We stand in the Convent of the Knights of St. John. Their allegiance is to the Order, not to their birthplaces."

Blaij spat up his wine onto the table and laughed. "You believe that?"

He was right. "No," I shook my head. "We have seen too much. Natheless, you sail with Romegas, a Provençal, and the best will not hold a man's country against him. *I* say again, I mean to free Lord Balthazar and I want your help."

Vergã now folded his arms across his chest, leaning back in his chair against the window. "Why should I help you, who stole my woman from me?"

"You yet nurse that wound, over a whore?" I scoffed, but this made no impression on Blaij and I went on: "If you will not help me, help him."

"Why should I help him?" Blaij shrugged.

I answered coldly. "Would you repay his friendship with a bastard coin? You would not now be wearing such finery—" I pinched the sleeve of his new silk blouse—"were it not for Lord Balthazar."

Blaij remembered a bash on the head from Lord Balthazar, and that a Spaniard should properly kill him, not help him. Still, Vergã was hard pressed to deny the large truth in my words and we both fell silent.

Finally, he said, "Señor, you are proposing treason against the Grand Master. Two years underground if we are caught and not killed in the attempt—"

"Two years is merely for murder. For treason we'll be executed—"

"You *are* rash. Have you spoken to Balthazar?"

I had not.

Now Vergã merely chuckled derisively. "Don't you think that might be a wise step?" he said. "In a few months Old One-Eye will try them and they will be released. That will be the end of it."

Only God and d'Homedes knew. Natheless, strangely, by keeping his head level, Vergã had given me good advice. I gulped down the remaining wine and set off for Fort St. Angelo.

The guard was playing cards with three of his mates. He grumbled loudly when I told him I had brought food for Fra Balthazar, but when I tossed him a few coins he broke off the game quick enough. Handing me a torch, he grabbed another and led me down through tunnels too low to stand erect in to a cell somewhere deep in the stone mass of the fortress. Against the sound of dripping water I spied Balthazar. The hour was past complines and he lay on a pile of straw against a wall covered with scribbling.

"Are you comfortable, Navarre?" I asked.

Balthazar at once rolled over. "Better accommodations could hardly be desired," he said lightly. "The shackles, to be sure, are a bit tight, but the readings left by previous occupants are excellent ... What took you so long? I'm famished."

I tossed him the bread in my hand. Happily the guard had departed for his card game and I could speak more freely. "We must get you out of here," I whispered.

"Why?" asked Balthazar, breaking off a crust and shoving it down his gullet.

The question and the matter-of-fact tone of it took me by surprise. "B—because you do not belong here!" I sputtered, finding no other reply.

"Francisco, my friend," he answered softly, "I have taken a vow of obedience and I mean to uphold it."

By now I should have expected nothing else from this Knight, tho' one might have questioned his vow of chastity. "There is talk of treason," I whispered urgently. "Don't you understand? d'Homedes will have you drowned in a weighted sack."

Tho' the torch, filling the passageway with an oily smoke, lit Balthazar's face inconstantly, I could see my urgency left him entirely unperturbed. "By the statutes of the Order there must be a trial," he said.

"Statutes! What prince e'er heeded the statutes he created?"

The Abbé refused to relent. "I say, let us not act rashly."

Rashly, the same word used by Vergã. Yet Balthazar, above all people, could hardly be blind to the designs of the Grand Master, and this fatal response would serve naught but to speed his own end. Ah, I waved my hand as the guard once more appeared to put a stop to the exchange.

"Not long ago you spoke to me of a passage of Niccolò that disturbed you," I said. "I'd advise you to contemplate his words." I turned from the prisoner and climbed out of the dark dungeon into the darker evening.

Twenty-Six

Pietru was waiting for me on the stairs to my room. He had no place to sleep and no money except the *denari* he had been paid for rowing that doomed expedition to Tripoli. I'd have preferred Flaminia in my bed but until he found lodging the farmer could share it. I would sleep little; Isabella's inability to accept the revelation of my past weighed heavily, and Balthazar's fate e'en more. The proverb says love offers the same end for joy and sorrow, but friendship is like a stone. Aye, if I could not have Isabella's love, I would never lose Balthazar's friendship.

The Chevalier wouldn't budge. Each evening I descended into the dungeon bringing food and each evening he refused to consider measures that might save him. His stubbornness continued even as talk about what the Grand Master had in store for the traitors swept the Borgo. The tempest of rumor spit forth such grave auguries that I knew I must seek powerful help. To whom could I turn? Of the Knights, de Valette and Villegaignon alone might recognize my name. I chose Villegaignon.

On a dull morning his servant saw me to his quarters at the auberge, where I discovered him at a desk writing a memoir in Latin. Like all the suites in the auberge, Villegaignon's two rooms were spacious enough, but Spartan in their furnishings; his armor occupied a full corner, on a stand, while a chessboard sat on a trunk of drawers. The Knight hardly rejoiced at the intrusion but permitted me to enter.

"Sir," I said, bowing, near quaking before this man who was said to have been a close friend of Rabelais and, incomprehensibly, John Calvin, the heretic, "I have come to petition your advice and aid."

Villegaignon set down his quill and bade me take the other chair. I spoke to him of Balthazar's plight, that he had been in Tripoli as much by accident as design, that neither he nor de Vallier could be held to account for the loss of the place and that a terrible injustice was being perpetrated.

Villegaignon got up, opened his door to be certain the corridor was empty, sat down again. Today he spoke with a certain scholastic reserve, strange for one of his heroism, and said he was well aware of Fra Balthazar's predicament. At the same time he reminded me, as Blaij had, that many of the Knights in Tripoli claimed he advised de Vallier to surrender the city.

"Do you know this for the truth?" I asked. Balthazar's own account had been of a different color.

Villegaignon smiled mysteriously. "I know the accusations. I also know the Monsignore has been meeting in secret with his most trusted men, that there will be a trial and that he will appoint his own creatures as solicitors."

"Your ears are keener than mine," I said. "Tell me, Monsieur, why does the Grand Master reveal such a tyrannical hand?"

The question obviously amused Villegaignon, who snorted disdainfully. "The loss of Tripoli is no trifling matter, boy. The Religion and perhaps all the Mediterranean now stand at the Abyss through his negligence in fortifying that outpost. Pope Julius himself advises Malta be abandoned for Siracusa or Messina. Under no circumstances can d'Homedes allow himself be held responsible for this catastrophe—especially before the Spanish Emperor, whose lackey he is." Hereat Villegaignon paused with a significant glance at me. "I tell you openly that I plan to fight d'Homedes, but I am a single man. The Italians and Spaniards, who resent the French domination of the Religion, have already sided with His Eminence. I am far from confident of the outcome. Tho' I have the most powerful friends, you know the expression, *Elohim bashamayim vehamelech bamerchakim*; and on Malta d'Homedes is a sovereign monarch of the Knights."

I dimly recognized the language as that of the Jews, but my ignorance of the meaning only brought down a sneer of contempt from Villegaignon. Natheless, his forecast could only alarm. "Cannot M. Parisot be of help?" I asked disquietedly. "You two are close friends, meseems, and he is a high-ranking Knight."

Villegaignon began tapping his fingers on the writing table. "Parisot's ambitions are high, but another year or two must pass before he becomes a Seigneur of the Council and he cannot afford a false step at this moment of his advancement. He thinks as I do and will act as required, but young man you are not to approach Parisot in this matter." His striking blue eyes bore into mine. "Do you understand me?"

As if written on the sky by God's hand. "What must I do?"

"Nothing, without my order."

Villegaignon picked up his quill, dipped it into the inkwell and I knew I had been dismissed.

More days passed as Balthazar languished in the black prison. I continued to visit him, but Villegaignon, conducting his own investigation by means unknown to anyone else, gave me no instructions. My hands were fast bound and I occupied my days with guard duty. Talk in the taverns had become fierce and Vergã was right: To a man the Spanish Knights had aligned themselves against the prisoners.

"Where do you stand?" one of those asked me, grabbing my collar.

"Unhand me, *puta!*" I replied. Before I knew it, my schooling had leapt to the fore; my offender was on his back and my dagger pointed at his throat. I slashed his cheek for good measure and the matter would have ended badly for him, had not the Order's penalties for duelling given me pause.

Not everyone paused. Villegaignon—in the auberges, in the squares— boldly questioned the Grand Master's actions, and the French, responding to this undaunted courage, began to rise to the defense of the Mareschal. Within days the French and Spanish were eating in different taverns; their bravi passed on opposite sides of the street.

"The Mareschal has fucked the Order!" some Spaniards spat out near the gate and at once a brawl ensued before my eyes. Those who weren't left lying on the street rushed out to the hills for single combat. A new civil war of the kind Balthazar had recounted would surely break out within a turn of the glass.

So alarmed was I that I approached Villegaignon a second time. He nodded, informing me that the situation was graver than e'en he had supposed: To prevent the Mareschal's story from being heard, His Eminence was ordering his confidents write letters to the kings of their countries. Villegaignon handed me a copy of one of these missives. I held before my eyes a letter to the Emperor himself.

"How did you get this, Monsieur?" I asked, incredulously.

The blond Chevalier shook his head and I read. According the Grand Master's insects, the French Knights were at this very moment besieging the Monsignore in Castle St. Angelo! The letter dropped from my hands. I knew then that my countryman d'Homedes would stop at nothing before having the heads of the French Knights on a plate.

Villegaignon yet refused to take direct action, believing that the important matter was to rally the opinion of the French Knights behind him. I left his quarters silently, knowing that if he would not act, I must. But I had no plan.

Providence intervened.

As I stepped from the auberge into the street an unfamiliar voice accosted me in Spanish. "How is the leg?"

I turned to see a man, scant years older than myself, dressed in a black habit and carrying a pile of books. For a moment I failed to recognize him, maugre his striking red beard. Only when he reminded me that he had treated my thigh wound on my arrival in Malta several months ago did I at last recollect Doctor Jean de Vigo from the Hospital. "I survived your treatment, at least."

"That is not a matter to be sneered at," he said cheerfully and went on to ask for my opinion of the current turmoil. Reluctant to reveal my mind to a Frenchman, e'en a good-natured doctor, I replied only that the entire affair was most unfortunate and that with God's grace it would be resolved without more bloodshed.

Vigo sensibly changed the subject. "Perhaps you might assist me in a matter of *some* importance to the Hospitallers," he said. "We physicians have lately learned that off the west shore of Gozo grows a certain fungus that the natives have known of for ... " he shrugged ... "*ages.*" He went on to explain that, as the Maltese told it, this fungus was remarkable in stemming the flow of blood in wounds. As it was the sworn duty of the Order's physicians to keep abreast of the latest medical advancements, the doctors and pharmacists often made expeditions to collect botanical specimens that might exhibit curative powers. Vigo was planning a short trip to the rock where this fungus grew. He required a few oarsmen and soldiers. Would I organize a crew?

I refused. As we spoke, the Order was about to collapse in strife. But Dr. Jean was as perceptive as one in his profession should be. Sensing my disquiet, he proposed that I could do naught about the conflict over

Tripoli, but I could assist in the first duty of the Knights: the treatment
of the sick. At length I agreed and enlisted Pietru and Vergã for the
expedition, as well as several other boatman.

We set off in the morning in a *luzzu* with four oarsman, two
arquebusiers and a doctor. The wind was fair and the going swifter than
on the day Isabella and I traveled along the same coast. As the shores of
Gozo came into sight, tho', Pietru's eyes dimmed and for a moment he
lost the stroke of the oar. We took the channel between Malta and Gozo
and by midday had reached the crag called fungus rock.

It stood just beyond the sheer precipices that formed this end of Gozo,
only a few easy strokes for a swimmer. The rock was perhaps ten times
the height of a man and covered with a brown growth. As our boat pulled
beside it, we saw the growth for a plant, a mushroom of a palm's height
and mottled appearance. Thereat Doctor Jean began to pull some of the
stuff from the rock and put it in jars he had bought, which immediately
brought cries of protest to Pietru's lips.

At first it was all Maltese: "*Ieqaf! Dan post qaddis!*" and we couldn't
understand anything. When the Gozitan saw our blank stares he managed
to growl with difficulty in Italian, "This grows nowhere else. Plant cure
wounds. Don't take it."

"Yes," nodded Doctor Jean with that pleasing hesitation in his voice,
"I have *heard* it cures wounds. I wish to *understand*. I will not take much."

Pietru did not much understand and began to yank the jars from Vigo's
hands. In the tussle, the doctor fell against Blaij, who in turn tumbled
overboard and struck his head against the rock itself. We hauled him back
into the boat, drenched and cursing and with a sensible gash right across
his forehead. Now Pietru wasted no time in taking the spongy plant from
Vigo. He squeezed it until a dark red liquid dripped onto Blaij's wound.
Miraculously, the bleeding soon ceased. "Best get juice from plant." said
Pietru.

"Yes," agreed Doctor Jean, "to ... distill it."

Tempers quelled, we put to shore on a level place to find something to
eat. During the hours on land I watched Pietru catch rabbits for lunch
and snare several birds with baited traps and silence. He had a name for
everything, each sort of thistle, each blossom, every lizard; none of them
said anything to me and most I had never seen. While lunch was cooking,

he took me a short distance up the deserted coast and pointed to a cove in the cliff, saying that this was where he hid after Dragut's *razzia*. A sadness descended over him, but once again he vowed to find his wife and we went back to eat.

On the return boat journey I asked Vigo about the Religion's medical expeditions. They were not well organized, he confessed, but the Order's physicians sometimes accompanied the Knights on caravans or did undertake journeys for the purpose of finding the best available drugs.

"Theriac and mithridatium are of course the *most important* of these," he observed, theriac being an antidote to poison and, besides, a universal cure, effective against dropsy, epilepsy, melancholy, plague, worms, ulcers and a host of other sicknesses. "Many physicians, myself among them, find ourselves somewhat, hmm ... *skeptical* of such claims and would like to test them on animals. But I must say Pietro Mattioli in his recent edition of the *Dioscoride* writes that if good theriac can be found, no other antidotes to any poison will ever be needed again. Unfortunately—" at this juncture Vigo sighed— "of the eighty-one ingredients many have vanished since the Golden Age of botany. We *must* continue the search."

To discover true rhubarb was particularly pressing. As its name made clear, rhubarb was believed to grow in barbarian countries, Greece or the Bosporus. With palms pressed together priest-like, Vigo also mentioned *Satyrion erythonium* from Aleppo, an aphrodisiac so potent that its mere touch had filled its discover with uncontrollable desire. This last quickly captured Blaij's attention.

As strange as it seems, while listening to Vigo, a plan for rescuing Balthazar began slowly to form in my mind. "Tell me, Doctor Jean, how many drugs do you keep in the Hospital's pharmacy?"

"Why, none," he replied. "At present we get them from local apothecaries, an impractical arrangement to be sure, which we hope to change shortly—"

"But of the drugs you get, are any of them harmful?"

At this naïve question he laughed brightly. "Of course. I would say *most* of them are harmful."

Nodding, I pressed him, still not knowing exactly where this inquiry would lead: "And do you employ drugs to make people ill?"

"Never by intent, if you remember your Hippocrates! One must admit, tho', that *is often* the way they do harm," said the doctor, stroking his beard and staring at me as if I were a bit simple. "Surely you have heard of ... *afione.*"

I shook my head, noticing how Vergã eyed me; he sensed something was up.

"*Afione,*" Vigo explained with animated gesticulations, as if he might be addressing an audience at the Sorbonne, "is an extract of poppy, introduced long ago to Malta by the Turks. They called it *Afion kara hissar,* and we the Hospitallers use it in *Filonio romano* and *Pille cenaglossa* ... "

"Yes, yes," I interrupted, already impatient with the doctor's Latin, "but what does it *do?*"

"Oh," replied Vigo, "that ... *depends.* We sometimes administer *Filonio romano* as a rectal clyster to combat pains in the abdomen and viscera ... "

"What *else* does it do?"

As a purple evening slowly spread over the sea, Vigo gazed at me with a like veil of perplexity. "Some surgeons here have recently begun administering *afione* to criminals ... while they are tortured. After all, it *is* very efficacious in relieving pain." Suddenly he broke off, having seen something. "Of course this does allow the questioner several *more* turns of the rack. In large enough doses *afione* can indeed cause sickness and ... death."

"Ah," I said. "Were it mixed with food or drink, what would be the effect?"

"Very difficult to say," answered Doctor Jean, squinting at me severely, e'en as Vergã glared. "But I can guarantee there would be one."

Now, at last, I put it to him: "Can you procure some for me?"

Here, tho', Vigo shook his head solemnly and decisively. "That would be a violation of my sacred vow as a physician. But any Turkish slave on Malta or *donna meretrice* can certainly find it *for* you. *Afione* is sold everywhere, maugre the penalties for using it, which for slaves is, hmm ... death."

Flaminia's concoctions were more potent than I had suspected, I suddenly realized. The discussion went no further. Soon thereafter we entered the Great Port and docked in Galley Creek. Vigo paid everyone for his services and bade us good night. Once the doctor was out of earshot, Blaij took me aside. "What are you about, Señor?"

By now the plan had formed and it possessed me. My idea was simple. The Hospital was required to treat anyone—including sick prisoners. All we needed to do was to make Balthazar sick.

"And then?"

"Escaping from the Hospital," I whispered, "cannot be difficult. It overlooks Kalkara Creek."

Blaij very nearly slapped me. "You are *esforzado!*" he said, using my old nickname from Granada. "We'll not only have to escape from the Hospital but from Malta—forever."

That was true. But he'd seen the state of things. What was here for us?

"As you observed," he replied. "I am doing well."

For me there was something as well, I acknowledged, but it was something I could ne'er possess. "I thought you had balls," I said to Vergã, then to the Gozitan beside me. "Xabaw," I asked, "What would you risk for a friend?"

"Everything," he said.

The conversation ended.

Twenty-Seven

"*Esforzado*." Ne'er before in my life, and rarely since, had I undertaken an enterprise so brave and so reckless. But once my mind had been fixed on't, nothing would deter me from Balthazar's rescue. Truly, having been guest of Sinan Pasha, having seen the imprisonment of loyal Knights, a letter declaring St. Angelo to be under siege and the removal of nearly every women on Malta—my plan failed to kindle in me the slightest awareness of madness. My design, tho', was flawed: With Flaminia among those missing, I possessed no knowledge of how to procure *afione* and, without it, I was as far from my object as January is from mulberries.

I might have spoken to Abdallah-al-Waryagli, but during our last meeting I'd tried to kill him and I guessed he would be ill disposed to the request. A few days passed. By then ships were arriving from Sicily laden with women who had been sent thither. Most of them, having no money and being unable to find work for the Vice Roy, had been reduced to begging or worse. Refusing to remain in exile any longer, they now returned to Malta of their own will and from one of these boats disembarked Flaminia. She came to my room distraught and weary.

"Must I be treated like a sack of oats?" she asked, throwing herself into my arms, "shipped back and forth at the pleasure of the Monsignore?" When her small anger at last had diminished, she asked what I had brought her from Tripoli.

A world of woe. I fastened around her wrist a bracelet I'd bought from a Mahometan slave in Birgu. Then I asked about *afione*. Flaminia of course knew a slave from whom she could get it, "*Ma perque, mio cuore?*" she asked, "*ellu ne far que dormir.*" I didn't care what it did so long as Balthazar would be released to the Hospital.

Cloves, wine, *afione*. Paracelsus had concocted such a mixture himself, Doctor Vigo said, calling it *laudanum*, and the famous alchemist carried *afione* in the hollowed crystal pommel of his sword. Others claim it was not *afione*, but a demon, Azoth. I do not know which is true, or exactly what concoction Flaminia procured, but a day later I had it. Not about to needlessly risk Balthazar's life with this mysterious drug, I tried it myself. Almost immediately a heavy drowsiness seized me, a pleasant torpor and strange visions, not unlike those I had experienced in church. At length I fell into a deep sleep from which I did not awake for on a full day. I gave Flaminia money to buy more.

If the undertaking were to succeed, we'd need a boat to Sicily. They sailed frequently enough, at least once a day. Money would buy passage for anyone, no questions asked. Forthwith I made arrangements with a captain who seemed no more untrustworthy than the rest, but a smaller boat would also be needed and help to row it. Believing I could not rely upon Vergã, I turned to Pietru, e'en as I knew that what I asked of him was unjust. "If we are caught," I explained, "it will mean certain death." He said he could get a *fregatina* or a *dghajsa*. Why he agreed to this desperate plan that held nothing for him, only he could say, and he didn't.

For another span of days I marked time. I knew the moment had arrived when the streets received news that d'Homedes intended to put the imprisoned Knights to death. Taking leave of Flaminia, I told her that if she did not see me on the morrow, she should find a new master. My mien unleashed a flood of tears such that I'd ne'er seen and she cast at me a gaze so filled with forlorn tenderness that for a moment I believed her caresses had been those of the truest love and that I was abandoning my one and faithful wife. But my lot had been cast. I admonished her to be a good Christian, to pray for salvation and I gave her all the money remaining to me after making the arrangements. She stared at it, if far from content, then placated.

At the prison, I handed Balthazar breakfast and some wine, and we gaily toasted his approaching trial and inevitable execution. Flaminia's philtre soon took effect, but the symptoms differed markedly from those that had afflicted me. Balthazar reacted with such violence to the drink that I instantly became convinced some other potion had been substituted and that his mortal life was in danger.

"*Picaro*, thou hast murdered me!" he ranted, with his hand to his brow, staggering around the cell in a rage and pounding on the walls. At length he collapsed onto the floor with his jaw gaping and for a terrible moment I thought I had truly killed him.

I sped to the guard in genuine fear, crying that Balthazar had become mortally ill from the food and needed to be removed to the Sacra Infermeria without delay. The guard, lighting a torch, showed no unseemly haste in descending to the dungeons, but once he espied the deep torpor of the Knight he called for his Captain and the three of us carried Balthazar on our shoulders to the Hospital, where we were instructed to take him to one of the upstairs wards.

It was as I had hoped—a ward directly overlooking Kalkara Creek through several large windows. An escape should prove simple enough. I left Balthazar with the doctors and made final arrangements with Pietru and the Captain of the Sicilian boat.

All might have gone according to plan had not later that day I heard a timid knock on the door to my room. Over the past weeks I'd avoided the Guasconi household, carrying within me Isabella's pained reaction to the events of my past. She, tho', had decided not to avoid me.

"Isabella!" I exclaimed, seeing her at the top of the stairs. "What are you doing here?"

She pulled aside her *faldetta*, "You have not come to my house of late," she said with a hint of sadness in her voice, "and I have been trying to find you."

The girl could hardly have chosen a more inopportune moment for this conversation, entirely occupied as I was. "Isabella, I am sorry. Seeing how you felt, I thought it best—"

"No, Francisco, it is I who am sorry. When you told me ... what you told me, I did not know what to think. I do not know what to think. Parisot is so strict in such matters, it is all difficult to grasp ... You have surely been slandered by some rogue, and you have acted honorably and with such bravery through everything. And your words about how you felt—"

With a wave of my hand I cut her off. "Isabella, it is of no consequence."

She looked up with a start. "What can you mean, Francisco?"

"I cannot speak now," I said firmly, ushering her out the door. "Please understand, and leave before your presence in this room causes tongues to stir."

The young lady refused to budge, digging in her heels with a fierce determination. "Francisco, tell me what is happening. Why are your words so harsh?"

"Remember me kindly, Isabella," I said. "Remember that a man once truly loved you." I slammed the door behind her and bolted it. The stamping and tears eventually ceased.

Late that evening, after the bell for *l'hora della ruffiana* had mostly cleared the streets, I walked through the Borgo toward the Hospital. On the street of the gunners a voice called out to me.

"Calla, picaro!"

Before I could ascertain who had accosted me, the scrape of a rapier being withdrawn from its sheath touched my ears. In my humor of utter determination, nothing would deter me. I drew my sword. Only as our blades crossed did I recognize the Spaniard I had recently scarred in the tavern when he had picked a fight with me. This time I would not pause. We fought. Surely the ring of the blades would bring other Knights and soldiers running to this deserted street near the city walls, but not a one appeared. A Spaniard, my foe fought little differently than I, circling until an opening would present itself. His blade caught my arm, cutting my shirt and my skin. The wound, slight enough, declared loudly that ours was a serious business. I'd waste no time this night and lured my enemy toward the back corner of the Hospital. A figure hovered there in the shadows. My opponent glanced in that direction and I, taking advantage of his distraction, ran him through the side. Thereon he fell to the street, as far as I could say, dead.

"There is no choice but for me to escape now," I said to Pietru, who now stepped fully onto the gun-smith street. "This is unfortunate. What do we do with him?"

Pietru shrugged. But at that moment, another figure appeared. Isabella had followed me. She brought her hands to her mouth, gazing on the scene with a mixture of fear and horror.

"Isabella!" I cried angrily. "By the Saints, why have you come—?"

"What I see cannot be sanctified by any saint," she said, finding her voice.

"I have no time for this," I answered with a sharp wave of my hand. "Señorita, leave us."

She shook her head, refusing silently but forcefully.

For a moment the three of us stood fixed on that street, unable to move any more than those mythological figures frozen by a god's touch. In that moment of inaction, I saw how Isabella's presence might be turned to our advantage. "If you refuse to leave," I said, "at least help Pietru get this man into the Hospital." After I whispered a few more words to Pietru, we dragged the Spaniard to the front door and pounded. I hid myself off to one side as a Serving Brother opened the door.

"This man has been hurt," Isabella said. The Serving Brother and Pietru lifted the body and carried it to one of the upper wards; I slipped in behind them, unseen. When his task was done, Pietru walked out of the front door, taking Isabella with him.

I remained inside, hiding behind the stone staircase. Luckily, the guard who had been posted at the door to Balthazar's ward joined the effort to move the body and, once realizing the fellow had been laid low with a blade, he ran out of the Infermeria to apprehend the criminal, passing not two paces from me. I crept upstairs and entered Balthazar's ward, bolting the door behind. There I found him on the same bed I had left him earlier, sleeping like a newborn babe. I stole to the window and whispered to Pietru, who now awaited me below on the back alley. He tossed one end of the rope we'd obtained right over the wall above Kalkara and threw the other end up to me. I fastened it directly to Balthazar's bedstead.

Shaking the Knight violently, I managed to rouse him, somewhat.

"What? You?"

"Shhh," I whispered, "we're getting you out of here."

Balthazar was too insensible to put up a stiff fight, and I quickly dressed him. Neither was he sensible enough to climb and so I well nigh hoisted him onto my shoulder. Out the window we went. I had intended to go right over the city wall to the creek, so close were those ramparts to the Hospital, but once more our makeshift plan betrayed us. E'en as I descended, the same guard appeared around the corner, searching for the murderer of the dead Spaniard. Suspended above the alley, I was in no position to defend myself. Pietru, tho', pulled from his belt a pistol I'd fetched him and the guard, seeing his chances significantly diminish, took to his heels.

I reached the top of the wall and paused there a moment with Balthazar on my shoulder. About to let myself down to the creek, I was suddenly aware that Isabella had yet again followed. She climbed up the rampart steps to where I stood. By this time she had fathomed the reasons behind everything she had heard and witnessed this day and made no protest. But neither did we exchange further words; at that moment a dreadful certainty overwhelmed us that ne'er would we see each other again. In tears she offered her hand, I kissed it ardently and was over the wall.

The bank of the creek lay only a few steps away, as difficult as they were, and we shortly had Balthazar sitting and faintly cursing in the skiff that bobbed in the water there. Pietru and I rowed for our lives out of the creek, into the harbor and to Gallows' Point. There, in the shadow of the rocks, we waited nearly an hour until a boat passed, as it should, heading for Sicily.

"Thank you, Pietru, I shall never forget this," I said as we helped Balthazar aboard.

"I come with you," the Gozitan answered.

"Why? There can be nothing for you in this flight."

"*Soldat mirar mi.*" That, assuredly, had not been part of the plan. "And I must find my woman."

I gave him my hand and he climbed aboard. The Captain set a course north for Sicily. In truth, neither of us expected to set eyes on Malta again.

Twenty-Eight

When Balthazar became fully himself again he said: "I'll kill you."

Seeing that the Abbé did not rejoice at his freedom, I handed him his *montante*, which we had thought to stow aboard the merchantman. From the fiery gaze he bestowed upon the weapon, for an instant I held no doubt he would use it. I lowered my eyes and vainly argued the escape by telling him that had I not acted he would surely have ended up in a sack at the bottom of the harbor.

"Do you presume to think I do not know the Grand Master's plans?" he answered. "Are you so simple to believe that in the coming months before the trial everything will not change? That Villegaignon is powerless?"

To no greater degree did the daring of our flight impress him and Balthazar went on with dripping disdain to recount at least ten recent escapes, employing every artifice: bribes, confederates, faulty locks, whores ...

"These prisons are as porous as a cheese. By not waiting for the moment when all hope is lost, you have not only endangered our lives, you have ensured that I will be defrocked and expelled from the Religion." Balthazar forthwith demanded of the Captain to return instantly to Malta but that one merely spat on the deck and told the Knight to go rot in Hell.

In this way we proceeded uneventfully to Sicily.

At Messina, Balthazar did not deign to take leave of us. It was left to me to run up to him on the quayside, after he had disembarked with his sword flung over his shoulder. "I hope someday you can forgive me," I said. "I intended nothing but to save your life."

He made no answer and continued to walk along the quay, his figure diminishing in the distance. The Abbé would surely have boarded the next round ship for Malta had he not espied docked there a galley as splendid as any that sailed the Mediterranean. On a pennon flying from the mainmast he could make out the words, *The Friend of God Alone*. Balthazar realized at once that he had stumbled upon the galley of Leone Strozzi, the Prior of Capua, and he climbed aboard.

Leone Strozzi would prove decisive in the long road to the siege, Your Majesty, and no man better represented his age. If he hadn't existed, surely someone would have invented him. Strozzi, a member of the most powerful Florentine family after the Medici, was a sworn enemy to the descendants of Lorenzo, tho' Leone's own great-grandfather was none other than Il Magnifico himself.

He had become a Knight of St. John, rising to the post of Prior of Capua, a post that assuredly brought him great riches. Strozzi's exploits were legendary. They began when arch-enemy Cosimo dé Medici captured his father Filippo, who killed himself rather than face the dishonor of a public execution. Leone blamed Emperor Carlos for Filippo's death and incontinently joined the service of the French. Becoming Captain General of their galleys, he laid siege to St. Andrews in Scotland and, after the French and the Turks captured Nice *anno* 1543, he escorted Barbarossa himself back to Patras.

Such acts—not to mention all the Spanish ships Strozzi seized—did nothing to endear him to Carlos or the Grand Master. Aye, d'Homedes defrocked him and expelled him from the Order. Only this year Strozzi attempted to put into Galley Creek and Old One-Eye threatened to blow him out of the water. Strozzi turned about and headed to Genoa, but found no refuge there, for Andrea Doria—in Carlos's service—also regarded him as a bitter enemy. The Prior discovered he was likewise unable to return to France, for King Henri's favorite, Prime Minister Montmorency, intended to make his own son Captain General and threatened to arrest Strozzi should he so much as enter any French port.

Strozzi, abandoned by all but God, took refuge on his own galleys and had been since cruising the Mediterranean from Italy to the Levant, putting in wherever he was allowed, raiding ports when he was not. That was when Balthazar spied his galley at Messina and climbed aboard. After several hours the Prior appeared, a bearded and handsome man having about five-and-thirty years to him, of middle height but sturdily built, with features softer than one would expect of someone with his reputation.

"Navarre!" he said, recognizing Balthazar from the French campaigns, "this is indeed unexpected, to find you in Messina."

"As it is you. What brings you here, Leone?"

The Prior replied that he had just deposited fifty thousand ducats in a local bank. "You see, Navarre, God has willed that I be made an outlaw. When d'Homedes forced me to turn about from Malta, I had but twenty quintals of bisket, which were smuggled aboard by a friend without the Grand Cyclops' knowledge. I have been reduced to plundering my way across the sea, seizing Christian vessels no less than infidel ones. But God will help me pay back every *scudo* I've captured from Christian ships. You and He know my loyalties."

"*Mort de Dieu*, we seem to have something in common," answered Fra Balthazar, "for I have also been made an outlaw." He went on to recount to Strozzi the extraordinary events of late.

"The sack of Gozo is unforgivable," the Prior of Capua said, making a fist, and there and then proposed that Balthazar join him.

The Abbé declined with gratitude, saying he intended to return to Malta to fight for his liberty, but Strozzi declared that no justice of any sort was to be expected from dog snout d'Homedes and that Balthazar's young friend had been right to effect the escape. Balthazar de Marans des Homes-Saint-Martin was no man to lightly abandon his scruples and he saw with clarity the injustice of his predicament. But with the same clarity he saw that in escaping the Convent he had violated his vow of obedience.

"Very well," Navarre said finally, thereby accepting the Prior's offer, but he never entirely came to peace with the decision he made at Messina and from that day forward the affair became one of those dark spots in his life, like the mysterious past love of which he never spoke. Having taken Strozzi's offer, tho', he saw no reason to prolong the disdain of his companions and sent for Pietru Galea and Francisco de Barai.

Of all men, only Balthazar would have given such matters a thought, yet alone the agony he bestowed upon them. It was his fate to be cursed by that eternal striving, striving after a perfection that must elude all mortals. The rest of us would have escaped Malta and pissed on it. This I say with certainty, for beginning that very day we entered with abandon the corsair's life.

The calendar was well advanced into September, already late in the season. Rain had begun and the sea was perceptibly rougher; unexpected storms became a present danger. Natheless Strozzi reckoned to go on until the going became impossible. October, November, even December—one never knew. And so, setting off in his two magnificent galleys, we plied the coasts of Sicily, Naples and Calabria, taking any ship that came our way. Sailing from Messina, we first captured a few small *caramusali* sailed by Turks and Armenians, which we looted and let go. The following day we boarded a ship flying the French flag bound for Alexandria and carrying a cargo of wheat.

"But we are subjects of His Majesty!" the Captain protested.

Strozzi nodded politely and ordered us to search the ship. We found no money, only some sacks of biskets. The Prior took five and, in the scrupulous way of his corsairing, commanded the *scrivano* to put down an exact account of what we'd plundered.

"Have no fear," Strozzi said to the Captain as we carried the biskets from his galleys, "you will be repaid every *sou*, by the Blessed Virgin I swear it." He crossed himself and gave the Captain a parting pat on the back.

A few days after, we entered a small port in the Morea, where we looted some round ships and captured forty men. We set the Christians ashore and chained the infidels to the empty places on our galley benches. Later that same morning, our watch espied a larger ship and we gave chase. The fellow turned out to be Venetian and put up an active defense, but Strozzi despised Venetians and at length we got the better of him. This time we took three hundred gold *zecchini* and, again, Strozzi's *scrivano* noted the exact amount in a ledger. The Prior crossed himself.

Such kindness did not satisfy the Venetian Captain. As it happened, the round ship was followed by an entire squadron and, after we departed, our prize managed to signal its fellows. Before we knew it, fourteen damned Venetian galleys were hot on our tail.

"*Remate cani!*" the *comito* shouted over and over, lashing the slaves mercilessly. The chase went on league after league for the better part of a day. It seemed finally that the *ciurma* would give out its last. In desperation, the soldiers themselves joined the slaves and convicts to help with the rowing. By the Grace of God we escaped. But at the moment we finally eluded the dogs, our watch espied a Turkish *fusta* and we went after it. A *fusta* should have outrun us, especially in our condition, but the barbarians lost their wits and ran the boat aground on an island.

"Hah, look at that!" Strozzi cried. We disembarked only to find that the infidels had fled inland. Christian slaves had been chained to the benches and we freed them, including a Venetian captain, badly scarred and on his last legs.

Strozzi, looking over this fellow, flew into indignation. "By God, how dare the barbarians treat a Venetian Christian like a dog!" The Prior then ordered the Captain fed and given new clothes and put the *fusta* under his command.

It went like that. Ne'er in my existence had I felt such a prolonged elation as during those few months at sea. I gave no thought to Malta. It was as if the past had disappeared and with it all the chains that bound one to earth. If any thought possessed me it was that Vergã had been right, that this was the life for a man to make his fortune. I became determined to best him in prizes, in booty, and I tried, counting every *scudo* that came my way.

At the same time my esteem for Pietru also grew. Ix-Xabaw, the Shabaw, proved himself to be an excellent sailor. Like every Maltese, he had been born to the water and swam like a fish. I watched, at first disdainful, then astonished by the amount of time Ix-Xabaw could spend under water. He rowed without complaint, and frequently showed off his always-hardening muscles.

"What do you mean, 'this is a good man'?" I asked once when I saw him chattering with the sea birds.

"He is good man," Pietru grinned toothily and pointed at the gull he was talking to. "He sings. You listen to what he says about wind and rain."

I laughed, thinking Ix-Xabaw weak in the head. Soon I realized he saw "men" everywhere, in rocks, trees, cattle. He would toss a sputtering log from the fire, growling, "He talk too much." Amusing, aye, but Pietru knew hours before the rest of us when to expect rain and from which direction the purifying winds would come. He also proved gruff, stubborn, and in the center of that stubbornness rested a place for melancholy. Each time we boarded a barbarian ship he searched for his wife among the slaves but never found her. I asked how long he would continue to hope and he shook his head, puzzled at the question. She was alive and someday he would see her again. The determined ferocity wherewith he searched showed us all that he could not accept what had happened on that terrible day on Gozo. He never uttered a word about it.

Alone among the crew Balthazar was less than overjoyed at our successes. Tho' he never failed to participate fully in our undertakings, no glimmer shone from his eye. We hadn't spoken as much as in former days, our friendship yet cool, but we did speak and I asked him why I did not observe his customary élan. He replied by lighting again on the passage of Niccolò: that it was impossible for a man to be good whose work required him to be fraudulent, murderous and rapacious.

"I see," he said, "that you have come to love it. You have become drunk with it, as you would be intoxicated by *afione*." Without mentioning valor, he picked up a sword and went into battle.

On Malta matters did not remain still. Soon after our escape, Nicolas Villegaignon walked into the one of the French taverns for lunch. Making certain no Spaniards were about, he sat down beside Romegas and said, "I am surprised you are not on the seas taking prizes."

"We sail tomorrow," the younger one answered, "and I'll find out what the damned Turks are up to ... Fra Nicolas, be on your guard. If you haven't heard, today d'Homedes ordered that a commission be formed to investigate the Knights. He's putting the trial in the hands of a secular judge and intends to have a speedy end to the affair."

"A secular judge, why?"

Romegas glanced about, bit into a fowl's leg. "'The offense, being so grave, a religious order ought not to deprive life of the accused.'" The sailor belched, wiped his lips. "À propos, the judge is a Spaniard."

"A Spanish secular judge," repeated Villegaignon, sitting back, "because a religious order ought not to deprive life in such a grave matter. Hmm, d'Homedes seems rather to believe *de minimis non curat praetor*. An ill design has been placed on the anvil, I can no longer doubt it."

"I warn you again, Fra Nicolas," Romegas said, half chuckling, "be on your guard."

"Fra Mathurin, you have spent years on a boat. I have sat through years of lectures in Paris, debated Calvin and argued over dinners with Rabelais. Do not presume to think I am to be cowed by a few commissioners. In any case, *megalon apolisthainein omoz engenez amartema*, but I suppose you wouldn't know about that. Please excuse me." Villegaignon took his leave without having eaten.

Romegas sailed in the morning. Two days later Villegaignon stormed over to the court building the Knights had raised thirty years ago at the center of Il Borgo, found the first of the commissioners d'Homedes had appointed from three different langues and demanded to see the depositions they had been collecting. The commissioner, one Escudero, stroked his beard and flatly refused.

"If you do not divulge the testimony in hand," the Grand Prior of France threatened calmly, "I will bring the issue before the entire Council."

Surely, the commissioner saw the spirit of l'Isle Adam blazing forth from the gold-threaded doublet before him, or the King of France, and he instantly handed over the documents. Standing in his place, Villegaignon shuffled through the parchments. Only a glance was necessary to reveal what was afoot.

"By custom," the Chevalier declared angrily, "any testimony to be used in a trial should be made only by persons of probity, but you see—" he thrust the sheaf under Escudero's nose—"you have collected depositions from villains, forgers and apostates who have sold their own children into slavery, among them those Spanish mutineers and Calabrian scoundrels who were the cause of the debacle." Villegaignon had not concluded. "What's more, I see no testimony here from de Vallier himself. How is such a thing conceivable?"

"S—Señor," replied the red-faced Escudero, confronted by this high-ranking hero, this blond devil, "I—it is true: d'Homedes has refused to allow de Vallier's testimony—"

"*Why?*" Villegaignon's voice cut him off so forcefully that the commissioner fairly turned white.

"O—on the grounds that his is a crime of state."

Villegaignon, assuming his full height, twisted his finger directly into Escudero's face. "This" he said, "is justice *alieni generis*," and he stormed out of the court with the testimonies in hand to seek the commissioners' witnesses.

Within hours he discovered one of the deposed Spaniards in the tavern under the sign of the pig. Sitting down with this drunkard, Moncayo, Villegaignon ordered a *mezzo*. Here too, while he filled Moncayo's tankard, Durand did not hesitate to make use of his celebrity, and if Moncayo was at first too far in his cups to understand that before him sat the hero of Algiers and recently of Malta, one of the most famous men in France besides, the Religion's Grand Prior of that country and favorite of the Queen, as well as nephew of the immortal Grand Master l'Isle Adam, he sobered up without delay. And by God, his interlocutor assured him, he, Nicolas Durand de Villegaignon, intended to get to the bottom of this subterfuge if it required enlisting the aid of the Pope and every cardinal in the Vatican. The Spaniard, by now uncertain whether d'Homedes or Villegaignon sat closer to Rome, stared dully at the Chevalier and confessed that much force had been put on him to denounce de Vallier. He had also been paid.

"By whom?" demanded Villegaignon, slamming his fist on the table.

Now Moncayo shrugged, pointing only to an intermediary whose name was unknown to him.

"By God I'll have you racked!" shouted Villegaignon, but at this Moncayo only shook his head, knowing that the Council alone authorized torture—and the Grand Prior was not going to get that without the consent of d'Homedes himself.

Furious, tho' hardly surprised by his discovery, Villegaignon shoved Moncayo aside and returned to Escudero, insisting that the witnesses against the Knights had been suborned. Escudero answered with upturned palms that he knew nothing about that. "My duty is merely to take depositions. You are welcome to produce your own witnesses for the accused."

Villegaignon had one week.

Durand regarded the round-faced man with ice. "By the Lord Almighty you are dogs, I would fuck your mother. Two months by custom is granted the solicitor."

"I shall report you for blasphemy," Escudero replied.

"Comme il uous plaira," said Villegaignon and departed. Natheless, enlisting the Frenchmen who had been slowly rising to his call to arms, Durand scoured the auberges, taverns and prison cells and interviewed anyone who had been in Tripoli and many who hadn't. Exactly one week after he had stormed out of Escudero's office, he threw testimony from threescore persons into the commissioner's face. Escudero, glancing calmly over the documents, replied he would pass them onto the judge, Agostino Combo.

The Grand Prior of France and nephew of l'Isle Adam observed with some satisfaction that he had forced the commission into a tight corner, so tight they were now sniffing their asses, as his friend Rabelais might have said. Truly, Villegaignon found himself in somewhat higher spirits a few days later when he donned his robes and proceeded to the Castellan's quarters atop Fort St. Angelo, where the judge Combo would announce his decision before the full Council.

The judge stepped forward before the assembled Seigneurs, each of the dozens robed in a black mantle faced by the eight-pointed cross. For a time the sweat rolling down his cheeks and the tremor in his hands prevented him from uttering the slightest word and he stood before the Bailiffs and Grand Crosses, rooted and quaking, until d'Homedes himself waved his hand and snarled: "Get on with it."

Clearing his throat and with a voice perceptibly quivering, Combo commenced reading the report. From the testimony of many persons of probity, he said, the commission had found that the loss of Tripoli did not *appear* to have been due to the Mareschal de Vallier. Here, after but one sentence, Combo's voice abruptly failed. He halted, glanced at the faces surrounding him, then turned his eyes quickly back to the paper in his hands. As far as the commission was able to determine, he said, voice fully cracking, neither de Vallier nor the other Knights were guilty of any acts that might be termed treasonable, and the misfortune was due entirely to the Calabrians who mutinied, making defense of the garrison impossible. Again Combo paused and with a silken handkerchief daubed the beads glistening on his brow. The commissioners were also unable to find anything in the constitution of the Religion that inflicted a penalty in such a case, which was certainly without precedent.

Without lifting his eyes a hair's breadth from the page, the judge went on. In opposition to this, the Order's statutes did *senza ambiguità* declare that any governor who abandoned a place with which he had been entrusted, without express leave from the Grand Master and the Council, should be degraded. Combo halted for no less than a third time, then, passing his tongue over his parched mouth, he bit his lip and announced his conclusion:

"It is therefore my decision that Mareschal de Vallier should be deprived of his habit and his cross and the same sentence should be passed on the Knights Fuster, Errera and Sosa, who fomented the rebellion."

Villegaignon listened to the sentence with mixed emotions. de Vallier had not been fully acquitted, but he had been spared a death sentence.

But d'Homedes was ill-pleased. Immediately he rose and declared, "Gentlemen, the judge's decision has been made in a slight ... *haste*. Each offense imputed to these Knights is of a different character and must be judged accordingly. I declare the decision regarding de Vallier should stand, while the sentence imposed on the others should be revisited."

He is trying to save the Spaniards, Villegaignon said to himself.

And without a blush of shame, Combo retreated. "His Eminence has seen the error of our considerations," he said, bowing in the direction of the Monsignore. "Let it be thus: Fuster, Errera and Sosa be removed from the sentence passed on de Vallier."

Immediately Bailiff de Schilling of Germany was on his feet. "Are you not the most profligate fellow alive!" he shouted in disgust at the judge standing before him, "to change your sentiments in a moment, at the least frown of the Grand Master!"

"He has spoken like the wretch he is," declared the Chevalier de Nuguez of Castille, also rising, turning toward d'Homedes himself. "I will never suffer the sentence that has been pronounced against the Mareschal to be executed unless the same penalty be inflicted upon the others."

Soon the entire Council had descended into a complete uproar, Villegaignon observed with pleasure, but the business did not end as he expected. The French Knights, on their feet, railed that justice had been suborned and that they were witnessing nothing less than an attempt to blame the Mareschal for the Grand Master's own negligence. But the Spaniards and Italians, also jumping to their feet, shouted that the Grand Master was in the right, that de Vallier had deserted his post and was guilty as charged. At length the Monsignore himself pleaded for silence and, in respect for his office, the Knights granted it.

With some artfulness d'Homedes explained, "As the one faction contends, it appears to me that de Vallier and Fuster's guilt is greater than that of the other two and I merely wish to delay the decision to another time. That is all."

This postponement the Council granted and Villegaignon understood that the game had not ended.

Twenty-Nine

During our undertakings we often put in at ports along the coast of Italy or at islands in the Morea. At almost every call, fisherman and traders told us the same: The Turks were this winter preparing another invasion to finish off what they had left undone. The further east we sailed, the stronger became the rumors. Such intelligence alarmed above all the Prior, yet one rarely knew who to trust unless they were known confidents or spies. Strozzi decided to investigate.

On a clear November day we sailed into Zakynthos, which some call Zante, a beautiful Greek island owned by Venice. To keep it, the Venetians paid an annual tribute of five thousand ducats to the Turks and there were rich Jewish merchants on the island who traded regularly with the Ottomans. Each time the Turks prepared for war, they demanded loans from the Jews. The closer the Jew lived to the Sultan's lands, the lower the interest. If the Jew lived in the empire, the loan should be without percent. Strozzi resolved he would talk to one of these merchants.

A landing party of sixteen put to shore, fully armed, and in the dead of night we climbed up the hill to a large house overlooking the harbor. We smashed open the door and kidnapped the Jew, his wife and children directly from their beds and dragged them screaming and kicking back to the caiques awaiting us. The merchant, one Jacob Levi, begged and pleaded the whole time for his release, offering anything if we would only let his family go, but we told him to shut his trap until we got him before Strozzi.

Aboard the galley, the Prior questioned Levi. Sure enough, the Ottomans had been pressing for loans up and down the Adriatic and Aegean, but Levi said he knew nothing of any invasions plans, whether the Turks were planning to invade Malta, or even Venice.

"He is lying, like the Jew-turd he is," declared Strozzi before the entire crew. "We should take them to Malta and ransom them."

"To what end?" objected Balthazar, standing there with the others on the poop. "We are unwelcome on Malta."

"The let us take them to Venice," answered Strozzi with a glance at Levi. The Jew shuddered, knowing his family would have a hard time of it there.

Balthazar appeared not to want to have anything to do with the Prior's course. "That is a long journey at this season. If you desire to ransom them, I say ransom them now. *Moy foy*, what can he tell us?"

"He knows the invasion plans—"

"I know nothing about the Grand Turk's designs!" Levi himself pleaded with tear-filled eyes.

Strozzi spat in his face. "How can a Jew agree to a loan without knowing its purpose? By God, let's torture him now and take him to Malta with the information. Then they must believe us."

By this time the pathetic merchant was on his knees and sobbing; natheless he yet insisted he knew nothing of any value. He was Greek, not Turk. In the end, after having strung him up for a short while, the Prior of Capua decided that Levi really didn't know anything and agreed to release the family for a thousand ducats. We held the wife and children hostage as several of the crew accompanied Levi back to the house where he had hidden some money. He paid it; we gave back his family and went on our way.

It must have been about the time we departed Zante when Nicolas Villegaignon's servant announced a visitor at his quarters in the Auberge de France. Durand, after all that had taken place, was hardly surprised to see standing at the door his acquaintance the Sieur de Bellon, a gentleman of King Henri's household. Bellon had arrived directly from France. Without prologue he declared to the Chevalier in the gravest voice that Henri was far from amused at the letters the Monsignore was circulating throughout Europe, which held Ambassador d'Aramont responsible for Tripoli's fall.

Villegaignon bade his guest sit. "*Ouy*," he breathed, averring that d'Homedes intended to go to his grave with a conscience free of Tripoli, but he would not die free of his tyrannical treatment of his fellow Chevaliers.

"Nicolas, you do not understand," said Bellon, taking the chair. "This has become more than a matter of honor between d'Homedes and d'Aramont. Spain intends to use the letters in its arsenal for continued war against France. Unless His Eminence recants, the accusations could quickly become a *casus belli* on France's part against the Religion. I have moments ago delivered a letter to the Monsignore from Henri, demanding that he prove the allegations against the Ambassador."

"Good. Let us exert all means to get an immediate response."

The urgency of his mission having deepened, Villegaignon the same day pressed d'Homedes's secretary for the Monsignore's answer, declaring to him that he intended to accompany de Bellon to France and deliver the reply to Henri by his own hand. But His Eminence had submitted Henri's letter, tho' addressed to him alone, to the full Council for deliberation. Villegaignon would need to wait for the reply. He waited.

And waited. Each day Durand approached the secretary in Birgu. Each day the secretary, glancing at him with fathomless eyes, told him, "Do not be concerned; pressing business of the Council has delayed the response."

"If we wait any longer," shouted Villegaignon when his patience had at last become exhausted, "the season shall be so far advanced that travel becomes impossible."

The secretary shrugged.

In this way weeks passed. "As I suspected," Durand said to Bellon one evening over dinner at the auberge, "the game continues and some new mischief is moving forward. I shall have to discover what it is."

But the Grand Master refused to receive the Knight, nor would the commissioners. The Chevalier's suspicions rested squarely on Combo, who had capitulated so shamelessly before the Council, but he had also been unable to see him. At a loss, Villegaignon decided to speak with Lady Emilia.

"Combo is a secular judge, not a Knight," she said, "and hails from Città Notabile. Master Falzon will surely know more about him."

Together with Isabella they rode out to Mdina to the house of Matteo Falzon. The landowner received them graciously, but when Villegaignon asked whether he had any information that might be of value, Falzon only laughed.

"You understand, Monsieur, that we in Mdina have as little to do with you Knights as possible, and I confess I wish for nothing more than to see the Order destroy itself in this imbroglio; and I say this with more sincerity than ever after the recent events that put my family and everyone else on the island in jeopardy of their lives."

Villegaignon found himself singularly uninterested in this Falzon's views of the Knights. "Surely you must know something about the scoundrel Combo," he insisted. "You sit at the head of the *Università* here and have dealt with him."

"Indeed I have," admitted Falzon. "We frequently have small squabbles among craftsmen or businessmen in Mdina. Combo has ruled in a number of these cases. I can tell you only that I have found him no better or worse than other judges; that if you scratch the surface of these dealings, one person has always bribed another, and that if the Knights are involved, the judge's decision is of no importance whatsoever, because the Council or His Eminence will overrule it."

Villegaignon nodded at Falzon. The last appeared true.

"You would do better speaking to the wenches in Birgu," interrupted Emilia, "than to the barons of Mdina, for the whores know everything that takes place in that town."

That was an idea, thought Villegaignon. Why had she not told him sooner? The Chevalier now made to depart for more fertile ground, but Falzon took him aside into his study. "I trust I have not offended you, Monsieur. You displayed great valor in coming to Mdina during the siege and for that I am grateful to you."

Villegaignon, however, appeared more interested in Falzon's library than in his apologies. "Who would have thought," he said, picking up one of the volumes he found on the shelf, "to have discovered such a collection on Malta? You have an interest in Erasmus ... ? My old debating partner, John Calvin, held great admiration for him. Of course on the matter of Luther they disagreed violently."

"I imagine so," Falzon answered, quite hesitantly.

Suddenly, Villegaignon with a curiosity Falzon could not comprehend asked, "Are there Lutherans on Malta?" Then he stopped himself and laughed at the absurdity.

Falzon smiled faintly. "As it happens, there was a French priest in Mdina named Gesualdo. Under his corrupting influence, two clergymen broke their vows of celibacy and ostentatiously married in public. Five years ago, Bishop Cubelles investigated and had Gesualdo burnt at the stake."

Villegaignon made no response, continuing to scrutinize the books. "Ah," he said at length, "I see you study the Cabbala. Have you come across the treatise by Paulus Ricius, his *Porta Lucis?*"

"No," replied Falzon, dragging out his words, "I have been unable to obtain it."

"I have an edition in Hebrew," remarked Villegaignon. "If you can read it; perhaps I may send it to you, with compliments."

Falzon shook his head as slowly as he had been speaking. "N—no, I am of course unable to read Hebrew."

"Ah, that is unfortunate," said the Knight with an audible condescension. "Perhaps one of the Jewish slaves ... "

"I think not," said Falzon with an audible finality in his voice.

Thereat Villegaignon merely shrugged, made his farewells to Lady Emilia and Isabella, who planned to remain at their residence, and departed for Birgu. Falzon gathered together his books and put them all in a trunk, which he then sealed with his strongest lock.

Returning to the Borgo, Villegaignon at once let it be known at all the inns and taverns that he was curious to learn anything about Combo or why the Grand Master's reply to the King of France had been so long delayed. Within a day he received a message that a certain *meretrice* wanted to meet him at the tavern under the sign of the chained goat. He could never remember her name. Like all Maltese women she was small and exclaimed, "O Madonna!" frequently. None of this interested Villegaignon. But when the wench told him she had had commerce with Combo, he was all ears.

She, however, wanted to be paid. He dropped a few *scudi* into her palm and she told him what Combo had told her.

It was not the Jew on Zante that convinced the Prior of Capua that a second invasion was imminent but the capture of another Venetian ship. Strozzi truly despised the Venetians. "Harlots," he spat the morning we sighted the merchantman, "who sleep with the Infidel. Nothing more or less." As the *fischietto* quickened the drumbeat, Strozzi went further: "It is our duty to search the Venetians, who think nothing of giving safe passage to Turks and constantly hold back their payments to the Religion."

Balthazar was less sanguine. E'en as he cast about for a buckler he reminded Strozzi that Venetian Knights belonged to the Langue of Italy, that a hospital of the Order stood in Venice. The Venetians had fought their share of wars with the Turks, losing to them Lepanto fifty years ago and half the Aegean after Prevesa—that calamity of which Vergã and I had been so laughably ignorant only months ago.

Natheless, Strozzi's pulse pounded. "The Turks have learned everything they know about artillery and shipbuilding from the Venetians!" he declared, spitting into the water. He was right: The Turks had stolen everything from the Venetian Arsenale, the greatest naval works on earth and, those who had seen it said, one of the wonders of the world. You can be sure Strozzi displayed no amusement when we boarded the round ship and found a cargo of heavy Venetian guns, the world's finest. The Captain admitted he was headed toward a rendezvous on the island of Chios, in Turkish hands.

"Do you tell me you plan to sell these weapons to the infidels so that our great enemy can imitate them?" Strozzi demanded.

The Captain was hard pressed to deny the accusation, but shrugged. "The Turks have copied Venetian weapons for decades, centuries."

"Dog!" Strozzi shouted. "Do you know that Clement pronounced excommunication and anathema on all those who sell weapons to the Infidel?"

"I know nothing of papal bulls," the Captain admitted after a long pause, "but trade is trade, and orders have been going fast up of late."

The reply was wholly Venetian—money—but the Captain's intelligence convinced Strozzi that a new descent was underway. He put the Venetian and his crew ashore, took a few culverins and sank the ship. Then, as we turned toward westward again, he gathered his senior officers to him. "It is our duty to warn the Convent about an invasion," he said, "and yet—"

"—if we appear in the Great Port," continued Balthazar, "we are likely to be blown from the water."

The discussion went on into the night, breaking off only when the officers decided to get some sleep. Sunrise brought a different resolution. As the light spread over the sea we aboard the vessels of the Prior of Capua awoke to find ourselves confronted by two heavy galleys approaching from opposite directions. One flew the standards of Religion and the other flew the colors of Emperor Carlos.

"*A fronte praecipitium a tergo lupi*," remarked Strozzi as the ships came into sight.

"Perhaps better: *incidis in Scyllam cupiens vitare Charybdim*," answered Balthazar.

"Under the circumstances," said Strozzi.

Strozzi and his Captain quickly discussed the best course of action but the matter was taken out of our hands: The Order's vessel approached rapidly, as for an attack, while the Emperor's vessel leisurely plied the calm sea. The Prior ordered the forward guns armed and took up a ramming position.

"*Eia!*" the *comito* bellowed. At the same instant the *fischietto* began pounding on the drum and the galley lurched forward, within strokes gaining top speed.

Our vessel and the Order's flew over the water, certain to collide.

"We are outcasts," said Balthazar on the poop, as he braced himself for the impending crash. "Natheless, I call it strange that the Religion should attack us."

"Perhaps d'Homedes has ordered it," replied Strozzi. "I hardly need tell you *viri infelicis procul amici*."

"No," replied Balthazar, "you do not."

But suddenly, as the enemy galley came within firing distance, it veered sharply to starboard.

"Why, I believe that is Fra Mathurin," observed Balthazar.

"Indeed," replied Strozzi and ordered the *comito* to halt the advance. At once the oars dipped into the water and the entire crew practically toppled over forward, so quickly did the boat come to rest.

Aye, it was Lescaut.

"Why were you attacking us, Romegas?" Strozzi said, embracing the young Knight as he jumped aboard.

"Your standards weren't visible, against the sun," Romegas replied. Then the tone of his coarse voice became darker. "Eh, friends, you are enemies of the Order and you must turn over your plunder to me this instant."

Strozzi put his hands on his hips and laughed. "By God, this man joined up with me not six months ago," he called out to all those within earshot, "and captured two Turkish ships near that accursed Los Gelves!"

"I don't jest, Leone," answered Romegas. "Hand over your plunder to me now or I'll take your ship."

Strozzi regarded his sometime comrade with increasing alarm. Could Romegas so quickly have forgotten their shared exploits? At that moment I noticed Vergã standing on the *ballestriere* of the other vessel. We hailed each other and he climbed aboard.

"So, Señor, you escaped Malta after all," Blaij said.

"No thanks to you," I replied indifferently.

"They say you killed a man."

"Kill or be killed," I answered.

Blaij nodded appreciatively. "If you return to the Convent now, *Esforzado*, you'll be arrested."

I shrugged. I, for one, had no intention of returning to Malta. "What are doing in these seas?" I asked.

"Much the same as you, I think. I like Greece. The women are beautiful there. I have several offers of marriage." We spoke for a few moments about our caravans and how soon we would become rich from plunder. Suddenly, Romegas waved to Vergã, ordering him back to the other galley. It appeared we would fight it out after all. Blaij and I saluted each other, preparing for combat.

By now, tho', the Emperor's vessel had pulled along-side and its Captain asked permission to board with another person, judging from his dress a high-ranking soldier. Strozzi, hearing out this man's urgent representations, asked leave of Romegas to postpone the battle for a short while and invited the stranger into his cabin. There they conferred for at least an hour as everyone else awaited the outcome of the mysterious business. At length the Prior emerged and called Romegas aboard once more, and surrounded himself as well with other members of his crew.

"The Emperor Carlos," he announced to the circle, "has offered me twelve thousand *scudi per annum*, the command of twelve galleys and a promise that I become Captain General after the death of Doria, should I join his service."

"I say," remarked Balthazar wryly, "what a *volte-face* on the Emperor's part."

Strozzi smiled faintly, moving his shoulders. "Carlos is an excellent judge of merit and, according to this Commander de Martines, as I am no longer permitted to set foot in France, the Emperor would be pleased to enlist me to fight his enemies—the French. Hah!"

"What have you told him?" asked Balthazar.

"Nothing as yet, but you must agree that the offer is too enticing to refuse."

Romegas, who had been scratching his beard throughout, now offered his advice. "Leone, at the Convent you have many friends, none above me. When you are in good graces with the Emperor, the ass d'Homedes will receive you again at Malta and make you a Knight again."

"As a member of the Order, I may not become Captain General of the Spanish fleet without the Monsignore's permission."

"Eh, spin out these negotiations," declared Romegas. "Don't decline or accept. Say you must confer with the Grand Master. Then I bet my balls Ol' One-Eye will lie down to please the Emperor."

The Prior informed de Martines that he must return to Malta to confer with d'Homedes about the proposal. However, this returned the slight difficulties which the officers had discussed the previous night: The Monsignore might well again see fit to blow the Prior out of the water; on a successful return Balthazar would surely be thrown into prison and, if Vergã was right, so would I.

The one eventuality seemed not to perturb Balthazar. Truly, e'en after the past months he rather welcomed it, a salve to his conscience.

"Do not fear, I shall speak on your behalf," said Strozzi to the Knight.

"And I shall speak on yours," said Balthazar to me.

I held fewer scruples than the Abbé and all our exploits had not left me more confident of d'Homedes's justice. So I refused, asking to be set ashore on the Calabrian coast. Natheless, Balthazar labored hard to persuade me and, with some unease among all parties, the decision was accepted. For several days we sailed up and down the coast of Naples and Sicily to the sound of trumpets, while Strozzi declared that he had deposited a considerable sum at Messina, along with a list of the Christian vessels he had plundered by dint of dire necessity, and all those persons to whom he was indebted might proceed to Messina and collect both the principal and interest, which he had computed to the exact taro. In the meantime, he had sent word ahead with Romegas to d'Homedes that he intended to return to the Convent. His Eminence replied that he would blow Strozzi out of the water should he attempt it. The Prior of Capua's galleys proceeded southward to Malta.

Thirty

After speaking to the wench, Villegaignon understood precisely why he had not yet received the Council's reply to King Henri's letter, and the reason horrified him. So disgusted was he that at first the Chevalier simply refused to credit that such actions could be laid at the feet of a Knight of St. John. In his entire existence he had ne'er felt the honor of the Religion to have been so wholly besmirched. Durand knew he must take every care, but equally that the time for care had fled. The only thing for it was to gather his words, his tongue.

Dressing himself and snatching up his rosary, he repaired to the Castellan's quarters atop St. Angelo where the Council was assembled. In the strong sea wind the Chevalier's black figure cut a moving gash in the grey castle walls under a grey sky. The guard, seeing Villegaignon approach, immediately offered to announce him; Durand waved him aside and strode in. At that moment the Seigneurs of the Council were in the full flight of argument, but when the Grand Prior of France bowed before the Grand Master, their tongues abruptly halted.

"What is the reason for this intrusion, Sir?" the Monsignore demanded angrily from his throne, with that sideward glare from his eye.

"Intrusion?" Villegaignon replied, bowing again. "Eminenza, as you well know, my rank entitles me to address the Council, indeed sit on it and, if I usually do not, it is only because of my infrequent presence at the Convent. As you also know, some weeks have passed while I have awaited the Council's reply to my sovereign's letter, and now with winter approaching, if I am to return to France, I must return at once."

"You, Sir," interrupted d'Homedes with dripping disdain, "are a Knight of the Sovereign Order of St. John of Jerusalem, and your allegiance is to the Grand Master, not to some secular prince."

Villegaignon well perceived his misstep. "My sincerest apologies, Eminenza, but the fact remains that the season is far gone and travel already dangerous. As I have not received the Council's reply and must depart imminently, in lieu of the absent letter it will be sufficient for me to take copies of all the depositions made to the judge Combo. Henri will see plainly that the capitulation of Tripoli was due not to any treachery on the part of Lord d'Aramont or the Mareschal de Vallier, but was caused entirely by the mutiny of the Calabrian soldiers."

"You dare presume!" exclaimed Senen-Lusarche from the Priory of Aquitaine. "Whence have you learned, Sir, that the Order is obliged to provide accounts of its criminal proceedings to secular princes?"

"That was not my intent," answered Villegaignon calmly, "but as the letter Henri requests is not forthcoming, I have little choice but to demand copies of the depositions. Is the envoy de Bellon to receive these depositions?"

"Nay!" cried the same Knight, joined by other followers of d'Homedes.

"And is he not to immediately receive the letter?"

A silence encompassed the chamber.

Villegaignon bowed once more to His Eminence. "In that case I must declare before this august assembly the reasons no reply has been forthcoming." Durand now drew himself up, facing the Grand Master alone. "There have for some days past, Eminenza, been reports spread about most injurious to your honor. They say that a private conference has passed between you and Combo, that after the previous court, which acquitted the impeached, the two of you natheless agreed to bring a renewed prosecution against Mareschal de Vallier. They say that this judge has engaged to put the Mareschal on the rack, and to force him by the violence of torture to confess to crimes he ne'er committed. Further, upon obtaining such false confessions, the judge is to condemn de Vallier to death and, after his execution, his confessions are to be substituted in lieu of the same letter that the Council has ordered to be written to the King. This, the reports have it, is the sole reason why the secretary, upon various pretenses, has delayed in delivering this letter to the King's envoy de Bellon."

No one in the chamber was able to listen to the accusations that flowed forth from Nicolas de Villegaignon's mouth with equanimity. The Grand Master, rage mounting throughout, at last began to quiver, to shake. Fire flashed from his one and only eye. "I command you," he shouted in his ancient voice, "to reveal before this assembly the author of these infamous reports!"

"The only question at hand," Villegaignon replied with every self-assurance and poise, "is whether the reports are true or whether they are false."

"Utterly false!" screamed d'Homedes in a sort of terror.

"Then declare, Monsignore," replied the Chevalier icily, "that you hereby acquit your judge, Agostino Combo, of the sum of five hundred ducats, which he stands bound to pay you, should he not pass a sentence of death upon the Mareschal."

As Villegaignon pronounced these terrible words, a gasp filled the hall and the Grand Master lost the ashes of his control. He fell at first into a complete confusion, so impossible was it to believe that an inferior had openly attacked a Monsignore, and his wits wholly forsook him. The old man began to twitch, as if possessed by St. Vitus's Dance itself, and for a moment everyone present was certain that his heart would give out and that he would fall, dead and destroyed, at the base of the dais. But he steadied himself on the back of the chair, and when after a moment he had sufficiently recovered, he loosed thereat a torrent of abuse on the Chevalier Villegaignon that had ne'er before been heard in the chamber.

"You are an infamous traitor!" he screamed, "sent by the Devil himself to destroy the Holy Religion!" He named Durand an enemy of God, a servant of the Dark One, a messenger of Beelzebub. Such was the stream of profanity that issued from His Eminence's mouth, that had any lesser Knight been guilty of them, he would have been arrested on the spot for contravention of the laws against blasphemy and thrown forthwith into the dungeon for half of eternity.

But Villegaignon, satisfied that he had at last revealed the whole perfidious scheme to the Council, merely bowed before the old man and quitted the assembly.

Later the same day the Council drew up a letter absolving d'Aramont of any guilt in the fall of Tripoli, forced the Grand Master to sign it, and delivered it to the Sieur de Bellon.

Two nights after leaving Sicily we put into the Great Port. The Feast of the Nativity had come and gone and a strong rain fell from the skies. Again the hour was late, past *l'hora della ruffiana* and, as on that other time, the great chain sealed off Galley Creek. I was certain this was an omen. Finding the road barred, Strozzi sent his *padrone* on a skiff under the chain to inform his friends he had returned to the Convent. He also sent with the *padrone* a gift for the church, a luxurious altar cloth he had ordered made at Messina, on which were embroidered the words of St. John: *He came unto his own and his own received him not.*

Surely the harbor watch had informed the Grand Master of our presence, and as the rain poured down everyone aboard waited in trepidation for the guns of St. Angelo to open fire. Nothing happened all night, but that the rain slowly turned to a drizzle and finally ceased. By morning a large crowd of Knights had gathered on the dockside to greet Strozzi and, in a gesture of the great esteem they held for him, they themselves lowered the chain for the Prior of Capua's entry. Without delay Strozzi, followed by this army of Knights, mostly Italians but with even de Valette among them, marched across the bridge into St. Angelo and to the Grand Master's quarters.

d'Homedes emerged from the Castellan's house, which he had surrounded with halberdiers, but if shock possessed him he well hid it. The two men faced one another other, the defrocked monk and the man who had defrocked him. Strozzi, like an expert *diestro*, allowed the Monsignore no time to collect his wits and call the guards; he immediately thrust into the old man's hand the letter proving that Emperor Carlos had offered him a high post in the Spanish navy. Standing in the puddles from last night's rain, Strozzi also at once informed the Grand Master *quia rumor classis turcice in dies augesci*t, that another Turkish invasion was imminent and that the Religion must not lose a moment in strengthening Malta's defenses.

The Monsignore gazed upon the man he so despised. He could arrest him but in the present circumstances a rebellion would not be ruled out. He could risk the Emperor's displeasure and turn him away. There, atop wet Castle St. Angelo, below overcast skies, His Eminence embraced the Prior of Capua like a long-lost brother, declared that he would send criers into the town and brigantines to the Vice Roy of Sicily to announce the restoration of Strozzi's knighthood, and he forthwith invited Strozzi to join him for refreshment inside, where they would discuss immediate improvements to the Convent's defenses.

For myself, I climbed the steps to my tiny room in Birgu only to find it occupied by another tenant. With a shrug I set off after Flaminia to give her some money toward the building of a house. I failed to find her, but one of the other *quiracas* told me she had taken up with someone else in my absence. Tho' hardly surprised, I confess to a pain sharper than expected at hearing the news. In the end it mattered little, for within several hours a friend of the Spaniard I'd killed recognized me in a tavern. The bells hadn't chimed before I was sitting in a cell far beneath St. Angelo, and not three days afterwards I learned, aye, I was to be tried for murdering the scoundrel and aiding Fra Balthazar's escape, Balthazar who sat unseen in the cell opposite.

The Abbé was in rare form. "*Ergo,*" he said, "*ex nihilo nihil fit,* do you understand, fool? Nothing comes from nothing. After four months, we are in a worse position than at the start. Not only am I locked up in this hole, but you and Pietru as well."

It was true. Pietru sat beside me against the dank stones. His fate, of the three, was the most perilous, for he had no protectors. He had nothing. Balthazar, tho', whose wit illuminated any dark corner, lacked the ability to remain indefinitely angered. "Imagine," he said at length, "they have arrested so many of us that I am forced to sit in the same dungeon as laymen! Unheard of! I shall protest! Natheless I say this is justice, justice! I well knew the risks in entering that castle at Tripoli and I accepted fully the consequences of my actions. Only your meddling deprived me of them. Finally, I am able to obey my vow of obedience, as I intended, and I yet expect to enjoy my newfound riches."

How is that? I asked. *O reniego de la Puta mi Suegra,* he could not look forward to being drowned in a sack or hanged.

"Nay. But, my friend, if one considers the course of recent events, it is high time Fortune turned her hand, for the Order's descent into a hell much of its own devising cannot continue indefinitely." He sighed ruefully. "I do hope she turns it in time to save our necks. Amen."

I was pleased to hear Balthazar call me "friend" as of old, and to see in this blackness he'd regained something of his former self. Yet, I perceived that if he had found himself again after these months, I had lost something. What, I found no words to describe.

Pietru's spirits were the most surprising. Failing to find his wife in those countless eyes we'd turned during our caravans, he'd also remained silent 'til the end about Gozo. Now I asked him directly about the devastation of his home, and what he would do upon his release.

Ix-Xabaw did not mourn or curse the Turks. He nodded slowly and answered, "Someday I plant the island again." As good answers do, his left much room for construal. For my part, I smiled, somewhat.

Shortly after, a torch lit up our subterranean kingdom. The guard had brought Flaminia. Upon catching sight of me, she pressed herself against the bars of the cell, stretching forth her arms, begging my forgiveness and swearing by the Madonna that she'd return to me if I'd have her, all the while crying in thanks for the fifteen *scudi* I had left with her neighbor. It seemed the neighbor had taken a cut. Flaminia had also brought bread, wine and *afione*. We shared the bread but *afione* had caused enough trouble and I passed it to Ix-Xabaw.

If the flickering torchlight raised a pity in me for my once mistress who depended fully on the good will of her masters, the pity was removed. The months at sea had left her a stranger, tho' she still insisted I attend the exorcism at Zurrieq, which had yet to take place.

In the midst of our reunion another torch appeared and, under it, Isabella. At once she shot a glance at Flaminia and said, "Begone, you common slut."

Flaminia, to my astonishment, proudly raised her head and retorted, "Common or uncommon, the only difference is the price."

Enraged at such a slander, Isabella lifted her hand and fully struck the *quiraca*, who laughing shrilly, natheless departed.

"Forgive her," I said. "She knows nothing."

Once Isabella's temper had cooled, she set her gaze on me and could scarcely disguise her shock. Before her stood a man, unshaven, lice-ridden, his clothes filthy, confined to a befouled cell, and whose stink signaled how many weeks he had gone without bathing. Natheless, she extended her hand and, as on that former time, asked whether I had kept her token.

I revealed the kerchief and Isabella managed to smile at it, but I might also have regarded her through a clouded glass. Recounting our exploits, I watched her face and saw how many leagues had passed between us.

"I did not think ever to set eyes on you again," she said when I had done.

"Nor I you."

"You've changed, Francisco. There is some hardness in you now, meseems."

"Yes." Isabella perceived what I had failed to cast into words. "You are right," I nodded and wondered if after a decade of campaigning Balthazar's laughter were not a pliant shield, mayhap, to spare himself an adamantine one. "What news from above, Isabella?" I asked, refusing to dwell on it.

The young lady lost no time in recounting Villegaignon's exertions, how he had nobly stood before the entire Council and exposed d'Homedes's evil designs.

"That is heartening news," I said. And puzzling. If Villegaignon had succeeded, why had Balthazar been arrested?

"We must get you out of here," Isabella went on urgently. "I shall speak to Parisot. It is the only hope."

"No!" I exclaimed, recalling my promise to Villegaignon not to involve de Valette.

"Then how can I help you?"

I saw we were speaking at cross-purposes. "Why, petition Villegaignon. He will have Balthazar set free, who can then plead on our behalf."

Now Isabella looked at me strangely. "Villegaignon is no longer here."

"¿Como?" I asked with mounting confusion.

"Some time ago, after he received the letter from the Council absolving Lord d'Aramont, he departed for France."

Utterly perplexed, I dropped into silence. At last I replied, "Do you intend to say that, after defeating the Grand Master, Villegaignon quit the island with the emissary de Bellon, leaving the Mareschal and all the other Knights in prison?"

"Si," Isabella nodded heavily, "that is exactly what happened. The Monsignore has not relaxed his intent to see the Knights tried."

I scratched my beard. "In the end Villegaignon was more intent to uphold the honor of the French Ambassador than to win freedom for his fellow Knights. What do you say, Lord Balthazar?"

Balthazar, who had bent his ear to the entire conversation from across the tunnel, replied, "I say I have always regarded Villegaignon as a centaur, half man and half beast, whose purposes remain unfathomable to me. Natheless, I say again, do not presume to judge one so far above your station. I cannot believe his exertions will have proved for naught."

With a sad tentativeness Isabella agreed. "The situation is yet more perplexing. Spanish spies, who were following de Bellon everywhere, captured them en route to Marseille. Whether this is d'Homedes's doing, I know not, but at this very moment I believe the two are being interrogated in Genoa about Tripoli." She sighed. "At the least, methinks, Nicolas averted a terrible clash with France, mayhap a war."

"*Mort de Dieu!*" exclaimed Balthazar. "Will every one of us end up in prison? But I do not fear for Durand. The Emperor will hardly dare keep him for long."

Regardless of his fate, it need not be said that Villegaignon's bartering had left us very much in the position we were in months ago, Balthazar exactly. "Then you must speak with Prior Strozzi, Isabella. He swore not to abandon us."

Isabella nodded faintly. "In these past days his talk of a new Turkish attack has terrified everyone. The Council has debated without cease the building of a new city on Mt. Sciberras to prevent the Turks from occupying it during an invasion, but no one believes the Order can afford such a project. I have heard no talk of the prisoners, not one word."

"'Tis true," said Balthazar with more cheer. "The finances of the Order are in no order to permit the building of a new city, however sensible the project may be. As for the charges against us Knights, meseems this sudden concern with defenses cannot help our case. The Grand Master will have a free hand to act as he pleases."

"It matters neither way to me," I said, seeing that e'en should God will the charges against the Knights be found untrue, I'd be tried for offing that drunkard in my own defense and for assisting a Knight escape whose imprisonment was laughable. Pietru's position was no better. "These shall be our walls for some years, I think."

"Do not believe that, Francisco," urged Isabella. "I will speak to Strozzi at once. Thou shalt not lose heart."

"Never."

Isabella prepared to leave. Pausing, she turned and thrust a folded paper into the cell. "A gift for you," she said and departed.

"What is it?" Balthazar wanted to know.

I unfolded the paper but the torch had gone and the only remaining light was from a small oil lamp on a niche in our cell. I could see almost nothing. "Verses, I think."

Balthazar's sigh was audible. "Did I not warn you to stay clear of that girl? Marriage negotiations proceed apace and her guardian, I declare with God as my witness, will brook no interference from you. He held her in baptism. Do you not understand?"

It seemed to me that the Abbé's advice reflected more than mere concern for a younger companion. "Tell me about the love you lost," I said to him.

It was in Italy, he said, Venice. She was beautiful, no less fair than Isabella, graceful and possessed of wit. She could speak on any subject and had a sense for numbers, which was well, for hers was one of the most successful of merchant families in the Republic. "I loved her as I loved the morning and the evening, the moon and the stars. We were to be married. Yet one day an acquaintance informed me that this family, which had come to Venice some years before, tho' to all appearances Catholic, was secretly Jews, and she a Jewess, a Marrano."

"H—how could you not have known!" I exclaimed, startled beyond words.

"Such things are not always evident, are they?" answered Balthazar severely. "I questioned her about the matter and she, in tears, confessed. I flew into a rage. How could she have lied so to me, not wearing the proper scarf, besmirching my reputation? I beat her, denounced her to everyone. Gossip did the rest and her family's lives became a living hell. At last word reached the authorities who intended to force them to the ghetto. Rather than face such a life, the entire family fled to Constantinople—where, I am told, they prosper."

Listening to this dark story in the equal dark of the prison, I sensed more than with his earlier tales that into this one were woven like parts of truth and telling, as if Balthazar had ne'er resolved to what degree diversion should cede to instruction. To further questions he made no answer, but along the history of his life I could hardly place such an episode. If he'd already professed as a Knight, he could not have married the woman. If he hadn't professed, wherefore had he come to Venice? Yet in his tale I found some commonness with the words of Abdallah the *chavush* about Constantinople, words that left me puzzled and ill at ease. Pietru, tho', entertained no doubts about what we'd just heard.

"Someday he find her," he said in his gravely voice.

For the Abbé's part, he merely shrugged and answered, "I hold no truck with Jews, yet I have ne'er forgiven myself for the harm I did those people, whom I loved. Afterwards, I swore to uphold my vows to the Religion, but I swore as well that I would ne'er do the other, if you take my meaning. In that, too, I have often failed, as I failed again on Zante."

Not entirely taking Balthazar's meaning, I questioned him no more on the matter. I retired to the wall of my cell where, crouching close to the oil lamp, I struggled through Isabella's poem:

Noi contro spietata e crudel Fortuna
Lottiam, mentre l'onda ci tien disparte:
Tu dal mar portato in lontana parte
Com'Ulisse erri con la vaga luna;
E'l mio cor piange sua acerba sfortuna
E gela al letto quando'l sol diparte.
Borea non si piega per nessun' arte,
E ogni navigio affonda in tal fortuna.

Lo sguardo mio su questa spiaggia parca
Chiede or se Ulisse stia cercando il porto,
Or se Iason giunga in colchida marca;
E io: con buona speme l'angoscia porto?
Medea la sua gran doglia ormai discarca?
Spira il vento: 'ogni tuo desio è morto.'

I was no judge of this young lady's verse, and to render its mournful sentiments in my own words I found too difficult. If to compare me with Jason or Ulysses, driven across turbulent seas, was too flattering by half, I natheless felt a sad comfort in knowing that Isabella, like me, struggled against Fortune's tempest, e'en as she despaired of ever defeating the forces that tore us, and our world, apart.

Thirty-One

The feeble light Flaminia and Isabella carried to the bowels of St. Angelo illuminated one thing with the brightness of day: Events were not unfolding as expected. Convinced to his marrow by Strozzi that Turgut would rise again above the horizon with the morning sun, Ol' One-Eye overnight appointed the Prior himself and two other senior Knights to survey the island's fortifications and draw up a plan of action.

"There is talk of it already. O Blessed Mother! I swear I'll not go to Sicilia a second time!" Flaminia was crossing herself under the torch in a frenzy. "They can throw me in this prison if they like. Malta is my home." The *quiraca* pronounced the last with a fervor that startled me after her recent dread. "But what will they do? If all the *quiracas* refuse to go, they won't do anything. How can I go now, when trade is finally beginning to grow again?"

Trade? I asked her sharply.

She mentioned a new love potion she made from a root "enula" plucked on St. John's Eve, a piece of orange and some ambergris, into which mixture she put a piece of paper bearing the word *sheva*. By her answer I took her to mean *afione*, but I let it pass.

Isabella had spoken to the Prior of Capua, importuning him to uphold his oath and intercede on Balthazar's behalf. Strozzi indeed brought the case to d'Homedes, but His Cyclops refused to release him, declaring that Balthazar would be tried with the other Knights.

"Do not fear," Leone Strozzi assured Isabella, "we are not defeated yet."

"The Prior would not reveal his exact plans," Isabella told Balthazar during her second visit. "I can say that his entire attention is directed toward the fortification of the island. Oh, he rides from one end to the other like a demon and has whipped up such a storm of urgency that the Grand Master himself is bending. As of this very day the commission has proposed not only to strengthen Birgu town, but to build two completely new fortresses to make Malta impregnable. They are well convinced it will take every man on the island to accomplish the task."

"Where are these castles to be?" asked the Knight with intense curiosity.

"As the Religion cannot afford an entirely new city, one is to rise on the tip of Sciberras, where the old chapel and watchtower stand. The other is to be built across Galley Creek on l'Isola."

Balthazar nodded, stroking his beard. At length he answered, "These are good thoughts. A fort on the tip of Sciberras will guard both the entrance to the Great Port and Marsamxett harbor. A castle on l'Isola will guard the inner reaches of the Port and protect Birgu and St. Angelo from a landward incursion. I say, my friends, someone has finally come to his senses and set Tripoli aside."

Isabella shook her head sadly. "*Oimè*, I fear not. The Prior visited my Godfather last night. Watching them together is to watch two evangelists in contest. They both swore by the Cross to wrest Tripoli from the grasp of the barbarian with their own hands."

"*Mort de Dieu!*" exclaimed Balthazar at hearing this. "For a heartbeat I thought the heavens had shone the holy light of reason upon these men. Ah, Folly's embrace is after all too fast to be loosed by divine guidance alone."

Before Isabella departed, she asked whether I had read her poem.

I had, I told her. "But my Italian is imperfect and you must know, my lady, I am deaf to the music of words and blind to the hidden meanings of things."

"Oh!" she cried, "you are impossible! I entrust you with a piece of my heart and that is all you can say?"

"Do not take it amiss, Isabella," I replied more seriously than I ought. "You would do better to show your writing to an ape than to me."

"I think so!" she said, with unfeigned harshness. "Perhaps you should be locked up in this cell forever, released now and again for oiling, so that the rest of us might know you are alive!"

With that she departed in a huff and Balthazar laughed. "My friend," he chuckled, "I say that was singularly clumsy. Here is a young noblewoman stranded on a barren isle amongst warrior monks, who soon will be given in marriage to a complete stranger. She has been raised on Petrarch and *Orlando Furioso*, with its singing of damsels and chevaliers and dimpled cheeks and incarnadine lips. She dreams of romance, of love, of a true courtier endowed with all the graces a man of station should possess. She yearns for poetry and you, unlettered peasant, give her the basest prose."

"Do you now advise me, Abbé?" I rejoined with irritation, "you who have constantly warned me to stay clear of her? Ah, you are right. Tho' I acknowledge to you that I love that girl with all my heart, I find no poetry within me. That is the bare fact of it. I have entered a life suspended between night and day, where the horizon brings only war and in which the sword is the only heeded voice. In that world there is no place for a woman."

"*Moy foy*, you sound like your friend Vergã," answered Balthazar, and fell silent.

For a few days more we lived on bread and water and were visited by angels. Suddenly one morning—I believe it was morning—into our pit descended a pair of Knights sent by Strozzi's commission. Such was the scale of the projects now being undertaken that these two had been charged with registering every capable male on Malta of age between manhood and deathbed—twelve and sixty, they said. That we were criminals hardly mattered. Aye, Pietru's role in the escape little concerned them and after they reported to the magistrate who held the depositions against us, the charges against Ix-Xabaw were abruptly dropped on condition he not leave the island. To our astonishment, of the three of us, Pietru walked free first to join the construction gang.

"*Il-fortuna tghin ic-cwiec*, we say," he told us as the gate to the cell was unlocked. "Fortune helps fools. I see you soon." And he cheerfully departed.

Several more days passed and the guard unlocked the cell again, this time telling me with a brusque wave of his hand that I was free to go. When I asked for an explanation, he only flashed at me the signed order for my release and when I hesitated, he shouted, "Go to the Devil for all I care, but get out of here!"

I stepped across to Balthazar's cell and said to him, "*À bientôt*."

"Before you ascend," he said, "allow me to apologize. These past months I have been harsh on you for your brainless rescue of a Chevalier. When I asked onto a year ago what was your valor, I did not foresee it would include such loyalty. That is as rare as it is stupid, but the best Knights would envy your devotion and for it you have my thanks. À *bientôt*."

Being unable to take the Abbé's hand, I bowed, overjoyed that our friendship had been fully restored. Then I gratefully left this dungeon. After days, tho', the Knight did not appear.

I felt more keenly than ever that I must aid Lord Balthazar but was granted not an instant to consider the matter. Scarce had my eyes adjusted to daylight than guards put me to work on the new stronghold that was to occupy the tip of Mt. Sciberras, a fort to be named after the old chapel there, St. Elmo. Once more I see astonishment fleeting across His Majesty's face. Yes, as work began on that castle, not far above the winter waters, no one could foresee that in a dozen years it would become the center of the most ferocious contest in the history of the world, a contest that decided nothing less than the fate of Christendom.

At the time, it appeared no more a distinguished place than many others of like character. We knew only one thing: None of us would be granted respite until the fort was finished. The engineer sent by the Vice Roy of Sicily drew up his plans in six days. Strozzi's commission ordered him to build it in six months. The Grand Master, convinced now to the marrow of his bones that the Turks would attack before summer, granted him not a day more.

"Very well," he said, "six months. I hold you to it."

Strozzi and the other commissioners personally supervised the work, which proceeded from dawn 'til dusk in periods. Masons and workmen arrived from Sicily. Under the dreary skies of late January, after the Feast of the Conversion of St. Paul, Knights labored side by side with peasants, townspeople and slaves, and hardly any distinction could be perceived amongst them. We quarried stone inland, hauled it on carts down Sciberras to the construction place, dug the foundations with pick and axe, carried the stones into position or raised them with machines in whose wheels tread people or horses.

"Six months," said a resonant voice near me. "Can you believe it, Señor?"

I glanced up from my labors to see a wine cup being held out to me by the dark hand of Abdallah al-Waryagli. I'd not set eyes on him since the night after the *razzia* on Gozo, when I'd attempted to run him through.

Now I looked at him with a greater dispassion. During the past months I'd fought many barbarians, but the fighting had become less a matter of honor or survival than commerce. One did not have to hate one's enemies; one merely had to kill them. Warily I accepted the cup.

As I stood there trying to find words wherewith to address him, al-Waryagli spoke: "I have been hoping to see you for some time, in order to make amends."

"It was I who tried to kill you."

The Moor nodded easily. "Yes, but in light of that terrible raid on Gozo, my words about the House of War only served to inflame, and I understand your fury."

As I surveyed the ceaseless work going on around us, under the gaze of Strozzi himself, I wondered that this infidel could offer the word "terrible." "Have you been treated well?"

He shrugged. "I now rent a tiny room at the bagno. I am allowed to move about freely, until nightfall; I pray as I see fit and I remain spared hard labor. A man in my position quickly learns to lower his hopes. This of course is the black humor of Destiny, and no intelligent soul attempts to fight against Fate. I do wish you infidels, on an occasion such as this when sweat drips from every pore, would learn how to make *sherbet* ... I have learned you were imprisoned."

"How did you discover that?" I asked with both amusement and surprise.

"Little escapes the ears of slaves on Malta—when they have ears."

I laughed. "So, it seems Fate treats you no worse than soldiers and Knights." Assuredly, after all that had lately happened, I found myself none too friendly with the Knights of St. John and I doubted the emissary's desire to be chained to this wretched island surpassed my own. "What of your ransom?" I asked, falling into that same easy tone we had found on a past occasion.

The Moor in his burnoose shrugged again. "No news. To their own disadvantage, the Knights lift not a finger to speed the process and a slave's letters are thus passed to the hands of strangers or untrustworthy merchants whose ships may never reach their destinations. I pity those captives lacking rank or wealth, for they have no recourse but prayer and will mostly likely die on this rock. Some pay me to write for them, but whither to send the letters? For myself, I write to some Jews in Venice who will give word to my family or, God willing, the Sultan." Abdallah al-Waryagli sighed deeply. "I begin to fear there shall soon be no Jews to write to. The Knights have recently taken sixty of them?" E'en underground, I had heard. "In any case, to this day—nothing—and certainly there can be nothing before summer. But Allah protects his servants and for that reason I am not fearful. "

"Mayhap the Order can sell you to a rich family. It will be easier for you ... I also find that escape from this island is not so difficult if one puts his mind to it."

With a raised eyebrow Abdallah demurred. "I give no thought to such adventures. The Knights need every body now and they watch the docks carefully ... Will this fort be finished before summer?"

I again surveyed the picture about us, with its hundreds of men racing to erect a miracle. The press of time had ensured that St. Elmo would be of small size, but the engineers assured us it was being built *alla moderna* according to the latest advances of military science. With our diligence, the outlines of the walls were already visible and one could see the form of a star taking shape. The reasoning behind such a design I did not know. I knew only that we had much back-breaking labor ahead.

"Yes, I think it will be completed in six months," I told Abdallah and got back to laying stones.

The entire Port was alive. When my period ended, I paid a *dghajsa*-man three *grani* to take me across the harbor to l'Isola. Unlike the occasion Vergã and I first set foot on Malta, today l'Isola was far from empty. A construction gang e'en larger than the one on Sciberras swarmed around the base of a second fort rising on the inward part of that tongue of land. This second stronghold, as yet unnamed, would prevent a foe from emplacing guns there, whence bombarding Birgu directly across Galley Creek. As far as I could see, the castle would resemble an ancient pyramid with its head lopped off, and would in a few months support a battery of heavy guns.

Vergã labored here and, as his hours were also ending, I collected him and together we crossed Galley Creek to Birgu, where we might find supper. Yet, e'en such a simple crossing was made difficult with the myriad vessels now crowding the Port and by the construction taking place on the opposite shore as well. As if two new fortresses were insufficient, Strozzi's commission also ordered the ditch between Castle St. Angelo and Birgu to be dug out and water let in, transforming it into a true moat running between Galley and Kalkara Creeks. Vessels might safely be moored there behind St. Angelo and the fortress would become completely separate from Birgu town. Birgu itself was being fortified with new walls and two new bastions on the landward side. Like ants, lines of workmen stretched to and fro, as far as the eye could see. I thought I espied Pietru among this gang, but was unsure. Mayhap he was one of the five hundred who'd been dispatched inland to repair the walls of Città Notabile so damaged by the Turkish guns six months ago.

No one could remain unimpressed by the scale of the work. Indeed, Your Majesty, it was during those days that the fortifications of the Great Port began to assume their modern outlines. "How does the Order expect to finance these projects, which must stretch its resources to the limit?" I said to Blaij as we sat down in a tavern. "An Egyptian pharaoh would not scoff at this undertaking."

Vergã nodded with some wonder. "Ah yes, Señor, you've seen no sun of late. The Council has sent fast messengers to every nation of Christendom, to all the priories of the Religion, with dire warnings of invasion and urgent appeals for ready money. Poor Knights who own nothing but their gold chains are putting them joyfully on the plate. Today I hear three rich Knights are en route to the Convent with their complete fortunes." Blaij spoke the truth. Within weeks we learned of old and infirm Knights who willed everything to the fortifications and converted their entire estates to silver, which they sent on to Malta. Then they died.

"I think it is shit," Blaij said.

What did he mean?

"All this," he waved as plates were brought, "is on the word of Strozzi. While you were on your womanly caravans, Señor, I sailed with Romegas. I spent enough nights with Greek whores to know about any Turkish plans—if there were any."

"We were further east than you," I objected, lifting my glass.

Vergã shrugged. "Perhaps. I'll wager you five *scudi* no Turkish invasion comes this summer. This is all an excuse to steal attention from the mess over Tripoli."

Now it was my turn to shrug. "I'll not accept. Everyone from Balthazar to Abdallah knows that an invasion will come—if not this year, then next. The great contest is hardly over."

"Aah," responded Vergã as he bit into a leg of rabbit, "the Order's intelligence is shit. They must devote the proper means."

That may have been true, but I then changed the subject. "What have you heard about the trial?"

"That d'Homedes remains out for blood. Your friend Villegaignon farted loudly and vanished. He saved the Ambassador's skin but did shit to save the hides of his fellow Knights. For his pains he's captured by the Spanish and sits a prisoner in some luxurious Italian villa. Hah!"

Tho' I came to respect Villegaignon, I'd ne'er presume to call him "friend" and his actions did remain inscrutable to me. As to his present circumstance, one could only wonder at so improbable a fortune. "What are your plans?" I asked Blaij, changing the subject again.

"To build a fort ... In a year or two I'll buy my own galley. If the Order lets me profess, I'll get letters and fly their colors. If they don't ... " He shrugged. "I can still sail."

"You still believe these Knights will allow you to profess?" I said with both derision and admiration, but Vergã only shrugged again, saying that he was giving money to Innocenza to build a house.

I answered that I was doing much the same.

"Why?" he sat back, wiping his mouth clean with his sleeve, as disbelieving of my answer as I had been of his. "You've fled Malta once; they've thrown you into prison; they pluck you out so you can lift stones like a slave. Why should you fight for the Knights?"

"One must fight for somebody," I shrugged, tho' to confess, I had lately been considering the same question.

Vergã snorted. "By the True Cross of Caravaca, you have changed. A year ago you would have held the piss of these Chevaliers to be gold."

"You as well," I replied, knowing Blaij was more right than I would admit.

"I still do," he answered with too much gravity. While I pondered this reply, he went on. "By the way, the year of our truce will soon be over."

At that I practically spat up my wine. "You yet brood over that long-gone whore!" I exclaimed with disbelief. "I cannot e'en remember her name."

"That's another thing I've ne'er liked about you, Barai. You think because your father bought a coat of arms you are a nobleman."

I should have realized that Blaij would not have put aside his mad grievance and that I would have again raise my guard. As complines sounded we rose, saluted one another and each set off to find his whore.

Thirty-Two

The next day my work ended before vespers and a small rain had begun. Only now was I able to tell Isabella of my mysterious release, but I was filthy after hours of hauling stones. To make myself halfwise presentable I stopped at Flaminia's room, where I'd left my other clothes, having yet to secure new lodging for myself in the Borgo. Despite the inexcusable insult wherewith she had besmirched Mademoiselle Guasconi, Flaminia conceded today that the signorina was a *bona anima*.

"You may thank her for your freedom," she said as she sponged the dirt and stone dust off me.

"¡*Como!*" I exclaimed, taken completely by surprise. "How do you know this?"

Flaminia offered no more than a demure smile and I quickly departed.

At the Guasconi mansion, the servants were gathering water from the large underground cistern filled by pipes running from the roof. For the first time I understood that the strange flat roofs of Maltese houses served a purpose—to collect the fresh water that on this island was near as valuable as gold. When Isabella and Lady Emilia caught sight of me free and standing, they both clapped their hands in joy and bade me enter the sitting room.

For a second time I discovered Jean de Valette here, now with the Prior of Capua himself. I hesitated to enter, but months at sea had stiffened me against the suspicious gaze the Knight cast in my direction and, for his part, Strozzi greeted me heartily as a comrade-in-arms. Thus I stepped in, taking a seat between Lady Emilia and Isabella.

"You have done splendidly, Leone," de Valette was saying. "Ne'er has there been such purposeful activity at the Convent. You have provided a shining example to all of what one man can do when he lets no obstacle thwart his will. By the Grace of God, you will become Grand Master when that Spanish ass dies. Do you wish it? Tell me and I'll throw my support behind you."

The Prior smiled, refusing a direct answer. "I have learned of late to thank Fortune's buffets and rewards equally, for one can ne'er say which wind will blow you into a fair port. A month past, I was an orphan on the sea."

At that Parisot took a glass from a tray the servant had presented and raised it to Strozzi. "May Fortune's buffets preserve your health, Leone."

"Sir," I said to the Prior, interrupting, despite the glower that lit up Parisot's face, "what can you tell us about de Vallier's fortunes and those of the other Knights?"

Strozzi glanced toward his friend, as if for aid. "I am not the best person to ask after that, having only recently returned to the Convent."

"Unless it be by armed insurrection," answered de Valette, his thin lips drawn up at me, "little can at this moment be done. The Order's statutes expressly forbid surrender of a place without authority, and there must be an accounting. The snake Combo reconsiders and we expect his decision in a few weeks."

"Did Villegaignon accomplish nothing then?" I blurted out with heat. "Will none of you grasp the torch where he let it fall?"

Isabella cast a worried look at me just as Parisot considered his response. "d'Homedes counts many supporters amid the Spaniards and Italians, more than a *nabot* such as you might perceive. Natheless, Nicolas put the fear of God into that judge and we may pray for a just outcome." Thereat, as if to spite the *nabot* who sullied his presence, he turned his head away. "Leone," he went on with hardly a pause, "perhaps you have heard that Nicolas has been released from Genoa—the Monsignore interceded on his behalf with the Emperor."

"Hah!" exclaimed Strozzi, shaking his head, "this is indeed difficult to fathom! that d'Homedes would do ought but let Durand rot in captivity after being so mercilessly exposed by him."

"I believe One-Eye has been so shamed by the affair that he desires only to do everything he might to cause Europe to forget it."

"Mayhap he recognizes that the Grand Prior of France is for all that a Knight of St. John," put in Isabella while the two men were laughing.

de Valette paid her no more heed than he did me. "Leone, we must consider in every detail how to retake Tripoli before our bitter enemy

Dragut ensconces himself there, which if I know Dragut must happen soon."

At hearing this, tho', Strozzi's fervor became more guarded. Scratching his beard he answered, "Yes, of course, Jean, but equally we must wait until the fortifications here are completed. We cannot spare a single man. Further, Tripoli itself is too strongly fortified—"

"Not against the Turks!" erupted de Valette without warning.

"Pâce, Jean. Let us secure another place near Tripoli whence we may launch an attack. Unfortunately, my enterprises have not made me so familiar with Barbary to suggest where the best place might be."

Parisot did not think long before replying. "I own several hundred galley slaves and many are not above the sin of avarice. If we pay them, if necessary offer them their liberty, we will learn where the Order might attack."

A servant then announced dinner and Lady Emilia rose, lightly placing her hands on Parisot's shoulders to interrupt the discussion. "Messeri, I would you find another venue to speak of military affairs," she said pleasantly, "for little bores women more than unceasing talk of fighting and bloodshed, and what we have beheld with our own eyes in this past year is enough to make a body shudder at the thought of it." Truly, a perceptible quiver shot through Emilia's frame from head to toe, and she crossed herself. For the moment she stood there behind Parisot, I was able to study his face. Again I saw nothing but the same man, whose severity left little room for greatness. For an instant, as he gazed up at Emilia, a smile crossed his lips and that stern, austere countenance gave way to the barest hint of tenderness. Then he got to his feet and afterwards I convinced myself I had imagined it.

Having not been invited for dinner, I excused myself, saying that I needed quickly to find a new room, which would be no mean feat with all the workers arriving from Sicily.

"We are not wanting for food, Francisco," replied Lady Emilia with her hands clasped before her, "and you are always welcome."

I protested that the grueling day's work had left me too exhausted to be a delight in conversation and bowed my leave. Isabella offered to see me to the door. There, on the threshold, I fervently kissed my deliverer's hands. "You have done me a great service, Milady," I told her, "and I am forever in your debt. I say this with all my heart."

But Isabella answered with a surprise well-feigned: "Whatever can you mean, Señor?"

I told her what my mistress had told me.

The young noblewoman scoffed. "You should not believe such gossip as dirties the streets of Birgu," she retorted sharply, "especially when it comes from the mouths of whores."

"In my experience their intelligence is the most reliable," I answered and now led her by the arm into the street. "You spoke to judge Combo, methinks. What exactly did you tell him?"

Isabella now glanced about nervously, still refusing to speak, and thereon I squeezed her arm tightly. "Unhand me, you beast!" she yelped, loosing herself, but I grabbed her again firmly, saying that I must know, for her sake above mine. Finding herself my captive in the mud and rain, she admitted, but no more, that she'd told the magistrate what she saw that night.

"And what was that, Milady? What did you see?"

Isabella smiled faintly, pulling herself free again. "That is between me, the magistrate and the Lord," she said.

The reason for this circumspection in large part eluded me and worried me more. "I trust you have in no way compromised yourself."

"How dare you suggest it?" she replied severely, shaking her head. Then she paused and touched my arm. "I beg you, Francisco, do not allow Parisot to discover the cause of your release."

Now I understood better. I swore, kissing my crucifix, and embraced this young lady who had become so dear to me and so unattainable. With the need to find a new room pressing, I took my leave.

Work on the fortifications proceeded with military discipline. As trumpets blared, halberdiers cudgeled idlers into service at the start of their hours. The first work began at primes, the second an hour before the noon Angelus and the third an hour after nones. In this way we labored throughout the spring, truly little different from the slaves in our midst.

With such rigor governing each movement of our lives, I saw Balthazar infrequently. He would hear no more of escapes, and stoically awaited the judge's decision. He smiled when I told him of Villegaignon's release from Genoa through the Grand Master's intercession. He listened with keen interest as I described by what amount Fort St. Elmo rose each day and with e'en greater attention when I reported d'Homedes latest edicts.

They were never-ending. Daily, to the sound of drums, criers would read the new *bandi* at the works and post them on the squares. One afternoon they announced all ships leaving Malta would be inspected. The next afternoon they announced that slaves would henceforward make up no more than fifty of the rowers in a galley's *ciurma*. "What can be the reason?" I asked Abdallah al-Waryagli when he made his rounds that day.

"You see how it is, this ceaseless, merciless toil," the Moor replied, casting his gaze over the rising fort. "They fear a revolt, of course. The situation is ripe."

Soon enough the truth of his words revealed itself. The Knights themselves joyfully put their backs to it, singing the day through, but the Maltese, tho' paid some coins, hourly cursed under their breaths and invoked the name of God, who in their language they call *Alla*. Worse, maugre the ships sent to Sicily for corn and grain, food for all the workers flooding Malta remained perilously short and the thousand slaves rarely received their daily three loaves.

Inside the bagno the infidels began to grumble, and more. One evening at l'Isola, they were being rounded up to be taken back to the bagno. Suddenly seized by the mad idea that they might overpower the guards, steal a vessel and escape, a slave picked up a rock and hurled it at one of their keepers. Another joined in and within moments a rebellion had begun. Whole lines of slaves seized the chains wherewith they were about to be bound and attempted to shackle the guards. Others cast about for picks and axes, intending to use them as weapons. Happily, all but a few of the tools had been stored away for the night and by the Grace of God no cannon were near; otherwise—In the midst of the disorder the crackle of arquebuses spit forth as soldiers ran toward the rebels. Within a few moments, as smoke filled the air, the rebels were surrounded.

"It was foolish," Abdallah said the day after the still-born revolt. "I myself faced them. 'Escape is impossible,' I shouted. 'Every ship is inspected. Allah will give you succours and punish your captors, but for now, I beg you, put down your stones.' Thankfully they obeyed ... Who knows what lives might have been lost?"

Some told me that more than one slave had been shot or quartered. Others said Abdallah had informed the guards of the slaves' plans in advance in order to secure for himself a better position. Whatever the exact truth, from that day on more guards were posted to keep an eye on the slaves. Thereafter, tho', for a small payment the *agozzino* did allow Abdallah near full freedom of the Port.

Aye, Abdallah made the most of his misery, writing ransom letters for profit, reselling bread and sometimes with the help of an innkeeper making this drink he called yoghoort. Sherbet was impossible because no ice came from Mt. Etna to Malta. Had circumstances been different, I might have become friends with the learned Moor. As he made his rounds during the work on Fort St. Elmo, he ne'er failed to speak of the wonders of Constantinople, which he averred to be the city of the world's dreams. He wondered about progress on His Majesty's mosque, which he said would be the grandest temple in the world, dwarfing the project on which we now toiled.

"Then be glad you are not working on it," I remarked at hearing the *chavush*'s words, "for you would be laboring for years instead of months."

"You would be working," he replied jovially. "I would be eating *sherbet*."

Thus with each passing day the Moor and I talked more familiarly, e'en as the situation around us grew more tense. Fortunately, the failed revolt awakened the Grand Master who decided not to risk a wholesale rebellion of the island's people. As Shrovetide loomed he decreed that work should cease and Carnavale be celebrated.

What a celebration it was! Birgu exploded. If the town was no more than a mote next to Granada, you would never have noticed in the midst of all the singing and dancing, the drunkenness and licentiousness that took place during that festa. For three days ribboned girls were available for the asking, musicians roved the streets singing bawdy songs, masked revelers danced into the night and on the church square in Birgu townspeople whipped a large stone hung from a beam.

Shrove Tuesday fell on the very first day of March and with Shrove Tuesday naturally came the climax of the festa, a custom the Maltese named *coccanga*. There being no trees in Birgu, the people had managed to find a number of long spars from the work sites and laid them between the roofs of two tall houses in the Borgo, facing each other across the street. They covered the beams with vines to make them resemble trees and hung from them ropes that nearly touched the ground, at the top tying up all manner of food—live piglets and rabbits, fruit and egg baskets, wreaths of oranges—everything you could imagine, presented by the Grand Master and the langues. The entire town was watching. E'en de Valette and Isabella mingled together in the crowd. At a signal from the Monsignore himself, a dozen youths careened toward this edifice, launching themselves onto the ropes and fighting off the others, each doing his best to climb up and seize the waiting prizes. The crowd cheered them on with shouts and laughter and the clapping of hands, and more than one of these boys, tumbling to the ground, gamely got to his feet and launched himself upward again.

In the midst of all this, I chanced to spy Abdallah walking off unnoticed with a young masked woman, who I perceived to be none other than my own Flaminia. Thinking this exceedingly strange, I followed, keeping a distance behind them. They left Birgu through one of the gates, walking along the dockside toward the new bastions that were this afternoon entirely deserted. I kept after them unnoticed for some moments, stealing myself behind barrels and boats. By the time they sensed my presence and turned, it was too late; I was upon them. I grabbed Flaminia's wrist.

"What is this?" I said harshly, forcing her fingers open.

She squealed but made no other reply. I am not certain what I expected, money, even *afione*, perhaps. Instead I found—a scrap of paper. Puzzled, I took it from her hand. "During the dog days you must pretend to cast his horoscope. Go with a staff of iron to the place where God grants requests and rub yourself with juice of vervain. Then the one you seek will be inspired with love." Yet another of her senseless spells.

"Is this what you do with your liberty?" I said to the Moor. "Trick innocent Maltese girls with useless potions and prescriptions?" Then I turned to Flaminia. "And is this what you do with the money I give you? Waste it on barbarian recipes that can do naught but put you in the embrace of the Dark One?"

"Do not be so certain they are useless," Abdallah replied calmly. "In my country many rely on such formulae to capture their heart's desire, and they are known to be highly efficacious."

"Do not be angry, *mio cuore*," Flaminia begged, "I only wanted to make you fall in love with me."

The *quiraca*'s words caught me off guard and I started, not knowing whether to laugh or cry. During Carnavale, tho', when lust ran through the veins like blood, no better incantation could be imagined. I saluted the Moor, took my mistress' hand and, replacing our masks, we ran to her room.

Carnavale only began the spring festivals. For three weeks more the forts rose, our labors bringing the Feast of the Annunciation. All Malta breathed a great relief, for with the Incarnation of Our Lord the black year of the *razzia* was, at long last, over. The Knights solemnized the New Year with a procession that began at the Hospital and ended at the church, but the rest of us marked the occasion with naught but a prayer for good omens, and sweat. Then, unexpectedly, a different festa intervened: A week before Easter, judge Combo announced his decision.

That day a palpable wave passed through the construction gang as the news swept past each bastion, causing the heads of the workers to rise one after the other. When at last the whisperings reached me, I hardly knew what to make of them: Combo had absolved the lesser Knights but pronounced de Vallier and Fuster guilty. He had sentenced Fuster to prison and the Mareschal to death, drowning in a weighted sack.

At that very moment, Balthazar and the other Knights set at liberty were walking from the prison, squinting in the light of day. Later when I found him we embraced, but the sun has seen more joyous reunions.

"By God!" I exclaimed as we found a tavern where we could sup, "e'en after Villegaignon exposed him, the damned judge would not relent. For five hundred ducats the Mareschal is to be executed! Why not thirty shekels, the dirty Judas!"

"The game has not ended, I think," Balthazar replied, looking little worse for his months of imprisonment. But tho' the Chevalier ate with an appetite one might have expected for one just released from the dungeons, he failed to reprimand me for blasphemy. He said hardly a word.

Had I but known of the other visitors Balthazar had received while imprisoned! Had I but known the words Balthazar spoke to himself, when he listened to the friends of Villegaignon: "We are dead men."

That next morning at terce the Grand Master rose from prayer at the Chapel of St. Anne atop the fortress and led a procession to San Lorenzo in the Borgo. Members of the langues carried their standards, the priest a

Bible, altar boys crosses and tapers longer than they. Behind them all walked the robed Mareschal de Vallier. He has aged one hundred years, thought Balthazar as he followed, reaching out to the Mareschal, who smiled faintly at his comrade.

Inside the church, with all the Knights gathered around him and the townspeople flowing out the doors, the Mareschal fell on his knees before the altar.

At the Monsignore's signal, the Master Equerry pronounced the ancient words: "Because you have by your crimes rendered yourself unworthy of wearing any longer the sign of the true cross and the habit of our order, to which we admitted you out of our good opinion of the regularity of your conduct, we do therefore according to our statutes and customs deprive you of the habit and cut you off from the noble society of our brothers, casting you away as a corrupt and putrefied member."

After this declaration, the Grand Master nodded and the Master Equerry put his hand on de Vallier's shoulder. His Eminence nodded again and the Equerry untied the strings of the Mareschal's sleeves. d'Homedes nodded a third time. Hereat the Equerry untied the strings fastening the mantle and lifted it from de Vallier's shoulders, and as he did so he pronounced these words that filled the church: "By the authority of my superior, I take from you the ties of the yoke of the Lord and the habit of our order, which you have made yourself unworthy to wear."

de Vallier, thus humiliated before the Knights and the people, rose to his feet with downcast eyes. The procession now left the church for the quayside at Galley Creek. The Monsignore himself remained behind at the altar in prayer, it not befitting a Grand Master to be present at an execution. But townspeople and peasants, unfettered by office, thronged after the line of monks to enjoy the rare spectacle of a senior Knight being drowned in a sack. By the time the guards marched de Vallier to the skiff waiting for him at the docks, the crowd had doubled its size, with hundreds of onlookers cheering, some for his death, others just to cheer.

What the Mareschal did not know was that beneath their habits, half the French Knights in the procession were armed with rare pistols and swords. Balthazar and his fellow conspirators now readied themselves for a mêleé. As the moment neared for de Vallier to be placed in the sack, he and two other Knights prepared to rush onto the caique and overpower the crew. The remaining French Knights grasped their swords, set to fight off the guards as they spirited the Mareschal onto a boat waiting nearby. Scant moments from now they'd be hauling for all they were worth with the Devil and every boat in the Port at their heels to Marsamxett harbor, where a brigantine awaited. Thence to Sicily.

"We are dead men," Balthazar repeated to himself. His eyes again met de Vallier's and for an instant they locked. In the older man's sad, noble resignation, Navarre knew that Gaspard de Vallier would ne'er accept this undertaking, no more than the Abbé himself had accepted a younger comrade's attempt to save his own life. As he found strength in the Mareschal's gaze, Balthazar understood the unfolding, desperate plot would fail.

The guards bound de Vallier's legs and struggled to put him into a grain sack, even as they cast about for the rocks wherewith to weight it. The three Knights from the Langue of France glanced at each other, ready. But e'en as they took their first step, a squadron of halberdiers emerged from the gates, marching at a double pace headlong into the crowd, parting it with curses and weapons.

Directly on the embankment's edge, their leader halted and read the proclamation he held in his hands: "By the authority of the Grand Master, the death sentence laid upon Gaspard de Vallier is hereby amended to one of perpetual imprisonment." A murmur swept through the crowd, a murmur that quickly swelled into a sea of derisive jeers. de Vallier himself collapsed with the sack half around him. The guards, once having convinced themselves of the edict, pulled the Mareschal to his feet and removed the sack from his head. They shackled him and led him away, into St. Angelo.

"Thus," Balthazar breathed with a strange mixture of relief and despair, "was Tripoli lost while face and five hundred ducats saved." The crowd slowly dispersed; afterwards Balthazar came to work at Fort St. Elmo.

Thirty-Three

"Silenzio, Udite! Silenzio, Udite!" The horsemen galloped up to those pouring forth sweat at Fort St. Elmo. Scant hours had passed since de Vallier was led off to the dungeons of St. Angelo and curses were still raining down upon the Grand Master from all quarters. Yet, despite everything, d'Homedes was issuing a new series of *bandi*. As the heralds commanded, we put down our tools and listened. What we heard from their mouths left every man among us with weakened knees.

Knights were to be sent forthwith to procure arms and thousands of quintals of bisket at Zaragoza and Palermo. All members of the Order residing at the auberges were to be fully armed by the first of May. A list of all men between eighteen and sixty on the island capable of bearing arms would be drawn up within the week. Two thousand useless people were to be sent to Sicily. From this day hence, no person capable of bearing arms was to leave Malta. No ship would depart. No fishermen were to leave the island without guarantee of return. Fort St. Elmo was to be fully provisioned with food, ordnance and ammunition—at once.

Turgut had risen; a Turkish onslaught was underway.

But Balthazar strode up to the nearest horseman. "Let me see those orders!" he barked, snatching the paper from the rider's hands. The Grand Master's signature was unmistakable. "By God, if he intends to divert attention from his perfidious treatment of the Mareschal, he will have surely succeeded." In the same breath, he marched over to Strozzi, who was inspecting the barracks under construction. "Leone," he said, "I see the imprint of your hand over this parchment. What has changed today?"

"Navarre, you do not dispute the measures. We are doing nothing more than you have ever advocated—strengthening Malta's defenses."

"It is not the measures I dispute." The Abbé halted abruptly, shook his head and went back to work.

To everyone's astonishment—not least we the laborers —the decree to
provision St. Elmo could be fulfilled. Such had been the speed wherewith
we had erected this fort that within weeks it would be ready to serve its
purpose. As Balthazar returned from his words with Strozzi, I surveyed
the stronghold I'd helped raise. Gone were the flat curtains and square
towers of antiquity. Low bastions with long arms replaced them. The
engineers had measured the thickness of the walls to the force of modern
cannon, and we now strengthened them with terre-plein from the rear.
The finished castle, resembling nothing so much as a great four-legged
starfish beached on the tip of the peninsula, would allow the defenders to
train all the power of their cannon and arquebus on any attackers caught
between the creature's legs. A ditch, nine or ten paces wide, surrounded
it.

Yet, as Balthazar cast his own eye over the work, he singled out the
imperfection that everyone understood e'en before the first stone had been
laid: "You see it clearly," he said, pointing upward to the heights of Mt.
Sciberras, "St. Elmo sits at the base of Sciberras and a foe occupying the
heights will lob balls into it as a child throws pebbles into a well. But
until we cover this mount with a city, or at the very least stand a fort on
the summit, this is the best answer to a problem with no resolution."

That evening, I jumped off a *fregatina* at Galley Creek and walked
through the gate toward my new room, which lacked the view of the old
but was otherwise hardly distinguished from it. Before the Bishop's Palace
one of de Valette's slaves accosted me and, with signs more than words,
told me his master commanded that I appear at once. Covered with the
day's dust, I was nowise presentable, but not for an instant did I think to
cross Parisot.

He received me alone in the sitting room, surrounded by his trophies
and image of the Virgin. Those rusted shackles above the door to the
dining room. The bird sat squawking from the kitchen. I bowed before
the Knight, apologizing for my appearance and remained standing. His
somber frown more deeply creased his face today and before he spoke I
knew why. "I have learned that my ward Isabella purchased your release
from St. Angelo," he said in Spanish. The word "purchased" struck me to
the quick.

"How might you know this, Señor?" I asked gravely.

Parisot briefly contemplated the glass of wine in his hand but did not raise it. "The kingdom of heaven holds secrets. Birgu ... " he shook his head, " ... few. Isabella refuses to speak on the matter, insisting she did nothing, and I shall not put her to the question."

That was a comfort. "I have no knowledge of her actions," I replied, leaving out the rest of our story.

Now Parisot stood, glowering, beginning to pace as I had seen before. "Do not take me for a fool, young man. Combo is such a rogue that I fear the worst and she *shall* be examined." He stopped and his eyes bored into me. "You are never to see her again, do you understand?"

Involuntarily I took a step backward. "Señor," I said, vowing not to retreat further, "your disapproval of me has long been plain, but on my sacred honor, I hold the greatest affection and respect for Isabella and would on pain of death do nothing in the world to compromise her in the slightest degree."

"You have already compromised her!" Parisot's words buffeted me, but the thunder of his voice was colored less by anger than concern. All the while the Knight's piercing gaze never left mine. "Malta is no place for a young woman of temperament, and Isabella is readily distracted by one from the rabble such as yourself, who has soiled his hands with vile and common labor, and with whom in a greater place she would never think to associate." For a moment he paused, then took up again, speaking with something less than the absolute surety that was his inviolable custom. "Lest you misunderstand, no one in this world is dearer to me than Lady Guasconi and her daughter my ward, and tho' the great press of the Infidel is again upon us, I must spare this attention for their well being. The wedding negotiations have been concluded and I will allow no servile interloper to jeopardize them."

"Señor," I said, not a little angered, "the Knights of St. John might not yet perceive it, but the age has passed when young ladies received visitors only by lowering their hair from the tower in which they were confined."

I regretted those words the instant I uttered them, but across de Valette's countenance flickered a near insensible change. The shadow that passed over his face was so slight that, whether it carried a fugitive smile or a rueful acknowledgement of a monk's life deprived of the company of women, I couldn't discern.

"She will be shipped within a week to Sicily with the other useless persons of the island and sent on to Firenze. Until then, I command you not to see her."

Hardly knowing how to respond, I half-turned to depart. Then, with no idea of what would follow: "Señor, you have said that I, a servile interloper, have compromised your ward. As I am not in a position to challenge you for that grievous insult, allow me the honor of requesting Isabella's hand in marriage. In accepting it she will at least marry the man she loves, and for whom she is destined." I bowed my leave.

I fully expected Parisot to pick up one of the swords standing in the corner and run me through.

He laughed. Laughed. "Love is neither her concern nor yours," he said, taking his seat again. By this time I was striding toward the front door with every determination to carry off Isabella. When I came to within a step of the threshold these words reached my ears: "Boy, I am not finished with you."

I halted in my tracks, pulse pounding and face flushed.

"Some weeks ago," de Valette said in a completely changed tone, "you heard the Prior of Capua and I discussing plans to retake Tripoli."

Only then did I turn toward him. *Si*, I nodded, attempting to calm myself.

Parisot himself was entirely calm, seated with the glass in his hand. "The Prior insisted it would be best to first capture another place whence we might launch an attack. We have yet to decide where such a place might be and plan to pay or free slaves who might advise us."

My confusion equaled in every respect my agitation. "Señor," I interrupted, struggling to regain my wits, "are we not expecting a Turkish invasion at any time? The forts—" I pointed to my dusty condition—"the edicts—"

de Valette waved me silent. "Yes, yes. The Grace of the Almighty shall see us through the Turkish invasion. After Dragut's defeat we must seize again our rightful patrimony. You are friendly with the Algerian *chavush*, Abdallah."

I caught my breath. "We speak on occasion, Señor. He is an interesting man—for an infidel."

"Myself, I have spent some years in Tripoli, much of it against my will—." Now, at long last, de Valette did concede a slight smile, in recollection of his exile. "But being from Algiers, the slave will know that coast better than I. Would he advise an expedition in return for his ransom?"

No question could have surprised me more, and I was forced to ponder it at some length. Finally I replied: "His loyalty to the Grand Turk is great, but he despairs of ever leaving this island. He might be persuaded, but this you will have to determine for yourself."

"We shall. Gracias. You will participate in the undertaking?"

"Of course." For a second time I bowed my leave from Jean de Valette; this time I departed.

The conversation left me ill at ease. At each moment my heart battled my head and I was at a complete loss to know whether I must disobey him and seek out Isabella, with the possibility of grave consequences for us both. The decision was forced upon me. Convinced of the immediacy of the Turkish invasion, the Grand Master decreed that those two thousand useless persons should be shipped to Sicily before Easter, which was but days away.

I sent Pietru to Isabella with a note, requesting that she meet me after complines on the wall behind the Hospital where we had last parted.

At the appointed hour I climbed the steps to the darkened ramparts overlooking Kalkara Creek and waited. With all the activity in the harbor, no place was deserted these days, day or night, but I discerned few women on the streets and none Isabella. The church bell sounded; one glass emptied after another. I prepared to go to her house and take my chances, climbing into her bedroom if necessary, and abduct her. At the last moment a cloaked figure approached.

"Forgive me," she said, pulling aside her *faldetta*, "escaping the house unseen at this hour has been no simple matter. Parisot is there—"

"Then you know ... "

"Everything."

She bowed her head and for a moment both of us fell to silently gazing onto Kalkara Creek, where the small boats plied the glistening waters. The sea breeze, as usual, was up and Isabella gathered herself close. In our awkwardness, I motioned her to sit beside me and ventured: "Parisot said the nuns would examine you."

"They have," she nodded, seating herself on the parapet. "A most unpleasant experience, but I pledge on my eternal soul they found nothing, nothing whatsoever."

I sighed in relief. "Neither would Parisot reveal by what means you paid Combo for my release."

"Nor shall I," she answered, looking straight onto me, "if payment by the truth does not suffice." E'en as I thought that truth was a small coin for a rogue like Combo, Isabella's expression abruptly changed. "Francisco," her eyes danced, "we have little time. How daring of you to offer to take my hand—"

"How reckless," I objected with a glance toward the distant gallows. "Your protector laughed. Laughed." After the better part of a year since they first set eyes on each other, both young people had come to better understand the forces pulling them apart—their stations, the past, a soldier's life, the shadow of the Turks. For all that, this girl, somehow, had become the only link to what heart still beat within my breast. "Isabella," I said rising, "I am prepared at this moment to flee with you, to put the whole world at our heels ... if you can bear the thought of a servile interloper."

An expression of childlike ecstasy at the vistas opening before us quickly spread across her face. But slowly her open-mouthed wonder faded to a bittersweet smile and she quietly laughed. "To put the world at our heels ... oh, what a beautiful dream! Francisco ... " Her voice suddenly grave, she glanced about, near frantic. "It is impossible. The Port is locked tight. No ship is leaving, except those ... "

"We can cross to Gozo and take a boat—"

"Shhh." She abruptly put her finger on my lips. "There is no place whither to flee, Francisco, and I will not be the one to jeopardize your welfare."

This did not sound like Isabella, I told her.

"Oh, were it only the dockside watch and the *bandi* ... " She looked away. When she faced me once more, the dance in her eyes had been replaced by the harder gaze I'd seen all too often. "Forgive me, Francisco, there is much standing between us, and I have of late learned that I am a small person who lacks the strength to fight every wave cast against her ... I cannot disobey Parisot. Nor am I opposed to a peaceful life in Firenze

... These events swirling about us ... Do you remember the words of the Knights at Rhodes?"

I nodded: "'When all human hope is gone, it is our duty to try to come to terms, so that we may vindicate our loss at another time and place ... '"

Isabella took my hands in hers. "We are not destined to lose each other forever."

Her conflicting emotions produced in me a like bewilderment. "Surely that cannot be God's pleasure," I managed to say, feeling she was already not the girl I thought I knew.

"Then let us part in good cheer. I have written for you a poem."

"Another, you dare?" I chuckled as I could.

"I dare. But you must promise to read it."

I crossed myself. "Isabella, you have given me tokens, poems ... " I cast about for something I might give her in return, other than heartache. At length, I remembered my crucifix, took it from my neck and pressed it into her palm. "I have worn it since beyond memory. Apart from a sword and a gun it is the only thing I own. Keep it safely."

She kissed it, then I drew her to me and kissed her as I might a lover. She accepted and returned the kiss, then gasping in shame, touched me lightly on the arm and vanished into the night.

The next day I read her poem:

Cerva selvaggia son in deserto campo
e crudel ferro trafigge il mio core;
verso il chiaro corre il mio destro ardore
poi fugge ove io sol l'arena stampo.
Come uccel che vola fra'l tuono e'l lampo
giro nella bufera del dolore;
con penne che mi traggon in errore
voglio smorzar la fiamma ond'io avvampo.
Ma il Colosso che s'alza avanti al porto
al solingo urbe sempre guardia face
e chiude mia fuga qual vecchia Sfinge.
Come fera in carcer non trovo pace
né vedo mia stella che dia conforto:
Invisibil fil mio cor e alma cinge.

She saw herself as a stag, with an arrow driven thro' her heart. She bounds this way and that, even takes flight as a bird, to no avail. The Port is closed and she flies from bank to bank, circling, ever lost.

Two days after, Pietru and I stood on the docks amid the crowds and watched all the useless people on Malta board the vessels that would transport them to Sicily. Pietru couldn't fathom how the Grand Master could do such during Holy Week. Good Friday was tomorrow.

"Good Friday or the Devil's Friday, it seems to make no difference."

No. We watched from a distance Isabella embrace her mother and Parisot, and step onto a galley with her servants. She turned briefly on the *ballestriere*, but was quickly lost amid the throngs of passengers. Once the ships had cast off and rounded the corner of St. Angelo, I glanced at the moat between the castle and Birgu, which Pietru had helped dig. It was now finished and from this time on the only way into the fortress was across the narrow bridge, or to swim. The sight of this moat reminded me that my hours were beginning and I crossed the harbor to St. Elmo.

On Easter day the Grand Master allowed everyone to attend Mass and enter the processions, but afterward the labor picked up at an ever faster pace. The proclamations flowed apace; galley captains must donate their crews and *ciurma* to the construction; new orders for corn and grain went out to Sicily. Men worked double hours, then treble.

One day, a few weeks later, the sound of picks, axes and chisels suddenly fell silent. The wheels and hoists abruptly stopped creaking. Balthazar and I quietly laid down our tools in a stupefaction. St. Elmo stood completed, the fort at the tip of Sciberras, fully provisioned, armed and manned, with the standard of the Knights flying proudly above it. A great cheer went up from the hundreds on the worksite as we wiped the sweat finally from our brow.

Then we crossed the harbor to l'Isola. A few more weeks passed when on the very day of the apparition of St. Michel, we laid the last stone of the castle there, and so it was christened Fort St. Michel in honor of the archangel. Another great cheer split the air as the standard of the Religion was lofted above the heavy gun battery that now overlooked Galley Creek to the northeast and faced the Corradino heights to the southwest.

Work on Birgu's new walls and bastions would continue for some time to come, but the joy among the Knights and Maltese at having completed the two fortresses knew no bounds. Had not so many of Malta's women been shipped off to Sicily, you can imagine the revels that would have taken place. But we drank to stupefaction, singing senseless ditties in the taverns about how the souls saved by St. Michel would come back as St. Elmo's fire to save us from Turgut.

Not to be drowned out by drunken workers, d'Homedes ordered a *Te Deum* to be sung in the Conventual Church, while fireworks lofted their own praises to the sky. In the midst of the festivities, Turgut's absence was scarcely noticed.

Thirty-Four

"Will the sack of Gozo and the fall of Tripoli go unavenged?" the Prior of Capua shouted to the crowd of Knights gathered around him under the sign of the Mule and Goose. "Will the Infidel carry Christians into slavery and steal our rightful patrimony?" Hardly pausing for breath, Strozzi quaffed down a tankard and was out the door.

"Strozzi's the Devil incarnate!" marveled one of the poor Knights nearby. "At this very moment I'd wager he's also in Città Notabile beating his drum!"

Strozzi's thunder was truly awesome to behold. Only yesterday had the booming of the fireworks over St. Michel's fallen silent and the last of the darkening cinders drifted to earth. Today Strozzi was taking command of the recapture of Tripoli, as had the proceeding six months been a sojourn at a pleasant villa.

"You see," Balthazar observed while the dust from Strozzi's cloak still swirled about us, "d'Homedes days are numbered. What better way for the Prior to demonstrate his fitness for the Grand Mastership than to take back what has been so grievously lost?" Balthazar paused, bringing his cup to his lips. "That d'Homedes cannot bear Strozzi's presence on the island, so greatly does it overshadow his own, must play no little part in His Eminence's own fervor for the enterprise. Scant wonder Strozzi has been chosen Captain General of the Galleys."

I could summon meager spirit for the undertaking. Isabella's strange parting weighed heavily, hardly less the knowledge that she had procured my release from St. Angelo by means God and she alone knew. Flaminia's baseless insults added to my suspicions, which tormented me day and night. That every criminal on the island had been set free to lend his back to the fortifications ne'er entered my mind.

The worst came to pass a few mornings after Strozzi's exhortation, when I encountered Lady Emilia outside her home. She took my hand and said, "You should know, Francisco, Isabella is married." It was just like that. "I know you had feelings for her, but she has eagerly accepted her wifely duties. The match with the Florentine was a proper one and both houses should do well by it."

Emilia's pronounced those words with an unfathomable harshness. I fair covered my ears and ran, to no avail. Fifty paces farther on I collided with Strozzi himself, who had just stepped out of his own large house, built here several years ago before the Grand Master had defrocked him.

"Ah, Francisco," he said, clasping me by the shoulders, "what ails you?"

"Isabella is married," I told him darkly, foolishly revealing my mind.

The Prior only shrugged. "What of it? The stars take their courses. Now, the expedition, will you join?"

"I've told Parisot I would," I replied, thinking the Prior right in showing no concern for secular affairs. I'd put my wounded heart aside. "But I have not heard in your speeches any firm plan. Have the slaves disclosed a suitable place to attack?"

Thereat Strozzi nodded with satisfaction. "Yes. The expedition shall fall on Zuara, a town lying not far from Tripoli. Some slaves are willing to guide us there for their freedom—a trifling price. They've already told us much about the town's plan, and how we might approach." Unexpectedly, Strozzi broke off, laughing. "Your friend the *chavush* has been especially helpful. Hah! he is ready to leave Malta."

"I'm not surprised," I answered, chuckling with a heaviness I could not shake off. "He is too accustomed to comfort to willingly remain a slave for long. But, Sir, do you have sufficient forces for the undertaking?"

Strozzi smiled confidently. "Soon I shall. Parisot will be Deputy General of the Galleys. Francisco, the best and the bravest shall be among us and we will right this great injustice that has been perpetrated on the Religion!"

Listening to the Prior, no one could doubt it. "I have wanted to ask this month past," I said, shielding my eyes from the now-bright sun. "Every day you swore that Turgut's galley would appear on the morrow. Where is the invasion?"

Strozzi shrugged again. "Be assured your toil has not been for naught."

I bowed my leave.

Despite the mask I'd worn before Strozzi, the news of Isabella's marriage had pierced my heart and a senseless rage consumed me. I found an inn and got drunk. To no avail. Moment by moment, my need to discover the means wherewith Isabella had secured my liberty mounted. Had she not done so, surely Parisot wouldn't have sent her off to Italy and this whole cruel fate might have been forestalled. Aye, I was thrashing about more like a bull than a man, but in my hard blindness I saw only red.

Unable to bear it any longer, I dashed to Flaminia's room, certain my *quiraca* would know what lay at the bottom of the affair. She was there. The wench had eluded the last roundup of useless persons by fleeing south to her village of Zurrieq, and when the fortifications were completed, she ran straight back to Birgu. As I stepped into the room, I put the question to her: How did my release from St. Angelo come to pass?

"You are drunk," she answered haughtily.

"Yes, and if you don't tell me what you know, I'll beat you senseless and you will forget your dream of a house from my purse."

"*Mio bove grande,*" she said, haughtiness ceding to caution, "you have no need to beat me. Mother of God! this Combo was terrified of being at the mercy of the Grand Master if he freed de Vallier—and he was terrified of being killed by the French Knights if he didn't. Madonna! after what he did, would I not be in fear of my life!" Forthwith she crossed herself. "I have heard that to free you Isabella guaranteed him safe passage from Malta."

In my stupor Flaminia's answer made little sense. "What are you saying?" I shouted. "How could Isabella guarantee that insect anything?"

"O wounded beast!" Flaminia answered, her high tone creeping back, "she'd met the one to make milk stink in her mouth and she would do anything to set him free."

"Anything!" I cried, slapping Flaminia soundly across the face. "Gossip-mongering whore, you have slandered her too often! Take back your words!"

Reeling from my blow, Flaminia desperately crossed herself again. "I am stupid, forgive me, *mio cuore.* But your Isabella has many guardians. She needed drop only a word to one of them."

I breathed, attempting to understand. Isabella would ne'er dare put the request to Parisot. Villegaignon had long since departed and only one possibility remained: Strozzi. Flaminia's story began to make too much sense, explaining even how the Prior of Capua seemed to know of the affair—and de Valette. Instantly I hurtled out the door and sped to Strozzi's house.

There I found him and barged like a madman past the servant who had opened the door for me. "Francisco!" Strozzi exclaimed at the sight of me, but I didn't allow him a word more. Instantly I demanded to know whether Isabella had importuned him with a favor for Combo to secure my release.

"*Piagato*, why torture yourself? She is married. *Finito*. Go home, sober up, prepare for a glorious expedition to Barbary."

"Did Isabella petition you?" I repeated.

"Yes," he finally admitted with a sigh of annoyance, "she asked for Combo's passage from Malta on one of my galleys, if necessary."

"And you told Parisot?"

But now Strozzi's answer came with a curious laugh. "I swore on the Cross not to speak to a soul!"

"Ah!" I exclaimed, running out of the house, more confused than ever. I found a horse in the stables, dug the rowels into its flank and galloped to Mdina, not stopping once for the heat or mosquitoes. I ran headlong through the town, boots clattering on the stones as I searched for Combo's office. Finding it, I fairly broke down the door.

"You swine!" I cried to this black-haired and bald-headed judge, "you have not only caused unbearable hardship on worthy Knights by your putrid corruption, you have caused the person who meant more to me than anyone in the world to be sent far from this island so that I would ne'er see her again! You'd best use that safe-passage soon, for I swear by the Hatred I bear toward all Infidels, I'll be revenged upon you!"

Combo, for his part, stared at me with an untroubled, disdainful expression and replied finally with a sneer, "Get out of my office, dog shit, or I'll have you thrown back in prison this very day."

I struck the pig across the face, knocking him straight to the ground. Taking a swig from the decanter of wine on his table, I smashed it over his head and departed.

At the time I did not know what consequences this episode would have. I didn't know anything. It was, simply, as had I lost my mind.

"Come to Zurrieq, *bove*," Flaminia insisted upon seeing Combo's blood splattered over my hands. "The castles are done and the friars are exorcising the spirit from the cave. The ride will cure you." A year ago I'd refused to have anything to do with the rite, but now, as if I myself needed to be exorcised from all the bile and disgust filling me, I rashly said yes. At her village, if naught else, I'd eat fresh bread and goat's cheese. Pietru had again been staying in my room and I brought him along.

Aye, the ride did much to put me in better spirits, and by the time the ceremony was to begin, I found myself sometimes laughing and singing with the rest of them. A good part of the village intended to take part in the exorcism. Everyone followed the two monks and a priest the short distance to the cave, which sat in a cliff towering high over the sea. That did not for a moment deter either the monks or Pietru, for the Maltese think nothing of flinging themselves over cliffs tied to a rope, and even suspending themselves at the end of a line, where they fish for hours on end above the waves. So over the side everyone went, lowering themselves down to a ledge just below the mouth of the cave.

The priest crawled in first, then the monks, then the rest of us. When as many of us who could fit into the cave where the spirit dwelt had gathered, the priest said, "I am lighting the candle of darkness." He lit this taper from a torch one of the friars had brought and, after his companions had dug out a little hole in the center of the space, the priest stood the candle there. All the while the friars were chanting: *Quicumque vult salvus esse, ante omnia opus est, ut teneat catholicam fidem ... Fides autem catholica haec est: ut unum Deum in Trinitate, et Trinitatem in unitate veneremur ...*

This went on for a little while. The friars frequently stumbled in their Latin, showing that they didn't really know their Creed, but had only practiced for this ritual. When at last they finished, they crossed themselves several times and that seemed to be the end of the ceremony. I tell you, I'd ne'er seen a true exorcism with my own eyes, but had heard enough about them from my mother to know that this bore no resemblance to the proper rite. In my present humor of disgust, my indignation at the blasphemy I'd just witnessed was tempered by the innocence of it, and I merely shrugged.

We left the cave and made to ascend. As Pietro and I awaited our turn at the ropes, we espied rocking on the sea below a small boat with but a single oarsman. He seemed to be waiting, tho' for what or who we could in no way discern. The boat lay too far to make out anything of its occupant, but when he understood we had caught sight of him, he quickly bent to his oars and began hauling for all his worth around the bend of the coast.

"Who do you think that is?" I asked Pietru.

"I think he is a slave," Pietru answered.

"What would a slave be doing at the south of Malta?"

"Escaping."

I glanced at the Gozitan and at the path winding from the ledge on which we stood down to the water's edge. "Come," I said to Ix-Xabaw, "quickly."

We scampered, nay climbed, down the steep path hand over hand, but it quickly ended—we were trapped high above the water. Pietru hesitated not an instant to dive in and, realizing there was nothing else for it, I was at once after him. By the time we surfaced from the blue, the skiff had passed out of sight to the west. Our way was blocked by another cliff and we swam around through a great rock archway until we were able to climb onto the land again. Again we ran, slowed now by our wet clothing, but after the next bend we spied the boat, already beached. Of the oarsman there was no sign. With a nod to each other Pietru and I began to climb another steep path up a new cliff. At the top, Ix-Xabaw pointed to some broken shrubs and footprints and we took off inland. We ran for hours, I swear halfway to Mdina, before I bade my companion halt.

"He has eluded us," I said to Pietru, panting and sweating, "but why was he watching the cave?"

"Something there," answered the Gozitan.

I stared at my comrade, thinking he was not so simple as I'd sometimes supposed. Why hadn't I thought of this?

We returned to Zurrieq and, with a torch in hand, once again descended to the cave's mouth. Inside, the candle of darkness was still burning. We searched every corner of the grotto, finding no one and nothing. Just as we were about to give up, I thrust my hand into a small hole in the wall and pulled out a sheaf of paper. It seemed that more than an evil spirit frequented this spot.

Once in daylight above I opened the papers. With the recollection of Villegaignon's execution of the two youths last year flooding back, I could naught but believe that the letters I held in my hands were written in

Turkish. Impulsively I showed them to Pietru, but the unlettered Gozitan shrugged, having no more notion of whether they were Turkish than Chinese. The only certain thing was that these missives surely contained some great danger and that I must bring them to Balthazar at once.

I found the knight only the next morning at the auberge, readying for the road. "Where are you going?" I asked, seeing his servant gathering up his master's belongings.

"To Rome."

"To Rome!" For all that I had witnessed during the past year, the idea of Rome was yet a conception too large for me to grasp. "Will you return in time for the expedition to Zuara?"

Balthazar laid his hand on my shoulder. "My expedition, my friend, is another, and one I trust not so desperate. His Eminence has ordered me to take part in a delegation to the Vatican, where with our Ambassador de Sengle there we may beg for money to help pay for the fortifications."

The implications of Balthazar's words descended quickly. "You will see the Pontiff himself!"

Balthazar could not but smile at the wonder written over his companion's face. "I shall see the Pope should he deign to see us. But the Pope has larger concerns than we the Knights—Lutherans and the battle for Italy, to mention but two. And tho' he is well disposed towards the Religion, to our misfortune, none of us are his close relatives."

"What do you mean by that?" I asked, for a moment forgetting my mission. "Are you schooled in affairs of the Vatican as well?"

Balthazar stared at me with a condescension that instantly transformed him again into Lord Balthazar de Marin des Homes-St. Martin, and he now loomed before me as tall as on that day I had first met him in a forlorn garrison in Africa.

"Schooled?" Abruptly he laughed. "Let us say, my young friend, that at least you cannot accuse our present Julius of murder, only that he has committed unutterable sins with that youth Innocenzo he picked up from the streets and on whom he bestowed the purple. And if he showers riches beyond imagining on his kinfolk, to his credit he has not carried out pagan rituals in St. Peter's like his predecessor. Ah, but why not? Did not Leo declare, 'God has bestowed upon us the Papacy, now let us enjoy it'? After all, what is the Council at Trento but an acknowledgement of corruption and vice ... "

Here Balthazar abruptly halted, making that selfsame quizzical expression he always did when his examinations brought him face to face with something new. "Yet for all that is vile and corrupt, faith is possible. One must find it within, somehow, somewhere … "

Balthazar said all this with scant attention of me at his side, or my mien, which moment by moment had became less amused, seeing that his discourse strode confidently across treacherous ground. Just as I was about to raise my voice, he finally took cognizance and said, "Francisco, your expression tells me you have come on a mission of some urgency, not to discuss papal comportment."

"Yes," I nodded soberly. "I found these letters in a cave near Zurrieq yesterday." And handing over to Balthazar the papers, I recounted all that had happened. "Is it Turkish?"

Balthazar shook his head. He did not read Turkish but could recognize it. "The letters are Greek, but I cannot make out a single word. I fear it is a cipher."

"A cipher?" I repeated dully, perhaps having heard the word in my life but having no clear notion of its implications.

"Yes you dolt, a code. The science of ciphering has advanced much in this our age and the Turks have lost no time in placing spies everywhere amongst their enemies. d'Homedes's edicts forbidding fishermen from leaving Malta have not been issued for lack of fish! Come, we must find someone to untangle these messages at once."

Balthazar instantly ordered his servant to inform the other members of the legation that their departure would be delayed. Letters in hand, he descended forthwith from his quarters in the auberge to the street, me at his heels. To my surprise, our destination was the Hospital and to my e'en greater surprise he sought out none other than Doctor Jean.

"Are you versed in the science of ciphers as well as medicine?" I asked as Balthazar showed him the strange missives.

"It is merely an … *avocation*," smiled the physician as he looked over the letters. "Yes, surely these texts are ciphered. You see the letters are Greek but the words have no meaning. Without a key this may take some time." Before the Knight could ask, Vigo shrugged. "My Greek is good but not … perfect."

"Do your best," said Balthazar, laying his hand on the other's shoulder, "get help and be careful. There is a spy on the island."

"Fra Balthazar, that there is a spy on the island no one has ever doubted," Vigo replied with a mixture of solemnity and amusement. "The only mystery is ... how many and for how many nations?"

Balthazar at once informed Strozzi and de Valette of the documents but word of them went no further, and while Vigo and his brethren labored secretly over the ciphers, the Prior and Parisot hastened the preparations for the expedition.

What an expedition it promised to be! As August loomed, Strozzi outfitted his galleys and *fregate*. de Valette offered one of his own. Romegas had been the first to volunteer. Neither did Commandeur Copier, who had stood with Balthazar to the last at Tripoli, lag behind. E'en ol' Bernardo de Guimeran, under who three hundred of us unleashed that hellish arquebusade against Sinan last year, stepped forward. The Prior's nephew had lately arrived in Malta and would also join the forces. Vergã signed up without prompting, Pietru as well.

By August two hundred of the bravest Knights and eight or nine hundred soldiers stood ready to sail to Barbary, yet Strozzi deemed this insufficient and continued his levy, appearing at every village and tavern on the island. But those of us who knew of the ciphers held our breaths for fear that the contents might compromise the expedition or prevent it altogether. At last, on the fourth day, Vigo came before Balthazar with several sheets of paper in his hand.

"We have, I think, seen through this cipher. It used but two replacements."

Balthazar read the messages, translated into French. They were not addressed to anyone. They described Fort St. Elmo as "a small castle in the shape of a star on the tip of Sciberras that has been built with haste with much soft stone." Fort St. Michel was "a castle on the tongue of land called Isola, which is otherwise unprotected." The reports seemed weeks old, mayhap months, which Balthazar reasoned might be due to d'Homedes' strict quarantine of the island. Everyone breathed in relief when Vigo pointed out that the letters contained no mention of Zuara.

"That is no guarantee that word of it has not left the island," replied Balthazar, but thereupon he sent word to his delegation that they might depart for Italy. He then asked if I planned to join the expedition.

"You know I will," I said gravely, aware of his misgivings, but for myself seeing it as an escape from this place that had of late become full of bitterness.

Balthazar's eyes welled with advice. He wanted to speak of valor when valor was impossible. He did not. He laid his hand on my shoulder. "I hope to see you alive someday," he said and, so saying, he embraced me and departed.

Thirty-Five

Two nights before the fleet's departure, the Ave Maria rang and Blaij and I sat down together at the nameless tavern where we had first supped a year ago. From every side the shouts were of Tripoli's loss and the unjust fate of de Vallier. "Gozo!" echoed constantly among the vaults. Strozzi's agitation had done the job: After a year of waiting, French blood boiled and the day of vengeance had arrived.

"I can taste this expedition in my mouth," declared a forceful voice from behind. Romegas. To my surprise, the Provençal sat—deigned to sit—down on the bench between us. "There is nothing I prize more than the wind at my back and inflicting every harm on the Infidel," he said, leaning on his elbow with a cup in hand. "Zuara is a big town and the slaves will guide us right to the plunder." I regarded Lescaut. Little of this Knight had ever pleased me. All muscle, not a dram of fat on him, aye, but that narrow dark face, framed by unruly black hair always gave him the look of a savage. His loud, coarse voice never brooked interruption and if his reputation for fearlessness grew by the day, I never heard a word from his mouth that showed he knew ought beyond the sea and ships. "de Valette has made me Captain of his galley," he said. "Vergã, you can sail with me, but remember, no one sets foot on my boat who knows the meaning of the word 'retreat.'"

"What language are you speaking, Romegas?" laughed Vergã, peering at him. "I've never heard the word before."

Lescaut thence cast his burning eyes straight at me. "You, I've forgotten your name. Do you have the balls? I don't think so. I can smell a man's balls and I don't smell yours."

I spat on the table. "You compare me with this scoundrel?" I replied, glancing at Vergã. "It was I who freed Fra Balthazar, I who escaped this island, I who sailed months with Strozzi and I who have sat in prison. What does this girl have to show for herself?"

E'en as Romegas smiled wickedly at my answer, both of us were slapped on the back by Ramon Caravajal, who I'd not set eyes on since Mdina. "Is your rapier sharpened, boy?" the jovial Knight asked.

"To be sure," I answered in like tone, with a second glance at Vergã. "I don't know what to do about all the noise my sword is making; it ne'er ceases to upbraid me for letting it be so long at rest."

Caravajal guffawed and slapped me on the back again, but Blaij, eyeing me darkly, drew his own sword half from its sheath and addressed it with a hot gaze at me. "*O Espada! si supiesses hablar, diziardes quantos Humbres matastes.*" If you my sword could speak, you would let the world know how many men it had let the sun shine through.

"*Excelente!*" Caravajal exclaimed, to be interrupted by Romegas.

"The French are polishing their armor," that one said, "while you Spaniards break wind. And so Strozzi is short of men. Parisot has agreed to speak at the ramparts. Let's get our asses over there and see what he says."

Forthwith we quit the tavern, careening with shouts and taunts to the landward walls of Birgu and there waited amongst the workers to hear Parisot, who did not often make so public an appearance. Shortly, tho', de Valette strode onto one of the new bastions in full battle dress, a splendidly engraved suit of half-armor, its shining cuirass covered by the blood-red field broken by the white cross. He stopped, resting his palms on the hilt of a one-and-a-half-hander, whose tip he had planted before him in the battlements. I wondered that a man of Parisot's age could swing it; mayhap it was for show. At first the nobleman appeared uneasy, as if for all his years he had ne'er walked among the rabble he so despised. His thin lips were drawn into their regular frown and for the briefest of moments a gossamer shadow of perplexity passed across his eyes. He did not know what to say.

He began then, slowly at first, using some words that I had heard before. "The Grand Turk," he said in Italian, "is bent on the destruction of the Holy Religion and it has pleased God to allow the Infidel with his insatiable appetite to seize our rightful patrimony of Tripoli."

He paused briefly, casting his eyes over the crowd, but saw his words had fallen short.

"Men," he shouted, pointing his finger at those below, "God is a father to warn us, not to punish us. He has chosen me, he has chosen each of you to fight the injustice that has been perpetrated against all Christians. Follow me to Zuara. Booty awaits you, but the greater reward is the reward of Heaven. I tell you, the Infidel shall not rest until he has devoured the last Christian on earth. We must not allow our swords to fall in this sacred war, which we wage in the name of Christ. We must feel him at our sides strengthening our arms. We shall walk in the shadow of death, as we have all our lives, but if we are victorious in this fight, God shall forgive our sins and on the day we are judged, we shall not be cast into the jaws of Satan but shall walk with Christ in the gardens of paradise."

Every word of Parisot's thunderings, warnings and cajolings carried an absolute conviction, and for the first time I glimpsed in his adamantine center a spark of greatness. If in this speech Parisot had fully found neither himself nor those standing below, his presence at least caused the men to shout and they cheered when he descended from the ramparts to walk amongst them.

At the same moment de Valette spoke from the ramparts, Strozzi employed his own methods. "Come with me to Zuara!" he shouted in the auberges and the barracks. " I offer two *scudi* for the head of every infidel taken!"

Enthusiasm for the venture swelled instantly. Three hundred of the bravest Knights would set sail for Zuara, as well as twelve or thirteen hundred common soldiers.

My feeble misgivings were now forgotten. I would go too and show this scoundrel Vergã and this Knight Romegas. But e'en as I walked back to my room with Pietru, a crushing fever seized me. By the time I staggered up the steps, several boils had appeared on my left arm and a carbuncle on my palm. As I threw open the door, I knew it for an omen. Flaminia, who awaited inside, took one glance at me and flew into a panic.

"For the love of God!" she said and made to run for one of her potions.

"No," I said, raising one hand as the other found its way to my brow. The room was beginning to swim. "G—get me to the Hospital." I managed those words, turning to Pietru. Then I passed out.

Sixteen *galere, fusti* and *brigantini* set sail from Malta on August sixth.

"When we ran into the *imbatti*, which blew us all to Hell," Blaij cursed, "I should have seen the omen and known we were in for shit." He remembered the smallest detail. "We could hardly make anything against those winds and didn't get to Barbary for eight or nine days. By then the pilots were fucked and when we sighted land everybody started shouting at once."

"Jesus, there's no town in sight! Where the Devil are we?"

"Shut your traps!" ordered Romegas. "We are where we are and we make the best of it. Vergada, get your ass into the water."

Blaij jumped into the surf and waded ashore with everybody else from the galley. It was late at night, and the waning quarter moon had already set. Romegas himself was cursing the pilots under his breath, but he hadn't been able to do anything against those damned winds any more than they could. Vergã glanced around him, shaking his head and thinking, So here we are—a thousand and a half men standing on a sandy beach at midnight somewhere east of the same place we almost got Turgut last year. Strozzi stood out in front with his beardless nephew, de Guimeran and Parisot, cursing with the rest while the pilots tried to reckon where the Hell the fleet'd landed.

After the pilots made their sightings and checked the charts, Strozzi's *pilota reale* walked up to the Commander. "We're at least four leagues from Zuara, Signore," he told him.

"By the Lord Christ!" exclaimed Strozzi, but he didn't lose his head. "If that's the way it is, that's the way it is."

That's the way it was—an all-night march. While the men got some bread in their stomachs, Strozzi divided the forces. First he sent ahead Maltese scouts dressed as Moors. Blaij couldn't get over how the Maltese sometimes understood the natives of these parts; Maltese was about the ugliest tongue he'd ever heard. It's as if they're spitting up their innards through their throats. It seemed the slaves back on Malta, and that Moor, had told Strozzi that Zuara was big, full of merchants of all nations who'd gotten fat off trade. They also told him it wasn't fortified worth piss on the land side and that the army could advance under a palm grove without being seen, right up to the ditch.

Palm trees there were, all over the place. So the scouts took off, to discover whether the slaves had bought their freedom or fucked the whole army. Then Strozzi's nephew, whatever his name was, stepped up to the Commander. "I'll lead some Knights ahead to take care of any trouble on the way." Strozzi agreed and sent his nephew off with a few dozen young Knights as an *avant garde*. The rest of the men he divided into three companies. The first was under Guimeran. Most of the Knights were in the second company, under de Valette. The common soldiers went into the third, which headed up the rear. Strozzi himself took command of this one.

Well, they set off. You've got to admire the old farts, was the only thought going through Blaij's head, especially de Valette. For all his years—how many, fifty-three, fifty four?— he took off in that suit of armor as if he was a twenty-year-old after a whore. He didn't bring that one-and-a-half hander of his, just an ordinary rapier. What would you want a *bastard* for anyway on a fucking midnight march along a beach? No, Parisot is iron. Guzman started singing that new song, "*Ningún humbre se llame desdichado, aunque le siga el hado ejecutivo ... ,*" and Parisot threatened to cut his throat if he didn't shut his trap. After that they tramped over sand and through palm groves, every *humbre* whispering, getting his blood up for the attack.

Romegas had already unsheathed his broadsword. "You might as well come to me, you Turkish bastards," he said over and over again as he cut off palm leaves in the dark like he was swatting flies. "You cannot escape Romegas."

The hired guns weren't bound by any vows of chastity. "I can't wait to put my prick in an infidel pussy and make some Christians," somebody said and everyone around laughed under their breaths.

It was like that, the strange rustling of the palm leaves in the wind mixed with the whispers of the soldiers and the swish of Romegas's sword. The armor of the Knights was so polished it reflected the starlight. Blaij couldn't get over it.

After some hours the army was getting close to Zuara and the scouts Strozzi had sent ahead came back. They were ravenous, and as they gulped down bread and wine, one of them said to the Commander, "Signore, to the left of the city we saw a camp with fires and pavilions. We think they're just Arabs. Most of them are almost naked and without arms."

"Let us attack them," interrupted the second scout.

"You say poorly armed?" asked the Prior.

"Yes," said a third, no less starved than the others. "They can hardly resist, and if they do we can fall on them with all the arms of the Knights and bring forth the weapons of the galleys."

Strozzi ordered one of the men to go ahead and find his nephew. After some time he had all his lieutenants gathered 'round. The nephew was for the attack. "This is a good idea and will bring us extra slaves," he said.

It was a strange council there, in a dark palm grove on a beach of Barbary with armored Knights surrounded by Maltese dressed as Saracens and an army that was moment by moment growing harder to keep in check. Romegas wasn't in that circle but he was also for an attack. "By the Saints, what are we waiting for? Let's get going."

"How many are there?" somebody asked.

Romegas snorted. "Didn't your whore-mother ever tell you that the greater the numbers, the greater the glory?"

Strozzi was still trying to resolve his mind when de Valette interrupted. "Leone," he said, "I see no advantage to this. A battle with these contemptible beggars on the beach will serve only to delay our enterprise and the noise will alert those in the city of our presence. Let us continue to our goal. It is only half a league now. But be sure the galleys are on the way."

"*Ouy*, Parisot, you are right."

They continued to march. The army reached the city in less than an hour, still under the cover of darkness. Blaij could hardly believe his eyes. The place didn't even have a guard house. The damned slaves were right! Not a single sentinel was standing watch and the gates had been left wide open! "We just walked in. The whole fucking army just walked in."

Pietru was in the third company. When the army entered Zuara, all the companies took up positions on the main square, where the streets met. Tho' Pietru had spent months on Strozzi's galleys with me, this was his first major undertaking. The same heat burned the Gozitan as it did everyone around him. No one had more reason to hate the Turks than he, but he hated them less than he feared them.

At that moment he remembered his mother saying, "*Jekk ma toqghodx kwiet, il-Bambin jibghaltlek gamra nar*—if you don't behave, God will send you a flame of fire." *Le*, he would send the Turks to Hell. Pietru ran his tongue over his lips, tasting vengeance, but more he wanted his wife back. She would surely be in this place, close to Tripoli. He was finding it difficult to remain still.

Strozzi, tho', was walking up and down the ranks, reminding the troops there would be no plundering until the town had been secured. "Do you understand me?" he whispered aloud. He was met by grumbling, a seething, which he answered: "I have offered you two *scudi* for the head of every Moor. For that you will obey orders!"

"You expect a head-price to act as a fetter, Leone?" asked de Valette. "Rather tell them that under pain of death they must obey you."

Strozzi laughed.

By now Pietru's arms shook in anticipation. The fellow next to him whipped out his tool and pissed on his own feet, so urgently did he need to relieve himself.

"Matches!" Strozzi cried suddenly, and with a wave of his arm motioned to the heralds. Instantly, the pounding of drums and the blare of trumpets filled the air. All over Zuara doors and window shutters began to open— and the alarm also set off his soldiers. It might have been a herd of stallions that could no longer be kept bound. The moment those trumpets sounded, all Hell broke loose.

"Order!" Strozzi shouted; not a man heard him.

The soldiers ran from house to house, smashing open the doors. Romegas dashed into the nearest place and discovered a Moor cowering among the sacks in the corn cellar. The Knight pulled him to his feet.

"Take this one to the square," he said, throwing the dog to the soldiers who had followed. They searched the house but found nothing of value. When Lescaut burst into the next house, he faced a raised sword. Laughing, he knocked the blade from the fellow's hand and cut off his head. His wife threw herself at the Knight, who caught her and with another laugh turned her over to the men, who sliced her burnoose to shreds and threw her across the table. Two held her down while the others raped her. While they were going at her, Romegas ordered her to tell him where the money was or he would kill her children.

Pietru kept an eye out for his wife. He didn't see her. But each time he herded a captive out to the square he made sure it wasn't her. As he ran back and forth he tried to look at everybody. In the darkness and chaos it was hard for him to make out what was going on.

He caught sight of Commander de Valette standing at the square with his sword raised, and for reasons Ix-Xabaw could not explain, he stopped for a moment to regard him. "Bring them to the square!" the Knight cried over and over again, ordering the captives to be tied up and marched down to the beach. "The galleys will soon be here."

Pietru did not know how far de Valette's voice carried in this tumult. With the reward as much butchering was going on as slave-taking. Pietru himself took two heads, but wasn't certain what to do with them, so he carried them back to the square, all the while shouting at them: "*Haqq it-Torok.* This is your prize for taking my wife! Serves you right!" At the square he spied Commander Strozzi and offered him the bloody trophies. "Here are some heads for you, Sir. Four *scudi*, please." The Prior chuckled, had his man make a note, and said Pietru would be paid later. Ix-Xabaw put the heads down where some others were piling up.

Vergã wasn't much interested in raping; he was more interested in money. He didn't find much, with all the competition around him. In one house he got to some jewelry before the others and took it. When the woman there pounded on him with her impotent fists, he knocked her out. At the same instant her husband appeared at the door and Blaij killed him with a dagger to the stomach. Then he cut off his head, for the reward. The blood splattering all over the place excited him. He undid his breeches, had a few thrusts in the senseless woman, finished quickly, threw her over his shoulder and carried her to the square. By now well over a thousand captives were huddled there. It was de Valette's duty to get them onto the galleys.

He stood in the center of the mayhem barking, "Get these dogs to the boats!" His men jumped at his command, and beat and lashed the barbarians without any distinction to their age or sex. Vergã put down his cargo, who was by now pummeling him, and shoved her in the direction of the beach with the others.

"It is a harsh necessity to repress the cruelty of the infidels," de Valette was saying to one of his Knights, "and to teach them to treat Christians better on like occasions."

Vergã saw the Commander knew what was what. He turned then to go back to his work, but halted in his tracts when two Knights leading a Moor by the arms ran up to Parisot.

"Sir, do you not remember me?" the Moor asked de Valette, doing his best to shake off the grip of the Knights.

de Valette took a brief glance at the dark man before him and shook his head, motioning for the Knights to take him away.

"Commander, I served under you when you were Governor of Tripoli!"

Hereon Parisot's expression changed. "Ah yes, I remember you now. You are Ali Benjiora, aren't you?"

The Knights let him go and the Moor bowed. "Yes, good Sir. I must tell you something, urgently ... "

Thirty-Six

I awoke in the Sacra Infermeria to see Dr. Vigo and Flaminia arguing at my bedside. Flaminia was insisting that the physician treat me with a concoction she held in her hand. Vigo sniffed it, making an expression of disgust, and told her she must quit the Hospital at once, for her very presence violated custom and probity. She stubbornly refused.

I raised my hand weakly, bidding them to cease their squabble, which violated decorum. "Get me out of here," I said feebly. "I must join the expedition ... "

Vigo shook his head severely. "You are not going anywhere, my friend. And there is no longer any reason to hurry; the expedition set off ... yesterday."

"No!" I exclaimed, to the extent I was able.

"*Si, por toda la Perdition del Mundo te lo juro*," Vigo replied.

Resignation forced itself upon me, and I told Flaminia that I put my faith in the Order's physicians and that she should inquire anon to learn whether I remained alive.

On that matter, Vigo was optimistic. "You are not suffering from the plague," he told me, taking my pulse, "but a lesser ... *indisposition*, which is not always fatal. I can feel your vital spirits flowing."

At this juncture I noticed the smallish room in which I found myself was empty. "Where are the other patients?" I asked.

"I am isolating you for forty days—*quarantining* you ... As a precaution."

I stared at him in alarm but the physician raised his finger to his lips. Threat he lanced my boils and filled them with a plaster.

Under Vigo's care my strength returned over the next days. Each morning and afternoon as I ate with the Hospital's sparkling silver utensil, I asked the physician for news from Zuara, but of course he knew nothing. Instead he waxed poetic about Vesalius, who had made medical progress possible. "What we have learned about anatomy and physiology since the publication of his *Fabrica* ten years ago! Dissections have become as popular as ... Punch and Judy! The Galenists have caused Vesalius *some* problems ... one must confess."

"Dr. Jean," I interrupted, reminded by his discourse of something that had been gnawing at me since our escape from Malta last year, "how is it possible that in one person *afione* produces sleep and in another the most violent reaction—or might I have fed Balthazar another potion altogether?"

"This is a deep question," Vigo replied. "Potions of course should *never* be compounded except by experts. But you are correct, *afione* ... *does* seem to produce diverse reactions. The Turks take it before battle and it sends them into the most extraordinary ... *frenzy*, making them heedless of danger." This last the physician pronounced with an extreme gravity; then after a momentary contemplation he added, "It is a puzzle."

At the word "puzzle," Vigo abruptly began to expound more cheerfully. "Since Alberti opened the doors a century ago with his cipher wheel, progress has been rapid. Trithemius's *Polygraphiae* is indispensable, but he has been accused of practicing magic and sorcery, and Cardano has just published in his *De subtilitate* autokey, a brilliant idea. The Pope's cryptographers—"

With all else, my strength quickly found its limits. "Dr. Jean," I pleaded wearily, "cease this lecture. I've ne'er had a head for puzzles and your speech is wasted on me." The physician graciously left off, allowing me to sleep, but as I fell into slumber I came to my senses. That I had ne'er given potions and puzzles any consideration explained why I had been so slow to see through a ruse that might have been taking place under my nose for months. Now Vigo had as if opened a door. When the next day Flaminia stole again into the Infermeria to visit her master, she did not find a sick, helpless man.

"Flaminia, *mio cuore*, you do not read a word, do you?" I said without waiting for her to inquire after my health.

"Of course not, Francisco. What would reading be to me?"

"Aye," I replied, sitting up, "but what to you do with those prescriptions the Moor gives you?"

She shrugged. "I give them to a fisherman who is skilled at making philtres. Then I sell them. You know that."

"But if you do not read, *mio cuore*, how do you know the ingredients are the right ones? They could be anything."

At this Flaminia fell silent, perplexed and saddened. I reached out my hand and stroked her hair. "Have you recently gotten prescriptions from the *chavush?*"

"Yes, until some days ago."

"Do you yet have them?"

"The last few."

At the snap of my fingers, Flaminia pulled the scraps of papers from her bag and handed them to me. Like all her recipes they contained ingredients I had never heard of and words that seemed to belong to no tongue at all. "Find Dr. Vigo," I commanded, but at that moment the physician himself entered the ward on his morning rounds.

"I have told you, you are not allowed here," he said to Flaminia with a severe reproach and, as she resisted, began to pull her toward the door.

"Dr. Jean," I said, raising my arm, "Leave off, I beg you. Look here." I handed him the papers and asked if they were ciphers.

After some study of the letters he asked Flaminia what the words *Kafé* and *Kasita* meant. She did not know.

"Nor do I." In a voice not much higher than a mumble, Vigo read the entire prescription: "'To make oneself beloved, wearing a talisman of one-quarter silver with copper, walk with iron past three towns towards sunset to the place of ritual and say the words *Kafé, Kasita non Kafela et publia filii omnibus suis*. These words said, make the person desired swallow the powder and marvelous success will follow.' Hmm."

Vigo fell into a pensive silence, stroking his beard. An eternity passed. He got to his feet, left the room, returned with a look on his face as had he been resurrected. "Yes," he said, "... it is a code. Silver, the alchemists' word for the moon. Copper for Venus."

"We have a quarter moon soon coming," I said, "with Venus near."

"Indeed. I believe *Kafé, Kasita* are the usual nonsense words in these potions, intended to distract. But 'iron'—Mars, the god of war; 'three towns'—Tripoli. With iron march west of Tripoli to the place of ritual. There seems to be a ceremony in Arabic lands called 'Zuara.' This is fairly ... *clever*." He turned to the *quiraca*. "How long have you been getting these?"

"Months," she squeaked faintly.

Vigo now studied the other prescriptions. They all differed but each contained the word "ceremony" or "ritual." "Yes," Vigo addressed me at length, "I believe you have shown our spies are yet at work."

Despite the physician's protest, I was on my feet, dressing. Breeches and leg hose on, I grasped my mistress by the shoulders. "Flaminia," I said, "do you understand? You have unwittingly put yourself in the gravest danger and the entire Order as well. Come, we must end this Moor and his fisherman." I grasped her by the hand and readied to leave the ward, e'en as Vigo attempted to block our exit, warning me that I was not entirely well.

"You are quarantined," he said sternly, pushing me in the direction of the bed.

Truly, the unsteadiness on my feet told me he was right. This would play no role. I shook Vigo away and led Flaminia out of the Hospital. First I stopped at my room where I retrieved my weapons, fastening on my rapier and slinging my gun over my shoulder. Without pause I set off to find the emissary, who under the guise of his weak physique and harmless demeanor had for who knows how long been sending messages to the enemy.

With my poor wench in tow, I went to his room at the bagno. Empty. I asked at the walls, the barracks; with increasing heat we ran across to St. Michel. Nothing. The day was strangely cloudy for summer and the wind gusting with unusual strength, as if a storm were brewing. For several hours we searched in vain under this tremendous sky until back at the walls, one of the halberdiers told me he had seen the Moor not a watch earlier and told him I was urgently seeking him.

"By God!" I exclaimed, "do you know what you have done? He must now suspect I have found him out and will be running for his life. Where can he have gotten to?"

"The fisherman," said Flaminia.

I glanced at her. "Yes, surely. Where is that one to be found?"

She said he lived near Cirkewwa, across the channel from Gozo.

"*O reniego del Spiritu Maligno!*" I cried, "full across the island!"

"Yes," Flaminia answered, "but his potions are of the best ingredients."

"By the Tomb of Lazarus, I hold not the slightest doubt! Come quickly. We've not a moment to lose." We ran to the stables for horses and with a

yell I spurred my mount into a gallop. As we put league after league
behind us, I thought it made good sense that the fisherman lived near
Gozo, for he could easily ferry messages to that island, whence the road to
Sicily or southward was not well guarded. We rode like the wind, or
would have, but Flaminia was no horseman and more than once she who
was to be leading fell behind. Neither did my weakness aid us. We rested
the horses at Mdina, but not long, sprang back into the saddles and were
off again. The road remained dry but for a few drops, yet the skies swirled
above us, an undeniable portent.

At length we reached the northwest coast of Malta and Flaminia
pointed out the fisherman's hut. Several horses were tethered outside. I
dismounted quietly, drawing my sword and crept up to the hut. Standing
to the side I pushed open the door and at once an axe came down, missing
me; I shoved the door violently aside and as my attacker made to recover
his weapon I thrust my sword through his bowels. A second figure rushed
at me with a long knife, but I turned sidewards, pulling my dagger from
its sheath at the small of my back, and ran him through the eye. Hearing
all the noise, Flaminia came running in and said I had just killed the
fisherman's brother and cousin.

I staggered outside, sweating with fever or fury, certain tho' that
nothing would deter me from my object. Flaminia followed without any
comprehension of what she'd witnessed. The hut stood on the coast itself
and from this vantage point I descried a small boat with two passengers
making across the choppy waters toward Gozo. The damned Moor was
one of them. Seeing no way down from this windy perch, I took the
arquebus from my shoulder, and knelt on the ground, losing an eternity
as I struck a spark over my tinderbox, finally lighting a sulphur match
and then the fuse. Luckily, the gun was loaded. I pushed aside the powder
cover, fixed the match in the dog leg, at last took aim and fired. The
fisherman slumped over and the Moor grabbed the oars from him, rowing
with all this strength, which would not be enough to save him from me.
I removed the match, charged the gun again from the flask, took another
ball from my bag and loaded the weapon once more, ramming down that
pellet with the scouring rod; instinctively I wiped the pan with my
thumb, from my touch box placed some new fine powder on it.

I did not realize I was standing atop one of those innumerable grottos
that line the Maltese coast. As I held the arquebus in my hand, taking

unwavering sight at my perfidious enemy, the wind-driven water rushed into the cave beneath me and forced itself through a hole in the roof, creating a great waterspout that roared into the air high above me. So powerful was this gusher that, just as I fired, it knocked me clean off my feet. I fell, hitting my head on a rock. When I came to, my head was in Flaminia's lap, and she gazing at me with an expression of tenderness and reproach. Unsteadily I got to my feet, but by now the boat had disappeared and with it Abdallah al-Waryagli.

"You are in the gravest danger," the Moor told Parisot. "The Agha Morat knows of your coming and is waiting for you on the beach."

"That camp of pitiful Arabs, you mean?"

The Moor regarded Parisot with astonishment. "Pitiful Arabs? Those are four thousand of the best Turkish horse and arquebusiers, sent by the Porte itself to Djerba. Told of your intents they have sailed here and have worked themselves into a fury to attack you."

Parisot put a gold ring in the Moor's hand and sped into the town again to find the Prior. No sooner did Valette tell the Commander of the situation than Strozzi called for his trumpeters to sound a retreat. "But look at this, Parisot," he said, surveying the chaos about him. "Who will hear the call?"

Vergã did not. With most of his comrades he was yet rampaging through the city's houses, tearing away women from their husbands, girls from their fathers, husbands from their wives and killing anyone who resisted. Or perhaps he heard it, but he was not about to cease his enjoyment. Neither did Pietru heed the summons. Like Vergã he was caught up in the plunder, rounding up captives. Only when he got back to the square, pushing a slave before him with one hand and carrying a head with the other, did he spy Strozzi attempting to order the troops there. The Prior managed to collect several hundred men behind him and make for the side of town without walls.

For everybody else it was too late. By now day was breaking and suddenly, by instinct, the soldiers as a man turned to the city's main gates. The same words escaped everyone's lips: "My God!"

Morat, having brought his cavalry up from the beach, was now walking into Zuara no more opposed than the Christians had been. When Vergã spied him across the square at the head of his horse and foot, he pushed the woman in his arms away from him and stood erect. Instantly he understood: They would have to fight their way to the ships. Enemy fire erupted and Vergã ducked through the door of the house next to him. He ran upstairs, found a balcony and began to return fire against the infidels. Blaij had thought to make up some charges ahead of time, but it was slow going. He thought he knocked off two Turks.

Vergã saw his only hope lay in getting to the southern side of town where there were some hills and the walls stood lower. Then he might join Strozzi. How? Below was complete mayhem. Soldiers and barbarians dashed this way and that. Escaping slaves were running into the arms of the Turks their deliverers. Of the soldiers, some scrambled for cover; others, having lost their heads, tore around in panic.

"Up here!" Vergã waved to those below. A few heeded him, running into the house, and he began to gather about him a small company.

The instant Strozzi sounded the alarm, de Valette made his way back to his column of slaves, which his men were already marching toward the beach. He put himself at their head again and marched them at a double pace down to the water's edge, but as the water lapped at their very feet a company of the Agha's troops caught sight of them. As this turbaned cavalry charged with drawn scimitars and high-pitched screams, and the enemy arquebusiers opened fire, the Knights at the rear of de Valette's column drew up to defend themselves. The captives did not need to be told that this was the moment they'd prayed for. As the Knights turned, preparing to meet the onslaught with sword and pike, the slaves at once began struggling with every strength to free themselves from the ropes that bound them.

When he'd spied Morat's cavalry preparing to charge the square and perceived no sensible resistance against them, Pietru well understood his own peril. He ran toward the south side of town and managed to escape before the charge. Now, panting for breath, he caught up with de Valette on the beach. Then the enemy sighted them. It was only several hundred of the Agha's horse and foot, but that force outnumbered the Knights. As the enemy cavalry galloped headlong, Pietru got off a shot from his arquebus; there was no time for another. He drew his rapier and a Turkish scimitar simply broke it in half. With only his gun left, the Gozitan began swinging. The slaves by now were escaping in droves and for a few heartbeats their very numbers provided a shield for the Knights, as in that panicked stampede they got underfoot of the enemy horses. Through everything, Pietru was somehow aware of de Valette, with the surf washing around his legs and his sword raised, never ceasing his forward march to the sea. At each step the Commander called his men to him and somehow, even while retreating, under his orders the Knights managed to prevent all the slaves from escaping.

Pietru could not understand de Valette's calm. The Turks continued to rain fire on the column's rear, picking off one Knight after the other. The horse charged and again. The Knights defended themselves with pikes planted in the sand. They took down Turks but with the numbers against them, Christian heads soon littered the beach. At the moment when all seemed for naught, de Valette's men spied the galley caiques sent out to meet them.

Everywhere the cry went up, "To the boats!" but this coast was too rocky to permit the skiffs to beach. So the men waded straight into the water, pushing what slaves remained ahead of them. As the cries reached his ears, Pietru too threw down his gun and dove into the water, hauling for all he was worth as balls whistled past. Most of the Knights didn't know how to swim and as they hesitated they were cut down by arquebus fire or lost their heads to the sweep of scimitars. Almost all those who tried to swim drowned in their heavy armor. By the time de Valette got to the ships, he had managed to put two hundred slaves aboard, but most of his company had been destroyed.

Vergã watched the entire massacre going on in the streets below him. He was running out of ammunition. "We've got to reach Strozzi," he said to the other seven or eight men he had gathered around him. At least three were wounded in the arms or thighs.

"How do you expect to do that?" one Roca asked. "If he's alive, he's on the other side of this fucking town."

"We can get over the roofs to a distance. Then we drop down over the walls."

"We'll break our legs."

"Take the rope from the beds. The walls on the southern side of town are said to be low and crumbling. Let's go there. Or would you prefer to stay cooped up in this place and lose your head?"

At once four of the men began punching their way through with swords and pikes, as the others cut the ropes from the beds and tied them together. The roofs were lightly made here in Africa and before long they had chopped a hole large enough to climb through. But e'en as he put a foot on the trunk they'd moved under the hole, Vergã heard a cry from outside. He glanced over the balcony to see a soldier trapped by two Moors who showed no interest in taking prisoners. One held a javelin and the other a scimitar and they had the fellow cornered hard against the next house, swinging his gun at them. Snatching his rapier, Vergã went over the balcony, landing not two steps from the Moors.

"Come here, you whore!" he shouted at the bigger one, the one with the scimitar.

The Moor advanced on him, almost laughing. "I'll slice you in half. Your ass stinks like a dead dog." With that he raised the scimitar; Vergã knew it would slice him in half. He grabbed an abandoned buckler lying on the ground with both hands and flung it at his foeman, knocking the weapon from his grasp. Then Vergã picked up his rapier and drove it through that's one's chest.

"Now you're a dead dog with a stinking ass," he said.

The action distracted the other Moor long enough that the cornered soldier was able to club him over the head with his arquebus. As the Moor reeled, Vergã snatched the spear from his hands and impaled him on it.

"Come on, comrade," he said to the nameless soldier, "upstairs." But that one was having difficulty walking and Blaij put his arm under his shoulder.

They got onto the roof, the ten of them, and began making their way to the landward side of town, crawling and running and helping those who could do no more than limp. There were not enough roofs to reach the walls. Below them fighting was all over the place, in every street, without order, hand to hand.

"So now you've gotten us trapped up here," growled Roca, lying flat on the rooftop.

"Another word out of you," answered Vergã, crouching near him, "and I'll throw you down. We know you'll drop like a rock." He thought for a moment. The nearest wall wasn't far—just a few streets away—but from here he couldn't see any gate or stairway. If they went down here, they might be trapped, and anyway, half the men couldn't jump. "We passed a storehouse just now. There must be a ladder. You two with legs, after me."

No one was immediately below and Blaij jumped down to the street with the other two following. They ran like the blazes to the storehouse several doors back and broke down the door. Sure enow, a ladder. The three of them carried it back to the other house and laid it against the wall. Blaij had thought they others would climb down but, losing their reason, they hoisted the ladder up to make a bridge across the street. Just as well. All the commotion had attracted the attention of the enemy and now four Turks hurtled around the corner as arquebusiers trained their weapons on the men trying to cross the makeshift bridge above.

The four barbarians lost no time in rushing the three Christians on the ground. Those scimitars weren't made to puncture armor, Blaij was thinking; they were only to slice, but God help you if you had no damned plate and got in the way of one. Sure enough, the soldier on his left went down, his chest cut wide open. Now it was two against four, but suddenly one of those on the ladder above fell, pierced dead by a ball, and knocked one of the infidels to the ground. Vergã slew him. The comrade on his right saw his sword arm sliced off at the elbow but managed to draw his dagger with his other hand and thrust it through his opponent's neck before one of the remaining Turks cut off his head.

Blaij was alone on the ground facing two foemen. This does not look good, he admitted and kissed his crucifix. A comrade above, by now across to the wall, took aim with his arquebus and felled one of the Turks. The last infidel on his feet brought his scimitar down on Blaij's rapier and, yes, snapped it in two. Vergã tossed away the useless weapon and his foe swung again. He missed and, as always with one of those of those blades, missed wide. Blaij launched himself in desperation at the off-balance Turk. It was only his sheer strength that saved Vergã in the end. He grappled with his enemy, pressing him to the wall. They fell, but Blaij did not loosen his grip and finally strangled the infidel with his bare hands. Utterly exhausted, he helped carry the ladder his mates now let down, and with this ladder and ropes they made their way over the nearest wall into the ditch.

Only five of them were alive now, every one wounded. They all slapped Vergã on the shoulders, naming him their deliverer.

"We aren't delivered yet," he said, looking around. No one was to be seen in this deserted spot under the palms on the south side of town. "If we head west, we are certain to run into the barbarians. Let's circle around the walls the long way to the seaside. Strozzi must be there." So they took off, trotting, limping, halting. Sure enough, to the north of the town, closer to the beach, they spied Strozzi's company and the red and white standard of the Order and they made for it.

Strozzi had gotten the only sizable body of men out of Zuara before Morat'd charged through the town, but he did not get far. On the beach a Knight from de Guimeran's company ran up to him. "Your nephew," he pointed east along the shore, "lies in the greatest peril. At this moment he is fully surrounded by Turks."

Strozzi instantly commanded his men to march in that direction, but God had taken the matter from his hands. The nephew and his small *avant-garde* had seen that their only salvation lay in reaching the galleys, but in their desperate flight to the shore, they'd been overtaken by the enemy. By the time the Prior reached the place of battle, only a few men remained standing, grinding their feet into the sand and fighting to the last drop of blood. Strozzi saw from a distance his own nephew struck down, and the Knight Sforza at his side.

The Prior let out a scream of anguish and ordered his men to wheel and attack the Agha Morat's main body. At the head of his troops, which now numbered no more than five hundred, Strozzi raised his sword and ran in full fury directly against the infidels. Inspired by this unexcelled bravery, his men charged close on his heels. Romegas was hardly a step behind.

Here Vergã and his comrades came onto the battle. When Blaij saw Strozzi's troops launch that hellish charge against the infidels, he knew that all their lives depended on the outcome of this action. He grabbed a broadsword from a dead Knight, discovered some reserve of strength within him and rushed into the mêlée. Vergã could hardly fathom what was taking place. Pike versus horse, broadsword against scimitar, arquebus fire all around. Mostly it was each man grappling with the enemy in his arms, here on the beach with the galleys visible in the distance, but without any way of reaching them. Blaij caught sight of Romegas wielding his sword with a Satanic wrath, surrounded by the smell of shit as it fell from the bowels of the barbarians who dropped everywhere about him.

Suddenly, the Turkish horse, surprised at the ferocity with which the Knights attacked them, withdrew to a distance, the foot following. For a moment it seems the path to the boats lies clear. Strozzi again raises his sword to lead the way. But the enemy's retreat proves only a means to allow the arquebusiers time to recharge. Before Strozzi's men understand what is happening, fire is raining all about them. At once the Prior himself is down, a ball lodged deep in his thigh.

"Save yourselves!" he cries as the Turks advance to dispatch the lot of them to the Devil.

But the Knights at this moment in no way contemplate abandoning their Commander and they close their ranks before him to form a rampart of men. The Turks charge again. Several of the Knights protecting Strozzi are killed immediately. Romegas, now wounded in the leg and arm, still swings his broadsword relentlessly. Vergã thinks that hope for the Prior is lost—and most probably for the rest of them—and the only thing to do is take down as many of the enemy as possible while they pray.

From that moment on, tho', things do not unfold as Blaij expects. A giant Majorcan Knight reaches the Prior and, as had he been a sack of feathers, lifts him into his arm, makes his way to the rear of the company and thence to the sea. The enemy levels at him a hail of gunfire. Is he hit? Vergã cannot tell, but from the corner of his eyes he sees the giant wade into the sea, hopping from rock to rock with the Prior in his arms, until finally in the deeper water he is met by one of boats from the *capitana*, and the two are taken aboard.

With the Commander gone, Blaij further expected that the company— what remained of it—would disperse in a panic, every man for himself. It did not. The Knight La Cassiere, holding the standard of the Order, now took charge. Quickly conferring with his fellows, they decided to march to the water, only sixty paces distant, and make for a narrow passage of rock that might protect them. They begin to move. It becomes kind of a running battle, the Turks initially surprised but losing no time to be after them even as they pick off any straggler lagging behind. But a few hundred have gained the rocks and the Turks regroup to charge again.

Once more the Knights confer. "My friends," La Cassiere shouts to the soldiers about him, as the screams of the infidels grow louder, "I would sacrifice a thousand lives before losing this standard to the infidels, which will certainly happen should we lose our heads to panic. We are decided.

You common soldiers have served us bravely and will be rewarded. Begone! Walk out singly between these rocks and save yourselves. The Knights will remain to defend this standard. If we are so fortunate not to be cut to pieces, we shall follow. Go!"

With the arquebus fire crashing into men and rocks, the common soldiers did not begin to walk singly: they ran, hurtled themselves through the passage, diving into the water, wading, swimming, hailing the boats, drowning.

Blaij refused. "I am with you," he said, stepping up to Romegas.

"Go!" the Knight ordered.

"No. I will make my end here."

There wasn't time to argue. Seeing their prey escaping, the Turks with Morat himself at the head of the cavalry, were again on them, fury redoubled. Those rocks prevented the horse from getting close, and the Agha ordered his men to dismount. They did, scimitars drawn.

Perhaps fifty Knights remain here at that passage leading to the water. They defend the place with pike and sword, which are constantly smashed by Turkish blades. Vergã glances about. The Knights have almost no weapons left, just their daggers, and the fighting is now mostly with bare hands. He and Romegas are back to back, struggling with their attackers as Morat Agha looks on, at once certain of the outcome and wondering at these Knights of Jerusalem. Finally, he orders his horsemen to remount and to finish them off.

Seeing that the last hope has vanished, the Knight Verdalle cries to La Cassiere, "Are we to stand here to be butchered and let our standard fall into the hands of these dogs? Our Commander has marked out the steps for us with his blood. Let us begone, I say!"

La Cassiere nods. "After me!" he cries and runs carrying the standard through the passage. Everyone bolts; the men keep as close together as they might and dive into the water when they reach it. La Cassiere and Poglieze hold the standard aloft, wading into the water with as much dignity as they can muster. Poglieze is shot dead, but before the standard falls, Verdalle grasps and rights it. Those Knights who aren't killed or drowned in this final retreat are met by the boats and taken aboard the galleys; hardly soon enough the fleet sets sail.

When the remains of the expedition reach Malta, they carry Strozzi to his home in Birgu on a plank.

Thirty-Seven

The Hospital's ward reserved for the wounded overflowed. Soldiers with gashed or missing limbs lay everywhere, on the beds, in the corridors, in the wards usually meant for the sick. The surgeons labored day and night. The smell of belladona embraced the air as screams filled the Infermeria.

I sat on the edge of Vergã's bed, listening to his story e'en while I examined the report of his condition the doctors had tacked to the foot of it. With naught more than a bandaged leg and arm he was wholer than most. At first I refused to credit his tale, yet others around lent their voices, and e'en Romegas, lying across the ward with a shoulder wound, assented.

"You can believe the sodomite," he declared boisterously. "None of the common soldiers fought with more courage."

"You will become a Knight after all," I said at hearing these testimonies, and was surprised at the strange color I found in my own voice.

Hereat Romegas abruptly changed his tone. "You think a few trifling wounds in one battle gives a man the right to be a Knight?" he scoffed. "In the first siege of Rhodes Grand Master d'Aubusson fought with an arrow in his thigh and a spear in his lung. Vergada here did well, but if he thinks to become a Knight of Justice—well, the bastard should take a dozen *caramusali* and get a dispensation from the Pope himself."

"A long road to plough," said Blaij, shrugging as his wound allowed. "As you said."

"Perhaps a confrater," continued Romegas, talking loudly, tho' as if to himself; a Serving Brother swiftly reminded him of the rules of decorum.

Suddenly, sharply, Vergã looked up at me. "And what happened to *you?*"

Leveling my gaze, I said: "I fell ill."

"A likely story," he snorted. "You knew Zuara would be too hot. Romegas saw it before we left: you don't have the balls. I've always said you were a cunt, right, Romegas?"

I refused to be drawn into it. "Go fuck yourself," I said.

Thereat I got to my feet and left. The year of our truce had expired and Blaij's ever uglier insults were a sure sign that he intended to bring things to a head—all over an imagined slight over a forgotten whore. I could not fathom whence his eternal contempt and shrugged.

His slanders natheless left me determined to discover with what malady I had been afflicted and I sought out Dr. Jean. I found him below in the surgery, engaged with others operating on the wounded. Two of the surgeons were tying up the veins in the stump of a soldier's amputated leg. They seemed not to be having success and blood was gushing over everything. Soon the patient drew his last.

"Dr. Jean," I said, watching him tie an animal bladder over the stump of another man's leg, "tell me, with what was I laid low these weeks past?"

"Almost certainly the plague," he answered carelessly.

"A lesser ... *indisposition* you called it!" I exclaimed in alarm.

"I saw no reason to disquiet you. There is no epidemic, thank God." He crossed himself. "*En cualquier caso*, you survived. Now as long as you are here, lend a hand." He motioned for me to help him ease a man's head into a helmet padded with felt. Vigo then whacked the helmet with a wooden hammer, knocking the fellow senseless.

"Hold this arm," he ordered and began to saw it off.

"I thought you were a physician," I said as I held the arm down, "not a miserable surgeon."

"The Sacra Infermeria employs only five physicians and five surgeons, and so in times of need one debases oneself." The doctor continued to saw. "Can you come by in three days' time? I want to collect a few bodies from the gallows."

"I should think there would be a surfeit here," I observed as blood from the surprisingly silent patient spurted all over me, Vigo and the operating table.

"Using Christian soldiers is ... *difficult* ... Now," he said, tossing the arm into a barrel, "get out of the way and go wash, we need to tie this up."

I walked back toward my room, passing by the stone walls of the Auberge de France and, as I passed by, who should step onto the street but Balthazar himself.

"Balthazar!" I exclaimed and we embraced. E'en as we regarded each other, I saw a changed man. I could not say why, but he seemed as from another world. "You have seen the Pope?" I asked cautiously, as we sat down in a tavern to eat.

"Aye," he replied with a sensible distraction, "that we did, but alas he has no money for we the Knights of St. John. He bids us to keep up the Crusade against the Infidel and prays that Mary Tudor will soon sit on the throne of England and put an end to the heresy into which that country has fallen."

"Balthazar, is something amiss?" I said with continued prudence. "You do not seem entirely present."

The Chevalier chuckled as bread and cheese was brought. "I am not. There is much construction now going on at St. Peter's Basilica, one reason the Pope has no money to spare for our endeavors, and His Holiness received our delegation in a small chapel built by Sixtus."

"Yes?" I shook my head, finding no significance in his words.

Balthazar gazed at me, or past me, I could not say which. "It has not long ago been painted by this Michelangelo."

"Isabella once mentioned his name," I recollected with sadness. "I know nothing of him."

Balthazar barely heard. "*Moy foy*, I cannot tell you my friend what an impression that ceiling, that wall makes upon you. It is as if heaven has come to earth. It is as if ... " The Knight trailed off, lost, and all was silence. I waited and waited for him to speak but he said nothing. Finally, after I had given up all hope of resuming the conversation, he returned from whatever place he was, shaking his head with wonder. "One man alone created that and now they are raising above the basilica a dome he has designed. It may rival Brunelleschi's in Firenze ... " Again the Abbé lapsed into silence, for a shorter space, soon chuckling. "I say, this Michelangelo, whoever he is, has talent. He may outlive us, my friend, he may ... "

Balthazar trailed off once and for all. I had never seen him rendered so ... speechless.

Nor did I comprehend any of this ecstasy—if that was the word—and would not for several years. "Have you heard about Zuara?" I said, passing to a more somber theme.

My question wrenched him to this world. He'd heard, tho' no details. "What part of the expedition was lost?"

"More than a third of the Knights and at least half the rest. They were surprised by Morat Agha. The *chavush* Abdallah had been sending him messages, for months."

"Truly?" Balthazar now asked with eyebrows raised.

I recounted the entire story. "I cannot say, of course, whether he was responsible for the exact messages we found in the cave, or whether his missives reached their destination. We will probably never know. I am certain he tried." Thereat I quaffed down my wine and poured another cup. "I am sorry I was not at Zuara with the others ... Once again Blaij names me a coward. It is all I can do not to kill him."

"God ordained your illness."

"Do you regret not having fought?"

Balthazar held out his cup, then looked at me severely. "Let us say, with Niccolò, *si guarda al fine*, one must examine the ends in considering the actions of men. What valor is to be had in a bad cause? Zuara was a bad end—in more respects than one. To think we could retake it in our present condition! Bah! This borders on madness. The Religion has lost sight of the end—what it wants, needs to become. Sometimes it is said of we the Knights that we know how to die as Christians, but not to live like them ... "

"Would you have joined had you not been sent to the Vatican?" I put it to him directly.

He did not answer.

"For what cause would you sell your life, Fra Balthazar?"

Now the Chevalier laughed merrily. "It is not the cause; that, Francisco, I have said—it is the moment. At your age, almost any will do. I choose more carefully. Fear not, the moment shall arrive. We do die well we Knights, don't we?" Now the Knight leveled his gaze at his companion. "Your trouble perplexes me. After glorious exploits at Città Notabile, daring escapes, months of corsairing, you allow Vergã to call into question your valor. Why? He is a poltroon."

"He is a poltroon who has gained the esteem of Romegas, to name but one."

"What is the cause of this ... *contest* between the two of you?" Balthazar asked, sitting back. "A common whore, no doubt?"

I conceded a rueful smile to the Abbé's perception, yet at the same time shrugged. "Since childhood he has nursed some grudge against me," I finally muttered.

Hereat Balthazar unfastened his dagger, placing it on the table. "I say this: true valor has no need to call attention to itself. I would also say, my friend, that a man who constantly provokes his comrade for so slight a reason has something to hide. Alas, if you remember Birgu's civil war, trifles do escalate. At this moment, tho', I am less concerned about Blaij Vergã than the Council at Trento."

"*¿Como?*" I exclaimed, startled.

"Surely you are aware of the great Council of Trento, now in its second session already?"

I had heard of it, of course, who had not? But such exalted matters had always been far removed from those of the small people. "Of what concern is this to us?"

"Of every concern!" exclaimed Balthazar, leaning across the table. "Now that Julius has convinced them to convene in Trento again without fear of the plague, they continue to design their answer to the Lutheran heresies that have convulsed Europe these past decades."

I did not see what the Knight was at.

"Their decisions will affect every aspect of our lives, every day, every moment, from the way we pray to the services in the church to what we read. I become a repetitious bore when I say that the Knights must remake themselves. As we speak the Church is remaking itself. Yet as I grow wiser, I perceive that such transformations are not always for the good. I am fearful."

"By the Angel of Peace, of what?"

"Listen to me, boy," he said, leaning over fiercely, "the Pontiff himself spoke of the Index introduced into Spain while we were off corsairing with Strozzi, the Index of proscribed books. Confiscations and book burnings have been a commonplace in your homeland for years. Now there is a list. Julius himself does not appear an avid prosecutor, but I say it will get worse. The Church condemned my old friend Rabelais's books years ago. I can hardly imagine why. Maybe they are offended at Gargantua pissing on Christians."

Despite the slight upturn of his lips at the last, Balthazar's concern struck me as strange and his words, as was sometimes the case in past months, to stride across dangerous ground. "Surely you do not oppose *El Santo Oficio*?" I said, dimly recalling my youth in Sevilla and my enthusiasm for the Inquisition.

"Nay, but one can be faithful to the Church without losing one's head altogether. Our age, we are told, is one of reason, but I ask again: Does the age looks forward or backward?" At this juncture the Knight sat back, his countenance growing darker. "I told you a story of Venice and a woman I once loved, that I would remain true to my vows but would not do the other. That pledge I affirm, my friend. But it is a mistake to believe that Christendom can heal the ills it has brought upon itself through the heretic Luther by its usual means. Remember the words of the prophet: 'This people hath wrought two evils. They have left me, the well of living water, and they have dug to themselves cisterns that cannot hold water.' The more we toil to pen the waters in shallow cisterns, the more rapidly the rain shall overflow them and run away from us. That much I know, amen."

"Do you once and for all style yourself a Cassandra then, Balthazar?" I asked, laughing uneasily. It was the first time, I thought, he had ever quoted scripture to me.

Balthazar shrugged, returning the laugh. "What else must an Abbé do?"

Thirty-Eight

Balthazar's prophesy began to be fulfilled at once, tho' no one knew it. Only days after our conversation I encountered Strozzi on the street, hobbling with a crutch. "Signore, you are already on your feet!" I exclaimed.

"Barai, you well know what we Knights are made of. Hah! I am organizing new attacks against the Barbary infidels. Will you join?"

My astonishment as I gazed on the Prior was unchecked. "Have you sufficient men?" I asked, believing it inconceivable after the recent disaster.

Strozzi merely shrugged, carelessly. "The hazards of war," he said. Aye, tho' a large part of his force had perished at Zuara, the Knights viewed this as an ordinary sacrifice. Moreso, such was the heroism and temper of mind Strozzi had displayed that while he still lay wounded in bed he had again been chosen Captain General of the Galleys.

This time I would go with him—and I did. Vergã as always sailed with Romegas. I cannot deny that the *contest* between Vergã and me, as Balthazar had named it, was high in my mind. The thought that Blaij might succeed in becoming e'en a confrater—a commoner rewarded for outstanding service who was entitled to wear a half-cross—was as intolerable as his baitings and threats, tho' his bravery could not but wring from me admiration.

Thus over the next months I proved myself, again. With Strozzi I sailed to Barbary, the Nile. So greatly did the infidels fear the Prior that they took every care to avoid him, all in vain, and we seized prizes, slaves and booty, including many items of luxury that we brought into the Great Port. I saw Vergã infrequently, when we counted out our loot in the taverns. Both Innocenza and Flaminia profited handsomely.

Winter of 1552 was already well upon us and we had returned from the season's last voyage. I stood on the dock while the galley was being unloaded of its cargo. "Good afternoon, Signore de Barai," said a voice behind me and I turned to see the landowner Matteo Falzon.

I bowed. "I am surprised to find you here, Signore," I said, coolly. "I did not believe you ventured from Mdina."

"Rarely," Falzon replied with equal formality, "but last night I heard that Strozzi has brought a cargo of rarities into the Port. I would be pleased to own that trunk." He pointed to a chest inlaid with brass and ivory sitting on the dock.

"You will have to speak to the *scrivano* about it, or Strozzi himself."

"I shall." Falzon boarded the boat, not long after returning with a bill of sale in his hand. E'en as he asked me to deliver the trunk to his house on the morrow, he regarded a necklace he had also purchased on board. "Do you believe that amber can detect infidelity in a wife ... ?" Receiving no answer, he said, "Be my guest for lunch."

Taking the paper from him I reluctantly agreed.

The next morning I found a cart and a driver, collected the trunk and set off for Mdina. The rain from the previous night made the going slow and we arrived in Città Notabile only in the afternoon. A servant greeted us, paid the driver and had the trunk carried into the house. Imagining I caught sight of that perfidious Combo on the street, I natheless followed the servant into Falzon's spacious courtyard with its trees, nymphaeum and twittering birds; here the guests had already gathered for lunch and were talking among themselves. I froze in my tracks.

"Francisco," she said with a warm smile, turning to me.

I bowed and kissed the perfumed hand. "Isabella." My surprise could not have been more complete. "I—I had not expected to see you again," I said, at last reaching the words.

She lowered her head bashfully. "You do not believe that, Francisco. We knew we would ne'er be parted forever." Now she looked up and gazed on me. "It has not been so many months, yet again I see you have changed." She said this passing her fingers over my arms and face, almost like a blind woman. "More scars. Your muscles grow ever stronger. They are now of iron. You are beautiful, Francisco, but your face has lost its expression and is like rock. Are you still able to read?"

It was only then that I noticed how Isabella herself had changed. She seemed grayer—somehow; the blush had gone from her face, and she was surely less a girl now than a grown woman. All in half a year. "Will you do me the honor of presenting me to your husband?" I asked.

"No."

"Why not? Do you regard me as unfit?"

She looked steadily into my eyes. "He is dead these two months past. The plague."

My heart went out and I told her with all sincerity how sorry I was to hear of such a cruel fate, if, I knew, a common one. Isabella herself seemed less in mourning than in confusion. She took me aside to the courtyard gallery, where we sat between the columns facing the nymphaeum. "I never knew him, not at all, and here I am at seventeen, childless and a widow."

Isabella was genuinely uncertain about what to do next. "I think I shall continue to live in Florence. Three paths are open to me: to become a nun, which would be proper; to become a courtesan, which would bring me renown. They frequent the highest society, have access to the most sparkling company and see their works published to wide acclaim. They are the best poets in Firenze." Isabella laughed softly. "The other choice is to remain a widow and manage my husband's affairs. And perhaps, God willing, remarry someday. For the present I think I must remain a widow."

"Do you continue to write?" I asked, my hand resting on a column.

"Yes," she said, surprised at the question, "my art improves with each passing day."

"Then your path is clear—you must become a courtesan."

Both of us smiled. "Truly, one must consider it," she replied, musing. "In Firenze the women carry their *Petrarchino* everywhere, tied to their waists with the most colorful ribbons, so great is their love of poetry. I do not believe I would enjoy, tho', the yellow veil the *cortegiane* must wear in public. Tullia has avoided that, so great is her fame ... Perhaps ... Have you returned to Granada, Francisco?" Isabella asked suddenly, "to retake your name?"

Still that. "After the castles here were completed, I intended to join the expedition to Zuara but was struck down—"

"With ... ?"

"The plague, but God willed my survival." At hearing this, Isabella glanced at me strangely, and no doubt we both perceived the Design in these events.

"Tell me," she said, with a tone balanced between playfulness and mourning, "has your heart become had hard as your arm?"

As the servant called all the guests to table, I rose, revealing to her the scarf fastened about my neck. "I have kept your token."

"And I yours." Isabella stood as well, pulling my crucifix from her bosom. "We will speak more of life later," she said, pressing my hand.

We did not. In the dining room Falzon said grace, giving thanks that the islands had been delivered from the Turks for another season. But no sooner had the first course been served than he himself inaugurated the complaints with a caustic protest against the exorbitant new taxes for the fortifications, asking whether the Knights intended to squeeze gold from the landowners' veins with the rack.

Naturally, Lady Emilia rejoined that it was for their own benefit, for after all the Knights protected them, but another guest riposted with a wave of his knife that she could hardly be serious, for the Religion forced the parish *università* to provision the militias and provide alms for the *poveri bisognosi*. Another wine-filled guest snarled that e'en when the councils elected bailiffs, the Grand Master appointed his own to supplant them.

"Bailiffs!" Falzon's wife scoffed. "Their mistresses are worse! They flatter themselves they rule entire villages. You can get nothing done at all without bribing them!"

E'en as Lady Emilia was gradually silenced, I listened to the barons with decidedly more sympathy than when I first sat in this house o'er a year ago. Late in the afternoon, when the mood was already glum and everyone well dissipated, the same Doctor Giuseppe Callus who had been among the guests that earlier time appeared at the door, his face so anguished that I thought he must have just escaped Turgut himself.

"Forgive me, all of you, for my lateness," he said, bowing to every side, "but I have had news of the gravest import."

Everyone set down their goblets and the chatter quickly subsided.

"d'Homedes has today ordered a commission formed to investigate *Lutheranam ac alias sectas impias*."

At hearing these words, Falzon inadvertently overturned his glass and his face paled to ashes. Everyone around the table turned toward him.

"*d'Homedes* has ordered it?" he asked at last, hands visibly shaking. "Does he have a papal brief?"

Callus shook his head. "Malta is too small and inconsequential for the Pope to send a ... " The doctor's voice failed him. "It appears that Bishop Cubelles will again take charge." At this Callus fairly collapsed into an empty chair. Casting about for a glass of wine, he poured himself one and held it up to the others. "Signore, Signori," he pronounced with the deepest resignation, "the Inquisition has come to Malta."

The guests did not remain long. With a shudder, Lady Emilia took her daughter by the hand and departed. I was after them, hoping to have a word with Isabella, when Falzon grasped me by the arm, bidding me to stay behind for a few moments. He led me into the courtyard, yet did not seem to know what he wanted to say.

"If I were you," I myself said finally, growing impatient, "I would flee."

Falzon shook his white face most slowly. "Signore, I fear you do not perceive the gravity of the situation that is descending. Only seven or eight years ago, Cubelles instituted a like process. Mayhap you know that a French priest here, one François Gesualdo, was burnt at the stake, as well as one of his followers." I had heard something about it, yes. "Perhaps you did not hear that Gesualdo was a ... *friend* of mine and that I myself was interrogated by Cubelles. Dozens were taken to the Bishop's Palace and submitted to the question. Due to my station, I suspect, I was released with a reprimand, but since that time I have been forbidden to leave Malta. Suspicion will fall on me immediately."

I found little sympathy for Master Falzon. "This surprises you," I answered, "when you keep works by Erasmus on your bookshelf?"

"Among my small circle in Mdina," he said, now beginning to pace, "there are those who ... read. Erasmus himself declares he never supported Luther, but did not feel prevented from engaging in a temperate discussion with him. He did not view it as a gladiatorial combat."

Confusion and anger had by now gotten the better of me and I involuntarily spat, "What has this to do with me?"

Falzon cast a mournful glance at the small statue within the nymphaeum. "The Inquisition is not a temperate discussion—may I address you as Francisco?"

"No," I shot back without thinking, "you may not."

"Then Signore," Matteo Falzon went on in the same mournful, impassive voice, "I say to you frankly that in the last moments I have become very afraid. I ask only that you forget anything you may have seen or heard in this house. I am the richest man on Malta and can pay you handsomely for your silence."

"You mean you can pay me not to denounce you to the tribunal."

It was strange to see this very rich, very powerful man simply terrified. Falzon lowered his head. "Early this year, while you sat in prison, Isabella petitioned me to find a means to release you. She thought I must know the judge Combo and could help. Indeed, Villegaignon himself had earlier sought my aid and to my shame I declined to intervene because of my enmity to his kind. But when Isabella approached me, I could not refuse her."

The landowner's words had riveted me to the spot.

"Do you know, Signore, the penalties for having carnal knowledge with an infidel slave?" Falzon asked.

"For a whore, yes," I answered.

"For a Christian man it is hardly less severe—for the first crime, ten years on a galley; for the second, hanging. A corrupt Christian judge certainly knows this. I needed only say to Combo that I had seen a certain scandalous woman enter his house on several nights and he was more than willing to free you."

"Did not Isabella petition Strozzi to give free passage to Combo?"

Falzon nodded. "Isabella in her desperation tried everything. But Combo, as uncomfortable as his situation was, never took the offer. As you see, he remains on Malta."

Falzon's words rang with truth. To my own shame I did not then recollect Balthazar's words, that he would not do the other. I only knew that I was reluctantly in Matteo Falzon's debt. I nodded feebly to him, bowed and departed from his house.

Thirty-Nine

I returned to my room to find Blaij at the threshold with a bloodied rapier in his hand. We had not set eyes on each other in weeks, and for a moment I thought he had finally come to call me out. But he stood there, still and impassive, blocking my entrance.

"Unless you have some business with me," I said, "stand aside."

"I've killed them," he said without the slightest emotion.

"Who?" Pushing by him, I unlocked my door.

"Innocenza and the dog I found her riding on my return."

I unfastened my own sword, tossed it upon the bed. "And what does this have to do with me?" I said, turning 'round, facing him.

Without leave my visitor stepped into the room. "Will you say you saw them *in flagrante?*"

I regarded the pale figure for a moment, poured a glass of wine, offered it to him. "Was he a Knight?"

Vergã took the glass. "No."

"Then the Council won't get involved. Leave Malta for a few months or tell the secular authorities what happened and that will be the end of it."

"You refuse to be a witness?"

The laughter that issued from my lips could not have been more derisive. "Do not jest with me any longer, Blaij Vergã. More important matters than you are afoot." I would have told him to get out, but he did that of his own accord, smashing the cup on the floor.

When Lady Emilia told Parisot of the coming tribunal, he was standing in his sitting room with his back toward her, feeding his parrot. At hearing her words, he calmly let the bird off his arm onto its stand, swiveled 'round to her and in a hushed, funneled voice said, *"Come?"*

She told him everything she had heard at Falzon's house.

"Does d'Homedes have a papal brief?" was his immediate question.

Emilia, seeing Parisot's narrowed eyes, shook her head quickly, in fear. She well knew Parisot's intractable hatred for Lutherans. She also knew that he'd never accept the proposition that the Order could be tainted by heresy.

Yes, de Valette had already begun to pace. "Another disgrace to the Order. Can the Grand Master truly believe that the Lutheran heresy has poisoned the Holy Religion itself? The Almighty cannot wish this, and a more preposterous thought is impossible to imagine." With that, Parisot donned his mantle and his wide-brimmed hat and set off for St. Angelo.

He found d'Homedes at prayer in the small Chapel of St. Anne next to the Castellan's house. Tho' the day without was cool, the chapel stones seemed to sweat and the air within was humid and stifling. d'Homedes knelt above the crypt where the former Grand Masters of Malta lay, among them l'Isle Adam himself. Out of a greater respect for l'Isle Adam than of d'Homedes, Parisot waited for His Eminence to rise. If the Monsignore was shocked to see de Valette standing at the pillar behind him, he disclosed nothing. Jean de Valette now stood face to face with the man he so despised. He bowed, formally.

"What is it, Parisot?" asked d'Homedes, walking from the chapel.

de Valette followed. "I have this hour been informed of the establishment of a commission to investigate the Lutheran heresy amongst the brethren."

"Not amongst the brethren alone," d'Homedes replied in his dry voice as the two of them stood on the summit of the fortress in the sea breeze, "but among the Maltese as well. We must be certain, mustn't we, that no French or German heretics corrupt the Catholic faith within the Order and in the country? Yes, four esteemed brethren shall carry out the investigation and they are to be taken in hand by Domenico Cubelles." The old man stopped, peering at de Valette in his cyclopean fashion. "You, Parisot, of all people, would never oppose this fight against the Lutheran pestilence, which is hardly less dangerous than that of the Infidel himself." d'Homedes paused again. "This wind is disagreeable. Let us pass to my sitting room." With that he led de Valette across the stones to a small room at the very tip of the castle. He parted the doors to the balcony and the entire Great Port now opened beneath them.

"I look to the future, Eminenza," answered Parisot, standing half on the balcony as d'Homedes seated himself. "The scandal of a tribunal will bring much unwanted attention to the Order, which is everywhere regarded as the purest in Christendom. We must never, never let it be said that the Knights Hospitallers of St. John of Jerusalem have sullied themselves with the bile of Luther."

"You, Sir, would prefer to do nothing?" d'Homedes hissed in disbelief, "when today whispers are everywhere. Against Villegaignon and that Balthazar—"

"Villegaignon!" shouted de Valette. "How dare you, Sir! No Knight among us is more noble or deserving of praise, he whose very uncle lies in the crypt above which you just now prayed!"

"The traitor reads Hebrew!" shouted d'Homedes, his eye flitting rapidly as all the disagreeable business of last year flooded back to distort his face. "He befriended Calvin himself, do you hear me?"

de Valette stepped fully onto the balcony now, grasping the *ringhiera* until his knuckles turned white, gazing into the grey waters far below. *"Vestri intemperance probat meus punctum*, Eminenza. No Knight is more learned than Durand, unless perchance it be Balthazar de Marans des Homes-Saint-Martin himself. Nicolas came upon Calvin at university, before that one even called himself Calvin. Had his confirmatory investigation revealed anything more, it is inconceivable he would have been allowed to profess."

d'Homedes's attempt to impugn Villegaignon's honor and faith disgusted him to his core, as much as the Grand Master's corruption itself disgusted him, but de Valette saw he must argue around this delicacy. "Take the step you are contemplating and, the Almighty will hear my words, Eminenza, you will see the Inquisition itself in the Convent, resulting in gross *inconvienti e scandali*. You will watch Knights accusing each other, slanders and calumny. You will watch young Knights accusing their elders, covetous of their fortunes; you will see murder to avenge false accusations ... "

Hearing this speech d'Homedes fairly cackled. "By the eye I lost at Rhodes, de Valette , your reasoning is as weak as your foresight is remarkable. Do nothing now—in that case we shall surely see the Inquisition. Far better to stamp our this pestilence today than to wait. A small scandal is much preferable to a large one. I have no more to say about the matter. *Alea iacta est.*"

He held out his ring for de Valette to kiss, but Parisot merely bowed and departed, thinking the wind up here was indeed disagreeable.

Flaminia sat on a stool before the Bishop in his palace, terrified. All the islanders knew of Cubelles and she had often seen him in processions or in church. She dimly remembered that time, about six years ago, when he burnt the priest at the square in Birgu. She was only a child then, but she saw herself skipping with her playmates around the big pile of sticks as the flames leapt up around the priest and his flesh blistered. Since then, every time she set eyes on Cubelles that picture came back. She regarded him as very powerful and probably to be feared, tho' she wasn't entirely certain why she should fear him; he just wanted to be sure everyone on the island was a good Catholic. Because she was a good Catholic she had been surprised when some men came up to her on the street and took her to the Bishop's Palace, a large building standing on the rise toward Kalkara Creek at the landward end of the town. They wouldn't let her tell anyone before they pushed her into a dark cell, where she spent two nights.

Now she was sitting in front of Cubelles himself and four other men, who faced down at her from their seats on a high wooden tribunal. Domenico Cubelles himself sat on a big throne-like chair in the center. She didn't like his looks at all. With fifty years, she guessed, he wore a square Bishop's hat as well as the mantle of the Order with its eight-pointed cross; she did not quite understand this because he was not a Knight. His thick Spanish beard was still nearly coal black and covered much of his face. What was left of that face bore the most severe expression she had ever seen. Flaminia wasn't sure whether Cubelles kept a mistress. The thought flashed through her mind that a mistress might cheer him, but she couldn't seize on the idea. As her breast heaved and pulse raced, her thoughts tumbled so fast that she could not seize on any of them except to wonder helplessly why she was here.

"You call yourself Flaminia and are from Zurrieq, is that correct?" said Cubelles himself in a voice that seemed to rise from the dead.

Flaminia nodded quickly.

"Do you know why you are here?"

"No, Monsignore," she crossed herself, "I swear by the Lord Jesus I don't know."

"Do you have any information you would like to give the Tribunal?"

The stones of this vaulted room somehow made his voice seem even more lifeless and Flaminia shook her head nervously, at a complete loss. "About what, Eminenza?"

"Address me as Eccellenza," said Cubelles. Flaminia knew the proper address, of course, but in her present state she had become too confused to remember. "This commission is gathering information about all those who have denied the Christian faith, and those who dabble in witchcraft, heresies and those suspected of heresy."

"But I am a good Christian!" blurted out Flaminia. "I go to church every week—"

"Are you not a common whore?" Cubelles shouted, cutting her off.

Flaminia reeled, frozen in terror. "B—but, " she replied after some time, "in my heart I have always been a good Christian." She now felt a wet spot growing along the bottom of her dress.

"Do you not accept money in return for carnal favors?"

What could she say to that? "I don't know a woman on Malta who doesn't, Eccellenza," she offered, causing the other commissioners to laugh under their breaths. "It is the only means to earn enough for bread. B—but I swear by the Madonna I have never taken money from a slave or a Jew—"

"*Silenzio!*" roared the Bishop at the top of his voice.

"—Even the nuns—" she tried to finish her thought, whispering—

"*Silenzio!*" the Bishop roared again and the stones rang.

Flaminia had stopped breathing. When the echoing of the Bishop's voice had ceased, there truly remained only dead silence and the buzz of a fly. One of the commissioners leaned to Cubelles, reminding him that whoring was not a contravention of the legal statues of Malta, except of course with non-Christians. He was not interested in the law, Cubelles replied; his duty was to protect the Faith. Again he turned to the wench before him: "Mistress Flaminia, do you fear for your immortal soul?"

She did, with the widest of eyes she most certainly did. Flaminia could not remember a day of her life when she had not sensed the dark spirits surrounding her, or when she had not imagined with certainty that when Death came for her she would be swallowed whole by the jaws of Satan as she tumbled into the everlasting fires of Hell. With every step she took through Birgu and in the countryside such visions followed her, and almost all of her little life was spent trying to find a way to escape the Inferno. She prayed and prayed. She could not understand why she was here. To Bishop Cubelles, she managed only to nod most fervently.

"You have been accused of dabbling in witchcraft."

The words struck her with a force as to make her dead. She could not speak. She tried; she faltered. Eventually one of the commissioners handed her a cup of water and she slowly drank it with both hands. When she finished, she managed to ask in a whisper, "Who has said this, Eccellenza?"

"That is not your concern. Do you deny being a witch?"

"May the Madonna burn me up if I am a witch!" she exclaimed hoarsely, crossing herself again.

Cubelles leaned over. "You see, what you have just said is sacrilegious—"

"I say the Lord's prayer every morning and the Ave Maria every evening," she cried, "and have an olive branch blessed on Palm Sunday to ward off spirits—"

She would have gone on, insensible to her own words, not understanding why she was saying anything, had not Cubelles raised his hand to silence her again. "You have been seen selling talismans and potions. Do you deny this?"

Still frantic, unable to think, to speak, Flaminia shook her head dumbly.

"You will cease this practice, otherwise your immortal soul will be forfeit. Now, can you tell us of anyone who practices the teachings of the heretic Luther?"

"No," she squeaked. "I have heard the name Luther, Eccellenza, but I do not know what he teaches."

"Where have you heard his name?"

"I believe in the taverns, Eccellenza."

"Who mentioned him?"

Again Flaminia shook her head. "I do not know."

"Any Knights?"

"No. Just people."

"Does the name Villegaignon mean anything to you?"

"No, Eccellenza."

"You must tell us names." Cubelles took up a sheet of paper passed to him by the other commissioners. "Did you join in a ceremony with a Carmelite priest and two friars to exorcise an evil spirit from a cave?"

"Yes, Eccellenza."

"Can you tell us who was there?"

Flaminia did. She had a good memory.

"What about your other friends? You must tell us what they have done of late."

Flaminia had already stopped resisting and just talked, not knowing at all what she was saying. "I saw Innocenza light a candle in front of an image of St. Anthony because she wanted to attract her lover to her again. She also told me that since the spell was cast on a Saturday, it would likely be in vain. I saw her eat pork on a Friday. That is all."

Cubelles decided that he was not going to get much of use from this whore, told her to sign her testimony and that she was sentenced to go to church four times a week and learn from the priest the correct recitation of her prayers. She got up but fell once—her legs would not hold her; again she rose to her feet, apologizing profusely, and put a cross where the clerk told her to sign. A guard led her away by the hand.

Later that day I laughed with a crowd on the main square as a woman walked through it with her head in an iron mask, fashioned to resemble the head of a pig. Only when the woman in this mask of shame stumbled through the taunts and dung being hurled at her and pressed her way directly up to me, all in sobs, did I perceive it was Flaminia. I would take her to a blacksmith's to remove this thing, I told her grasping her arm, but she refused, saying she must wear it all day as part of her penance. She left me then, saying it was time to go to church to pray.

By now the warp and weft of Balthazar's prophecy had become manifest to all.

"They're gathering everyone," said Isabella that same evening at the Guasconi household, "from the lowest to the highest."

I recalled the jubilation in Sevilla when Luther had died, and the enthusiasm with which the book burnings had been greeted. On Malta, nay. The entire island was swept by confusion and panic, no one being able to conceive whether this Tribunal was a good thing or a bad thing, certain only that two people had burned at the stake seven years ago. Lady Emilia was frantic with indecision.

"Perhaps it is necessary," she said in her sitting room, as the saints looked on. "If heresy should come to the Convent itself, then no place in Christendom is safe. Parisot is enraged beyond reason at the very thought of it."

Ill at ease as I was, standing before the Guasconi after Parisot's ban against my presence, I had felt compelled to come, to warn. "You must not visit Falzon again, Lady Emilia, Isabella," I said, "for he will without fail be questioned."

Emilia agreed at once. "None of us must see him again, even go to Città Notabile, at least until all this is behind us. Do you understand, Isabella? Isabella?"

Isabella made no answer, so possessed was she at that moment by her own divided mind. "I understand," she said at length, then feverishly clasped me by the arm. "Francisco, the Bishop expects denunciations, requires them. Do not present yourself before the Tribunal to denounce Falzon. Do this for me, I beg you."

Isabella felt trapped between her desire to avoid trouble and her debt to Falzon. "I have no reason to denounce him," I said truthfully.

Matteo Falzon was hardly surprised when his servant answered a knock on the front door of his house and ran to his master with the news that two halberdiers were waiting outside with a summons to accompany him to the Bishop's Palace. Falzon kissed his wife good-bye, mounted his horse and set off for the Borgo. He knew the questioning would be difficult. Seven years ago Cubelles suspected, not without reason, that he and his father had been disciples of the impenitent Gesualdo. Both he and the elder Falzon had been let off with a slap. Cubelles was insusceptible to bribes, which had been attempted, and Falzon could only imagine that the sentence had been so light because of his position, head of the Mdina Council, the *Università*.

With each step toward the Borgo the shiver in his bones grew deeper, and well before they trotted up to the Bishop's Palace, Falzon found himself quaking and sweating in the saddle. When he was led into that arching stone room and Cubelles barely deigned to glance at him, his bones told him that the Pro-Inquisitor would spare him nothing.

"Matteo Falzon, you are accused of spreading the Lutheran heresy in Malta," Cubelles began without prologue.

Like Flaminia, Falzon had the impression that the Bishop's voice was not that of a living thing, even that the dry hollowness emanated from somewhere beyond the figure facing him. "Who has made such an accusation, Eccellenza?" Falzon finally answered, feeling with every breath and heartbeat that he had been cast back seven years.

Cubelles refused to be taken in by the insolence. "You are not to put questions. We are to put the questions. Are the accusations true?"

"No, the accusations are not true," Falzon answered flatly. Already he felt possessed by a powerful weariness, as if the entire process were one of utter futility, the outcome ordained. At the same time he admitted to himself that the accusations were not entirely untrue. It was, in truth, a matter of nuance.

Cubelles pressed forward. "I exhort you to say the truth about whether you have ever engaged in the spreading of Lutheranism on Malta."

"I have not," Falzon replied, searching, casting about for any strength within him.

"Do you own writings of Erasmus and Cardano?"

The question hardly surprised Falzon and he saw naught to be gained by denying it. "Yes, I do, Eccellenza. I am unaware that the Italian Cardano is a Lutheran, or Erasmus either. As His Excellency knows, Erasmus condemned Lutheranism for its excesses and was even forced to flee his home for fear of persecution."

The simple response sent Cubelles into a rage. "Do not dare presume to lecture me on history, Signore Falzon!" he shouted, rising to his feet. "Erasmus's works are presently under suspicion! Should you hold any doubts, visit Spain!"

"I am not permitted to leave Malta, Eccellenza," Falzon replied in a whisper, "as you know." He felt certain that Erasmus's works had yet to be condemned by the Vatican but had not the strength to argue it.

Nor did Cubelles, who saw that the interrogation risked going down the wrong road, allow Falzon time to think about it. "What are you views on the doctrine of transubstantiation? Do you view the celebration of Mass as a repetition of Christ's sacrifice on the Cross? What is your view of the sacraments? Of papal infallibility? Do you deny that you were a disciple of François Gesualdo?"

The questions issued forth from Cubelles' mouth, evenly, unhurriedly, without expression. Falzon merely sat on the chair provided, doing his best to look beyond Cubelles and trying to decide in his own mind what he believed. His detestation of the Knights colored even this. How they had raped his small island for their own ends! How they had slowly enslaved the *università* and overturned the laws! Matteo Falzon's contempt for the usurpers grew fiercer each moment he sat before this illegal Tribunal. He thought back to the execution of the impenitent Gesualdo. The priest was a man of strength. At the instant the image of Gesualdo's burning body flashed through his mind, Falzon's thoughts lit on Luther's own summation of his teachings: *sola fide, sola scriptura*. But never, never by the word of these corrupt Knights and their lackeys. Yes, he was a Lutheran. Falzon remained silent.

"Torture him," said Cubelles.

A guard led Falzon down below into a cell. Nothing happened for several days while some formalities were seen to. This was undoubtedly intended part of the torment, for as each instant dragged on Falzon imagined with mounting dread what awaited. By the time the guard led him into a room with a tall ceiling, terror fully consumed Falzon; he could not think, he could barely speak and he knew not by what force he remained standing. A physician from the Hospital had been brought as witness. The young man, with a striking red beard, held a glass vial in his hands, containing what Falzon didn't know. Cubelles asked Falzon a last time for a confession, but Falzon only shook his head and continued to mutter the twenty-third psalm, which had never left his lips since the cell door had slammed shut days earlier. At a sign from the Bishop, the guard bound Falzon's wrists behind him and tied a weight to his feet, and now Falzon's bowels finally deserted him. The mess made no impression on the guard, who laughed and went about his business. He pulled down a rope from the hoist and hooked it to the one binding Falzon's wrists. Then at the signal from Cubelles, he and another pulled.

Falzon had never felt such pain. It seemed as if his shoulders were being ripped from his torso. He screamed, screamed for every moment of this eternity, but his cries did nothing to ease the agony. He saw only a whiteness before his eyes and he prayed for deliverance. Then the guards dropped him. And caught the rope. From his mouth issued such a cry that no human could make. Then, thank God, he passed out.

Forty

The Carmelite friars were summoned to the Bishop's Palace, reprimanded and taught how to perform a proper exorcism. Balthazar, too, was called. His arrest at the hands of d'Homedes concerned the Bishop for a moment, but Tripoli and its aftermath did not fall within the commissioners' charge. They interrogated the Abbé briefly, found an inquisitive mind but no evidence for the taint of Luther, released him. Vigo was summoned the following day.

"Identify yourself for the record," Cubelles said in the same hollow, expressionless voice.

"I am Dr. Jean de Vigo, Eccellenza," the witness replied, sitting before the Tribunal in a chair, "a physician in the employ of the Order of St. John."

One of the commissioners handed Cubelles a paper, which he briefly examined. "Is it true that you have recently engaged in the dissection of the bodies of criminals?"

Vigo made not the slightest attempt to discern through what channel Cubelles received this information; too many people knew of the demonstrations, and he was far from alone in performing them. "It is true," the doctor replied calmly, thinking this room was excessively damp. "The statutes of the Order make it quite ... *plain* that the Religion shall hire only physicians and surgeons who are skillful in their profession."

Cubelles stared down at this physician with a certain curiosity. "And you regard the practice of dissection ... "

" ... as necessary to increase one's knowledge and skill, yes."

"Do you believe, Doctor," the Bishop went on with no discernable change in his voice, "the practice to be consistent with Church dogma?"

Vigo did not know how to answer the Bishop's question and shrugged. "If you are referring to the celebrated papal bull of Boniface, Eccellenza, I believe the bull merely condemned the unseemly practice of boiling dead

Crusaders to extract their bones, which of course ... *facilitated* their transport homeward for burial. However, Eccellenza may recall, Sixtus IV more recently authorized dissection for the purpose of the medical art. I know of no formal interdict against dissection."

"If there were such an interdict?"

Vigo hesitated, then answered: "I would cease."

At this juncture one of the other commissioners raised his voice . "Tell us, Doctor," he said, "what is your considered opinion of the number of ribs in Eve's body?"

"Ahh," replied Vigo, nodding in comprehension. "As a physician I can only reply that my observations agree with those of Vesalius: a woman has the same number of ribs as a man."

A second commissioner now joined the questioning. "Do you believe that within the human body rests a bone, imponderable and incorruptible, which is necessary for resurrection of the immortal soul?"

"Vesalius, Sir, has not been able to locate such a bone," replied Vigo as he flicked a crawling insect from his sleeve and looked up. "Neither have I."

Cubelles here interrupted with a raised hand. "You are aware, Doctor, that Vesalius fled Italy—"

"—for Spain, Eccellenza. However, I believe it was less a matter of persecution than ... *invitation*—by the Holy Roman Emperor Carlos."

"Can you comment on the status of dissection in heretical countries?" the Bishop asked.

"Hmm," the doctor hesitated, flicking away the same insect a second time. "I believe the Lutherans embrace it, Eccellenza."

After some discussion among the commissioners, Vigo was released and the Tribunal issued no opinion on the matter of dissection.

The secrecy behind the doors of the Bishop's Palace quickly poisoned Birgu's air. Not a person in the tiny town did not know one who had been called before the Tribunal, and anyone who had been called immediately became suspected as he who denounced the next. The taverns quickly emptied and innkeepers complained to foreign merchants that business was bad.

"Is it true Falzon was put to the question?" Isabella asked the afternoon following Vigo's interrogation. We had gone out riding to escape the foul air and hoped to find a village where life went on unaffected. But neither of us could avoid speaking of it.

"So I have heard," I answered. "People suddenly say his name as if he were Lucifer himself. Nobody admits to have ever spoken to him and today they claim he has magic powers." I had been unable to repay my debt to him, I thought, and if I had not betrayed him it was mere circumstance. "Isabella, we will be called, I cannot doubt it any longer."

"I pray you are wrong," Isabella answered, crossing herself as we trotted southward under those dull winter skies, then with a sudden intensity exclaimed, "Francisco, we have nothing to hide! But Parisot ... "

She trailed off, with close to a gasp. "What of Parisot?" I asked, not comprehending anything. "His zeal is unsurpassed. Surely no one—"

Isabella shook her head, too violently. "Never! But Parisot knows full well that this Tribunal can bring only harm to the Order, and it will surely bring him into conflict with Cubelles. They already begin to detest each other ... "

At a loss, I managed only to mutter feebly that Parisot had not granted me leave to speak to her.

My words caused Isabella to laugh with a laugh that came less from a woman than from a wounded animal. "Parisot surely views me as damaged goods, not so much in need of protection as in former times." Thereat her eyes bore into me. "Is that what you think, Francisco? What has your whore led you to believe?"

"Isabella," I replied, more confused, "forgive a simple *quiraca*'s stupid insults. As for me, every man dreams of a virgin bride, but be assured, damaged as you may be, I am yet prepared to marry you."

My remark calmed Isabella to a degree, but I saw from her pale smile that her own journey had hardened her no less than my exploits had me. Six months had forced innocence to cede to experience. We came upon the same stone altar upon which we had danced o'er a year ago. This time it elicited only a bittersweet smile from both our lips. Determined, natheless, not to let innocence completely die, we danced again that pavan. Our fears, tho', would not be held at bay.

"Francisco," my partner said as she circled around me, "if you are called before the Bishop, what will you say?"

"About Falzon?" I replied, backing away from her, "What might I say? That I scarce know him and we have discussed no matters of faith."

I bowed and she curtsied. "Will you say you met him through my mother and me?"

Feeling an accusation, I asked sternly what she would have me tell them. And what would they believe? We circled again as the birds perched on the great stones eyed us curiously.

"Don't you see, Francisco?" she said. "The Tribunal will want to know whether Falzon has spoken to *us* about Luther, whether *we* are tainted with heresy. That would impugn Parisot himself. I cannot allow it ... "

Again Parisot. Once more we parted and bowed and I shook my head at her harsh tone. "Why? Parisot can defend himself."

"Do not speak so. He is my Godfather and has raised me from birth. Do you think I could betray him, jeopardize his advancement in the Order?"

"Isabella," I broke off the dance, standing erect with hand on my hip. "You see how these suspicions corrupt us. You must know I would sooner undergo torture than betray you."

Isabella herself stood erect and again smiled wanly. We embraced and spoke no more about the Tribunal.

Two mornings hence I was summoned for questioning. The guard led me into the audience chamber and I sat on the same stool from which Flaminia had earlier faced the commission. This Cubelles presented a terrifying aspect indeed, resembling in his black mantle and full beard a frozen idol of some legendary people, but I assured myself he and I were of one faith and that he did naught than perform his duty with the zeal required of him.

"Do you have anything you wish to tell the Tribunal?" he began according to custom. The three other commissioners scarcely seemed to be paying attention; rather they seemed more occupied with keeping themselves warm on this chilly day.

"No, Eccellenza," I replied, not entirely perceiving what the Bishop was at.

"Do you wish to denounce yourself?" he went on with little pause.

The question left me speechless, puzzled and more than a little fearful. "For what reason, Eccellenza?" I ventured, knowing instantly from the Bishop's countenance that I was not to set questions myself.

"Have you carried out any acts that should be judged by this Tribunal?" Cubelles went on, posing the question as one a schoolboy might comprehend.

"I do not believe so," I replied, shifting on the stool as a schoolboy. "When in port I attend church regularly and say prayers daily."

From the distracted expressions of the commissioners, which were more drawn to the sensible damp on the walls, I sensed all this was custom. One of them then asked abruptly, "Are you acquainted with Matteo Falzon?"

The question, dispassionately put, in no way surprised me. "No," I said plainly.

My attempt to divert the commissioners from this road failed instantly. "Do you mean to say you have never eaten a meal at his home?"

I sat rooted to the stool. Someone had betrayed me to the Tribunal. Betrayed. It was the only word. The thought that someone I might admire, trust, love could betray me, and that by necessity I would continue to admire or love him, was ... I hardly know how to say ... a true loss of innocence. While such venom coursed within, to the Tribunal I remained outwardly passive and retreated a step. "I meant only to say that I am in no way on intimate terms with Falzon. I have met him on two or three occasions, Eccellenza."

"Two or three?"

There was nothing for it; I swallowed. "Three, one being only for a few moments during the siege of last year."

Hearing this answer, the Bishop leaned over slightly. "Did he attempt to inculcate you with the doctrines of Luther?

"Not at all, Eccellenza," I said, regaining my footing. "I know nothing of his beliefs."

"Did he ever speak to you of magic?" one of the others raised his voice again, interrupting.

I instantly remembered Falzon's strange question at the docks, whether I believed amber could detect infidelity in a wife. My pulse raced, e'en as I realized I may have stumbled again. I became aware that Cubelles was repeating the question and I shook my head slightly, thinking that the stones in this chamber produced a sensible echo.

"You are lying," said the same commissioner.

At the force of his accusation, I retreated another step, feeling the sweat on my brow. "He wondered whether amber could detect infidelity in a wife."

"Did he say whether he believed in the efficacy of amber?" asked the commissioner.

At last I was able to shrug easily, for Falzon had not.

"The witness indicates no," Cubelles said to the secretary and abruptly went on: "In what other circumstances did you meet Falzon?"

"I was his guest on two occasions for lunch," I answered.

The Bishop immediately asked who else was there.

Feeling pressed to a wall, I yet sought an escape. I told him I happened there by accident and that the guests were unknown to me. Cubelles was in no way convinced.

"You intend to say you stumbled into the richest manse on Malta and you, a commoner, were admitted without question?"

"No, Eccellenza, he asked me to deliver a trunk to the his house and kindly invited me to stay." This half-truth served not at all.

"Were not Lady Guasconi and her daughter present at these gatherings, the same Guasconi with whom you are on such intimate terms?"

Much to my displeasure, I saw that the Tribunal knew more than I had surmised. "I met them at the first luncheon," I replied. "They are neighbors of Falzon in Città Notabile, as I am sure you know."

"What was discussed at these lunches?" another commissioner asked flatly.

With the chasm opening, Balthazar's vow hit me with force: the Pro-Inquisitor would get nothing more from me. "I don't remember very well," I replied. "The guests spoke Italian, and at the time my understanding of it was imperfect. I paid little attention. Mostly they spoke of taxes."

Truly, one of the commissioners laughed at that, only to receive a glare from Cubelles. Thereat, they quickly perceived I was going to be of little value to Tribunal and let me go, thanking me for my cooperation and with the admonishment to continue attending church regularly.

I wandered away from the Bishop's Palace in a bafflement and walked into the Church of San Lorenzo. Kneeling there before Our Lord Christ, I asked forgiveness for not having fully acquitted my debt to Falzon, yet gave thanks that I had caused little misfortune to those I held dear to me. The following evening gave me reason to doubt even this success when a servant led me into the Guasconi household and I found Isabella weeping in the sitting room.

"Get out of here!" she cried savagely. "I never want to see you again!"

At once I knew she had been interrogated. "Isabella, tell me what has happened!"

"Tell you! It is you who betrayed me to the Bishop!"

Her words slew me. "Betrayed! How? Isabella, they knew we had been at Falzon's house together; I could not deny it. I told them not a word more. You must believe me." I crossed myself.

My oath did not in the least assuage her. "Why should I believe anything you say?" she continued to shout through her tears. "You denounced me, you denounced Falzon!"

"This is incredible!" I shot back. "I told them nothing. There was nothing to tell. Nothing said at Falzon's in my presence was of the slightest import. The heretic Luther's name was never mentioned. Isabella, what are you hiding?"

By now she was beside herself and scarce listening. "Do you not understand? You have put us under the Tribunal's suspicion. They believe we are disciples—because of you! It is impossible to prove one's innocence."

"Because of me?" I cried, wounded and astonished by the madness of her words. "Is it not possible they have lied to you for their own ends? Is it not possible that your own frequenting of Falzon's house before we met was the cause of this misfortune?"

For a moment I thought my reason had an effect and Isabella ceased her accusations; yet her breath caught in her throat and she continued to sob.

"Ah, Isabella," I said, kneeling beside her. "You see what all this has done to us, and for no reason under God's Heaven. Let us leave this bitter place once and for all—"

"No one can leave during the Tribunal. It is regarded as an admission of guilt. The stain—"

"Let them believe what they may. We will go to Florence together, be married."

"Go, leave me. I wish nothing more to do with you."

Isabella pushed me aside with her arm and covered her face. E'en then I dimly perceived that whatever had taken place before the Tribunal had terrified her so deeply that she would sooner die than reveal it. Natheless, I had said my piece and left. I would depart Malta on my own.

My departure became a headlong flight. I stopped for something to eat at one of my habitual places and found Pietru there, munching on bread. He, thankfully, had not been called before the Tribunal and because he was a man of few words we were spared the necessity of speaking of it. Together we walked back to my room. As we climbed the steps we heard a lot of noise above. Thinking thieves were about, we unsheathed our swords and ran up the stairs to find three men upturning the room.

"Hold!" I cried, preparing to take them on.

At that moment, one of them pulled a book from under the mattress. Brandishing it in my face, he said "Erasmus. You're in it now." The three barged past us and down the steps.

Pietru and I stared at each other. "Some *kelb* wants your ass," he said.

"Yes, and I have no intention of letting him have it. I am off, Xabaw, at once." I hurriedly stuffed my few possessions into my bag, made certain I had all my money and bolted down the stairs with Pietru behind me.

He said he would go with me.

"Why, Xabaw? This is not like the other time. You have nothing to fear by remaining on Malta. The island is your home."

"The climate is bad this year," he replied.

I slapped him on the back and we dashed down to the docks to find any boat that would take us anywhere. At the embankment we encountered a crowd of people boarding a round ship. Their dress surely marked them as Jews—and so it was: The same sixty who had been captured a year past had succeeded in paying their ransom and were now departing.

As we stood among these passengers, tho', from the gates emerged three guards. Instantly our swords were out. Pietru took on one and two charged at me. I kicked a barrel into the first and he stumbled; then I bashed him over the head with the hilt of my rapier and he fell unconscious onto the dock. The second one was upon me. Our swords crossed and we struggled amidst the barrels and grain sacks, falling together among some bags of corn. We wrestled there, first he on top, then I. Only after I managed to pin his arms with my legs could I free my dagger and off him. I got to my feet, intending to aid Pietru, but at that moment Blaij Vergã suddenly stepped out of the shadows and into the center of this ill design.

"As the guards have failed to take you, I shall have to do it myself." And with those words he threw himself at me.

"So you are behind this!" I shouted as our rapiers struck and sparks flew.

"Let us rather say," he answered, backing off, circling, searching, "you are in ill-favor with a certain judge who questioned me about a certain dead whore."

"You sold me to Combo for your own freedom? Judas!"

With that scream I lifted an empty barrel that stood nearby and hurled it at him with every strength. But Blaij dodged it and it smashed harmlessly on the ground. Now we were all over the docks, among the barrels, atop the sacks and crates. Nothing stopped us; this fight was to the death. Pietru had finished with his man and approached, but halted in his tracks, so furiously were Vergã and I attacking each other. We wrestled, punched, fell. At one moment he was strangling me, but I kicked him in the balls and we sprang again to our feet. We lost our swords; with eyes slanting we regained them; we swung at each other with the back end of the weapons. Neither would yield. In the midst of this panting desperation, I thought I spied Isabella on the docks, but I paid no heed; I could not.

Suddenly Blaij, gasping for breath, cried, "You are a blind fool, Barai. All this time you thought it was about a whore."

"What say you?" I shouted, lunging at him.

He jumped aside. "Isabella, She was the cause."

"Isabella?" I could not fathom this.

Now Vergã stupidly swung overhand at me. "In Granada. She was mine."

I caught his blade on the guard. "You are mad! How could a bastard have hoped for her?"

"That is exactly it, you spoiled *coño.*" Vergã now retreated under my onslaught. "Everything was yours." Still I pressed forward. "It was I who put Agacio up to denouncing you. He was my cousin, after all."

"You!" I cried. "You caused this entire train of misfortune?"

"Thank me!"

Vergã laughed liked Satan himself and I let out the roar of a wounded beast, losing all reason. Seeing nothing I swung madly, which was exactly what Vergã wanted. His blade passed between my ribs and I fell into blackness. The last word I heard before the darkness closed about me was—*Venezia*.

Forty-One

When Vergã ran me through, Pietru was instantly upon him with his dagger and stabbed him in the shoulder. My enemy staggered off, dripping blood, while Pietru and some other passengers carried me aboard the round ship. Isabella, watching everything in horror from the nearby gates, suddenly lost her mind. Without thinking, she lifted her dress and dashed through the piles of cargo and bodies littering the dock, gaining the boat just as the gangplank was raised.

I have no recollection of any of this, for I was completely senseless.

By the Grace of God, among the freed Jews was a skilled physician and he saved my life. But neither he nor Isabella thought it prudent that a man in my condition be subjected to a winter voyage through to Venice and they carried me ashore at Catania.

For well o'er a month Isabella and Pietru nursed me in a hospice. Fortunately I was young and like the Knights themselves, God had granted me a strong constitution and willed that I should be difficult to kill off. Day by day I recovered my strength but soon it became apparent that Isabella had not forgiven me for my imagined betrayal of her before Cubelles's Tribunal. She treated me with an extreme coldness, barely deigning to speak, and again I sensed she had been terrified into renouncing me.

"It is not enough that you are a Moor," she said at last, "you must falsely accuse me to the Bishop! Of course I needed to denounce you."

"¿Como?" I cried from my bed. "So it was *you* who gave me up to the Tribunal!"

Isabella, shocked at the slip of her own tongue, made no reply and our trust of each other was in that instant destroyed.

From then on a bitter silence reigned. Isabella had written to her mother that she was safe and intended to go on to Firenze. When my strength permitted, Pietru and I escorted her by boat up the coast of Italy to Toscana, where at a place called Piombino she nodded to me, saying that other passengers would see her home. Thus we parted, not enemies, not friends, not lovers. As I watched the wind fill the sails and the oars dip into that haven's waters, I turned to Pietru. "By the Passion of Jesus," I spat, "a pox on tribunals that do naught but destroy love and friendship!"

"Do not hang your head like a dog," he replied forcefully, laying his hand on my shoulder. "You find each other again."

"I despair no longer," I answered plainly. "Any man has but a certain reserve of grief, and these two years have drained me of mine. Perhaps Isabella has said it rightly, I have grown hard. So be it. Let us look to the future."

The question was what to do. E'en as we stood at the harbor of this small coastal town, I perceived that my life had reached a crossroads as significant as the day Blaij and I had fled Granada. I thirsted for revenge against that scoundrel who'd wrested my life from me, and vowed that the next time I set eyes on him, I'd kill him. To my rage, under no circumstance could I now return to Malta. A wiser man might have bolted after Isabella, but I still had only twenty years to me. So bitter were my feelings at water's edge that the thought of chasing her to Firenze ne'er entered the fool's mind. Toscana, as Isabella had warned, was no safe place to be, with Siena in open rebellion against Carlos and Cosimo dé Medici, and it seemed ill-considered to remain in these environs a moment longer than necessary.

"I say we pick up the road where we left off—*a Venezia!*"

On our caravans with Strozzi, everything I had heard about the strange city—or country, I hardly knew how to name it—had increased my curiosity to see the place that was ruled by no monarch and despised by popes and Knights. As Fate had put me on a ship bound thither, it seemed we should follow the omen and continue in the direction we had begun. In any case, I was Esforzado.

Pietru nodded. "To Venice, good."

With some of the silver I'd brought we purchased horses, sheathed our arquebuses in the saddle holsters and set off overland. The day was clear and pleasant, with each step our cares fell further behind us and our spirits began to take wing. We had traveled only two or three hours along the road, singing and joking, when on the outskirts of some ancient town the most peculiar sight greeted us; to be sure a more peculiar sight would have been difficult to imagine. We stopped in our tracks. At a distance before us, several men carrying picks and shovels on their shoulders followed another who, holding a forked twig in his hands, wandered hither and thither over the rocky earth. He seemed not so much to pay attention to where he was going as to keep a close eye on this branch clenched in his fists. Pietru and I watched the procession with no little amusement, for this little band of men circled and spiraled over the landscape, suddenly changing direction every few steps with no apparent plan whatsoever.

"Eh, they run around more like mice than men!" Pietru laughed, pointing, and I agreed. Certain by now they were neither bandits nor marauding soldiers we hailed them, asking what they were about.

"Shh!" one of them answered with a finger to his lips. "*Silenzio!*"

At length the leader abruptly halted, pointed to a spot on the ground not far from a grove of trees and the rest of them began hacking at the tough soil with their tools. The leader, loosening his grip on the twig, wiped his brow and greeted us. We dismounted.

"I'm called Georgius," he said, offering his hand, and explained that a copper mine was located nearby and that he and his men were prospecting for new veins of ore.

"With that?" I exclaimed in astonishment and curiosity, pointing at the piece of wood. "By these whiskers grown with cannon smoke, what magic is this?"

Georgius, a muscular fellow wearing a long dirty shirt and a full beard, shrugged. "There is these days the greatest contention among miners," he responded. "Some say the forked twig is of the greatest help in discovering veins, others deny it completely. Some say one must cut a branch of hazel, as I have; others claim it is best to use a different sort of twig for each metal."

Pietru eyed the stick, at which Georgius handed it to him. "Let me try," the Gozitan said, revealing his missing teeth.

"Your fingers must be held to the sky," the miner instructed, "so the twig is raised at the end where the branches meet."

Pietru was off, wandering across the ground. Georgius chuckled, turning his blue eyes to me. "I have not told him what he must look for." Some people, he recounted, say the power of a vein will twist the twig in

the hand, much as a magnet draws iron to itself. Others say the twig is of
no benefit to good and serious men.

As we sat down on large rocks near the grove of trees, I asked whether
he found it of value.

Once again the miner shrugged. "I thought to examine it on its own
merits. It is certain that the twig does not work for everyone, and to this
many explanations have been given. Those against it say that the proper
incantations said over it by wizards give the stick its powers. Other
opponents say that metals have no ability to draw to them plain wood and
branches. Rather, the warm and dry exhalations of the veins cause the
twitchings. Proponents of the twig explain its failures by claiming that a
hidden quality of a man may weaken and break the force from the vein,
just as garlic juice weakens and overcomes the strength of a magnet."

All this was new and fresh to me and, mayhap because we were on the
road and loosing ourselves from the past, every word carried with it an
intrigue. "What do you believe?" I asked.

"As I say, I examine it on its own merits. Italian lands are not rich in
ore. Here where there is copper we have had some success with it, other
times not. But I do not know any wizard's incantations and it would be
unseemly for me to use them."

At length Pietru came back, saying that, truly, the branch had turned
for him. Georgius instructed two of his men to dig where Pietru indicated.
After a few hours, they hit a vein where he had pointed, but not where
the twig had twitched for Georgius himself. The miners didn't know what
to make of this. I did. "This man," I said, slapping Pietru on the shoulder,
"can talk to birds and the winds. I have no doubt that he can talk to copper
as well."

Georgius then invited us to sup with him at his home in the nearby
town and asked whither we were bound.

"Venice," I said.

"Good," he replied. "We are headed thither ourselves with a shipment
of copper. Our way lies by Siena and the more men we have the better."

I asked him what he would do with copper in Venice.

"Sell it of course—to the Arsenale."

Ten wagons set off the next morning at dawn. The road indeed lay by
Siena and our train gave it a wide birth, for Georgius, enlarging on what

Isabella had told us, explained that not many months ago the Sienese had rebelled, throwing the Spaniards out. Now with some inconstant aid from French troops, the city was engaged in a desperate struggle against both Carlos and Cosimo. Mayhap because winter lingered fighting was infrequent, but to our good fortune our wagons encountered no armies of either side.

When Georgius told his fellows that I'd spent the past two years on Malta with the Knights of St. John and that Pietru had survived the sack of Gozo, the miners' questions were immediate and never-ending. I could not help but think I sounded much the same two years ago.

"Signore, is it true," a man of my own age called Niccolò wanted to know, "that the Knights once had a ship greater than all others?"

"*Sì*," I nodded, telling them all of the carraca *Santa Anna*, whose main mast was so big that six men couldn't encircle it, who carried fifty large cannon, held stores for six months at sea and an armory that could outfit five hundred soldiers. I confess I discovered a great pleasure in playing the role of an authority on the Knights, tho' if some affectation found its way into my voice I shouldn't be surprised.

"Is it true, Signore Francisco," a beardless youth called Sebastiano asked with an awe-struck air, "that the Knights have never retreated in battle?"

I laughed at his question, at the same time nodding. "Truly, no one makes a better death than a Knight of Malta, and some would sooner give their heads than take a step backwards. Natheless, when all hope is lost, they have been known to make a hasty getaway." In pronouncing these words I recognized my debt to Fra Balthazar and a shadow crossed my face at the thought I would likely ne'er see him again.

Our good-natured companions could hardly believe I had been at Mdina two years ago, and when I told them that, aye, I'd been close enough to Turgut to strike him, they all cried together, "*Bugiardo!*" When I recounted the building of the forts, they urgently asked whether those works would hold against the Turks.

"With the Christian princes all at war with one another," said Sebastiano, "the Turkish Sultan seems unstoppable."

To this I shrugged. God alone knew the outcome.

Most of all the miners were astounded to meet a survivor of the *razzia* on Gozo, which had left all Europe speechless, and they tortured Pietru to learn whether everything they heard was true. "*Sì*," he grunted, "the island is empty now." They called him a hero for living through that terrible day, but this powerful man who near resembled a legendary dwarf only shook his head and said, "*Le*, I was afraid and hid in a cave, like a *kelb*."

In this manner, trading tales and jests, our caravan of copper crossed the Appennino to the environs of Rimini and made its way up the coast to Choggia; there we loaded the cargo onto a boat and sailed into the Venetian lagoon.

E'en as we crossed that grey expanse and watched the city slowly emerge from the waters before us, I understood we were approaching an extraordinary place, one constructed more of imagination itself than of material wood and stone. Just how extraordinary it was, I would not know for some time, for we hadn't come to ply the Grand Canal or gawk at those splendorous sights that lead many to call Venice the most magnificent city in the world.

We had come to sell a cargo of copper at the Arsenale, and made straight for those works on the eastern end of the island. But one glance at them convinced me we had arrived at the marvel of marvels. The Arsenale was a city unto itself. As we docked on a canal next to the foundries there and began unloading the metal, Georgius remarked that it covered fifteen *salme*.

From our location I could not make out the Arsenale's full extent, but Pietru and I turned to each other and exclaimed with one astonished voice, "The whole of Birgu would fit inside!"

This estimation was not far off the mark. A foreman appeared from the nearest building, greeted Georgius and directed his workers to help us bring the copper inside, where it was weighed and stored in a special room for copper. Once the task was done, Vannoccio, as the foreman called himself, led us through an unending series of storerooms for saltpetre, for pitch, for iron, for sailcloth, for wine; shops for lancemakers, shops for cuirass makers, shops for swordmakers, the foundries themselves.

When we had traversed, truly, the length of Birgu town, Vannoccio said, "These are the minor industries. Come." He then led us out behind these shops where before us spread a great basin, in which five or six galleys and round ships had been turned on their sides for repairs. Beyond this basin stood a row of several dozen giant sheds, in each of which sat the hull of a new ship.

"Come," the foreman said again and we walked beyond this row of sheds to a second basin, e'en larger than the first, where yet more galleys were under construction and repair. On the far side of this second basin stretched another row of gargantuan shelters, longer than the first one, and in each a ship.

Both Ix-Xabaw and I were shaking our heads. After the past two years I thought I had become fully a man and nothing more in this world could surprise me. The Arsenale surprised me. Nay, it astounded me. And yet Vannoccio was not done. "Come," he said and took us past a galley through this second row of sheds. Lo! Before us spread a third basin, greater than the other two, this one filled with water, where some ships floated.

I stood stupefied. I had simply lost the power of speech.

Vannoccio slapped me on the back. "Messeri," he said with pride beaming from his voice, "the Arsenale in which you stand is the base and foundation of the greatness of this Republic, rather the honor of all Italy. Nay, let me say it with more honesty, of all Christendom. It is the bastion and bulwark of our faith against the Infidel."

His words made a profound impression on me. "Sir," I said in my best Italian without warning to him or to myself, "I have spent two years fighting the Infidel with the Knights of Malta, who have purchased much ordnance, galleys and methinks e'en a great chain from this place."

"Indeed," said Vannoccio.

"They believe their faith to be the bastion and bulwark of Christendom; you believe Venetian ships and arms to be the same. I tell you honestly I cannot return to Malta and have no place in this world to go. Will you let me work here, in the foundries, to decide for myself where the bastion and bulwark of Christendom resides?"

The foreman, who had at least forty years to him, regarded me from head to toe. "A fine speech," he said at length with a chuckle. "But you could not pass for fourteen. If nothing else your scars give you away. It is against guild rules to take you on as an carpenter's apprentice, or an oarmaker's or a caulker's. Grown men learn slowly. The Arsenale has stood here for four hundred and fifty years and we have learned something in that time. You wish to build ships?"

I shook my head. "Nay, I have had my fill of ships. I am a fine swordsman and not a bad arquebusier. I would make swords—or guns."

"Georgius, has this lad really spent two years with the Hospitallers?"

The miner nodded, saying that if I hadn't, I was the best teller of tall tales he'd encountered in many a season. Again Vannoccio turned to me. "Have you training in the metallic arts?"

"None, Signore," I answered honestly, "you must buy a pig in a poke, but if I learn more slowly than your other apprentices, you may throw me headfirst into the nearest canal."

The foreman stroked his beard long and hard. He was, evidently, taking a great risk. "You are doubly fortunate today: not only is the cannon foundry less watched than the major arts, but as the Turkish threat rises, the Arsenale is in need of ever more workers. We are now in a constant state of danger and employ several thousand under these roofs." Finally he pursed his lips and said, "Very well, I'll take you on as an apprentice. If anyone asks, tho', tell him you are my long-lost son, returned from the wars."

"What about me, eh?" Pietru asked.

Vannoccio eyed the Gozitan suspiciously and sighed. "And what can you do?"

"Anything," Pietru said.

Vannoccio took our hands. He led Georgius to the *casa corrente* to get paid for the copper shipment and then we all went for supper. Thus it was that Pietru and I put Malta behind us and became *arsenalotti*—sons of the Arsenale.

End of Volume 1

For sales, editorial information, subsidiary rights information
or a catalog, please write or phone or e-mail
iBooks
Manhanset House
Shelter Island Hts., NY 11965, US
Sales: 1-800-68-BRICK
Tel: 212-427-7139
www.ibooksinc.com
bricktower@aol.com

For sales in the UK and Europe please contact our distributor,
Gazelle Book Services
Falcon House, Queens Square
Lancaster, LA1 1RN, UK
Tel: (01524) 68765 Fax: (01524) 63232
www.gazellebookservices.co.uk
email: melanie@gazellebooks.co.uk

www.ingramcontent.com/pod-product-compliance
Lightning Source LLC
Chambersburg PA
CBHW050122030726
47505CB00007B/1999